YOUNG ATLANTEANS

TWO TRIBES ·

T STEDMAN

ACKNOWLEDGEMENTS

A special thank you to my readers, who, I'm sure, are some of the best in the world. And as always, my team, Nicky Lovick, Daniela Orwegoor and Jane Harrison.

PROLOGUE

Ballygowan Castle – West coast of Ireland

Xavier exchanged a wary look with his sister, then nodded at the Santalini guard to say they were ready. JJ stood, hands in his pockets, and looked down at the floor. He wished JJ took this more seriously. Punishment was coming and he always made it worse. They'd gone too far this time.

The guard grinned, revealing a gleaming gold tooth and fangs and announced their arrival at their father's study into his head-set.

'Send them in.' The richly accented Irish voice said through the heavy oak door.

It was a harsh reminder that they were very definitely back in the Atlantean world where normal rules didn't apply. Here, their father ruled absolutely and while the six foot five, muscled vampire, dressed in Special Ops black, didn't scare them nearly as much as he should have, their father was pissed off and that was cause for concern. The guard pushed the door open wide with a wink and the three teenagers trooped inside.

They came to a standstill in a 'usual suspects' line up, directly in front of Dante Dubonnetti, the Atlantean king, on a cobalt-blue rug. At almost forty, he was still a remarkably handsome man, with olive skin that crinkled at the corners of his lively slate-coloured eyes and black curly hair, identical to Xavier's. Although Dante's was now tipped with grey. He was writing something seated behind the huge carved desk, placed in the middle of the room lined with books and ancient charts – like a judge. Which he was, really. He didn't look up from his papers and continued to work, making them wait a full five minutes.

Xavier looked across at his father's best friend, sitting in a large ox-blood leather armchair to his right. He was drinking something from a heavy glass, with his expensively tailored leg crossed at the knee, looking stonily straight at them. *Jay.*

Sharply dressed, blond and handsome, Jay was the biological father of JJ, who shared a mother with the rest of them. It was a weird setup – even they knew that. The two men acted as father to the three of them and their two younger siblings, Roman and Zander. And while Jay was cool and cared for them all as equals, there was no sympathy in the directness of his steely-blue gaze today. He could often be even more strict than Dante.

The minutes ticked on.

'Where's Mum?' Alexia said, eventually. 'Shouldn't she be here for this?'

At last, their father put down his pen, sighed and looked at them over the gold rim of his glasses. Xavier recognized the hard expression and shifted uncomfortably. There was no cheeky glint in his eyes. No amusement playing on his lips. There was going to be no winning him around, even with Alexia's little girl wiles.

'I don't remember giving you permission to speak, Alexia.'

She huffed, rested her weight on the other hip and went

to protest again, but the king held up a hand. 'Shut up girl, your mother is fully aware of what's going to happen.'

Xavier stood a little straighter and felt the others become alert next to him. Everything had suddenly got a whole lot more serious. If their mother wasn't there it meant the king had made up his mind and he didn't want to be swayed. There was no telling what he would do. People often remarked on how their father was a great king because he was tinged with a little madness. Some said it was from all the power that surged through him, bestowed on him in his youth by his mother and her four sisters, but their mother had scoffed and said he'd always been that way.

Xavier looked across to gauge their second father, Jay. He was usually the colder, quieter one out of the two and some would argue the more stable, but sometimes that just made him more ruthless and harder to deal with. Like right now. They were in big trouble.

'You – Xavier! You're the oldest. You can explain what the hell you were playing at,' Dante said.

Xavier closed his eyes and looked at the floor. Everything always fell on him in times like this. How was he to explain to their two fathers what JJ was really like when he was away from them? They thought they had them all pegged, with him, Xavier, the popular ringleader, Alexia the girl who effortlessly got what she wanted and JJ, the quiet, brooding genius. The reality was that while JJ had inherited his father's charming, cute, choirboy good looks, he was a boy hell-bent on self-destruction. He was dangerous and volatile and completely determined not to fit in. And, most of all, Xavier was angry that he'd spent the best part of a school year covering for him and was about to get the blame. In the end, he looked at his father, the king, deadpan. 'I'm not sure what you're asking me for exactly, Father?'

Alexia giggled.

Xavier knew it was from nerves, but he willed her to shut up. He wasn't trying to be clever. This would go a whole lot better if their father thought they were truly sorry.

'Are you trying to be a joker with me, Son?' the king said, narrowing his eyes at him.

Xavier looked across at Jay for some help and all he saw reflected back was the same, nonchalant expression.

'What happened at the school?' Jay said, in his quiet reasonable voice that could be just as menacing.

Xavier blinked and remained silent. They were going to get punished anyway. He reckoned an unwillingness to speak would inflame his father slightly less than any kind of half-arsed explanation of what went on.

'Maybe JJ can shed some light?' Jay said.

Xavier breathed a little now the heat was off him, but in a whole lot of ways it was worse. He, at least, could do some damage limitation, whereas JJ wouldn't care less what trouble he landed them in. He didn't care about punishments, what people thought of him, he didn't care about pain. JJ didn't feel anything.

JJ shrugged. 'I dunno … I just didn't get on there. It was full of rich, self-important, entitled, snobs. Just buy them a new science wing or something. It will soon be forgotten.'

Alexia clamped a hand to her mouth. Xavier looked at the ceiling.

'Some might argue, you should all be right at home there,' the king said, now clearly livid.

Xavier saw his father's point. 'Xavier!' his father barked, making him jump.

'Like he said.' Xavier tried to look anywhere but his father in the eye.

Dante let out a blast of air, still glaring at the three of them. 'Have you any idea how bad this looks? The US government gave our nation those school places for you and all your cousins to train you into the diplomats you're meant to one day become. For feck's sake, it's part of the treaty between our two races that you integrate.'

Xavier fidgeted awkwardly. His father was right. And it was a good school. He and Alexia would have been fine there. But Alexia doted on JJ and Xavier felt responsible for them all. It was kind of an unwritten rule that they stuck together in all things. Despite everything, they fiercely loved each other.

JJ stared blankly ahead of him as if it made no difference to him. What their fathers never seemed to grasp was that it didn't.

Alexia was looking at her nails. Xavier could see her crafty mind working on a way out. 'Why can't we go to school in Murrtaine? Keefer and Dannon go.'

'You don't learn about the human world there. It's not so important for your cousins,' Jay said softly.

Xavier was relieved. Murrtaine was OK for holidays, but he had no wish to spend any length of time in the underwater city. It was so cut-off. The human world was far more exciting.

'Neither do you from home schooling. It's turning you into brats,' Dante continued, his thick Irish accent stronger than ever when he was angry.

'I won't go back,' JJ said, calmly, looking the king insolently in the eye.

Dante laughed in a single blast, and looked at Jay as if to ask, 'can you believe this kid?' Then he looked back at him; amused this time. 'Hey, you won't have to, Son. After you went through the whole of the eleventh-grade females like a pair of whirling dervishes and subsequently ruined the end of the semester's Meet and Greet for new students with a western bar brawl, they won't have you back.'

Xavier found his father's whole demeanour disturbing. Like he had something truly bad up his sleeve.

'None of that was me!' Alexia said, immediately.

Xavier wanted to tell her to shut up. This wasn't something she could whine and bat her eyelashes out of.

'No, but you like to stir it up, Alexia, and you certainly didn't help.' Dante sat back in his chair, furious, withering her with a look. 'Now get out me sight,' he said, wearily, with a flick of his hand.

Part of Xavier wanted to follow his siblings and hurry to leave, but he knew his father hadn't delivered the blow yet. 'You haven't told us what's going to happen,' he said, his heart speeding up in his chest.

Dante smiled with narrowed eyes as if at least he'd got that right. Then, with malicious delight, his father delivered the news. 'That's right, I almost forgot. The three of you can pack your things. You'll be starting a new school on Monday.'

They all groaned. Xavier closed his eyes. His mind was already ticking through the possibilities and implications. *This wasn't too bad. It was to be expected.*

'Where?' JJ asked, cutting across his thoughts.

'London!' Jay and Dante said together.

Xavier stared at his father along with the rest of them. Then he heard JJ distinctly swear under his breath and he exchanged a weary look with him. They could just imagine the type of place. 'I'm not going to another posh school,' JJ said.

Dante grinned wickedly. 'Well, that's just as well then, coz you're going to the Marcus Garvey High School in South London. You'll be fine there.'

Xavier looked over at Jay to make sure it wasn't a joke. He just raised his eyebrows with his typical, no-nonsense look. They all knew it was pointless to even protest. Xavier numbly followed the others out of the room.

. . .

WHEN THE DOOR CLICKED SHUT, Jay looked over at Dante. 'You think they'll settle any better there?' He was sceptical. They were all a handful, but ever since they'd learned of the Darkly Begotten prophecy, his son troubled him.

Dante bobbed his head, 'Probably not, but never let it be said that the Atlantean monarchy is afraid to get its hands dirty.' Dante batted his hand as if it was of little importance. 'We can get our people in there to keep an eye on them and if anything happens it'll remain under the radar. This time, we'll be in control.'

Jay nodded and took a sip of his drink. He guessed it could work. A school like that would have had its share of troublemakers. Their three would be chicken feed. 'What about the other cousins. Their parents might not be as enthusiastic about your choice in school' he said with smile. The children of all the Siren sisters were meant to follow theirs into mainstream education. An inner-city school in a deprived area of south London would not be their first choice.

Dante grinned, like he whole-heartedly agreed and was going to enjoy every minute of it. He'd been the same since he was a kid.

'And there's Ronnie,' Jay reminded him. He was the son of their kids' mother's bodyguard. He was a good kid and certainly didn't deserve to be pushed around with their miscreants. But by simple association, he'd be forced to change schools too. It wasn't very fair.

'Ah, he'll be alright,' Dante said with a flick of his hand. 'He might get some sense into our kids.'

Jay smiled. He knew when it was impossible to argue with his best friend. And in his usual, roundabout way, he guessed he was right.

'We'll let these three go for starters, then filter the others in when they settle down a bit. That should keep the parents quiet for now. We'll sell it as an environment under our complete control that will benefit the poorer kids in the area.'

Jay nodded. The school would be struggling with the meagre financial allocation they got from the government. They would jump at the chance of a cash injection. Then, before they knew what had happened, Dante would own the school. They wouldn't see it coming – and neither would the kids. With a deep sigh, he weighed the alternatives and conceded to the fact that there weren't any. Suddenly, he felt very weary with it all and pinched the bridge of his nose. 'What do you think is going on with those two?' he said, waving a hand at the door their children had just gone through. Despite their closed ranks, he could clearly feel the friction between the two boys.

Dante leaned over and topped up his drink. 'Apart from being chips off the old block, you mean?' he said, laughing. 'No, I think we have ourselves a little power struggle going on there.'

Jay nodded thoughtfully. He was probably right. Despite him and Dante being like brothers for most of their lives, there had always been friction and rivalry between them. They had been brought up privileged and gone to some of the best schools and colleges in England and hadn't exactly taken full advantage of their opportunities. Looking back, maybe Marcus Garvey High School would have suited them back then too. He let out a single blast of laughter. 'Hence the school.'

Dante nodded. 'I think this could be just the right place.'

Jay sighed, sitting back in his armchair and thinking of the many times they'd been hauled up in front of headmasters in their youth. Except their children had more than just money and privilege. They had certain mental powers they were barely able to control. He knocked back his drink to sear his doubts away with the amber liquid. *I hope you're right ...*

CHAPTER 1

eeting the opposition

Xavier daydreamed, unseeing, out of the grey-tinted window as the limo edged through the South London rush hour traffic. Two Santalini guardsmen rode in the front of their car, four in the SUV escorting them ahead, and another four behind. Even out of their red and black uniform, the black fatigue-wearing members of the Santalini royal family looked more like Marines than escorting family, which he was sure was the story his father had told the headmaster. To try to pass off the soldiers of the race as that, family or not, was laughable.

Professor Max Brunswick, his father's human advisor, sat uncomfortably in the back with the three of them. He rarely left the cloistered walls of the castle or their secret retreat of Filfla, where his father kept all his precious books.

'How are we supposed to blend in arriving like this?' Xavier said, tutting.

JJ rolled his eyes, shook his head and looked out of the window.

'We will be very early, and it's just for your first day,' Max explained, pushing his round spectacles higher up his nose with his finger. 'You'll have other accommodations after today, much closer to the school. Your fathers want you to have a totally immersive experience.'

Xavier frowned. That didn't sound good. They'd spent the night at Jay senior's hotel in Soho. He assumed they would be based there while they were at school. They knew it well and Jay could come and go keeping an eye on them. It made much more sense.

'No, you'll live here. Your father gave strict orders you're not to be coddled and it's simply not practical to do this journey every morning. This arrangement is much more time efficient and safe.'

'He doesn't expect us to board with the locals, does he?' Alexia said, pulling a face at the dirty shop fronts and grimy bricked buildings passing by.

'This isn't a boarding school,' Max said without elaborating.

Xavier watched the shock seep into his sister's face. It would be funny if he wasn't as alarmed as her.

'What, a state school that we have to drive to every day?' she said in absolute horror.

'Walk,' Dr Brunswick corrected, flatly. 'You will walk there and home again every day.'

Xavier and JJ had Googled the school straight after the meeting with their fathers. It was a regular everyday secondary school, ethnically diverse, and about second to last in the league tables for the whole of England. He and JJ had both agreed their father was simply trying to teach them a lesson to be grateful. They would go through this charade, spend the day roughing it, and then pitch up in front of the posh boarding school, in keeping with their royal status. Now, the closer they got, the more nervous Xavier became that that wasn't the case at all.

JJ looked across their sister at him, obviously thinking the same thing. 'Where are we staying, then?'

'With a local family, just a ten-minute walk from the school. Your father has arranged everything. Your bags will be taken there while you are at school, then, when your day finishes you will go back there, OK?'

'Oh no!' Alexia whispered, as if she'd just heard someone had died. 'Surely we'll get lost or kidnapped in the ghetto.'

Xavier laughed and JJ shook his head. Their sister was so dramatic. She would make sure she was treated like a princess wherever they ended up.

'Don't worry unduly, Alexia. The kind lady you will be lodging with has three children at the school. They'll be able to act as guides and show you about the place.'

They all looked at each other, more uneasy by the minute. The whole thing was fast becoming a nightmare. Their old school in New Hampshire didn't seem such a bad place after all.

'What's her name – this woman looking after us?' Alexia asked on the verge of tears. 'I guess she must have a big house with the three of us and three kids of her own,' she said.

'Her name is Valarie Johnson. She is a nurse and has two smaller children too.' He ominously left out the size of the house.

'And the kids?' Xavier said, watching Max's discomfort closely.

'Erm…' Max opened his briefcase and sifted through some papers. 'Ah, here it is. Richard, Latitia and Dwayne… Erm, the ones under five: Joseph and Marcus.'

Xavier and JJ exchanged another concerned look. Surely this must be some kind of joke.

Xavier sat back in his seat. This wouldn't be for long. He knew his father. This was just a ploy to teach them a lesson. It was all to make them appreciate their old school when they were sent back. 'Chill out, Lexie. We'll be out of here in no time.' *Yeah, two weeks – a month, tops.*

JJ WAS SEETHING. Not because all this was beneath them – far from it, but from embarrassment. If they wanted them to immerse, why stick a beacon on their heads? Their motorcade was waved into the staff car park by the police, as if they were visiting foreign dignitaries. It was so conspicuous that peopled were stopping in the street to check out who it was. They came to a halt, right in front of the steps to the main doors of the old red-brick building, where they got out hurriedly and were ushered in by their guards, forming a shield from the onlookers and talking into headsets.

A small stocky man with a huge moustache and wearing a tweed jacket met them and introduced himself as Mr Lingham, Deputy Headmaster and Head of English. He led the way down the old parquet-floored corridors that smelled of boiled cabbage and sick.

JJ bit down his hatred for the place already. It wasn't that he was a snob and wanted a better school; he didn't want any school. He knew who he was and what he was meant to become and didn't need all this bollocks. There were easier ways of bringing him down a peg or two that didn't drag his brother and sister down with him. This whole exercise was a waste of everyone's time. *To hell with it.*

As they went down endless poorly lit corridors, with shiny green paint to waist height and peeling magnolia to the ceiling, his morbid thoughts somehow went hand in hand with the place. It felt kind of homely. Flickering lights lit tatty noticeboards. Door signs that should have said Humanities Block, had the 'ities' scrubbed out and the BL scribbled over with a C. Ceiling tiles were missing, revealing the wiring running above and finally the library that had no more than about fifteen books in it. It really felt like a middle finger to the establishment. By the time they came to a stop outside a door with a crooked 'Head' sign on it with 'gives' diagonally scrawled across it, he decided he liked the place. He'd just go along with it and do his own thing anyway. If they wanted to waste their time trying to teach him what he already knew, then let them. It made no difference to who he was, anyway. He didn't give a shit where he lived or who with. His life was preordained. In short, there was no point in getting involved, making connections, or weighing himself down.

Mr Lingham smiled and knocked on the shabby door.

'Come in,' a deep voice said.

Mr Lingham held open the door and they followed Max into the office. A huge, overweight, cheerful-looking black man stood up from behind his desk and couldn't look more like Professor Clump if he tried. JJ flashed a look at Xavier, who gave a small smile of recognition back.

'Please sit,' the headmaster said, indicating three chairs opposite him. Another was brought in for Max. Mr Lingham perched on the edge of a sideboard and four of their guards stood, arms crossed, at the back of the room, which was ludicrous as they would leave them to fend for themselves when this meeting was over.

The headmaster smiled at each of them in turn. 'Hello, I know who you all are. I am Dr Henry, your headteacher. Your fathers have explained everything, and I understand you will be staying with a local family, which I'm sure will be fabulous. I want you all to feel right at home here.' His laughter boomed, even though there was nothing funny, after almost every sentence he said. But the guy seemed OK, upbeat and positive. Heaven knew why, in this shit hole.

JJ yawned.

The headmaster narrowed his eyes on him, not missing a

thing. 'I can see we have an active mind here. We'll soon have that put to good use. Can't have you getting bored now, can we?'

Alexia sniggered. Xavier hid a smile behind his hand. The guy was a smart aleck – *so what.*

'Let me welcome you, and let you know how pleased we are to have you all here.'

'Thank you, Dr Henry,' Max said. 'Here is the first donation to the school from the children's father. I trust it's in order?' Max passed a small envelope to the headmaster, who took it with a smile. 'There will be a similar donation each term.'

The room was silent while he took out his letter opener, slit it, and took out what looked like a cheque. His eyes went wide before he could school his features. 'Bloody hell,' he choked. Then rubbed his two chins. 'Please pass on my sincerest gratitude. Every penny will be put to good use.'

'His Highness thought it would go some way to help in refurbishing the sports facilities here?'

'Of course,' Dr Henry said, having to re-read the cheque again.

Xavier and JJ exchanged a worried look. Suddenly the move here wasn't looking that temporary.

A knock at the door brought their eyes back to the headmaster. Max took it as his cue to leave and the guards stepped forward. 'We will leave you to your day, Dr Henry,' Max said.

'Very good. That will be the children's new brothers and sister,' Dr Henry said, laughing.

JJ baulked. *Not likely. This would be good. Time to suss out the opposition.*

Max went out with the guards and JJ heard them come in, but didn't turn round.

'Come here where we can all see you?' Dr Henry said. The three traipsed in and joined him next to the desk.

Both boys were black, with trendy faded haircuts and deep-brown eyes. They were big, good-looking guys and knew it. In a second, JJ had taken in the Beats earphones, looped around their neck, the black bomber jackets and navy-blue sweatshirts, at least three sizes too big, with the school logo in a semi-circle over their left breast. Their black trousers hung low and bunched over their beige Chelsea boots and were the final proof they conformed but pushed the uniform boundary to the edge of what was allowed. He locked eyes with each of them. Impressions would be formed and there was no point in giving any notion of weakness.

That was as far as his study of them went, before a bubble gum pop brought his eyes over to the girl a little out of view.

Xavier and Alexia were saying hello. She nodded back and shook both their hands. JJ was too busy taking in her long cane-rowed hair and hooped earrings the size of saucers. When her eyes finally rested on him for his introduction, they were a lighter shade of brown and her heart-shaped face had smooth skin the colour of caramel. His eyes dropped; he couldn't help it. Her waist was cinched in with a large belt to emphasize her perfect hips and her white shirt was knotted just above it. Her black trousers were rolled to halfway up her shin to reveal a black boot far chunkier than her brothers'.

She looked him up and down, moodily, as if to ask what the hell he was looking at, blew another bubble and raised an eyebrow.

A small smile crept over his face. *Well, hello beautiful ...*

CHAPTER 2

The rest of the morning went by like a bad dream for Alexia. Their host brothers and sister had been excused and gone off to their classes, and they were all subdued. The headmaster insisted on showing them around the school himself, making them stand out even more than they did already. She was sure it was for their father's benefit and wasn't the norm.

They started their tour in the large reception area. Kids of all ages, colours and nationalities streamed through in two lines through two metal arches. 'Oh look, airport thingies!' she said laughing. 'Why do they need those?'

'Concealed weapons,' Xavier said in her ear.

Shocked, she looked at JJ for confirmation. He just raised his eyebrows without answering. She took that as a yes. 'Shit!' she said, a little too loudly.

A boy was pulled to the side, patted down and something confiscated. 'We have to ensure pupil safety,' the headmaster said.

Suddenly, their old school seemed a much better place, even though they'd been in a rush to leave it. Here, the kids seemed louder and more boisterous. Their uniform looked drab and ill-fitting, the girls' bags cheap and their coats, if they had one, tatty.

Xavier was grinning at her. He always took great enjoyment in annoying her. JJ was bored as usual.

Then followed endless departments – English, Maths, Art, etc. Everywhere looked dilapidated, needed fixing and a new coat of paint.

Eventually, their depressing tour came to an end. The head needn't have bothered; one shabby classroom looked pretty much like another and the teachers reminded her of aging hippies. He explained that science was their next class before lunch and gave them instructions on where they needed to go.

A bell rang signifying the end of the period and the corridor suddenly swarmed with so many kids they found it difficult to move. As obvious newbies, they were pushed all over the place. Xavier grabbed her arm, so they weren't separated. JJ shoved a few people back and got into some minor scuffles. Thankfully they were herded along until they reached a staircase. They made their way up to the second floor, along the corridor, to the classroom marked 'Science 3'. Another bell sounded, the door opened and the kids behind them pushed them into the room.

Inside, the desks were long wooden benches, carved with names and initials all over them by some sort of sharp implement. A compass, she guessed. They were arranged in four rows, with an aisle down the middle. Xavier pulled her along with him and they sat together by the window. He was always protective of her. It felt more like possessiveness – especially around other boys. She had actually been closer to JJ growing up, but they had grown apart lately. He sat behind them.

A balding man in glasses, wearing a brown tweed jacket

and corduroy elbow patches, briskly entered the classroom and slapped his worn satchel onto the desk. Then he issued orders to open the windows even though the room was freezing.

Alexia sank down in her chair when she saw his eyes rest on her and then check in his folder. He closed it and perched on the edge of the desk. 'Don't get too comfortable, you lot, I want you to stand up.'

Everyone groaned and their stools scraped as the whole class slowly stood. She noticed several kids still on their phones. 'Phones off and away or lose them till the end of the day,' the teacher said with a no-nonsense look over his glasses. Then he smiled and surveyed the class. 'Hello. For those who don't know me, my name is Mr Benson. I'm going to take the register and where I point to is where I want you to sit. That is where you will sit every time you come to my class. You're going to have to humour me, it helps me learn your names. There will be no chatting, no turning around to the person behind you and absolutely no checking your social media profile while in my class. Is that clear? You aren't that popular.'

The class grumbled a less-than-enthusiastic 'Yes sir' when he finished speaking. He was about to open his mouth to begin when the door opened and one of the boys they were staying with came in. 'Dwayne Johnson, you're late! You're here,' he said, pointing at a desk just in front of Alexia. Then he pointed at her. 'You are?'

'Alexia,' she said, blasting red with the spotlight on her.

He rolled his eyes. 'Alexia, who?'

'Dubonnetti,' she said, looking at Xavier to save her.

'You're next to him.' He pointed to the vacant chair next to Dwayne.

She looked at Xavier imploringly.

'Excuse me,' Xavier said, partially raising his hand. 'I am also a Dubonnetti, shouldn't I be next to her?'

'No, you will sit behind her.' Mr Benson flashed his eyes at him and went back to his register.

Someone sniggered.

Alexia moved slowly into the seat next to Dwayne and looked at him warily as she sat. He gave her a friendly smile, but she averted her eyes. He seemed OK, but she'd never been around ordinary humans before. The ones in New Hampshire were pampered and spoiled and predominantly white. She swivelled in her chair to look for JJ and saw he was now near the back of the room. He chose to use his father's name of Gardiner and not any of his royal names of Dubonnetti, Santalini, Bonaci or Florianna. He was stubborn like that.

'Right, open your exercise books to page thirty.'

Alexia looked around her; they hadn't been given exercise books yet.

'Here ... you can share mine,' Dwayne said, scratching his head awkwardly. His stool scraped as he moved in closer. Her eyes caught his and held them for a long moment. They were very dark brown and seemed honest. They reminded her a lot of her cousins' eyes; Keefa and Dannon. All the Murrs from the Borge family had eyes so black you couldn't distinguish a pupil. He gave a small smile, which she returned shyly.

The door to the classroom opened and closed, breaking the spell.

Dwayne looked over his shoulder at who'd come in and tutted. It was his sister Latitia.

'Sit!' the teacher said and pointed to the chair next to JJ. She groaned and he smirked.

Alexia didn't miss that look – she knew it well. She glanced at Dwayne, who'd clocked the same thing. 'How come you and your sister are in the same class?' she said, to get his attention.

'I could ask you the same thing.'

He was right. All three of them were exactly the same age. It happened a lot with the royal children of Sirens. But he wasn't to know that. For a moment she was lost for words.

'Twins,' he said, answering her question with a smile.

She smiled awkwardly back. 'Same.' This was going to be harder than she thought. He seemed quite nice, but she had no idea what he knew and she was sure she knew even less about him.

XAVIER SAT at the bench behind his sister, in a science lab last refitted in the 1950s, and watched what was fast becoming flirtation between her and their new foster brother and he didn't like it one bit. He wasn't sure what was bothering him exactly – probably that she had never really been interested in anyone before. This new school was unnerving. The building seemed to function on a wing and a prayer and its pupils were from a corner of society they had absolutely no training or experience with. He'd never felt so far out of his comfort zone.

A boy was sat next to him and he'd forgotten his name already. He needed to get out of there fast. His father already had the headmaster in his pocket. If they left it much longer it would be impossible to get expelled.

He turned in his seat to communicate with JJ, only to see him getting all gooey-eyed over the girl, Latitia. He'd seen it a hundred times at their old school and turned back to face the front in disgust. *Was everyone taking leave of their senses?* It was the look that got them into fights time and time again. Then he narrowed his eyes on his sister; looking coyly at that boy again. Perhaps that was their ticket out of there.

. . .

JJ SAT BACK in his chair and openly appraised Latitia. She was something he'd never come across in his life before. All he'd ever mixed with growing up were other Atlanteans and they were invariably rich, royal or both and at the last school, they were their human counterparts. Spoiled little rich girls whose Daddy brought them everything and would save their pretty little arses should they waste their expensive education. All they did was parade around in designer clothes and bitch about their friends. The minute they opened their mouths, he was bored.

This one reminded him of a dancer out of one of the rap videos he and Xavier loved to watch – all attitude and swagger. *Hot!*

She turned and looked sideways at him when she sensed him watching her. She kissed her teeth loudly. 'What's the matter ... not seen a black girl before?'

He grinned. 'You're not black, I'd say you're a milky coffee colour.'

She frowned and shook her head as if he'd offended her, which made him laugh loudly.

'Care to share the joke with the class, Jason Gardiner?' the teacher said, loudly. 'What did I say about chatting?'

'My name's JJ,' he said, turning back to Latitia as if he'd been rudely interrupted.

She didn't turn around, but a scarlet red blush entered her cheeks and he knew he had an effect on her.

'Share your books with JJ, please, Latitia,' Mr Benson said. 'And need I remind you about the school policy on inappropriate jewellery?'

She huffed, pulled the hoops from her ears and slammed the books down on the table between them.

He edged closer, not able to hide the smile creeping over his face.

'We don't want you here,' she whispered.

'Maybe not yet,' he said back. The place had got a whole lot more interesting. 'I'm like a song that grows on you.' He laughed at her look of horror.

* * *

'HURRY UP, Mum, I've already missed Maths and Science. It'll be lunchtime by the time I get there.' Paige slammed down the phone.

Both her younger brother and sister were sick today and her mum had to work. That meant the job of free babysitter fell to her. She understood that her mum had to work three cleaning jobs, and she helped her keep the simple maisonette clean and tidy, but it was really hard when she missed so much school. On days like today, she had to wait for her to come home to relieve her, then rush back after school.

Her hopes rose with the doorbell. She peered through the peephole, just in case, and was met with an eyeball, making her jump. 'Jade!' she shouted, throwing the door open. 'Bloody hell, Jade, why aren't you at school?'

'I got up late. Ew!' Jade said, pointing at her four-year-old brother, his nose running with yellowy-green snot.

'Hang on, mate,' Paige said, grabbing a fistful of toilet paper from the loo for him to blow on.

'I thought I'd come here first. When's your mum home?'

'She reckoned by twelve.' A rattle and crunch of keys made both their heads turn to the door.

'That's her.'

Her mum bustled in, weighed down with a couple of shopping bags she'd hauled all the way on the bus. She looked worn out already. Wisps of blonde hair were escaping her ponytail as the kids hung off her denim jacket to see what she'd bought. 'Hello, Jade.'

'Alright, Linda.'

'Get off then, you two.'

Paige didn't need telling twice. She grabbed her coat and a biscuit from the new packet her mum had only just put on the kitchen side and they went out of the door of the second-floor maisonette. At least it was only the first day back so she wouldn't have missed much.

She slipped on her coat as they leisurely walked. The day was grey and it would probably rain. They didn't want to walk too fast to make sure they arrived after the dinner bell went. It was less conspicuous to slip in unnoticed that way. Paige had written her own excuse note saying she'd been at the dentist. Jade hadn't bothered. The school would ring home, but her mum didn't care and would cover for her.

'Thank god it's the last year,' Jade said, as they walked in through the gates.

Paige just smiled at her friend, then looked up at the old red-brick school building that had been pebble-dashed black from a century's worth of exhaust fumes. She slowly climbed the steps to the main entrance, thinking sometimes that she envied Jade. All she wanted to do was leave school and get a job. Life was so simple and uncomplicated for her. Paige wanted more. She wanted out of this shithole. She'd decided years ago that she'd work hard, get her exams and someday be a nurse or even a doctor. Although it felt like an uphill battle at times, with all the missed days and having to catch up all the time.

A feeling of hopelessness descended on her when they walked in through the doors of the school canteen. Jade shot off to chat to someone she'd seen. Paige sat down alone at one of the long trestle tables and fumbled in her bag for some change. Maybe she could scrape up enough for some chips. With her hand in the crumbs and crap at the bottom, she absently looked ahead of her. That was when she caught sight of him. He was sitting with another boy and a girl – the only kids out of uniform. But it didn't matter because they were silently apart from the madness around them anyway. Alone and beautiful, all three of them. But he stood out completely.

Jade came back with several friends, chatting animatedly. She slammed down a plate of chips between them and followed her line of vision. 'You owe me 70p. Who are they?'

'Not sure,' one of the others said.

'They turned up this morning.'

'They don't look like they come from round here.'

No they didn't. They all could be models. Her boy (as she referred to him from then on) and the girl next to him looked Latin and exotic. His hair was long and curly, for a start. Not many boys their age wore it like that. His clothes looked foreign and expensive. The girl was a female version of him and obviously his sister, *thankfully.* The other boy was blond and good-looking, but still seemed equally apart from everyone else in the room. It was the strangest feeling; as if they literally glowed.

He must have felt them watching as he turned to look straight at her and their eyes met. Completely captured, she wanted to look away, but she couldn't. His were the most unusual shade of pale green she'd ever seen. He neither smiled nor looked away. They just openly stared at each other until they were interrupted as another boy joined them. He was one of the Johnson brothers who were in her year. He'd brought back a tray piled high with snacks for them all, and the boy became distracted and looked away.

Bloody hell. Her heart was beating like a train. *Who the hell were they?* No one had ever had an impact on her like that. There had never been a single boy in Camberwell who had lured her off track. She tried to shake herself out of it because she couldn't stop thinking about him and the look they'd shared. She hated to admit it, but she was very interested in finding out everything about him and that just wasn't in her five-year plan.

Her eyes strayed to their table again. The Johnsons obviously knew them and, somehow, she just knew she had to get to know them too.

CHAPTER 3

JJ was relieved when at last the final bell went. The day had been long and boring. Xavier and Alexia had been constantly moaning and trying their mother and fathers' numbers unsuccessfully, and resorting to ranting to their younger brothers, Roman and Zander, and any of their cousins who'd bother to pick up and listen to the tirade.

The last class filed out and the three of them stuck closer together this time, in the throng of kids crowding the corridor.

'Where are we meeting them?' Xavier shouted over Alexia's head, while they were pushed and jostled along.

'I dunno,' JJ said over his shoulder.

'Dwayne said he'd meet us by the front gates,' Alexia said.

JJ didn't miss the angry look on Xavier's face. It did seem as though their sister was getting pally with her foster brother already.

The day was still dank and grey with the dark clouds of evening drawing in to add to the gloom. The two Johnson boys were already there. Richard or Richie, which he seemed to be known as, was laughing with a friend, and Dwayne was on his phone. His face lit up with a beaming smile when he saw Alexia.

JJ grinned knowingly at Xavier. This would be entertaining. He didn't see the harm and wasn't going to make life harder for his sister. Especially as he took in Latitia's banging hot body walking towards him, haughtily tossing her braids back over her shoulder. All he could think was *let's live and let live*, with a smirk on his face.

Latitia scowled at him.

Instead of responding, he looked straight at Dwayne. A moment only men understood passed between them. He looked pissed off – not so much because JJ was ogling his sister, but because he now understood JJ held the bargaining chip for Alexia. He almost laughed out loud.

'Let's walk!' Dwayne said. 'It's not far.'

JJ nodded once, sealing the deal, and they began to walk. They went all the way along Denmark Hill onto the High Street, then a few turns later into a rundown housing estate.

Alexia's face went from unease, to concern, to absolute horror, and JJ put a comforting arm around her shoulders. They continued to walk in silence, taking in their surroundings. He'd never seen anywhere look so neglected. All the cars seemed dented and shabby and were all more than five years old. Graffiti tags of varying talent were spray painted onto many of the grey concrete walls. Chewing gum dotted the pavements and litter speckled a small recreation ground. It consisted of just two old swings and a roundabout, with some discarded plastic bottles of cider propped up around the posts. Suspicious little metal cartridge tubes glinted next to them. The Johnsons seemed blind to it. He guessed you would be if you saw it every day.

Eventually they came to a bleak, grey concrete block of five stories arranged in a quadrangle with three others.

Alexia looked at JJ in alarm as they entered the stairwell that stank of urine.

'Lift's broke,' Richie explained.

JJ took Alexia's hand and gave it a squeeze. Xavier followed sullenly behind. The stairs were dark, with gloomy yellow-film covered lighting to illuminate the name-tagging that continued all over the walls.

Thankfully, they only had to climb to the second storey.

'Are we visiting someone?' Alexia asked, with a plea in her eyes.

'No,' Richie said, putting his key in the cracked front door.

JJ squeezed Alexia's hand again when her eyes went wide. He knew she was trying hard not to cry. Xavier's face was unreadable.

'Mum!' Richie called, while they stood awkwardly in the plain, magnolia-painted hallway.

A little kid ran in to greet them from another room, closely followed by a naked toddler wearing just a saggy nappy. The place didn't seem big enough. *Five kids, plus them, made eight.*

An attractive black woman joined them, drying her hands on a tea towel. 'Welcome! Welcome!' she said. 'I'm Valarie.' She grabbed Richie, Dwayne and Latitia, one by one, and kissed them, despite them squirming. 'Well, come here. She opened her arms. 'If you're gonna be my kids for a while, you all get treated the same.' And she squashed JJ against her ample bosom and kissed him loudly on the cheek. She then proceeded to hug the life out of the others. Alexia let out an involuntary yelp.

'This is Marcus and this little rascal is Joseph,' Valarie said, introducing the two little ones. 'What lovely-looking children you are – so like your beautiful dads,' she said, shaking her head.

JJ quirked an eyebrow at Xavier. The connection to their fathers was intriguing. Xavier widened his eyes in answer back.

'Right, let me show you to your rooms.'

There couldn't be many bedrooms. JJ hoped – if he had to share – he'd be near Latitia. He looked about him and realized she'd already disappeared.

'Put the kettle on, love!' Valarie shouted. 'Right, follow me.' Then she walked two steps to a door and pushed it wide.

JJ and Xavier poked their heads into the room. Not only was the room smaller than they were used to, but there were two sets of bunk beds, one on each side of the room. It was painted a sky blue, in a paint that had seen better days and there was a rug and a small pine chest of drawers between the beds with a clock on top of it. That was it.

'You boys are in here with Richie and Dwayne.'

'We're on this side,' Dwayne said, pushing between them and staking his claim on the right side of the room.

'JJ and Xav … you take the beds on the left. You can slide your bags underneath,' Valarie said, then turned her attention to Alexia. 'Alex … come with me. You're in with Latitia and the babies.'

Xavier looked stunned. JJ shrugged. *Guess he didn't need to unpack.* There was nowhere to put anything anyway.

'Alexia, my name's Alexia.' Her lips were a tight line when she glanced at JJ as she followed Valarie.

JJ kicked off his shoes and claimed the bottom bunk by lying on it with his hands behind his head.

'Don't get too comfortable,' Xavier said, putting his phone to his ear. 'We're not staying.'

JJ let out a blast of air in amusement. It was no surprise when Xavier immediately swore.

'Bloody answerphone. He's been deliberately not answering all day.'

'Of course. Just chill out, Xav. Go with it for a while.' JJ closed his eyes and absorbed the throbbing bass coming through the wall from the flat next door. It was kind of relaxing. It didn't matter where he was. His whole existence was mapped out for him and had been from the moment he was conceived. There was no free will where the Fates were concerned. No point in fighting it. Xavier was just tediously slow in learning this.

FORTY-FIVE MINUTES later and Valarie shouted, 'Food's in ten, guys!'

JJ eventually roused himself with a deep sigh and wandered out into the living room.

Richie and Dwayne were sitting at the small dining table doing homework. The two younger kids had their heads stuck into some kids' programme on a prehistoric TV. Xavier and Alexia were sitting on the battered black leather sofa, texting like mad on their phones. Latitia was the only one missing.

The opportunity to speak to her alone wasn't going to come up often, so JJ turned quietly before anyone noticed him and went back out into the hallway. The clattering of pans told him where Valarie and the kitchen was, so he knocked on the only other closed door.

'What?'

'Can I come in?' JJ said as quietly as he could.

There was a long pause. 'What do you want?'

'Just to talk.'

Another pause. 'Make it quick and then go.'

Smiling, he went in.

.   .   .

LATITIA WAS SITTING with her feet hanging over the top bunk. She had homework books around her, but was texting on her phone.

JJ looked around. The room was laid out exactly the same as his, except this one was girlier; purple, filled with stuffed toys and pictures, obviously drawn by an under-five. 'Can I come up?'

Latitia looked a little alarmed. 'No. Don't you understand boundaries where you come from?'

He laughed, not at all offended. He wouldn't mind betting she was prickly with all the boys. 'Ah come on. I only want to talk. It's kinda hard for us being away from home.' He was shamelessly playing the sympathy card, but *all's fair ... and all that.*

She narrowed her eyes. 'Five minutes.' And moved her books to make room.

JJ grinned, climbed the small ladder and sat next to her. It amused him when she shuffled up the bed to make the space wider between them. 'Texting your boyfriend?' he said, pointing at her phone still in her hand.

The pause before she said, 'Yes,' gave it away as a lie.

'I don't believe you,' he said with a smirk.

Latitia sat up straighter. 'Why? Don't you think I would have a boyfriend?'

He was trying not to laugh as he'd really offended her. His face got serious. 'Of course I do. It's just I think you wouldn't bother with the average boy around here.' It was obvious flattery, but she *was* beautiful and deserved the best.

For a moment she looked stunned; studying him for a hidden joke or insult. 'That's right,' she said eventually. 'So don't even try it.'

Laughter escaped him before he could stop it. Then he wiped it off his face with a hand. 'The problem with that is, I'm not from around here.' A frown crossed his brow. *Why was he bothering?* Then he shrugged the thought away. He was here to have fun. 'And I'm far from average.'

When his eyes returned to hers, she'd been studying him closely. 'My mum knows your dad.'

JJ nodded. 'Yeah, probably both my dads.'

Her eyebrows rose for a second. 'The other two … different dad?'

It surprised him how easily she got it.

'Me too … the two little ones have a different dad.'

JJ smiled at the simplification. 'Mine's slightly more complicated.' How do you explain to someone how your mother carried them all in her womb at the same time? And that it was a miracle he was conceived at all. It was pointless going into it, and so he leaned back against the wall. 'So why no boyfriend then?'

Latitia shrugged. 'I'm too busy, I don't want the distraction.'

He conceded with a nod. 'What do you want to do?' There weren't that many people in his life who were ambitious. Everyone in his family had their lives mapped out for them.

'I want to be a dancer.'

Her words were defiant, but he could tell she expected him to laugh. His eyes roamed over her body, appreciating every toned muscle. He could totally see her doing that. 'My aunt was a dancer.'

Her eyes lit up in surprise. 'Really?'

'It was before she got married.'

'What about you, what do you wanna do?' Her animosity suddenly gone, she turned towards him, waiting for his answer. *But what could he say?* That he and Xavier would someday have to battle it out for the crown? It didn't matter what he wanted, or who he met. Everything would turn to crap anyway.

With a deadpan face and a deep sigh, he said, 'I'll have to

go into the family business.' His eyes flashed to hers and he decided he didn't want to talk about it anymore.

She was staring at him and sensing his unhappiness and he didn't like it. It made him feel exposed.

Then Richie burst into the room, without knocking, and the heat was taken off him. His beaming smile dropped for a second when he saw JJ on his sister's bed, but his excitement got the better of him. 'Tish, come and see. It's massive.'

Latitia was already climbing across JJ to get down the ladder. He slid down straight after.

'What is it?' Latitia said

'A massive TV.'

'A Game Station! A Game Station!' Little Marcus was saying, jumping up and down.

In the living room, they were all gathered round while Valarie pulled the last of the packing from the huge TV, satellite box and games console.

JJ cast a look Xavier's way, who rolled his eyes. It was obvious who'd sent it.

The Johnsons were thrilled.

'Set it up, Richie. We'll have dinner on our laps tonight.'

Valarie left the room, wiping her eyes. It left JJ with a strange, confusing ache in his stomach. He couldn't tell if she was happy or upset. It didn't take much to guess there wasn't a lot of money coming into this house. He'd never been around people this poor and it made him angry. Whether it was Dante or Jay who sent this, it didn't matter. They were riding rough-shod into people's lives and affecting them enough to bring a nice woman to tears.

THEIR FOOD CAME on patterned plates of varying sizes with cutlery that didn't match, but they ate quickly. The fish and rice were cooked in a way JJ had never tasted before. Valarie explained it was Caribbean food. He liked it and guessed she'd been warned to avoid serving meat as their bodies had trouble metabolising it. Still troubled by Valarie's reaction to his dad's gift, JJ went to clear up the plates and take them into the kitchen.

'Don't worry, love,' Valarie said. 'Richie and Dwayne can do it tonight. I'll draw up a rota tomorrow. You go and put your feet up.'

He just shrugged and went back into the living room. Latitia had gone back to her room.

'It's the pits,' Alexia said as soon as she was sure they were alone.

'If Dad thinks sending all this means we're staying, he's wrong,' Xavier said.

JJ sighed and kicked back in his chair, vaguely aware there was a knock at the front door. 'Does it matter where we are? It all ends up the same. I don't mind it. At least they're not fake.'

'We'll see if you feel the same when you've humped her,' Xavier said.

JJ flashed a warning look at Xavier's unapologetic face and went to come back with something, when he heard raised voices coming from the hallway.

All three of them leapt to their feet to go and see what the shouting was about.

There were two huge white blokes, almost the size of his father's guards, standing in the hallway. One, with tattoos covering a shaved head, was pushing Richie and Dwayne back, telling them to, 'Back off!', The other, fatter with pale skin, freckles and ginger hair was holding back Valarie. It was clear the boys were trying to push them out of the flat. Latitia held the two little ones against the back wall, crying to get to their mother.

'I told you, next week. I'll have it by then,' Valarie was

shouting.

'We'll just take something now to help you remember,' the bald one said. Then, when the boys realised what he would inevitably take, they renewed their efforts to block him. He simply tutted, pulled back his arm and punched Dwayne squarely in the eye, sending him flying. The Johnson boys were big, but still only youths and no contest for the two gorillas pushing their way in.

JJ immediately stepped forward into the hallway, barring their progress, and Xavier was right there with him.

The two men pulled up when they caught sight of them. 'What do we have 'ere?' the bald one said, laughing.

'Please go into the other room, boys. I can deal with this,' Valarie said.

'Maybe I can be of help?' JJ said.

The bald guy was looking mildly amused. 'And what can you do, Son, eh?'

JJ felt Dwayne come up to the left of him, rubbing his jaw. 'What do you need?' JJ asked.

The bald debt collector pointed past him into the open door to the living room. 'That telly for starters.'

'I'm afraid that's mine.'

The two men faced each other and laughed. 'Oh, I'm frightfully sorry,' the bald one said, mimicking a posh accent.

'How much money do you need?' JJ said.

'No JJ,' Valarie said, shaking her head.

He wasn't sure if she was scared or embarrassed at owing these goons money.

'Five hundred quid!' the bald one said as if throwing any figure out as a test.

Xavier came closer and touched JJ's hand. The minute they touched, they could project each other's thoughts. They'd practiced since they were children and did it often –

A gift from their grandmother's side of the family. *How much do you have?* JJ asked.

About four hundred. You? Xavier replied.

About the same. JJ put up his hand. 'One minute.'

The bloke waved him on to continue with a regal hand, still making fun of him, and Xavier disappeared to get the money. The two men exchanged a look.

Xavier returned a few minutes later and put a wad of money in the bald one's hand. 'There … Five hundred pounds.'

The man did a quick count and grinned. 'Same time next week then, Son.'

Valarie put her head in her hands. He wasn't sure if it was because he'd paid for her, or because the bloke knew he had a source of real money and was going to be back.

'No!' JJ said. 'When you come next time, it will be for the final balance. Do you understand?'

They turned to each other again. 'Do you understand?' he mimicked again. 'Can you believe this kid?' Then his arm flew out and grabbed JJ by the throat.

CHAPTER 4

The four huge Santalini vampires sat parked up conspicuously in the street, in the blacked-out SUV. It was almost dark and the streetlights had just come on. They'd been watching the flats. One picked up his phone. 'Dante?'

'Keenan … everything OK?'

'Yeah, we're outside the place now. Two local characters have just gone in. What do you want us to do?'

There was silence for a beat. 'Watch … do nothing yet. I want them to handle it themselves. I don't want them to assume we'll bail them out every time they mess up.'

Keenan wasn't sure, but Dante was the king, so, with a deep sigh, he agreed and clicked off his phone, throwing it on top of the dashboard.

Dante had really lost it this time. Keenan was a prince of the Santalini royal family, revered as the special forces of the race. He was also mated to the queen's sister. They'd been brought up in a place just like this and he knew how dangerous it could be. Life was cheap, and spoiled, mollycoddled kids like Dante's and Jay's could be crushed like bugs. They were mad leaving them here like this.

'They've been a while,' Reeve, his guard mate said, interrupting his thoughts.

Keenan nodded absently. Those two low-lifes had debt collector written all over them.

LATITIA WATCHED in horror as the bald one walked forward, forcefully lifting JJ off the floor by the neck, and smacking the air out of him against the wall.

JJ's face went red, holding the man's wrist, trying to loosen his grip, while he held him seven or eight inches off the ground. The other boys shouted and went to take a step towards him, but the ginger one held out his hand and shouted, 'Keep back or he'll snap his neck!'

Everyone was forced to watch as JJ went limp in the man's hold. The man's partner smiled smugly as if it was a normal day's work for him. Xavier watched nervously, and Dwayne and Richie caught Valarie in their arms before she made matters worse by flying into them.

'Now listen, you little shit. You're gonna have five hundred quid for me the same time every week. You understand?'

Latitia was watching JJ, hoping he'd agree just to end this nightmare, but apart from being red at the lack of air, he seemed relatively relaxed in the guy's grip. He'd completely stopped fighting.

She wasn't sure what happened exactly. The guy holding him began to shake his head. Then he seemed to stagger forward, loosening his grip enough for JJ to slip down onto his feet. As JJ's colour began to return to normal, an awful noise started to come from the bald man's throat.

His friend went to take a step forward. 'What the—?'

Xavier moved for the first time and barred his way. In a weird reversal of roles, he shook his head. 'Leave them.'

JJ and the thug seemed to be having a private chat. But that definitely wasn't the case because JJ hadn't spoken a word. Then the thug released his grip and doubled over, legs buckling, and JJ eased him down onto the floor until he was lying flat on his back and staring up at the ceiling.

Xavier went to JJ's side and touched him on the shoulder. 'Enough, JJ.'

JJ still hadn't let go of the arm that had held him. Blood began to trickle from the man's nose, and down the side of his cheek.

Everyone had witnessed something, but none of them were sure what it was.

Valarie hitched a breath and covered her mouth with her hand. The guy's partner looked uncertain and agitated. 'What you done to him?'

'Stop now,' Xavier repeated, quietly.

But JJ appeared fixated on the unmoving body at his feet.

Then, from nowhere, Alexia pulled JJ back by his free arm, breaking his stare and forcing him to let go. He blinked, appearing to wake up from a trance.

The other guy left standing was now looking like a trapped animal, not sure what to do. JJ turned to face him, now breathing as if he'd been running. 'Take him! And have the final bill next week.' His voice was cracked and dry, as if it was a strain speaking.

The guy stooped and struggled to pick his partner up, not allowing his eyes to leave JJ for more than a second. Then he threw him over his shoulder in two hefts, like an old carpet. Dwayne got the door and the man left as fast as he could.

Dwayne shut the door and locked it after him. Latitia allowed herself to breathe. The little ones slowly slid down her leg now it was safe and ran to Valarie. They stared up at the newcomers, as shocked as they all were.

JJ suddenly staggered and held his head. Xavier and Alexia rushed to him and got under each of his arms to take his weight. Before they led him away, JJ looked up to find Latitia's gaze and held it for a moment. His was exhausted, holding such sadness; an unspoken apology, almost. Somehow, she knew it was for far more than witnessing what just happened.

Her hand went to her mouth in horror as a trickle of blood ran from his nose.

Valarie saw the same thing and ran to him. 'He's bleeding. Let's get him straight to bed. I'll call the doctor.'

'It's OK,' Xavier said. 'It's a migraine. He'll be fine after he sleeps it off.'

Latitia swapped a look with both her brothers, who were following the scene as closely as she was. They raised their eyebrows at each other; none of them sure what just happened.

KEENAN STEPPED out from the gloomy stairwell at the foot of the stairs into the path of the two men he'd seen going into the flat. Except, this time, one was carrying the heavy weight of the other in a fireman's carry. 'Need a hand, mate?'

He stopped in front of Keenan.

The man went to step around him. 'Nah, you're alright, mate.'

Then Reeve stepped out from a doorway blocking his way again.

The bloke sagged, knowing he wasn't getting out of this easily. He let his partner down till he was lying on the floor at his feet. 'What do you want?' His eyes were flat, waiting for the inevitable violence.

'Your pal don't look so good,' Keenan said, flashing a look Reeve's way. Reeve understood and bent down to put two fingers to the side of the unconscious guy's neck. He nodded. 'He's alive.'

Keenan gave his attention back to the man in front of him. There was no point in wasting time asking what they were doing in the flat; he'd seen his type a hundred times. It was, however, intriguing how a woman and a bunch of kids managed to incapacitate a grown man built like a doorman. 'What happened to your friend?'

'Walked into a door.'

Keenan didn't miss him tensing and ready to fight. He could smell the spike of adrenalin and his fear. He smiled and took a step into the guy's space. Almost six inches taller, it wasn't hard to intimidate him. The blood that washed over his eyes and flash of elongated fang made his eyes widen and any bravado disappear.

The bloke recoiled. 'Look, I dunno what happened. There was a kid up there. One minute my mate 'ad 'im by the throat, the next he doubled over like he'd snuffed it. That was it … no one done nothin'.'

Keenan frowned. 'Which kid?'

'I dunno … some blond, posh kid. I've never seen him before.'

Keenan was beginning to lose patience. 'And that's it?'

'Look, what do you want?' the bloke said, mirroring his impatience.

Keenan answered by taking another step closer. 'You don't go back there, OK?' he said in his most quiet and reasonable voice.

The bloke was already shaking his head. 'Look, it's not up to me, mate. They owe money.'

Keenan relaxed his stance slightly. The bloke was shitting himself more about the consequences of not going back than he was of him. He was just the messenger and if he didn't go, someone else would be sent in his place. It was better to deal with someone he knew.

'Did she pay today?' Keenan asked.

The bloke looked uncomfortable. 'The kids paid.'

'How much?'

'Five hundred quid.'

Keenan quirked an eyebrow at the amount of cash the kids had on them. 'How was it left? Apart from the obvious,' he said, bobbing his head at the body at his feet.

'We told 'em we'd collect the same amount next week. The kid said no and to come back the once for what they owed. That was when it kicked off.'

Keenan exhaled loudly. The boy was so like his dad it was untrue. He narrowed his eyes on the bloke. 'This is what you will do. When you come next time, you'll come alone, and you'll come here and not to that flat … are we clear?' Their boss, whoever he was, was not going to let the family off by paying up what they owed. It wasn't how they worked.

The bloke frowned. 'Yeah, but what about the money … how will I find ya?'

'I'll be around. Don't worry 'bout a thing.' Then he let a swirl of blood into his eyes as a reminder. 'You'll get the money from me. But don't get greedy.'

The bloke went to stoop to pick up his partner, but Keenan reached out a hand to stop him. 'And you won't say what happened up there … just make something up,' Keenan finished with a polite smile.

The bloke frowned slightly as if to say he didn't much know what went on anyway, but agreed.

Reeve helped him put his partner back across his shoulders. The bloke couldn't get out of there fast enough.

Keenan watched him leave the entrance to the building and hurry along the path as he put his phone to his ear.

. . .

XAVIER HELPED VALARIE put JJ to bed with a cold compress on his forehead and a bucket next to him in case he was sick. They drew the curtains and left him in peace and went back out to the hallway. The others had dispersed.

'Will he be OK?' Valarie whispered. She looked drained and her eyes fearful and bloodshot.

Xavier nodded, deciding that for a human, she was really quite a nice woman. 'He'll just sleep now.'

She seemed genuinely worried about him. He had to remember that she was a nurse and, for a human, blood from the nose could suggest something a lot more sinister than a migraine.

'I won't pretend to know what just happened, but I'm grateful, OK? To both of you.'

Xavier smiled wanly without answering. The least said, the better. He walked into the living room where everyone was sitting in stunned silence. Even the little ones were subdued and looking at everyone to gauge whether they should still be scared. Dwayne was holding a cold flannel to his eye and cheekbone.

Xavier sat on the sofa next to Alexia. 'I want to go home,' she whispered, a tear escaping the corner of her eye.

Xavier just patted her leg. He didn't want to upset her with his disturbing realization that they really were on their own here. No cavalry was going to gallop in and save them. Their father's message had come through loud and clear; they had to grow up.

The embarrassing silence seemed to go on forever – even when Valarie brought them all a cup of hot sweet tea for the shock.

'Is someone gonna address the elephant in the room?' Richie said, in amazement.

'Richard!' Valarie hissed, flashing him an angry look.

He frowned like he couldn't believe no one else was asking the same thing. 'In case you didn't see what I just saw, a bloke the size of a brick shit house just keeled over in our hall, with just a look from the Boy Wonder in there.'

'We all saw, Richie,' Valarie said in her strict parenting voice, trying to shut him up.

'JJ done something to him – we all saw it,' he persisted.

Xavier felt rather than saw Alexia look at him. All the children of sirens had strong telekinetic abilities; partly due to genetics and partly because they were brought up closely with the Murrs – the purest family of their race, but JJ was an anomaly. With the weakest bloodline, as his father was more human, he seemed to have the most developed mental abilities out of all the offspring and had had them since he was really small. No one could get in his head if he didn't want them there and he could easily control things around him. The problem was that his gift came at a price. Whenever he used it aggressively, as he'd done just now, he always suffered a terrible backlash effect, normally in the form of a debilitating migraine. It could put him out of action for days. 'You've got a vivid imagination, Richie,' Xavier said. 'The guy must have had a stroke or a heart attack.'

Dwayne looked exasperated. 'But we all saw ...' he said, glaring at them all.

'Leave it, Dwayne,' Latitia said, coming to Xavier's rescue.

But the look Latitia gave Xavier told him she didn't believe him for a second. Without saying anything else, she got up and left the room.

LATITIA CLOSED the door to the living room and padded over to the room the boys shared. She opened the door and slipped inside. It was quiet and almost dark, just a blueish gloomy light coming in through the curtains. Then closing the door silently, she approached the bed next to the window and could just about make out JJ's form, lying on his back with a blanket over him.

She knelt down next to him. He was fast asleep, but frowning as if he was in pain. The compress had slipped off and lay on the pillow next to him, so she put it back on his forehead.

His arms were outside of the blanket, resting by his sides. A golden bracelet, about an inch wide with strange engravings over it, circled both his wrists. It was the first time she'd noticed them. They fit so snugly, she wondered how he got them on and off.

'Who are you?' she whispered.

His chest continued to rise and fall, peacefully now. He seemed a lot more comfortable than when she first came in.

He'd confused her and intrigued her from the moment she'd set eyes on him. A good-looking teenager who appeared confident and wealthy, but underneath was harbouring some strange and tragic secret. She saw it in his eyes tonight. There and then she made up her mind to put her misgivings aside and get to know him better. Tonight he'd proved he most definitely was not your average boy.

CHAPTER 5

$\mathcal{A}$lexia left for school with Xavier in a noisy bustle with the others the next day. Everyone grabbing a last-minute slice of toast, drink, or a biscuit for on the way. JJ was still out for the count, so they left him in bed. Xavier tried to explain to Valarie that it was normal for him, but she wasn't convinced. Alexia heard her already calling someone as they left. 'Sorry it's such short notice, but one of my kids has been so sick in the night ...' No doubt her father would be her next call.

At school, Alexia followed Xavier from class to class in a daze. She couldn't stop thinking about the previous night's events. Everything terrified her: living in a city where no one appeared to care – the dirt and the mess – the knowing no one. Huge men, able to simply push their way into the place where they lived and having absolutely no royal protection. It all went to prove they weren't getting out of there any time soon and were all alone.

Every time she looked up from her textbook, Dwayne was watching her closely. It wasn't fun like before. Now his expression held the question: *who was she?* The sheer heat of his gaze made her feel uncomfortable.

The morning passed agonizingly slowly, until it was lunchtime at last. The five of them sat down at one end of a trestle table in the school cafeteria. After five minutes of silence, Dwayne stood up. 'I'm getting some food. Anyone want anything?' But his eyes were directly on Alexia when he said it.

Xavier's stare burned her in a silent warning, making her face heat in anger. There was no way she was letting him play dad with her here; life was already bad enough. 'I'll come with you,' she said, standing up and flashing Xavier a defiant look back. Xavier's eyes narrowed: don't push it. She didn't need skin contact to know he meant to have The Chat with her when they were alone. She'd heard it all before and it was boring.

Leaving Xavier with a final glare, her stomach fluttered when Dwayne gently touched the small of her back to guide her towards the food counter. As they neared, Dwayne leaned down to her ear. 'What say we get out of here?'

Alexia flashed a look up to his eyes in shock. He was smiling wickedly with an adorable dimple in each cheek. After a moment to settle her butterflies, she glanced over her shoulder at Xavier. He was saying something to Latitia and still looked moody.

'Quick, before he sees!' Dwayne said.

She swallowed and gave him a single nod. Dwayne grabbed her hand and pulled her through the queue to an exit on the other side of the serving counter.

'Where are we going?' Alexia said, having to run alongside him to match his long strides. They burst out of the doors and reached a path to the street. The light felt bright, but it wasn't sunny; the air smelled of tar and the streets were noisy with cars and people. It felt like the world was full of life while she'd been cooped up in that school.

'I know a great little fried chicken place,' he said, at the crossing just outside the school gates.

'Oh,' she said, coming to a standstill and frowning up at him. 'I can't eat a lot of meat.'

His eyes narrowed, then he nodded. 'Veggie eh?' Er, let me think …'

The beep of the crossing sounded and he pulled her across, forcing her to run again. 'Noodle bar?' he said, as they passed many shops before she could see what was inside.

Now they were a little way away from the school, he slowed down so she could walk. She shrugged. 'I can try them.'

Dwayne smiled quizzically down at her, as if he was a little puzzled by her answer but didn't want to push it. 'Well, you don't know what you've been missin''

A smile crept across her face with the warm glow spreading inside. This boy made her feel good in a way she never had before. He didn't seem to judge her for where she came from, he seemed to take her on face value and that made her feel alive. Brave. Here, she was away from her brothers, enjoying the freedom of it. Never really analysing it before, it dawned on her that there were loads of things in the world she'd never tried.

For the first time real embers of excitement fired up in her stomach. Suddenly, living in Camberwell in the dingy flat, being there, walking along with a cool boy from a rap video, didn't seem nearly as bad as it was before. Instead of feeling punished, a feeling of liberation began to steal through her.

All too quickly they reached the little noodle shop that was more like a canteen. It was tiny with three trestle tables like the ones they had at school, with a Chinese chef and young girl serving. It was quite busy even though it was early lunch and only just after twelve. Sweet, spicy, unusual smells filled the room and made her stomach rumble. She'd skipped breakfast that morning.

Dwayne ordered two bowls of a steaming hot soup and they went and sat side by side on the long bench that ran the length of the table. Looking at the bowl he placed in front of her, all her new bravado disappeared. She was in a place you could hardly describe as a restaurant, with a strange boy, and something in front of her she had no idea how to eat. Thinking that perhaps she should treat it like spaghetti, she looked around at the other people. They all seemed to be eating something different.

Dwayne got up again and went to a small island at the edge of the room and came back with a plastic spoon and a piece of wood wrapped in a paper serviette.

OK... She took them from him gingerly, put the napkin in her lap and used the spoon to taste some of the clear liquid around the noodles. It was a tiny sip and tasted like nothing she'd ever tried before. It was sweet with an aromatic tanginess that wasn't unpleasant.

Alexia became aware that Dwayne's eyes were on her the whole time.

'Good?' he asked and smiled. His eyes were soft – as if he knew she was sampling something for the first time.

She nodded shyly, her lips turning into a small smile. Then watched as he picked up the piece of wood, ripped it from its paper envelope and twisted it in two with a snap. Holding them easily in one hand, he plunged them into the mass of noodles and pulled out a bundle. She watched, enraptured, as he used the sticks as a pincer, easily picking up clusters of vegetables and noodles and bringing them to his mouth.

Dwayne paused when he realized she was watching him.

Suddenly embarrassed, she quickly looked down at her own bowl.

'You really haven't eaten noodles before, have you?'

Alexia looked back at him nervously, but he was smiling. Shaking her head a little and feeling heat flood to her cheeks, she returned to scooping the liquid of her soup in her spoon.

'Here,' he said softly, and scooted a little closer to her on the bench. He reached for her sticks and broke them in the same way he'd done before. 'These are chopsticks ... you've never seen them before?'

She frowned. 'Kind of.' They weren't like the ones here. One of her aunts had been brought up in Japan and she remembered seeing her cousins Dannon and Keefer eating with something similar.

'Where you been livin', princess ... locked up in a castle or something'?'

He was grinning at her again. She smiled wryly. It wasn't so far from the truth. The thing was, there wasn't much call for chopsticks at the palace of Murrtaine where she had spent most of her childhood. Completely submerged in water, everything was different. A pang of longing hit the centre of her chest for her safe and familiar former life. 'Something like that.'

Dwayne was holding out her chopsticks for her to try.

Alexia took them from him and jabbed them into her pile of noodles. Spiking a huge bundle, she brought it to her mouth and pushed the whole lot in, biting off the ends. 'Mmm!' She was unable to close her mouth properly.

Dwayne burst out laughing. 'Not like that, you nutter.' He reached over and closed his hand around hers, placing the sticks the correct way between her fingers. She swallowed, acutely aware of his closeness. The now-familiar, warm feeling vibrated through her from his touch. Her cheeks flamed and her heart hammered. She prayed he couldn't hear it.

'Like this,' he said softly next to her ear, moving his fingers on hers so the sticks moved like tweezers.

It felt as though her insides melted. His voice was like a caress that moved through her body, lighting it up all the way down to her toes. Seeming oblivious to the effect he was having, he gently guided her hand to the food, pincered a small amount of the noodles and lifted them from the bowl. 'See?'

Alexia couldn't move. His cheek was so close to hers she could feel the warmth of his skin. Afraid to breathe, let alone speak, she wondered if he too was aware of the silence and suddenly charged atmosphere. It felt like a moment – one of those in a film – when the two teenagers kissed. Her chest was rising and falling in anticipation.

Instead, he released her hand, drawing away to resume eating his food. Even with his dark skin, she could see the blush in his cheeks.

It was confusing. She suddenly felt foolish for thinking he would kiss her and fumbled again with her chopsticks. Letting out a long breath to steady her nerves, she arranged them again in her hand like he'd shown her. Then she haltingly managed to get some food into her mouth. Strangely, she felt a real sense of achievement and, forgetting her embarrassment, she couldn't help grinning to herself.

Dwayne was looking at her now and smiling again – the previous awkwardness suddenly gone. They then ate their food in companionable silence.

When they'd finished eating, he ordered a couple of cokes and passed her one. 'What's with your brother?'

Alexia nearly spat out her drink and was suddenly alert again. Still, it had only been a matter of time before one of them questioned her about JJ.

'He watches over you like a Rottweiler.'

Pleasantly surprised he meant Xavier, she let out a breath and relaxed a little, pushing her finished bowl away from her. 'He's a bit protective, that's all.'

'That's all?' Dwayne laughed, but he was studying her.

He was confusing. She darted a look at him, aware they were sitting very closely again.

'Look, you can trust me, OK? He said, his eyes meeting hers. His voice was almost hypnotic in its softness. 'We're kind of brother and sister now.'

She searched his face; surprised at the feeling of disappointment in the pit of her stomach. *Was that how it was between them – brother and sister?*

They held each other's gaze for what seemed like a very long time. His eyes were deep and honest. Close up, they were a warm mahogany brown. She could see the small flecks of fire in the irises. Unusual. The kind of eyes a girl could lose herself in.

His lips parted slightly while she studied his face and she couldn't help wondering how the softness would feel pressed on her lips.

'Have you got a boyfriend someplace?' he asked.

Her heart began to beat at the very forward and not at all brotherly question. She swallowed hard, frowned and shook her head.

The beautiful smile he beamed transformed his face. He was so cute, she couldn't help smiling back.

Without pushing it, he changed the subject, instantly lightening the atmosphere. 'So where you from?'

Xavier had ordered her to say nothing, but she figured it was safe to say: 'Ireland.'

He looked surprised. 'You don't sound Irish?'

'Oh, how do I sound then?' she said, a little puzzled.

'Posh!' he said, laughing.

She couldn't help laughing along with him, and he bumped shoulders with her playfully. He really was easy company. It made a real change from the dark intenseness of JJ and stifling protectiveness of Xavier. 'We don't mix much … you know. Went to school out of the country.' She averted her eyes before she gave too much away.

'And you ended up at Marcus Garvey,' he said, with baffled amusement all over his face. Then he shook his head. 'What did you do to deserve that?'

Alexia laughed at his mock-horrified expression.

'Must have been bad, man.'

'We got expelled from our last school,' she said, giggling along with him.

He laughed loudly at that. 'What, all three of you?'

She laughed, nodding. 'Well, it was mainly my brothers … I kind of got the blame for making it worse.'

He nodded with an amused frown. She could tell he was puzzled, but didn't ask for more details and she was grateful. Instead, he changed the subject. 'Listen, I'm DJing at the youth club at school this Friday night. Wanna come?'

She brightened immediately. 'My mum is a DJ. We used to play with her decks as kids,' she said animatedly.

He was genuinely surprised and looked impressed. 'Really? What music she into?'

'Oh, she played House mainly … before she met my dad. In you know, places like Ibiza and the Ministry.'

His eyebrows popped. 'Serious?'

She nodded.

'And she taught you?'

'Yes … well I can do it, but not as good as her.'

He nodded sagely. 'I think I found myself a new partner.' He grinned and bumped her shoulder with his again. 'So you'll come?'

Her heart sank suddenly, guessing Xavier's response.

Seeming to read her mind, Dwayne began to stand up and held out his hand to help her. 'Don't worry, we'll invite the Rottweiler. And if anyone misbehaves, JJ can zap them with his x-ray mind!'

She laughed loudly then and stood up as well. Her heart fluttered as she nestled her hand in his. He held it all the way back to school and she let him.

CHAPTER 6

*X*avier found himself alone at the table with Latitia. She really was hot. He totally got what JJ saw in her. It even crossed his mind to go for her himself, but that would be repeating history. It had been a pattern between him and his brother since they'd become old enough to care. She wasn't his type – not really. And he didn't plan on hanging around long enough at this school for his usual fights with JJ. *Then again ... it was their ticket out of the last school.*

'Will JJ be OK?' Latitia asked, interrupting his thoughts.

Xavier looked at her with heavy-lidded eyes and could hardly bother to reply. *She was hooked already.* 'He'll be fine,' he said on a bored exhale. He looked around him at all the kids dotted around the cafeteria. Some alone, some in huddles, most on their mobile phones. All itching to catch up with their friends and perpetuate their fake social media lives.

Latitia narrowed her eyes. 'What's the deal with you two?' she said, bringing his attention back to her.

'Don't worry about it ... we'll be out of your hair soon.' He wasn't being particularly friendly, but it was easier than going into the whys and wherefores of who and what they were.

'We're not stupid, you know,' she said, getting angry.

Girls like her were used to boys crawling all over her. Xavier just smiled and searched her face. 'Aren't you?' he said with a chuff of laughter. 'And yet we've been here all of forty-eight hours and JJ has you in the palm of his hand.' He finished laughing as her face changed to outrage. It didn't hurt to hamper JJ's progress a little. But he wasn't under any illusions. One or the other would have her; it was just a matter of time.

'You prick!' she growled furiously.

It only made him laugh harder.

At that point her brother Richie came back from the counter with a tray of food and sat opposite him. Xavier smirked at Latitia, deciding to leave her alone for a bit. It was boring tormenting her anyway, and his eyes strayed again to the rest of the room.

The dinner hall was now full. *Alexia had been a long time.* 'Was Alexia with you in the queue?' Xavier said, suddenly sitting up straighter, alert in his chair.

His eyes went to Latitia, who was now smirking. 'Well, posh boy,' she said, her eyes glittering. 'Looks like Dwayne and JJ are peas in a pod.' She widened her eyes in mock fright.

Xavier seethed. He hated that she was right. While he'd been busy tormenting her, Dwayne had used the opportunity to get Alexia away from him.

'Where has she gone?' he demanded, looking furiously at Richie.

He just shrugged. 'Dunno ... probably gone down the High Street.' Then he continued eating as if it were the most natural thing in the world.

Well not in his world. Xavier's brain raced. She was away from him, *god knows where,* with only a human to protect her. He seethed again that his father could have done this to them.

'Whatsup?' Latitia said, clearly enjoying herself. ''fraid Dwayne'll get his grubby paws on her?'

'Latitia!' Richie said, with a look of apology directed at Xavier.

Latitia just grinned, leaning back in her chair, satisfied that nothing more needed to be said.

'She'll be fine. He'll look after her.' Richie said, looking him directly in the eye in all seriousness.

Xavier acknowledged him with a small nod, but he wasn't happy at all.

Richie finished eating and pushed his tray aside. 'You know it would help us if we kind of knew what we were dealing with?'

Xavier studied the boy for a long moment. He was sincere enough, and probably a good kid. But he couldn't handle the truth – not yet anyway. 'Like what?' he said lightly, looking around him, knowing his avoidance would piss the boy off.

'Well, for starters, you're obviously not from round here?' Richie said.

Xavier narrowed his eyes. 'We're not.'

'Where you from?'

Richie was trying to be as upbeat as he could to put him at ease, but Xavier was not comfortable with where the conversation would inevitably go. 'Ireland.'

'Aaand? … You gotta give us a bit more than that.'

Xavier didn't answer. Just gave him a blank look.

'Look … you're living with us. You've obviously got a few bob – if the presents from your dad are anything to go by, and what was last night all about?'

There it was … Xavier sighed deeply. It was bloody typical that this shit was left down to him to deal with. Just as he was about to fall into the practised spiel about JJ's migraines, Richie cut across him.

'Before you say a load of bollocks, let's cut the crap, OK? We all saw JJ did something to that bloke – don't get me wrong, I'm grateful. But don't you think it would be fairer and safer to let us in on it a bit?'

Xavier laughed and wearily shook his head. He actually liked this kid – and he didn't take to people that easily. 'Whatever you think it is, you're wrong, OK.' He sighed, worn-out now. 'You have no idea what you're dealing with.' He flashed a warning look at Latitia. 'You have nothing to fear as long as you don't piss us off.'

'Who, JJ you mean?' Richie said, looking suddenly alarmed.

'Any of us.' Xavier directed his look straight at Latitia, hoping to scare her when she joined the dots.

Latitia narrowed her eyes. 'Dwayne,' she said, more to herself.

Xavier raised his eyebrows in surprise. 'She's cleverer than she looks.'

With impeccable timing, Dwayne and Alexia walked back into the dinner hall. Xavier checked his watch just as the bell rang. They'd been out for the whole of lunch. *Where the hell have you been?* He projected, standing up and grabbing her by the wrist.

OW! Out to lunch, she glared back at him.

They glared at each other, inches apart.

You went off on your own to the middle of god knows where? Have you taken leave of your senses?

It's OK, Xav, I was with Dwayne. She raised her arm, showing she still held onto Dwayne's hand.

He laughed spitefully, out loud, at the ludicrousness of the situation.

Then, remembering they weren't alone, he and Alexia turned their heads to the other three watching them closely.

'You all saw that, right?' Richie said to his brother and sister.

Latitia and Dwayne both nodded.

Xavier sagged. *Shit!* In his anger he had just had a telepathic conversation so obvious that the three Johnsons, who were already majorly suspicious, had clearly seen and worked it out.

The second bell sounded, saving him. He tutted loudly and yanked her away from them by the wrist he still held. *Nice one, Alexia!*

What did I do? She whined.

Xavier took a quick glance over his shoulder to see the three gobsmacked Johnsons standing shoulder to shoulder, watching them go. They needed to get out of there.

'Oops!'

Not paying any attention to where he was going, he slammed straight into a girl. Not just any girl, but the one who had stuck in his memory from yesterday.

Her tray with dirty plates clattered to the floor. Alexia tutted and took the opportunity to skulk off through the crowd. Deciding to let her go, he bent down and helped the girl pick up the pieces.

Strands of her honey-blonde hair escaped her ponytail and fell into her face and, as they finished, she looked him straight in the eyes. They were big and blue, but something in them told him she was sad – no, more than that, dissatisfied. But she was also determined and strong. He'd always prided himself on reading auras well and hers made him jolt with electricity at the strength of it. He'd never had such a powerful impression from a human before. They were always so weak and insipid.

Picking up the last broken piece, he made sure his finger

gently brushed against hers. *Yes.* It confirmed in one second everything he'd just thought.

She snatched her hand away as if she'd got a static shock from him. Then she looked embarrassed. Her peachy-clear, pale face went a rose pink and looked beautiful against her blond hair. She wore no makeup at all, he noticed. She didn't need it. 'I'm sorry,' he said, his voice suddenly croaky.

They slowly stood and he put the piece of cutlery in his hand on her tray.

As soon as he spoke, Paige felt her cheeks go red again. He was the most beautiful boy she'd ever seen. Like model beautiful, times a hundred. Those green eyes that were so green they didn't look real. Soft black curls of hair reaching his shoulder. Literally no one wore their hair like that – not around here anyway. Today he wore uniform; meant to make everyone the same. It had failed because, this close, she could see it was the right colour – navy blue like everyone else's, but he actually wore the blazer. To a girl whose mum moonlighted as a seamstress, it was obvious from the cut, the material and the buttons that they were handmade. The boy looked like he had literally walked out of the pages of a magazine.

And when he spoke, his voice was raspy and so well spoken she almost swooned.

'That's OK,' she heard herself saying, after way too long. Then felt idiotic when she flushed red again.

'Here,' he said, passing her what looked like a real square hanky.

A little confused at first, she realised to her horror – when he pointed at the front of her cream-coloured shirt – that she had what looked like ketchup all down the front of it.

She nearly died a thousand deaths; she was so embarrassed in front of this demigod, this vision of beauty. It didn't matter that it was his fault that it had happened in the first place, all she could think about was that he should see her like this and she needed to get away from him as fast as she could.

Instead of taking his hanky, she side-stepped around him, slammed the tray down on a table instead of the finished pile and ran out of the room, barely containing her tears. His eyes followed her. She knew it because they were burning a hole in her back.

CHAPTER 7

J J opened his eyes and, for the first time in days, the pain didn't feel like an axe slicing through the side of his head.

He remained still for a few moments, just to make sure. He listened to the hiss of air brakes and the beep of a lorry reversing through his open window. Then the heavy metal clang of what he guessed were the dumpsters being emptied in the carpark below. He moved his fingers and then his toes. No numbness or pain, everything seemed in working order.

Now for the real test.

Bracing himself for the tidal wave of nausea, he lifted his head slowly from the pillow until he was looking at his toes and shifted his weight onto his elbows.

After the initial wave of dizziness, the world stilled and there was still no pain.

It had passed.

His curse: the debilitating pain that had plagued him whenever he lost his temper and used his telekinetic powers, was over.

Gaining confidence, he swung his legs over the side of the

"

bed and slowly sat up. He took a minute to let his head adjust to the change of angle.

Something rattled in the next room. Someone was home.

JJ stood slowly and lurched for a second, grabbing hold of the bedpost. His legs were jelly and he was as weak as paper. God knew how long he'd been out. It had been a long time since he'd lost his temper like that.

After a moment, he walked unsteadily to the door, opened it quietly and peered outside. He wasn't sure who was home or whether he could handle talking to them.

Valarie walked out from the kitchen and pulled up sharp. 'JJ! You're awake.'

He smiled a little at making her jump. 'Sorry … how long have I been out?'

'Two days.'

Not bad. It could have been as long as a week.

'I'll make you a hot sweet tea,' Valarie said, turning back towards the kitchen. 'You must be dehydrated.'

JJ followed her. 'Where is everyone?' He had no idea what time or day it was.

Valarie looked up at the plastic wall clock. It said 4 o'clock. 'They should be home from school soon.'

She poured two cups of tea. 'Come and sit down. You look a bit shaky on your feet. Then you can tell me all about it.'

JJ sighed and followed her into the living room. Memories were coming back to him thick and fast. Filling him with a progressive sinking feeling that he was not going to escape having to give some sort of explanation.

They both sat down in the living room, he on an armchair and she on the sofa.

'We've got about fifteen minutes before the kids get back. I wanted to thank you privately for what you did.'

It wasn't what he was expecting. He smiled wanly. 'Didn't really think much about it.'

'Doesn't matter. You were brave. It wasn't your battle and you bought me some time. I can't thank you enough.'

He put up a hand to stop her. 'Please … it's OK.' Just then a wave of hopelessness washed over him. It wasn't OK, although not in the way she thought.

'What is it, JJ?' she said softly. 'Look, you don't have to tell me, but it helps sometimes, you know.'

JJ took a deep breath and looked into her eyes. She was looking at him so kindly, but she had no idea. There wasn't a whole lot she could do. *Shit*, there wasn't anything anyone could do. Nevertheless, he could trust her. 'How do you know my dads?' he asked, looking up through his eyebrows.

A smile instantly transformed her face. 'Oh yeah. I know both your dads from years ago.' She leaned back into the sofa with a sigh. 'A pair of real heartbreakers. I used to work in a small walk-in clinic for iffy diseases, in Soho.' She was smiling, until he fell in. He should have seen it. She was a nurse. 'The girls from the local establishments would come in and they all adored your dads – particularly Jay. He kinda looked out for them all. He lived close by and I got to know him very well,' she tacked on, slightly embarrassed. 'He donated quite a bit to the clinic.'

JJ wasn't stupid. He knew where his dad's hotel was, and what the bars were like around it.

'Everyone knew them on the club circuit – they were real celebrities. But we always knew there was something very different about them … something …'

JJ remained still and looked her dead in the eye. 'Something, what?' he said flatly.

Valarie sighed deeply. 'We were never sure exactly. But you kids have it,' she said, nodding. 'I knew straight away.'

He held her gaze for a long moment, then looked around him. 'How come we're here … now?'

'Dante contacted me last year.'

JJ frowned. Last year was way before they got expelled.

Valarie read the confusion on his face. 'Jay had the business there, but Dante … well, we had a bit of a thing back in the day.'

His eyes widened in shock. It was the last possible thing he expected her to say.

She held up her hands. 'Nothing serious, I promise. And it didn't go on for more than a few months. Before your mother. You couldn't even count it as a relationship – just when he was in town. You know … that type of thing,' she skated over, assuming he disapproved.

JJ shrugged it off. It was a surprise, yes, but he had no illusions about either of his fathers. They had a complicated relationship with his mother and it was none of his business. All three had been there as parents, and in the dangerous world he came from, that was what mattered. Knowing what he and Xavier had been like, he guessed his fathers weren't much different when they were younger.

'He kind of kept in touch ever since. Every couple of years, just to see how I was doing. That kind of thing.'

Dante acquired people like possessions; he never really let them go. He studied her face and felt quite sorry for her. She was back-pedalling in the hope she hadn't offended him. The truth was, he seriously doubted whether Dante had gone behind his mother's back. It was one of the things he admired about them – their ability to be honest in most things.

Valarie seemed to read his mind. 'There was only ever one woman on both your dads' minds. I knew that.'

He guessed by the wry, regretful smile, she wasn't the

only person his dads had had flings with. It must have been hard for her or anyone else knowing his mother was with both men at different times. They would never understand what had happened. That it wasn't his mother's fault. It had cost her dearly with a lot of heartache and he wasn't about to discuss it with a stranger.

Valarie seemed like a really nice woman, and he was grateful she didn't push it any further. 'Thanks for taking us in,' he said eventually.

She smiled in relief that he wasn't angry with her. 'No problem, honey. I was glad to be able to give something back to your dads for everything they've done for me over the years.'

JJ stared at her again. He wanted to scan her brain to find out exactly what his dads had done for her, and how much she actually knew about his race, but decided against it. The process could be painful for the subject, and he couldn't risk sparking off his migraine again. He opted for the old-fashioned way. 'Did they ever … you know, explain anything to you?' he said, leaning forward, glancing at her warily, elbows on his knees.

Valarie looked at him steadily. 'They knew that wasn't necessary. I saw things no one could explain,' she continued, staring at him with meaning.

JJ studied her intently. He could see what Dante had seen in her. She was making this whole thing a lot easier for him. 'What about the others? Dwayne, Richie and—?' he said, letting his voice trail off.

'Latitia?' she finished for him. Then she shook her head. 'No. But I'm gonna trust that you know they are my babies, and I want them to be safe … you understand?'

He nodded thoughtfully. He understood why his dads trusted this woman. 'Of course.' It was a bargain on a need-to-know basis, and he accepted that.

The front door rattled and opened with the crunch of keys. With the sudden barrage of noise and voices, their heart to heart was at an end.

THE FIVE TEENAGERS blustered in chattering or texting on their phones, waking the little ones from their nap immediately. Soon the small flat was full of people with the volume switched up to maximum.

JJ smiled to himself. He kind of liked it. Even though he had many cousins, he'd been brought up in castles and Bond villain lairs the size of football stadiums. This kind of felt real and homely.

It didn't take long for them to realize his bed was empty and pile into the living room where he was still sitting. Richie and Dwayne marched straight in and loomed over him.

JJ didn't move a muscle. Ready for trouble, he looked up at them and waited.

Richie nodded and put out his hand. 'Dunno what crazy-assed shit you pulled, mate, but I'm glad you're on our side.'

JJ held out his hand slowly and they shook. Then his eyes tracked to Dwayne. Richie nudged him, and he nodded once in agreement but didn't say a word.

JJ nodded back. It was an unspoken truce and they weren't giving him the third degree – for which he was grateful. Valarie's voice rose over the younger ones' din from the kitchen, and their attention was soon on something else.

JJ's gaze found Xavier, who simply rolled his eyes and looked away. He understood. Xavier had powers too, but kept his firmly under wraps. It always looked like JJ was bragging or showing off, but that wasn't how it was. Xavier was angry, but he was the only person who understood. Xavier had made it clear that he had no intention of clearing up another of his messes and hanging around there was making it a whole lot more likely. He got it. Xavier didn't want him getting too comfortable.

His gaze fell on Latitia. She was standing just inside the room looking on, waiting to say something, quietly. Her expression said it all: Fear. Amazement. Pity. How JJ hated that.

Thinking she somehow had a right to put her two pence worth in, she walked over and stood right in front of him. 'Got a minute?'

He laughed and frowned up at her. 'Why?'

'I'd like to talk to you in private.'

'I'm busy,' he said, blinking, shaking his head slowly and looking away. It was brutal shutting her down like that, but there was no way he could go there now. Xavier was right. She knew too much about him already. He felt exposed and he didn't like it. It was better if she hated him than this soppy, compassion shit that was coming off her in waves.

'So you're ... you know, OK?' she stammered, shifting her weight uncomfortably.

JJ nodded moodily, without looking at her. She was confusing him and wouldn't go. He was angry she was forcing him to hurt her because she refused to get the message.

'Asshole,' she said under her breath. Then she turned on her heel and stomped from the room.

The mission, though accomplished, felt hollow. Xavier was watching him coolly. JJ covered it by laughing on an exhale, but there was no real mirth. He satisfied himself that the equilibrium was restored with Latitia at arm's length. There was no point in letting anyone close, because when he went down, they would most definitely be dragged down with him.

· · ·

LATER THAT EVENING, while Alexia was on the phone to their younger brothers, getting the news from home, JJ managed to get a minute alone with Xavier in the bedroom. 'What have I missed?' he asked, flopping down on his bunk.

Xavier climbed the ladder to his bunk, while the bed complained with a creak. 'Not a lot. Alexia is getting too close to Dwayne. She sloped off to lunch with him today.'

JJ sighed, put his hands behind his head and absorbed the information. He weighed up all the angles, the pros and the cons. It probably wasn't a good idea for her to get close to anyone, any more than it was for him. But he was also aware that Xavier was far too protective of her. If he didn't start letting her breathe, they could have more to worry about than Dwayne. He was OK and at least someone they knew. 'Dwayne's not so bad,' he said, thinking aloud.

'Are you insane? He can't keep her safe,' Xavier spat, leaning over the side of the bunk to glare at him.

'You gotta let her have a life, Xav. She'll only fight you … surely better the devil you have half a chance to control,' he finished wearily.

Xavier relaxed back down in his bed and was silent. It went on for so long that JJ thought he was actually considering what he'd said.

'No one's coming for us, JJ,' he said, eventually.

JJ didn't answer right away. The penny had finally dropped for Xavier. Their fathers were determined they would have to change and grow up and they were completely alone there. It suddenly made sense why Xavier was holding on to Alexia more tightly. 'I know,' he said. The conversation he'd just had with Valarie went through his mind again and the way he'd savagely cut off Latitia. He closed his eyes, hating himself. 'This is our life now, Xav. We've got to find our way here. Gotta get used to it.'

JJ felt the bed shake as Xavier angrily turned on his side. 'It's OK for you. You're the blue-eyed boy with Valarie, the one who saved the day. And it's only a matter of time with Latitia.'

JJ let out a blast of air. 'Noooo, not going there.'

Xavier didn't answer. He was quitting while he was ahead, knowing something had changed, and didn't push it. JJ was grateful; he immediately deflected the conversation. 'There must be someone you have your eye on?' JJ said, putting his forearm across his eyes. Xavier was the more conventional and serious out of the two of them, but he was a good-looking kid and got just as many girls interested in him as he did.

The silence that followed went on a moment too long to have nothing of interest. He dropped the arm from his eyes. 'Well?'

'There is this one girl.'

JJ smiled. *He'd kept that quiet.* 'Who?'

'I don't know her name. I managed to knock her dinner all down her today,' Xavier said, not able to keep the laughter out of his voice.

JJ grinned. 'Nice … made sure you're on her radar then.'

They both laughed, just like when they were kids, getting into trouble over something.

'Yes. I guess she won't forget me.'

JJ stopped laughing. 'Make the most of it, Xav,' he said, more to himself. Latitia came into his mind again. He squashed it instantly, not sure why she was bugging him.

Xavier misread the silence for him plotting one of their games. 'Keep your bloody hands off, JJ.'

He laughed. 'Get a move on then, brah … I'm getting bored.' He wasn't sure what made him say that – probably because it was their usual MO. But he had no real desire to steal Xavier's girl.

He felt Xavier shift in the bed. 'She's mine.'

It gave JJ pause for thought though. Xavier must really like this one.

Let the games begin ...

CHAPTER 8

*X*avier got a call from his father, Dante, at around 5 p.m. He looked at Caller ID, composed himself and put his phone to his ear. 'Dad?'

'How's it going, Son?' the soft Irish voice said.

Anger suddenly surged through him as he thought of his father sitting back at his desk at Ballygowan Castle, lounging on his secret private island of Filfla or lazing in one of his Italian villas, while he lived out of a suitcase and had to queue for the shower. 'How do you think it's going?' he huffed, swearing under his breath, as there was literally not a single room to go to for privacy.

'You're up next,' Valarie said, nodding towards the bathroom door as he slipped outside the flat to talk.

'OK, you've made your point,' Xavier hissed through his teeth. 'When are you going to pick us up?'

There was no smile in his father's voice when he said on a weary exhale, 'There will be no pickup, Xavier. You need to learn, as the crown prince, that this is what it's like for most people your age. You need to understand and walk in their shoes if you're going to be any sort of leader.'

The reasonableness of it made Xavier want to smash his phone before he got another of his father's ridiculous life lessons. 'You'll wish you listened when one of us winds up dead in a crack den, or Alexia gets pregnant, or JJ's up for murder.'

There followed a satisfactory beat of silence while he waited for Dante to take in what he said, then he realized that his father was trying not to laugh, when he could no longer hold it in. He quickly coughed and composed himself. 'Then you'll have an awful lot of explaining to do, won't you, Son. If you're to rule a nation, you are going to have to find a way to keep your own family out of trouble. I wasn't much older than you when I won the crown.'

Xavier wanted to scream at him that their family was hardly conventional, but he thought better of it. There was a tightness in his father's voice that told him there was no bending him and he wouldn't help his case. The more he pulled against him, the tighter the restraints would get. So instead, he changed tack, trying to keep the emotion out of his voice. 'So, do we get to come home for a visit?'

'The end of term. You can come home for the holidays.'

'Where's Mum. I want to speak to her.' As he said the words, moodily, he already knew the answer. She wouldn't be allowed to plead their case. She was too soft where her children were concerned and his father's weakness, so he would only allow it once they'd settled into their new life. So he wasn't at all surprised when his father said she was busy. 'So, I'll say goodbye. Jay wants a word,' he said as his parting words.

Xavier slumped against the wall and nodded, even though no one could see. It wasn't unusual for him to speak to JJ's father. Both had had an input in their upbringing. And weirdly, despite Jay's hardball reputation, he often found it easier to talk to him. Maybe it was a ploy and they had a good-cop bad-cop thing going on, but, most likely, it was always so near a nerve with his own father. Jay seemed to instinctively give him the distance to open up. As soon as he heard Jay's clear British accent, it all came pouring out.

'My father is impossible. He's lost his mind,' Xavier said, immediately.

'Is it really that bad, Xav? You're away from home with all the freedoms someone your age could want. Do you really want to go back to boarding school?'

Said like that, Jay, annoyingly, had a point. Although he was trying to tie him in knots and deliberately skating over the issue, Jay was, indeed, a skilled negotiator. Tears of frustration welled in Xavier's eyes and he turned to the wall to hide them. However, Jay seemed to cut through it all with the soft reasonableness of his voice. 'I need you to be the big brother you have always been to JJ, Xav. I know how hard he can be.'

Xavier sniffed, mildly placated. The fact Jay understood, seemed to help. 'He makes it too hard, sometimes,' he said, gaining a little confidence. 'He's hellbent on going his own way and he drags Alexia with him. They constantly back each other up.'

He heard the smile in Jay's voice, as if he could completely imagine what it must be like. 'But you handle it better than anyone I know, Xav.'

Xavier sank against the wall, defeated. He was right. He did. 'I wish my father thought that.'

'Trust me. He does. More than you think.'

Xavier let out a deep breath and nodded. As usual, Jay had restored his equilibrium. Part of him knew it was clever manipulation on Jay's part, but another knew Jay would kill for him, literally, too.

His next words gave him more comfort than anything. 'Seriously though, Xav. If you need anything; if you get into any trouble at all, you can call me, OK? I've arranged my schedule so I'm in London for the rest of the school term.'

It was a huge relief to know. 'Thanks, Jay,' Xavier said and ended the call.

He walked back into the flat thinking deeply about what both his fathers had said, and the difference between the calls. He went back into the bedroom and flashed angry eyes at JJ lounging on his bed. He grabbed his towel and wash things, needing the bathroom as the only place in the whole flat to escape to.

JJ's PHONE rang and by the look in Xavier's eyes and his hasty retreat, he'd already spoken to their fathers. He reached over for it on the chest of drawers and Jay flashed on the display. He stared at his phone, momentarily debating whether to ignore it. However, he knew if he didn't answer, his father would turn up for a visit and not in a good way. He knew he loved him, but he took nobody's shit, least of all from his son. 'Dad?' he said.

'JJ, Valarie said you had a migraine,' his father's clear, direct voice said immediately.

It was no surprise that Valarie would give his father regular updates. He wondered if she'd been as upfront about the debt collectors. He quickly hedged that she had and opted for honesty. 'Yeah, I lost it, but I'm OK now.'

'And you dealt with the situation?'

'I think so. He wasn't dead.' JJ frowned. It was a completely bizarre conversation to be having in any walk of life, let alone with a father. He could almost hear the cogs of his father's mind working, thinking of possible witnesses and getting rid of bodies, rather than a teenager's emotional stability.

Jay answered with a simple, 'Well done.' Then surprised him by suddenly asking, 'Are you happy?'

JJ was so taken aback, all he could say was, 'I guess,' before he could think too deeply about whether or not it was true. And for a moment it shocked him, because, for the first time in a very long while, he guessed he was relaxed. 'The people are OK.' He stood up and began to undress for his shower, still a little troubled by the revelation. 'Dad?'

'Yes, Son?'

JJ put his head into the hallway to check Xavier was still in there. He'd be coming out soon and he didn't want to miss his slot. 'How's Mum?' It felt like a lifetime since he had spoken to her.

'She's fine.'

There was a distinct thawing in Jay's voice at the mention of his mother. It had been a long time since they'd been a couple and his father was married to someone else, but there would always be a bond between them no one else shared. It had been a source of comfort for him growing up in such a strange household.

'Does she know where we are?'

'Yes, she does.' The amusement was evident in his voice; he could never hide it where his mother was concerned. 'She's under armed guard at Dante's orders.'

JJ laughed and Jay laughed along with him. Both knew she would be furious. Otherwise she would have been straight there, causing mayhem and ruining Dante's idea of discipline. He could so imagine the conversation between the two of them. Talking about his mother left them on a good note. 'Listen, Dad, I have to get in the shower. It's a military operation to get a turn here.'

Jay laughed easily. 'I'm proud of you, Son. Don't make it too hard for Xavier, OK?'

JJ grinned. He was left looking at the Call Ended message

on the phone. He put it down with sigh, finished undressing and tied a towel around his waist.

'JJ!' Valarie shouted. 'Next up!'

JJ snatched open the door before someone jumped in his place, straight into the path of Latitia coming out of her room. Her eyes widened and dropped to his bare chest in shock.

LATITIA SLAMMED into the warm honey skin-covered muscle with an 'Oomph'.

'Sorry,' JJ said, catching her by the elbows and searching her eyes, concerned.

She wanted to swear at him to look where he was going when she was caught off guard by the depth of aquamarine in his eyes. *Who the hell has eyes like that?*

Then, remembering who it was and the harshness of their last conversation, she took a hasty step back. She felt strangely cold after the warm comfort of his body. Her eyes dropped to the bare skin of his chest. He was half naked, except for a towel hanging low on his hips.

However, it wasn't just the trim athlete's physique that held her attention, it was the array of black and grey tattoos that covered his chest and abdomen. She counted five in all, looking remarkably like intricate coats of arms, in wrought-iron curls and flourishes. Then, as he secured his towel, it drew her eye to those golden bangles around his wrists. They were intriguing in that they seemed impossible to get off.

Her mouth had gone sandpaper dry when she looked into his eyes again. He was still waiting for a signal that she was OK. 'You're sixteen. It's illegal for you to have all those,' she blurted, pointing to his chest. It was lame and uncool, but seeing him without clothes seemed to render her senseless. He made her angry and confused. Feel things she had no business to feel and she realized she was shaking and had a pain in the pit of her stomach.

However, he seemed completely at ease. 'Not where I'm from,' he said, softly.

There was a moment, when their eyes held each other's, that lasted a lifetime and was over too quickly. You knew it meant something, but you couldn't exactly say what it was. But they had one. There and then in the cluttered hallway, with kids' toys strewn all over the floor and music blaring from the living room.

Then the bathroom door opened, Xavier walked out in a cloud of steam and the moment vanished. JJ dropped his eyes and, just for a second, she thought he would say something. Instead, he nodded, went straight in and closed the door.

She simply looked at Xavier, dazed. He was grinning. His apple-green eyes were alive with amusement as if he were very aware of what had just passed between them. His skin was wet, painting his tanned skin with a sheen. He was beautiful, and it made her heart sink in defeat. The gods had truly sent these boys as a test or punishment or something. He was a couple of inches taller than JJ, but muscular, toned and tattooed. He had just one, over his heart; exactly the same design and placement as one of JJ's. His wrists were bare. No bangles on him.

She suddenly became aware that it was obvious she was ogling him, but before she could turn away, and make for her room, he took a dangerous step closer. He was so close she could see the droplets of water dripping onto his chest from the curls of his black hair. He stared down at her, smiling, testing what she would do. 'What do you want?' she said, but her voice came out a croak.

His grin widened and he searched her eyes. 'Still deciding,' he eventually said. Then he laughed, stepped back and as he went to go into his room, she got a clear view of the crown and spread eagle wings across his back.

Then, just before he disappeared, she called, 'The one on your chest … the one that's the same as JJ's. What does it mean?'

Xavier turned in the doorway, still grinning. 'It's my family crest: Dubonnetti.'

Latitia frowned.

The smile suddenly disappeared from his face and he began closing the door.

'But JJ has five,' she persisted, unsure why it felt so important.

He shook his head as the door closed, 'Ask lover boy.'

ALEXIA WAS FALLING in love with Dwayne. She knew it because she took every opportunity to look for him and the cramped accommodations she'd loathed began to seem quaint and charmingly homely. She noticed the arresting colour of his deep brown eyes, the softness of the voice he reserved for her and the rich dark-brown colour of his skin. How his neck sloped kissably into his shoulders, how his defined pecs met ribbed abs and tapered into a narrow waist and strong legs. He was built far more solidly and manly than either of her brothers.

Alexia was even getting used to their routine. They left every morning at eight after he took care of the little ones, washing and dressing them, while Latitia and Richie tidied so their mother could do an early shift or sleep in if she'd been on lates. Every night he'd insist on doing homework at the dining table before getting distracted by making dinner and bathing the little ones. He did it all, encouraged her to do the same and never seemed moody like her brothers did all the time. By day four and five of walking to school, he was openly holding her hand.

It was no surprise Xavier noticed immediately and his face darkened like thunder. She was ready for it and had warned Dwayne. He let go of her hand for her to walk first through the school metal detectors, but it was JJ who met him on the other side. She held her breath while they stood nose to nose. It struck her that JJ wasn't much taller and they could stand eye to eye. Xavier watched curiously while JJ stared him down. A crowd began to gather as if there was going to be a fight, but there was no shoving or shouting. The conversation was internal; JJ was scanning him for his motive and intentions. It was not cool. Her brothers had to stop running her life as if they were her fathers.

She watched nervously as Dwayne didn't step down. She prayed JJ was being gentle. Beads of sweat were forming on Dwayne's brow. A full scan could be painful, especially for a human. Then, without warning, JJ stepped back and she could finally breathe.

JJ smiled and Dwayne wiped his arm across his forehead, angrily. 'What the hell was that?'

Alexia immediately came between them.

JJ shrugged and swung his book bag over his shoulder. 'Nothing … look after her. Xavier won't be so nice.' Then he turned and walked off down the corridor where he got swallowed by the crowd.

Dwayne looked down at her and, for a moment, she thought he was deciding she wasn't worth the hassle. Then he seemed to relax and pulled her into a hug. 'Your brothers are such bloody weirdos.'

They held hands down the corridor and she knew she'd just received the nearest thing her brothers gave to a blessing and she felt like the happiest girl in the world. Too happy.

Then why did it feel like someone would take it away from her any minute?

CHAPTER 9

Xavier simmered on his sister's budding relationship all morning. He tried to think more like JJ and failed. Every time, his mind would drift to them getting physical and he'd want to pulverize his brain until it was nothing more than mush. He'd warned JJ from that very first day; the way they looked all gooey-eyed at each other. Then sitting together in class until they were brazenly holding hands. It was too much; he had to put a stop to it. JJ had simply been quicker this morning, saying he'd handle it. Well, he didn't. Scanning him superficially and declaring him not an idiot, was not enough. He'd have to take over the situation himself, like he always did. JJ was copping out and he was forced to look the bad guy again.

'You completely let him off,' Xavier said, at the end of morning class. 'You know what he's trying to do.' He couldn't even put words to it, it sickened him so much.

JJ stopped dead in the corridor and turned as the flood of kids swept around them. 'Leave it, Xav. Let your sister have her life, otherwise you will regret it.'

Xavier glared at him, taking in the hard implacable look

he'd seen in his father, Jay, and there was no moving him. In the end he tutted, swore under his breath and walked off in the direction of the canteen.

There was no sign of his dumb sister. She'd gone off somewhere with panther boy to help organize his stupid after-school party and JJ would avoid him now for the rest of the day. *Now who was sulking?*

In the end, he went to the counter, paid for a salad, an apple and a can of coke and went and sat at an empty table. He took a few bites of his celery, mulling how best to approach his sister, when he spotted the blonde girl from the other day, carrying a tray towards him. She was with the same girl as before, talking incessantly and gesturing with her hands next to her, but his girl walked purposely, eyes forward as if she would rather be anywhere else in the world. It was utterly captivating to watch. He didn't think he'd ever witnessed someone more out of place.

She was almost level to him and ready to walk past, when in a quick decision, he stood up.

The two girls came to an abrupt halt in front of him – his girl only just recovering her tray. The other one finally stopped talking and they both openly stared at him. 'You!' his girl said, her eyes wide with surprise.

'Hello again,' Xavier said, his mind racing to salvage the situation. 'Sorry, I wanted to apologize again for walking into you the other day.'

'By doing it again?' Her eyebrows went up and a pink flush entered her cheeks. He couldn't tell if she was angry or simply caught off guard. She looked at the girl next to her who shrugged and looked back at him. This wasn't going to be as easy as he'd thought. 'Can you give us a minute?' he said to the girl next to her. 'I just want a private word with—?' He looked at his girl enquiringly.

'Paige,' she said, with the same completely dumbstruck

look. He needed to talk fast and he wasn't going to get anywhere with her sidekick in tow. 'Please—?' he said, giving her one of his most brilliant smiles.

'Jade,' she answered, taking the tray from Paige and grinning over her shoulder, all the way back to their crowded table of girls giggling towards the back of the hall.

He held his hand out to the vacant seat opposite to where he'd been sitting. 'Please, sit with me for a bit.'

Bewildered, she did as he asked and he helped her in with her chair. He noticed the wisps of honey-blonde hair escaping the tight braid that hung from the nape of her neck. She completely intrigued him. Everything about her was neat and functional. No big earrings or jewellery of any kind. Just a neatly pressed white shirt, tucked into the waistband of black trousers, gone slightly shiny from the constant washing and ironing. Her shoes were a black soft material trainer that would be comfortable but completely inadequate for the weather. Her tatty canvas bag full of books, dumped on the floor, confirmed what he suspected; that she was bright but had very little materially.

He moved around the table to take his seat and spotted Latitia on the other side of the hall, moodily eating alone. He should really go over and begin his campaign to get back at JJ, but there was something about Paige that captivated and moved him deeply. He couldn't quite put his finger on what it was. He sat and smiled at her and she fidgeted with her hands in front of her. She was a pretty, blue-eyed seemingly unremarkable girl, but she exuded something. His eyes went to Latitia, exotic and beautiful, then back to Paige. That could wait.

In the end, it was Paige who spoke first. 'You don't need to bother with all this, you know,' she said, holding her palms up. 'I mean, it was annoying, but it washed out.'

Xavier nodded, thoughtfully. He bet she washed her own

clothes too. 'Of course. I just wanted to begin again after getting off on the wrong foot. It was such a poor introduction. My name is Xavier.' He held out his hand across the table for her to shake.

She looked at him properly for the first time, as if he'd lost his mind, and gingerly took the hand offered. 'I know who you are. Word gets round quickly here.' She blushed, looking at their still-joined hands.

Xavier was reluctant to let her go. He was scanning what he could like crazy, trying to learn as much as possible before she pulled her hand away. He ached to go deeper, but he didn't want to alert her to what he was doing.

As soon as she frowned and her eyes flickered in pain, he released her. It had been enough and he hadn't been disappointed. She was a cacophony of contradiction. Church mouse poor but strong principled, sweet but direct, honest but clever and caring but hard-working. In short, like no one he'd ever known, just like he'd suspected. 'Forgive me, I don't know that many people yet.'

'Except the Johnsons. How do you know them?' She smiled in confusion and for a moment he had to work really hard not to show his distaste for them on his face.

He recovered quickly. 'We don't. Not really. Their mum is friends with our dads. We're just staying with them for a while.' The minute he said it, he knew how weird it sounded. They didn't fit in. His father was mad to ever think they could. The best he could do was change the subject. 'Dwayne is DJing at the after-school party this Friday night.'

Paige nodded, back to not looking him in the eye. 'I heard.'

Xavier looked at the bare table in front of her and suddenly realized she had no lunch. 'Forgive me, would you like me to get you anything?'

She immediately shook her head and went to get up. 'I don't really eat lunch. I really need to get back.'

He put out a hand quickly to still hers. 'Please. A little longer. You're not in that much of a hurry to get to Benson's class, are you?' He pushed his unopened can of coke towards her. 'Here.'

She eased back into the chair and cracked open the can. 'Science is my favourite class. Are you aware how much sugar is in this?'

Xavier grinned. He might have known she was a science geek. 'I'll switch, I promise.' She smiled for the first time and took a sip. It transformed her face from pretty to stunningly beautiful. He got a glimpse then of the woman she would one day become. 'Why do you like science so much?' he found himself asking.

She toyed with the ring on the can. 'It's the answer to every-thing; what we know and what we're yet to find out. 'I'm going to be a doctor someday … or a nurse, if I'm not clever enough.'

Xavier's heart dissolved just watching her. It was exactly the profession he would put her in. She fit it perfectly. 'Doc-tor. Definitely,' he said, knowing it absolutely.

She laughed; a soft, melodic sound. 'How would you know, doofus?'

He laughed out loud. Never in his life had he been called that. It was charmingly not insulting. 'Listen, my sister is going to this party and I refuse to let her go with the Johnson boy alone, would you like to come with us – with me? I don't do third wheel.'

She laughed again and studied his face. He watched her, hoping she'd say yes. That was completely new to him. Her smile faded and she looked doubtful.

'At least let me buy you a drink to apologize for ruining a perfectly good school shirt, even though the designer wants shooting.' He was grasping at straws, but as she laughed, he found himself wanting to hear that laughter again and again. He got the impression she seldom did it.

'It's not that I don't want to, it's that my mum does her cleaning job on a Friday evening and I have to look after my younger brother and sister.'

His heart sank. Suddenly what his father had said had meaning. She couldn't automatically go off and do what she wanted to do. Some kids had to work or help parents so they could make enough money to live. He wanted to offer to pay for a babysitter, but he knew he'd be overstepping. Instead, while he said, 'That's a shame,' he was racking his brains to make it happen. 'Let me give you my number, just in case. Then, if you can make it later, or if something changes, you can let me know.'

She was openly staring at him as she passed him her cheap smartphone. He tapped in his number and then passed it back. 'What?' he said at her curious expression.

'Nothing,' she said, shaking her head and getting to her feet. She was looking all around her, nervously. 'Is this some sort of dare or something?'

For a moment, Xavier had no clue what she meant. Then he understood, appalled. It felt like she'd kicked him in the gut. 'No! I was actually serious. It's a genuine offer.' He picked up his bag from the floor, flashed her an angry look, turned and walked away. His cheeks burned that she thought that of him. So little of him. So little of herself.

By the time he got outside to the autumn sunshine, he'd calmed down. It was totally something he and JJ would have done in the past. What had stung was not that she had read the situation so wrong, but that she'd read him as a person so well. To her, that was the type of guy he was. He wanted her to like him. Striding out through the wrought-iron school gates and past a vagrant being moved on by the police, he decided he'd had enough and went home.

ALEXIA WAS SITTING on her bed, in her robe, doing the final touches to her make-up. Dwayne had gone ahead to set up for the after-school party. Latitia was in the bathroom and the younger ones were in the living room with Valarie, watching TV. Recognizing the rare opportunity for privacy, she hurriedly put her make-up back in its bag and dialled her mother. She'd tried several times and got the message 'the phone may be switched off'.

This time, she picked up.

'Hello, Mum. I've been trying to call you for ages.'

'Hello, sweetheart. I know. Your father confiscated my phone. How are you? Is everything going OK?

'It's not bad. I just wanted to hear your voice.'

Her mother tutted. 'Your father went too far this time. Don't worry, I'm working on him—'

'It's OK,' Alexia said, cutting across her. 'Honestly. It's not that bad. A bit cramped, but the people are nice. Dwayne, one of the boys here, is a DJ, actually. He's DJing later tonight.'

'Wait! Backtrack a bit,' her mother said. 'You have a boyfriend?' She sounded excited and not a bit angry, just like Alexia knew she would react. She was the coolest mum ever. 'How did I not know this. Are your brothers OK with it?'

She knew them all so well. Alexia had to laugh. 'Mum, I haven't had a chance to tell you, and he's not my boyfriend. Not yet. But I do really like him.' Suddenly everything lost its humour and she felt serious about it. She hadn't said anything to Dwayne because they were going to have to fight to be together and she wasn't sure he'd think she was worth the hassle. 'They've been awful. Well, mainly Xavier. But even JJ gave him the whole mind scan stare down thing yesterday. I was mortified. And tonight we've got this school party where Dwayne will be DJing and I'm nervous as hell about it. There will definitely be trouble.'

Her mother listened quietly to the whole thing, then she sighed. 'I know it's hard having protective brothers, but, in a way, it is nice that they care.'

Alexia knew she was thinking of her own lonely childhood in the foster system and she was right, but her brothers were insufferable when it came to letting her have any kind of life.

'Look, go there tonight and just be you. I know you would have chosen a nice boy because you're a nice girl. And as much as I'm angry with your father and Jay, they are good judges of character and chose that family, so you tell your brothers that you've spoken to me about it and if they have a problem, they're to come to me.'

A wave of love, gratitude and relief swept over her. How she loved her mother. She always understood what she was going through. 'Love you, Mum.'

'Love you, darling,' her mum said softly, almost making her cry and her new make-up run. 'Now go get 'em.'

CHAPTER 10

JJ walked in through the school gates with Alexia and Xavier and let out a weary sigh. It was now dark and the rain from earlier was slowly drying on the pavements. A streetlamp fizzed above them and the air smelt damp. Alexia was fidgeting with a childlike excitement that not even Xavier's sour face could dampen. *Joy.*

He had to hand it to the school; it looked like a good turnout. Kids were streaming in from every direction and congregating around the harassed teachers, sitting at a desk at the door, taking everyone's money.

JJ eyed the dressed-up girls in short skirts, wearing far too much make-up than was necessary. The boys looked 'hip hop', in their lairy oversized shirts and seemed to have taken great pains over the designs of their faded hair. The damp air was soon a heady mix of sickly perfume and aftershave that made him choke. He was glad his sister's cute little black dress was modest in comparison. Although Xavier had already told her that her butt looked big in an attempt to get her to change it – which she ignored, of course. He and Xavier had opted for conservative blues and greys in Gucci and Armani, teamed with black leather jackets, respectively.

Even he wasn't immune to a pang of excitement when they neared the front and the heavy bass beat a rhythm through the walls. He paid the three pounds cover charge for the three of them with a ten-pound note and guessed it would go part way to buying the new gym equipment he knew their fathers would end up paying for anyway.

The school gym seemed full already when they got inside. The tacky paper bunting and single glitter ball over head was a far cry from their last school in New Hampshire, whose proms and mixers were like fantasy film sets. It was kind of quaint, but the disparity made him a little sad.

Alexia quickly said, 'See you later,' as soon as she spotted Dwayne.

Xavier went to stop her, but JJ grabbed his arm. 'Let her go. She's safe here.'

Xavier pulled his arm out of his grip and glared at him.

'Pick your battles and chill out,' JJ said, already scanning the crowd, wishing he could relax so they could at least enjoy the evening. He opened his senses wide like a net – a natural habit for Atlanteans to pick up power pulses or projected speech. It was no great surprise when there weren't any. They were deep in Homo Sapiens' territory. He glanced across at Xavier and could tell he was doing the same. The look he returned was tinged with sadness. They were far from the madness of home, but where they were had its own dangers. *Latitia.* Strange how his eyes landed on her. She was dancing with her group of friends, in a monochrome top and skirt that skimmed all her curves and already looking the worse for wear. 'Look for your girl,' JJ said, already moving in Latitia's direction. 'I have a feeling she might turn up.'

He didn't catch what Xavier said back. He was already focused on Latitia and the way she moved on the dance floor.

She was wearing trainers even with her cute little outfit and wasn't putting in much effort. Just trying small manoeuvres and dissolving into giggles with her friends when she stumbled or almost fell over and still managing to look frustratingly hot.

A boy with short dreads leaned in and spoke to her just as her eyes met his. JJ saw the moment the idea sparked in her mind. Her arms went up around his neck and she moved in closer in time to the music.

JJ sped up his progress through the crowd, not taking his eyes off the way their lower bodies crushed together as one. It was ridiculous to get angry. He had no claim on her and he knew she was drunk and trying to get a rise, but she had to learn not to demean herself like this in front of others. That was what he told himself, anyway.

He came up right behind her and she pretended not to know he was there. She gripped the boy tighter to her and he responded by doing the same. In the end, JJ swore and tapped her roughly on her shoulder. 'Come and get a drink, Latitia.'

She infuriated him by snuggling into the boy's chest. 'Can't you see I'm dancing?'

The boy, who was tall for a human and at his eye level, read the situation correctly and didn't look so sure. It was that wise decision that saved him a spell in the hospital. He held up his hands in the universal language for surrender and walked off, leaving Latitia to turn and scowl at him. 'You had no right to do that.'

'It's only nine o'clock,' JJ said, already seeing the slight smudge to her eyeliner and lipstick.

She shrugged.

'And you're drunk.'

She rolled her eyes and went to turn away again. 'You're

not the boss of me.' Her hips were already moving as she began to dance again.

His eyes dropped to the temping midriff she was showing as she moved provocatively around him. In a moment, the familiar fierceness rose in him. He snatched her roughly to him and whispered in her ear, 'Then let's dance.'

Latitia allowed it stiffly, as if it took a moment for her mind to catch up with whether she should or not.

JJ relaxed his hold, knowing the instinct was too strong for human company. Strong territorial emotions were normal for Atlanteans when it came to a mate. *Mate?* He instantly shook the thought away. That could never be what was going on here. 'It's just a dance,' he said, a little distracted by the revelation, and began to move with her.

He absorbed the feel of her; soft and warm. She smelt gorgeous, and it was more than the cheap perfume. There was an underlying note to her skin that drove him wild. It overwhelmed him so much he was grateful when she decided to try to keep her anger with him. 'You're too ... too—'

Her expression made him laugh. 'What?' he said, resisting the urge to cover her mouth with his own. The strength of his urges around her shocked him.

She was no more than a few inches away, looking bleary-eyed up at him. 'I don't get you. One minute you've got the whole loner thing going on and then ...'

'There's nothing to get,' he said, swaying with her and looking off into the crowd. But even he had to admit he was sending mixed messages. 'There's just no point in me getting close to anyone. Doesn't mean I don't like you.' *Or want to share you,* he finished in his head.

JJ was glad when she tutted and rolled her eyes, too inebriated to see how she was affecting him. 'You can't have it both ways, Mister.'

The exaggerated way she pointed at his chest made him

laugh because instead of pulling away, she pulled him closer to her afterwards, as if she refused to let him go. She was too drunk to notice but he revelled in it, breathing in the scent of her hair at her hairline. 'If only it were that simple.'

He said it more to himself, but she heard and pushed apart to look him in the eyes. 'Well, what is it then?'

Her lack of coordination had disappeared and her chest was rising and falling in anticipation. As if she knew, even in her drunken state, that they were at a monumental cross-roads. 'Tell me. You can trust me.'

He stared down into her eyes. The noise and the bustle of the party had already receded around them and he wondered how much truth she could handle. Did he want to share any of himself with her? Could she handle that – *could he?* Because he knew, if he did, then he'd have to throw in his whole lot with her. It was the only possible way it could work. But that would be a real relationship and that was something he had little or no experience with.

He was torn. She'd only seen a very small part of his power and knew nothing of his race.

He almost spiralled off in anger at his fathers for putting him and her in this impossible position, when she touched the side of his face to pull his attention back to her. 'If you don't want me to dance with other boys, you have to at least give me something.'

The irony made him feel sad. The reality was he was strong enough to do what the hell he wanted, and that was at the bottom of his fear with her. That she understood so little of that. But before he could say another word, her hand was behind his neck and her mouth was on his.

Strangely, it was only at that point, he remembered where they were. Her friends were nearby, pointing and whispering, but he was soon lost. The kiss bloomed and opened into the deepest, most drugging kiss of his life. She became pliant and soft around him and tasted sweet, like the cherry alcohol she'd been drinking. He had to call a stop to it and pulled apart, breathing heavily.

She was looking at him wide-eyed with wonder and tinged a little with fear, proving she was a shocked as he was at their reaction to each other.

It wasn't his idea to come to the school and it certainly made no difference to the scheme of things, but for the first time, as he gazed down into her uncertain expression, he questioned the need to face the future totally alone.

He nodded to the seating area arranged in the corner of the room. 'Do you want to get some water and talk?'

She nodded, clearly pouncing on it as progress. So he led her by the elbow in the direction of the chill-out area of low gym benches, grabbing two bottles of water from a table nearby. It sparked a gaggle of gossip as the crowd closed the gap behind them. He didn't care. His mind was already scrambling on what on earth he was doing; off-piste and making it up as he went along.

JJ sat down heavily on a bench, while another kid scooted along at his stern look. Latitia sat gingerly, angling herself to face him, leaning her elbow on the wall. He cracked the top off a bottle of water and passed it to her. 'Here. Your mum will kill you if you get home smashed.'

Latitia took it from him and brought it to her mouth. 'I didn't think you were coming tonight?' she said in between gulps.

He smiled a little. He and Xavier had never arrived to anything early in their lives. And in all honesty, he hadn't been sure he'd come himself. Xavier had demanded it in the end so he could stalk Alexia, but he was sure he was also checking whether the blonde he fancied, really didn't come. In the end, JJ opted for as honest as he could be. 'I wasn't sure myself.'

Somehow, the idea of getting into trouble with Xavier, flirting and fighting as they'd done at their last school had lost its appeal. He sensed it in Xavier, too. Maybe their dads had been right and they were growing up. But as he sipped his drink and studied Latitia's stunning, expectant face, it still didn't alter the fact that their worlds were poles apart and neither could play much of a part in the other's. 'What do you want, Latitia?' he asked, suddenly so weary with it all.

Her eyes widened and she immediately balked. He was sorry how arrogant he sounded, but there was no other way of saying it that wouldn't insult her. 'I mean, where do you see this going between us?' he said, motioning his hand between them.

Too late. Her eyes lowered to a scowl and she went to get up. He quickly grabbed her arm. 'Sorry … please … let me explain.' He said the words softly, suddenly conscious of the eyes on him, restraining her.

'Explain then. You kissed me back, remember?' She slumped back onto the hard wood and glared at him. 'You've got precisely five minutes.' She checked the time on her phone and folded her arms.

His grin soon turned into a frown at how he would do that, exactly. In the end he let out a deep sigh. 'How much did your mum tell you about us?'

Latitia shrugged. 'Dunno. Not much. Just that she knew your dads back in the day. And she owed them a lot.'

JJ bobbed his head. He'd guessed as much. He had no idea where he was going with this.

Latitia started to look bored and checked the time again on her phone.

It made him smile. He admired that she didn't take bullshit. 'OK,' he said, leaning back onto the wall. 'Don't say I didn't warn you. I'll tell you a little, otherwise we'll be here all night.' He scratched his head. 'And quite honestly, I'm done with the whole thing.'

He looked up at the coloured lights bouncing off the ceiling from the cheap glitter-ball and wondered how on earth he'd put it in terms she'd understand. But when he looked at her again, her impatience had been replaced with a look of sadness.

'It's OK. I'm tough. I can take whatever it is. I promise.' She stroked the back of the hand resting on the leg he had bent at the knee.

He looked at it as if it were an alien thing on the end of his arm. He felt completely thrown. 'It's hard to explain.'

'Try me.'

He took a deep breath and began with the three of them. 'Well … you know I have a different father to Alexia and Xavier?'

Latitia nodded and waited.

'Well … we are still part of one family – a very important one.' He shifted irritably. 'Like one who has the President of the United States on speed dial kind of important.'

Her eyes went wide and then narrowed with scepticism. 'What are you doing in this dump, then?' She was starting to grin as if he was going to deliver the punchline of a joke.

'Our fathers' last-ditch attempt to force us to grow up.' Then he frowned. 'It strangely appears to be working.' He focused on her face again, looking more and more bewildered. 'We're too old to be tutored and we messed up at our last prep school in America, so here we are. Left to fend for ourselves and clear up our own messes.'

She stared at him a long moment after he finished speaking, no doubt weighing whether she believed him. Then she swallowed, now sobered, and frowned. 'OK. Suppose I believe you, why does that stop you having a girlfriend?' Then, immediately seeing her mistake, she corrected it to,

'Or getting close to anyone?' Her face went a deep shade of purple.

He smiled sympathetically, understanding and feeling immediately sorry for her. It did seem the easiest thing in the world to an outsider. 'Maybe, if it was just a roll in the hay, but I don't think it would be anything that simple with you, would it?' He widened his eyes mischievously, but his meaning was serious enough.

Latitia laughed and visibly thawed in front of his eyes and he hated himself for it. A less scrupulous guy could swoop in and take anything. Her inexperience, despite a level of street smarts, meant the kind of honesty that humbled him. She was the trusting fawn gradually taking scraps from his hand, only to find out his world was a far more dangerous place than any of London's streets. She had no idea.

'I don't understand then. Why can't you?' She was sitting forward, now openly holding his hand.

JJ looked down at their joined hands across his leg. The music vibrated the walls around them and when he looked into her eyes again, all he could think was how unbelievably light brown they were for a human and how they set off the glow in her dark skin, perfectly.

He ran a finger over the top of her hand, then it just began to come out. One word after another, like a train, with no conscious thought to it. 'My father and Xav's father grew up together like brothers, but they weren't blood, you know?

'OK,' she said nodding slightly.

'When Xav's father grew up, he took over the family business. He was the oldest and he won his birth right fair and square.'

She nodded, her face clouding a little at his choice of words, but she didn't stop him.

'Then, a few years ago, when we were young, something

happened where a guy took it from him. He was from another family and *my* father saved it for him.'

Her face was a rainbow of expressions, trying to follow every word. He knew how it must sound. That she probably thought they were some Mafia-type family in a turf war, or something. He simply didn't quite know how else to put it. 'Everyone thought my father would take it over, but he didn't. He handed it back to Xav's father. He loved him.' For some reason a lump came up in his throat as he saw the concern in her eyes. He couldn't look at her and toyed with the bands at his wrists that symbolized all his hopelessness. It was impossible to tell her it all.

'That's good though, isn't it?' she said, gently rubbing his hand. 'They were like brothers and your dad did a great thing.'

JJ immediately snapped out of his wallowing and sat up with a sharp intake of breath. 'You don't understand. To lead the—' He almost said nation and swapped it for company at the last minute. 'You can only pass it on to your eldest son. When we grow up, it should be Xav's.'

Latitia looked at him, completely bewildered. He wasn't doing a good job at explaining it at all. He tried to dig a fingernail under his wristband and failed. It was a habit in times of stress. 'We're a big family and because of what happened, some say it should come to me.' His eyes went to hers, any warmth in them completely gone. 'Xav is my brother and I really don't want it.' When she just stared at him, at a loss for words, he added the killer blow: 'But I won't have a choice and we'll have to fight for it someday. So all the posh schools and all the studying for some pie-in-the-sky job won't change a single thing.'

He'd stunned her into silence and even that made him angry. He pushed his hand back through his hair.

Surprisingly, she made no comment on what he just said,

simply pointing at the gold bands on his wrist. 'What are those?'

It almost made him laugh; that she should home in on the very symbol of everything he'd just said. He held both of them up so she could examine them closely, but pulled them out of reach before she could touch the metal that would burn her. 'They tell my people who I am. That no matter what I do, I'm on this earth to mess everything up. So that's exactly what I do.' His anger was rising in his chest. 'So, me, you, here,' he said moving his hand between them and getting to his feet. 'It's not going to happen.' He stood, turned his back on her and pushed roughly through the crowd. He had to get away before he said something he'd regret. She'd forgive him, let him love her and then he'd mess her life up too.

CHAPTER 11

*A*lexia stood up on the dais with Dwayne and surveyed the crowd. She'd done it many times with her mother when she was small, but this meant so much more. The tacky decor in the shabby gym, in the run-down school, full of happy, partying kids, forgetting all their problems in their simple lives, made her heart glad. She was grown up, with the cutest boy ever, having the best night of her life.

She was proud of him; the crowd adored him. He was truly master of ceremonies. He instinctively knew what they wanted and played it to cheers every time. People's problems, how someone was dressed, no matter what background they were from; nothing existed except the music. In the dance everyone is created equal. Knowing that was what made a great DJ; her mother had taught her that. He was without doubt the coolest boy in the room.

She was so excited, she called her mother and held out her phone so she could see the delighted crowd. 'Just like you, Mum,' she said, almost crying with happiness.

'He's great, darling. I can't wait to meet him. Put him on,' her mother said.

'She wants to speak to you,' she shouted to Dwayne.

He pulled his earphones down and turned his back to the worst of the noise. It was really tough to hear. 'Hi, Mrs Dubonnetti. Thanks. Yes I will.' Then he laughed and handed Alexia back her phone.

'Bye, Mum. Love you,' she said and ended the call. 'Hey! What did she say?' she asked, intrigued.

'She congratulated me on a great set and told me to look out for you and hold my own with your brothers.'

Alexia clapped her hands and laughed. 'She loves you. I knew she would.'

Dwayne grinned, covered his ears again and dropped his next tune. Then he swept her up and kissed her in front of everybody. Alexia couldn't ever remember being this happy. It lasted no more than about three seconds, but it was enough to get a cheer. She didn't care who saw. It was proof Dwayne felt the same as she did. Not even her brothers could ruin that.

Dwayne put her away from him with a grin and told her to stop distracting him, making her laugh. He selected his next song and picked up her hand. 'Come on, we deserve a break.' He went to walk towards the steps down into the crowd when he paused to look out to the doors at the back of the room. He squinted as if he was focusing on something, or someone.

'What is it?'

He shook his head and began going down the steps. 'Nothing. Someone got let in that shouldn't have. That's all.'

Alexia tried to see who it might be. Nothing seemed out of the ordinary, but Dwayne's mood had completely changed. Something was very wrong. He seemed loath to move too far away and grabbed a couple of juices while they stood at the foot of the steps. A few partygoers congratulated him and patted his back, then the crowd parted as a group of boys approached that she didn't recognize.

There were five boys, ranging in varying shades of black skin and all dressed in the trendiest, eye-catching clothes, like models on a catwalk. Dwayne gripped her hand and pulled her into his side. It was his reaction that made her more nervous than anything.

One of the boys eyed her up and down and kissed his teeth, loudly. 'Where you been hidin' this one, Johnson?'

'You shouldn't be here, Trick. This is a school party; you don't go here.'

The one Dwayne had called Trick moved in uncomfortably close to Dwayne. Alexia's heart pumped as the others moved in behind him. She'd seen enough of nights out with her brothers to know there would be trouble. He kissed his teeth loudly again and sneered. 'I don't need to get physical, everyone knows I rule the decks,' Trick said right in Dwayne's face, making him blink.

'That's right,' another boy said, posturing and pointing behind him.

Alexia was now shaking. Her eyes dropped to a boy taking a square black box out of a bag. He bounded up the steps and plugged it into Dwayne's equipment. The music stopped abruptly and another, louder, more aggressive song kicked in. Trick laughed and followed him, producing another set of earphones while another boy began shouting down a mic.

The crowd responded, instantly assuming the change was planned and began chanting the offensive lyrics back to the rapper.

Alexia moved into Dwayne and he put his arm around her. They were forced to watch what looked like madness until a flock of teachers swarmed the stage and the electricity was cut.

Trick dropped the mic to an eruption of cheers and grinned widely as the five of them were escorted off the stage. He fixed Dwayne in the eye as he passed with a smirk and even Alexia could see that he'd completely stolen Dwayne's show.

One of the teachers approached Dwayne angrily. 'It's over, Dwayne. We're calling a halt to it before there's trouble.' The lights came on and Dwayne pulled her away, obviously furious. Alexia couldn't believe he'd been blamed for the whole thing.

XAVIER MADE three or four circuits of the room, just to make sure Paige hadn't lied to him and come after all, then grabbed a can of Coke from the drinks table, leaned against the wall and watched Alexia and the Johnson boy on the stage.

He didn't get it. She was a spoiled princess that had always had everything she wanted, two brothers and loads of cousins who doted on her and here she was living in poverty, in the back of beyond, and he'd never seen her so damn happy. It made no sense at all.

The thing he hated most of all was that the source of her happiness was Dwayne. He was an ordinary boy from an ordinary family and yet he mixed up everything he wanted to feel about this place. Dwayne was a boy – a teenager with raging hormones, like any other. Something Xavier fully understood, especially wanting to get close to a ten out of ten girl like his sister. But every time he convinced himself of that and was ready to pound him into oblivion, he had to do silly little things that proved he was as attentive, sappy and totally into his sister as she was him.

She passed him a CD and he kissed her cheek as if to

prove a point. It made him grind his teeth and seethe. It was clear where their little union was heading; it would be so much easier to split them up if the guy was a dick.

He took another swig from his can and watched Dwayne lead Alexia down the steps from the stage. Then something lit up his senses and made him straighten up from the wall. It was a change on the air currents, a shift in the mood of the room.

Xavier homed in on a group walking through the crowd towards them. The partygoers shifted and parted and he started to move parallel to them to reach his sister.

Almost immediately, the music was yanked off and replaced with hard rap that got the place jumping. And not in a good way. The mood in the crowd had become over-excited and aggressive, like an unlicensed firework display where the dangerous, unpredictable explosives could go off and hit anyone.

Thankfully, just as he reached his sister by the stage, teachers seemed to appear from every corner of the room and the plug was pulled from the sound system. Dwayne was already moving away, pulling Alexia by the hand.

'What happened?' Xavier called after them. Alexia looked upset.

It was difficult to see if she heard as the whole crowd seemed to be herded out at the same time. It wasn't until they were free of the school building and almost to the school gate that he managed to break into a jog and get in front of Dwayne to stop him.

Dwayne glared at him. 'You saw what happened. It was a takeover.'

Xavier made a quick assessment between him and his sister and gauged that the harm was mainly to Dwayne's pride. He relaxed a little. 'Do they go to another school?'

They were soon joined by Dwayne's brother, Richie and

then Latitia. JJ sauntered in through the school gate. It threw him for a moment. He hadn't even realized he'd gone.

'It's finished already? What happened?' JJ said, joining the circle of their group.

'Gate crashers. It got pulled,' Richie filled in for him.

Dwayne still appeared to be furious and began walking again towards the gate. They all fell in behind him, Xavier nudging his sister along by the small of her back. It was dark, they were out in the street and suddenly he was reminded of just how vulnerable they were.

Richie had caught up with his brother and was in deep conversation. Obviously talking him down, just as he'd done with JJ many times before. He was glad to see JJ the other side of Alexia, both now in their usual protective positions with her. Except this time, Latitia was brought into the middle of them too. That was new.

Xavier looked ahead, scouring the street for danger, his mind still on JJ and Latitia's joined hands. Everything was changing. They were changing and he hated it.

It had stopped raining and the roads were shiny, reflecting the streetlamps. It gave the air a kelp-like smell and made the orange glow in the windows of the stacked dwellings almost inviting. It gave JJ an overwhelming ache for home. Although where exactly, he wasn't sure: his mother's family castle in Ireland, his father, Dante's, Island of Filfla, his father, Jay's London hotel? He guessed it could be any or all of those places. It was the people he missed. Comfort. The familiar. They were so far out of their comfort zone that it sank in what a genius decision it had been on Dante's part.

They were a sombre crew walking home. All the earlier excitement had been sucked out of the evening. Dwayne and Richie were in heated debate as to how Dwayne should save face, with Latitia chiming in every so often to not lose their heads.

Alexia looked sulky and angry. However, a sideways glance at Xavier's tight expression made JJ suspect it was less to do with her spoilt evening and her boyfriend being taken down in front of the whole school, and more to do with Xavier using it as an opportunity to berate her. Judging by her face and the way she stopped and glared at him a couple of times, Xavier was clearly having a go at her in her head.

'Leave her alone, Xav. It wasn't her fault,' JJ had to say in the end.

Latitia looked at him strangely.

JJ instantly realised his mistake. Then, after everything said between them earlier, a reckless wave of spite whipped through him. 'We talk in our heads,' JJ said, without further explanation.

'Oh, that's it, tell the bloody world,' Xavier said, throwing his hands up in exasperation.

'I'm sick of lying,' JJ said, without breaking stride. 'Stop picking on Alexia just because you feel so shit.'

Xavier's face dropped and darkened, and Alexia seized her chance. 'Yes, Xavier. They are our family now; we should be able to be honest.'

They turned into the road they lived on and, thankfully, Xavier didn't outwardly react. However, he looked across at Alexia who widened her eyes at him. Xavier was furious. His aura was an angry pulsing red and his face had hardened to granite. He clearly hadn't settled in as much as the rest of them and was becoming more unhappy and volatile.

They walked past the rubbish-strewn playground, now deserted except for a huddle of teenagers, congregating after the rain on the small roundabout. Something insidious niggled at the edges of his consciousness and formed a feeling of dread in JJ's gut. It wasn't them, eying them curiously, and it wasn't Xavier, now ignoring him completely. It was something else.

He could smell it.

He felt it in a current of polluted air.

Fear. Anticipation. Excitement. Very human and very close. 'Slow down!' he called out to Dwayne and Richie. 'Something's wrong.'

They immediately stopped, looking around them to see what he meant. There was nothing there. Not yet. There was something else, too, that he didn't have time to process. The imminent danger was something only an Atlantean could detect. 'Do you feel it?' he said to Alexia and Xavier. They nodded.

'What is it?' Latitia said. She looked scared, trusting his instincts explicitly.

'Stick with me,' he said.

They turned the last corner. A souped-up SUV with music thumping was idling next to the curb. Its windows were blacked out so he couldn't see inside. A neon-blue light ran around its skirts, screaming that someone had a lot to prove. Unfortunately, there was only one way into the building and they had to walk past it, so they stuck closer together.

Nothing happened.

Their apartment block was now in view. 'Do you know that car?' JJ whispered. It was still there, just waiting.

Dwayne and Richie nodded. 'One of Trick's friends.'

He'd guessed right. They were walking into some kind of ambush.

Xavier had fallen into formation with him, coming to the same conclusion. He didn't need to say a word. They both knew the ones who had broken up the party were waiting. They came into view on the low wall at the entrance to their building. There were a couple of girls with them. They were laughing and chatting until they went silent when they saw them approaching.

'Let me do the talking,' Dwayne said.

JJ nodded, pulling Latitia and Alexia in tighter between them.

Trick pushed one of the girls off his knee and stood up from the wall. 'Ah, there they are. DJ Tame Dwayne and his micro-crew of toffs.'

His followers laughed loudly and gathered around him.

JJ did a quick count: five boys, including Trick and two girls. There was at least one keeping the engine running. They were outnumbered and he didn't know about Latitia, but Alexia couldn't fight. She'd managed to slope off every time his father wanted her to learn.

'What do you want, Trick? It's late. We just want to go home,' Dwayne said, in a last-ditch attempt to be civil.

'Late?' Trick mimicked in a fake posh accent. 'Why, the night is young?'

His followers sniggered.

'What say we continue our little battle from earlier upstairs?' Trick said, holding out his arm for them to lead the way.

Dwayne took a step back. 'No! My mum and little brothers are inside.'

JJ stiffened. Everything was fast becoming out of control. Trick walked up in Dwayne's face and two of his friends barred Richie's way to go to his side. Trick pointed at the small silver box Dwayne was carrying. 'Do you mind if I take a look?'

JJ knew most of his music would be on an SD card or a USB, but DJs still coveted those rare grooves on CD that they could reliably transport to shows and showing Trick was the last thing Dwayne would want to do. No DJ wanted to give access to his arsenal to a competitor – particularly a slime ball like Trick. But he left him little choice and he handed over the box.

Trick turned and grinned to his friends at his small victory and took it over to the wall to open it.

All the while, JJ bided his time in the hope this petered out and racked his brains for a way to handle it if it didn't.

Can't you do something, JJ? Alexia said, desperately, in his mind.

We can take them, Xavier said.

Not unless we have to. There's too many of them. We're better off protecting the girls.

Xavier shuffled his feet in agitation and was spotted by one of Trick's friends. 'Stand still, posh boy.'

'Mmmm-mm,' Trick was saying, looking intently at a CD case he'd pulled out. 'Nice track.' Everything he said was in the same exaggerated, mocking tone. 'Must be worth a few quid.' He took it out of its case and fumbled, almost dropping it, catching it just in time. But his hands were all over it which, of course, was deliberate.

Dwayne took a step forward in reflex to save his beloved property and one of Trick's friends stepped in to bar his way. Now Dwayne's temper had flared up and he bumped chests with him.

JJ readied himself to jump in but the two girls had circled behind them and he didn't trust what they would do to Alexia and Latitia.

'Give me back the box,' Dwayne said, his patience now gone.

Richie shoved the boy out of the way, who'd been holding him back, to stand with his brother.

The boy ran back and shoved them both in the chest. 'Who d'you think you are? ... get back in your place!'

Suddenly, they felt surrounded. JJ looked across to Xavier and they had to turn their backs to the girls to keep watch behind them. Everyone seemed to be turning and moving, trying to protect their backs and keeping an eye on everyone else. It was impossible to keep track.

The boys were now roughly shoving Dwayne and Richie from all sides. Under ordinary circumstances, JJ and Xavier would have been in the thick of it, but Alexia and Latitia were now being stalked by the two girls from the opposite direction. To take their eye off them would leave them exposed.

The shoves became rougher. 'Leave us alone!' Dwayne shouted.

JJ kept an eye over his shoulder.

Too late. A punch was thrown at Dwayne.

Xavier took a step forward to intervene, just as one of the girls lunged and pushed Alexia in the chest, almost knocking her over.

No, Xav! JJ projected. *The girls!*

Xavier turned his head and saw the danger at the last minute. He switched directions.

'Don't you push me!' one of the girls squealed when Alexia had barely touched her.

JJ and Xavier had spent their childhoods learning to fight. They were surrounded by soldiers and guards – their own aunt had been a government assassin. Unfortunately, Alexia was into ponies and braiding hair and was totally vulnerable here and Latitia's abilities were completely unknown. It wasn't ideal.

Dwayne and Richie were now separated and in the middle of the boys who were still pushing them around. 'You're nothing!' Trick was shouting in his face. 'You're not a DJ … you're only good for school discos and weddings.' Dwayne was shoving back, but it wasn't having much impact.

JJ quickly assessed that their best defence was in one

group with the girls in the middle. They were too out in the open where they were.

Xavier had seen the danger too and made sure he pulled Alexia between them.

Then JJ felt a familiar tingle on the edges of his senses. He'd felt it faintly a few times while they'd been in south London. Something they took for granted as it was so prevalent at home. Here, starved of everything they knew, it was as easy to sense on the air as bonfire smoke. Atlanteans were close by.

CHAPTER 12

our huge males stepped out from the shadows. Alexia and Xavier saw them at the exact same moment. The others stopped pushing Dwayne and Richie around and the grin dropped from Trick's face.

Dwayne tugged his brother back out of the way of the boys and Trick pulled out a knife that had been tucked into the waistband of his jeans.

'Don't be silly,' the rich, deep, familiar London-accented voice said, pointing, completely unfazed by the knife. 'Evening, guys,' he said to JJ, Xavier and Alexia.

Keenan, JJ projected, allowing himself to relax for the first time, recognizing the guy who was married to his aunt. The lively blue eyes quickly surveyed the situation. The three other males nodded a greeting behind him. They were easily six and a half feet tall, dressed completely in black and packed with muscle and various weapons: a compact 9mm MP5, a Glock and several lethal knives. And that's just what JJ knew. The huge men belonged to the Santalini royal family of soldiers, loyal to his fathers and had always been an object of fascination to him growing up.

JJ let out a breath and Keenan came forward and touched him and Xavier on the shoulder; the closest thing to a hug from the big guy. He approached the group of boys. They parted, exposing Trick standing there brandishing a knife.

Keenan tilted his head to the side to indicate to Dwayne and Richie to join the rest of their group. They obeyed. 'Do we have a problem here, guys?' he said, turning his attention back to Trick. When he didn't answer, he glanced over his shoulder at Dwayne and pointed to the silver box, still sitting on the wall. 'Yours?'

Dwayne nodded vigorously. It was hard to tell who he looked more scared of.

Keenan clicked his fingers and signalled for Trick to pass it to him. 'Do you mind?'

Trick looked around him, completely bewildered, until he saw the futility of holding out. He walked over, put the CD he'd taken out back in its case, and handed it to Keenan – making sure he kept himself out of reach. JJ saw his powers of reasoning already at work even through the shock, as Trick tried to calculate who the big guys might be. He was recovering quickly. 'Who are you? Don't recognize you from around here.'

Keenan immediately took a threatening step forward, making Trick take an evasive step back. Not before the horror registered on his face. He'd given him the smallest glimpse of him: a flash of fang, the smallest swirl of blood in his eyes. JJ had always wished he could do that to intimidate his enemies. 'Oh, we're always around. You just don't know it.'

It was just the right amount of threat to make Trick swallow. JJ couldn't keep the smile off his face.

Then, without breaking eye contact, Keenan pointed back at the road, to the waiting car. 'I think we're done here.'

Trick nodded and, without a further word, skirted a wide

radius around Keenan in the direction of the car. The others followed. Although, just as he went to pass JJ, he gave him a last warning glare. As if he thought he was somehow responsible for what had just happened. It was by no means over.

The four Santalinis turned and didn't relax until the seven of them had squashed into their friend's car and it screeched off into the night. Then Keenan turned back and grinned.

Alexia ran to him and hugged him tightly. 'Uncle Keenan. You saved us.'

JJ rolled his eyes. She was so dramatic. Still, she was probably right. Even with his power, there were simply too many of them.

Keenan kissed the top of her head and ruffled Xavier's hair. JJ shook all four of their hands in thanks and noticed Latitia, Dwayne and Richie looking on uneasily. He had to remind himself that he was used to Keenan's longer canine teeth and sheer size. He guessed they did look pretty badass to a bunch of ordinary teenagers, even if they did appear to be on their side. He quickly introduced them.

Keenan nodded and smiled, careful to cover his teeth this time. Then he gave JJ a wink when his eyes rested on Latitia, making him wonder how much he knew. 'What are you doing here?' JJ asked, deflecting the heat away from his personal life. 'Not that we're not grateful to see you.'

'Just passing by. Thought we'd just pop in to see you,' Keenan said in that easy way he had about him. 'Lacy sends her love.'

JJ smiled at the thought of his doting aunt, who spoiled them all rotten.

'Are you coming up?' Xavier asked. There was a light of hope in his eyes that maybe their father had sent the Santalinis to get them.

JJ doubted that very much. Somehow he couldn't imagine

any of them in the tiny flat. They seemed to dwarf everything around them.

Keenan smiled kindly and bowed his head. 'No, thank you. We have somewhere to be, but we'll see you around.'

The light faded instantly from Xavier's face. JJ hadn't realized until that point just how unhappy Xavier was. He wasn't fitting in at all and that was worrying. It was usually the other way around.

Dwayne and Richie looked up at them with awe when they shook both of their hands and thanked them before they went. They watched them right out of sight, until they blended in with the shadows and disappeared as if by magic.

They left an eerie quiet. JJ looked up and down the street and ushered them all in the building before they got into a thousand questions.

'Who were they?' Latitia said as they climbed the stairs.

'My uncle and cousins,' JJ said, keeping his answer to a minimum. But, of course, it wasn't enough.

'From your family business?' she persisted.

JJ looked at her close to his shoulder to see if she was mocking him, but she was looking down at the steps, thoughtfully, absorbing it all. 'No, they're from another family, loyal to our father. They're the guards.'

She was processing it even though it was quite shocking, perhaps becoming more and more convinced they were Mafia or something. It seemed the simpler option, so he let it slide.

'Your dad is really important, isn't he?' she said as a statement.

JJ smiled and nodded at her trusting expression and finished in his head, *more than you know.*

· · ·

FOR ONE SINGLE, wonderful moment, Xavier thought the Santalinis had come to escort them home and by some happy coincidence had stumbled upon them in trouble. However, it soon became apparent that his father had no intention of moving them anywhere and Keenan was simply 'around' so the king's children weren't roughed up too much.

It meant they'd been there all along.

Leaving them to a life of hardship. Only stepping in when they appeared to be making a hash of it.

It made him furious and sick at the same time.

He and JJ had done their best, but they were outnumbered in strange, hostile surroundings and to do anything they would have had to leave the girls unguarded. Dwayne and Richie were about to get their arses handed to them and Alexia was almost in tears. It was so unfair. How his father could do this to them was beyond the pale.

Everyone else seemed so pleased to see the guards, they couldn't thank them enough. He wanted to scream at them that they shouldn't bloody be there in the first place.

He hated this place.

He hated his father.

He hated everyone right now.

'Xav!' JJ called, as he started to walk off into the night. 'Where are you going?'

Xavier glared at him over his shoulder and continued walking. He was too angry to speak. He had no idea where he was going, only that he needed some space between them. Before long, he was alone and he had to remind himself that the area was rough. However, in his current mood he dared anyone to come up to him and see what they got.

The pavements were slick and wet, making his footfalls echo against the graffiti-strewn walls. It gave the impression of quiet over the constant traffic hum of the city. The air smelled fresh, as if the rain had washed away the city grime.

Even the clouds had gone, leaving a clear sky; if that counted with the yellow-grey light pollution.

With his hands firmly shoved in his pockets, he walked down every alleyway and cut through. Past rows of tightly packed cardboard houses, rusty old cars and through the car parks of high rises. It felt like he'd covered quite a distance when he turned a sharp corner and went straight into someone, almost knocking them over. 'So sorry.' *Girl, blonde,* 'Paige?' His brain scrambled. He couldn't believe it. That she should be there, right then. Right now. He openly stared at her, at a loss for words.

For a moment, she appeared to do the same. 'What are you doing here?' she said eventually.

'I could ask you the same,' Xavier said, still reeling.

'I live here,' Paige said, pointing at the four floor building behind her. 'I was just going to see if I could catch the last hour of the party. My mum only just got home from work.'

Xavier's heart spiked for a moment. It was a lot of effort to go to for an hour. It was then he realized how nice she looked. Her hair was down for the first time and she wore the palest-pink lip gloss. He found himself hoping she'd done it for him. 'It got broken up about an hour ago. Some DJ invasion or something.'

He watched her absorb the new information. 'Poor Dwayne.'

'Yeah, he's furious.' As he said the words, a rare pang of shame hit him. She barely knew Dwayne, and here she was showing more empathy for what happened than he had – his supposed adoptive brother.

She shifted her weight with embarrassment at the silence. 'Well, I guess I'm all dressed up with nowhere to go,' she said, looking down at her thin beige jacket, black skinny jeans and boots. She was far from overdressed.

It made them both laugh – for the first time since he'd

come to this godforsaken place. 'We could go for a walk. I believe the recreation ground has one working streetlight and is more de-littered this time of year?'

Paige laughed again – a delightful sound that bubbled out of her and was incredibly infectious. She looked around her, seeming less sure. 'Maybe not. There'll be hordes of kids roaming the streets after the party, not wanting to go home.'

'Like the Zombie Apocalypse,' he said, making them both laugh again. He saw what she meant, though. She was right.

Another awkward silence followed, where neither of them could think of an alternative.

'You could come up to mine … I mean, if you want?' A range of emotion crossed her face in a couple of seconds; like she didn't know if she wanted a no or a yes.

Xavier looked behind her at the row of 1960s council maisonettes in white plaster and light-brown brick. They were little houses built on top of one another, making four floors in all. He couldn't see the point. *Why did humans feel the need to pile everything high?* He didn't want to miss the opportunity to spend more time with her. 'Sure,' he said.

She turned and they walked shoulder to shoulder down the path and into a stairwell and the now familiar stench of urine. 'Just two flights. No lift needed, luckily,' she said, her eyes darting nervously.

He felt sorry for her embarrassment. Still, he guessed he must like her a lot to be going through with this.

As they reached the top of the concrete steps, he wasn't so sure. He was going into the unknown alone. She was cute and intelligent and all that, but she didn't fit in with these surroundings any more than he did. 'Who's inside?' he said, dragging his feet.

She stopped and turned him to look at her and really studied his face.

Suddenly it was really important not to reveal his trepidation with the whole thing.

'Just my mum and my little brother and sister, who will be asleep by now.' She was watching his reaction carefully. She may not be able to go beneath the surface, but she was scanning him as well as any Atlantean. It made him pull himself together. He didn't want to embarrass her. 'Your mum?' he repeated.

She seemed to relax, automatically taking his reticence the wrong way – or rather, the way he wanted her to. In the end she rolled her eyes, linked her arm through his and led him along the gangway. 'Don't worry, she'll love you.'

He allowed her to lead him while his mind raced. He'd always avoided meeting a girl's family – even in Atlantean circles. Knowing who he was always made them want to race to engagements and marriage. They all wanted stronger links to the royal family and for their daughter to be queen one day. *And humans?* Well, he simply avoided it. He was unsure what they would want from him, or whether he could give it at all.

They reached her landing and his mind raced for an out, but there wasn't one. Instead, he walked the concrete gangway and passed the rows of alternating doors and windows to his left and the open brick balcony to his right, wondering if it was too high to jump down into the courtyard of parked cars. Ironically, the top was painted with a white stripe so people could see it at night and not fall over.

Noise came through each inadequate plywood door: loud TV, music, shouting. Paige looked up at him and smiled apologetically. He found himself smiling back at her to reassure her. They reached her front door and his opportunity to run had gone. He tried to swallow, but his mouth was sandpaper dry. He looked each way along the landing while she

put her key in the lock. Then she pushed the door wide.
'Come in,' she said.

CHAPTER 13

Xavier took a step inside and was immediately engulfed in the orange glow from the square plastic lampshade on the ceiling and a wave of heat as balmy as the tropics. A faint smell of cooking hung in the air.

'Shall I take your jacket?' Paige said, taking off her own to reveal a black 'Science Geek' t-shirt. It was so her, it relieved a little of his tension and he slid his small leather bomber jacket off his shoulders.

Paige took it from him. 'This is nice,' she said and hung both their jackets on a hook by the door. He smiled and waited while he looked around the fairly large, square hallway and the stairs that led to the second floor and her bedroom. She put her fingers to her lips and made a 'Shh' sound. 'If we wake up my brother and sister, they won't leave you alone.'

He smiled less than enthusiastically and wondered what he was doing there for the umpteenth time. He didn't do regular girls, families and certainly not snotty little siblings, but then she picked up his hand and something stirred in his chest and all he could think of was how much he liked it when she did that.

She slipped off her ankle boots on the dark patterned rug, so he did the same with his Italian loafers. Then she knocked lightly and went in one of the doorways and peered inside. 'Mum?' she said.

The last thing he was expecting was for her mum to be up. He considered bolting for the exit, but she held his hand firmly and pulled him with her. 'I've got a friend with me. The party got broken up before I got there.'

'Oh, come in, come in,' a soft, quiet voice said.

Paige gave him such a yank on his arm that he couldn't help stumbling inside. A very pretty young woman smiled at him and quickly got to her feet from an old sofa, dragging her fingers through her mousy-blonde hair to make herself presentable. He put her in her mid to late thirties, judging by her clothes, but she had dark circles under her eyes like she was worn out before her time. She approached, straightening her blue shirt and smoothing down her jeans, obviously not used to receiving guests. 'Hello there, I'm Linda.'

'We were going to go to my room,' Paige said. 'We'll be quiet.'

'No, no. You stay in here. I was just going to go to bed anyway.'

As she held out her slim hand, no jewellery and no nail varnish, she looked him in the eye for the first time. She openly stared, as humans often did. It was why he usually avoided eye contact. Today, he held her gaze for her daughter's sake. Somehow it felt important that she liked him.

She didn't just look tired. It was in her whole aura. Atlanteans could read the colours that leeched out from a person's soul and hers were dull from fatigue, but were threaded with warm red and earth tones, proving she was hardworking and kind. In other words, a good mother.

He reached for her hand for the necessary skin contact. It confirmed what he thought. She was a good person, struggling through a tough life. 'Pleased to meet you, Linda, I'm Xavier.'

Her hand jolted slightly at the current of electricity, but her eyes remained glued to his while he held her mind. 'Oh, my god, Paige,' she said, flustered. 'I don't think I've ever seen a more beautiful boy.'

He smiled. It was the reaction he was expecting, but he was sure she hadn't realized she'd spoken out loud. A scan often confused a human subject and he didn't want to cause pain, so he quickly left her mind and released her hand.

His own mother had explained when he was just a small boy that the gene pool of Atlanteans produced beautiful children, but it had held no significance until then. He couldn't think of a single ugly or even a plain one. He inclined his head and said a simple 'thank you'. Then, with a small bow of his head, 'It is an honour to meet you.'

She finally dragged her eyes from him to look at Paige, amazed. 'Such beautiful manners. Where on earth did you find him? Certainly not at that school.'

Paige simply nodded, looking bewildered at her mum's strange behaviour.

Xavier felt he had to cut in. 'I do go to the school. In fact, I go there with my brother and sister. We're new to the area.'

She looked back at him, shaking her head in shock. 'I can see that.'

'Mum?' Paige finally said, tipping her head in the direction of the door.

She seemed to snap out of her stupor and immediately headed towards it. 'Yes. I'll leave you kids to it. So nice to meet you, Xavier. You can come around any time,' she said, turning and backing out as if to royalty.

He bowed again and this time she giggled like a school-girl, before she hurriedly left the room. Paige followed her to make sure the door was firmly shut. 'I'm so sorry about that. I don't know what got into her.' She walked back towards him and he noted she'd gone a charming shade of pink.

Xavier felt a little sorry for her mother. He was probably the first Atlantean she'd ever seen. They must be a rarity in this part of the city, but his mind quickly strayed to the curve of Paige's hips that she normally kept hidden under loose-fitting uniform. 'Don't worry about it,' he said, grinning. 'It's you I'm here to see.'

Paige's eyes shot to his, as if she was gauging what he meant. It struck him that she had no idea just how attractive she was. In another setting, with good clothes, she would be a real beauty, but she hid it in plain sight, behind the cover of books, baggy shirts and serviceable ponytails. Seeing she was clearly unnerved, he took a step closer.

'Do you want a drink? Tea, coffee, er, squash. I think we've got some biscuits somewhere.' He picked up her hand and it was shaking.

'Tea would be nice,' he found himself saying.

She visibly relaxed and nodded, then turned for the door. He followed, out into the hallway and into the small plain white kitchen. The floor was covered in some kind of laminate tile, in grey, and the fridge was decorated with drawings done by a toddler. There were little touches of blue in the caddies and jars on the countertop, but despite being a little dated, everywhere seemed tidy and clean. *Well ordered,* he found himself thinking. Like Paige, herself. 'No milk or sugar, just weak and black.'

She shot him a glance as if she was forming an opinion from that alone. 'You certainly don't belong around here, do you,' she said as a statement, not a question. She poured the boiling water over a teabag and quickly whipped it out and into the bin. 'OK?' she said, showing him the cup.

He nodded. 'Perfetto.' He took it from her.

'So, you're Italian,' she said, adding milk and two sugars to her own cup and returning the milk to the fridge. 'Should have guessed with the hair and clothes and everything.'

It made him smile, but he bobbed his head and didn't correct her. It was partially true. He'd spent a lot of time there and his name had its origins in that part of the world. 'Close,' he said, not meeting her eyes.

There was a moment of silence when they both took a sip from their cup. Then, sensing the drought in conversation, he held out an arm for her to go first. 'I have some questions I've been meaning to ask you about the science homework.'

As intended, she immediately relaxed into comfortable territory. 'OK, I'll grab mine. I did it earlier.'

Of course she had. He smiled to himself and went and sat down in the living room and waited for her. His eyes skated over everything. There weren't many trinkets. There weren't many surfaces to put anything on. Just a child's efforts at pottery on the windowsill and a few photos of very young children in a multi-photo frame. A couple of cheap tourist prints of boats in a Mediterranean marina hung on the walls and pointed to at least one holiday abroad. However, they seemed to be placed to fill space or to cover the hideous painted woodchip wallpaper rather than for their own appeal. It made him consider ordinary lives for the first time, where power and possessions clearly meant very little, except to live and survive. It was unsettling.

She came back and sat at the coffee table with armfuls of stuff: pencil case, ruler, textbooks. His heart sank. He hated schoolwork. He lacked the necessary concentration. The effort always felt so pointless to him – especially when he could simply lift the answers from somebody's head.

'I absolutely love genetics. It's fascinating. Don't you think?'

He tried to look keen as he smiled back at her. She did look gorgeous when she was animated about something. It was as if she had suddenly come alive. It made him sit down on the sofa next to her and lean forward to look interested. She sat on the floor and spread everything out on the low table in front of them. The clean, neat, delicate fingers quickly sorted through one of the textbooks to find the right page. They were indicative of her; well-kept, functional and yet barely containing a passion few people in this god-awful place ever noticed. Suddenly, he felt very privileged to see it. It was illogical, he knew, but he edged a little closer and smelled clean soap instead of perfume radiating from her skin where she was warm. His pulse raced as it had never done before.

He wanted to move the gold silk of her hair behind her ear and gently kiss the curve of her neck and have her moan his name, but he stopped himself in the nick of time, coughed and quickly asked, 'So blue eyes are always recessive?'

He'd intended for it to take his mind off wanting to kiss her, but she looked at him sharply with perfectly cornflower blue irises and, for a moment, they stared at each other. His eyes dropped to her mouth, now devoid of lip-gloss. 'What about green. Are they recessive or dominant?' It came out more as a husky whisper.

She continued to stare into his eyes as if something would reveal itself there. 'They are a mutation that produces low levels of melanin. There is no real green pigment, they just give the appearance of green—' She stopped mid-sentence and frowned. 'I think I would have to argue in your case.'

That was it. His lips crashed into hers and he was kissing her wildly, hands in her hair and crushing her to him. All in a second and it was over. As if he'd dived into a whirlpool and hauled himself back out again. They both stared at each other, out of breath, until he swallowed. 'Can you write the answers down, so I don't forget them?'

For a moment she gazed at him, in shock, until she blinked, nodded and scribbled the answers down quickly on a pad. It was stuff he'd covered years ago with one of his tutors, necessary for understanding the human population, but it was all he could think of on the spot to spend more time with her. He wanted to see the way she put her hair behind her ear when she was thinking, how close she came to the paper when she wrote. All the while, reliving the kiss of his life, over and over. She, on the other hand, became absorbed in her subject. The facts and the figures. She had a delightfully quick and enquiring mind. She gestured with her hands and laughed with her rosebud lips when he asked ridiculous questions just to see what she'd say, and when she answered something eloquently, he reminded her to write it down.

Then, as suddenly as the revelation came, he felt utterly deflated. He was so weary with it all. The unsettling feeling he'd had earlier came back to haunt him. It wasn't the inane school assignments, the area or even the people. It was her situation – the utter hopelessness of it. There didn't appear to be another parent – as seemed to be the norm for many at the school. It was just that the more her aura burned brightly, the more he was reminded that in her world, a lack of money and resources was the difference between being trapped in a soul-destroying job or being able to break her shackles and reach the potential of her dreams. It was unlikely that a girl from her strata of society, with her handicaps, would ever attain the level of doctor. Her well-meaning mother was holding her back already. Add on the cotton for brains friends and possibly some idiot boy getting her pregnant and her lifetime cage would be sealed. He found he wanted to shake her and warn her, but it was futile. It was simply the lottery of birth.

He sat back in the sofa and watched her talking on the subject she loved, gesturing to make a point with her hands and it hit him he was as trapped as her. He was at the opposite end of the social scale and as trapped as she was. He could attain six doctorates with his resources and have the backing of his father to do it, but at the end of the day, no one would listen to what he wanted. He would take his place as king of a world that had no idea his race even existed. *What was the point of that?* It only became a self-built, more sophisticated cage, but a cage nonetheless. For now, all he could do was feel privileged to observe the wonderful sense of joy this insignificant human girl still had in her. But something shifted inside him.

A COUPLE of hours passed in a flash. Paige was easy company and Xavier forgot the differences of who they were. He was enjoying himself. She was witty, with strong opinions he enjoyed challenging. It made their conversations the most lively and interesting he'd ever had. Unfortunately, when he caught sight of the time, it was almost twelve o'clock and he didn't have a door key. 'I'd better get going before I get locked out. Don't want to outstay my welcome with your mum,' he said, getting slowly to his feet, feeling stiff from sitting in the same position.

Paige got up with him and stretched out her back from being hunched over the books. They really had lost track of the time. 'Don't worry. I think she's ready to adopt you,' she said with a grin.

The easy way she now spoke made him pull her towards him and kiss her again. She felt perfect in the circle of his arms, completely encased and just the right height. She tasted of peaches. He had to stop himself before he needed more.

Xavier cupped the side of her face and ran a thumb across her lower lip. 'Sorry,' he whispered. 'I simply can't help myself.'

She looked up at him with dilated, enquiring eyes; so fragile and unsure. It was madness between the two of them, he knew. He would have to tread very carefully so as not to break her. It struck him that, for the first time in his life, he had to act responsibly and he wasn't sure how he felt about that, exactly. 'I'd better go,' he whispered again. 'I'll see you tomorrow.' He reluctantly released her, keeping hold of one hand as he headed towards the hallway. His mind was already preoccupied with whether it could ever work between them.

They stopped at the front door and he slipped on his shoes, while she opened the latch for him. 'Are you sure you know where you're going?'

He frowned a little because he didn't. He'd found himself outside her place by accident. He laughed a little. 'Actually, I have no idea where I am.'

She gave him instructions back to the main road that would take him to the Johnsons' place, while he pulled his jacket back on. 'I can draw you a map?' she said.

He put his misgivings aside, took in the pink of her cheeks and her slightly ruffled hair and kissed her again. She responded easily as if they'd been close forever. He pulled out of the kiss before he crushed her against the wall, right there in the home she shared with her mother. His body temperature rose to feverishly hot – a physiological change that often happened with Atlanteans – and rose ferociously with her.

Xavier put her away from him suddenly before she noticed, and more roughly than he would have liked.

She looked bewildered and disappointed. 'Are you OK? You look angry. Have I done something wrong?'

She'd taken him pulling away and the redness of his face as anger and rejection. The ridiculousness of it exasperated and frustrated the hell out of him. He had to get away from her to get his head straight. He had to think clearly about what he was really getting into with this girl. It wasn't going to be simple. He was going to have to be responsible and he wasn't sure he was ready for any of that. He ran a hand up through his hair, pushing it back.

'Are you OK? she was saying. 'Can I get you a glass of water?'

He wanted to shout at her to get away from him, but he managed to take a few gulps of air and say, 'I'll see you tomorrow,' in a gruff whisper.

Now she looked frightened and he wanted to shout at the kind doe eyes to stay away from him if she knew what was good for her. Instead, he half turned away, hating himself.

Then he felt her soft hand clasp his and he was kissing her again. One last incendiary kiss that seared through his body in white heat. The kind that could drown her if they were anywhere near water. The need to protect her reared up and shocked him; even then when he was lost to the world, absorbed only in the sensation of her. She was too close and addictive. In the end he had to push her away, rush out of the door and make sure he pulled it shut behind him.

He ripped off his jacket and breathed easier for the first time in hours. He relished the cool, drizzly air on his burning-hot cheeks. He'd been with a lot of girls – particularly at their old school. Girls who gave themselves to him simply because he willed it. His father had explained the heat and what it meant for them as ancestors of an underwater race and he'd experienced it many times. Often using a swimming pool or a cold shower to cool off. But this – what he'd felt with Paige tonight – was on a whole other level. It scared him half to death. Everything was so far out of his control.

His thoughts whirled and tumbled over it all the way back to the Johnsons'. It seemed the walk took no time at all. Maybe he'd been walking in circles before. His heart raced between abject terror at what he could do to her if he didn't get a hold, and the excitement of having his own girl who was clever and beautiful and responded to him so beautifully. She liked him for him, not who he was. She had no clue about his money and title. She'd simply invited him into her home and helped him with his homework. She was motivated and driven and had no idea that one wrong move and he could kill her.

Then there was the real truth. That even more infuriating than his father making them live there in the first place, was that it would inevitably be temporary. Just as he was making a life, he would have to leave. His and Paige's paths would separate, both to be ruined by the circumstances of their birth.

It struck him then that she would, without doubt, meet someone else. *Of course she would.* She was gorgeous. Anger flashed through him in a tempest so hot, it dwarfed the heat of earlier. If he'd come upon someone at that point he would have killed them on the spot.

Thankfully, he rounded the corner to the Johnsons' apartment block. He vowed to himself right then, that, however selfish it was, he would not allow that. Paige would never belong to anyone else. He took a moment to calm down, then, with his decision made, he messaged JJ to let him in.

The door opened in seconds. 'We need to talk,' Xavier said immediately.

'Agreed,' JJ said, as serious as him. 'The three of us need a meeting.'

Xavier stared into the weird aquamarine eyes that always seemed to know everything.

'I'm guessing we all have the same problem,' JJ said.

CHAPTER 14

J stepped back while Xavier moodily pushed past him into the flat. One look at his face told him all he needed to know. 'In here,' JJ said, overtaking him and heading for their bedroom.

Richie came out of the kitchen, biting into a slice of toast.

'Can you give us a minute, mate?' JJ said. 'We've got a family thing to discuss.'

Richie rolled his eyes and immediately diverted his steps to the living room without comment.

JJ pulled Xavier into the room and put a chair under the door handle. Alexia was already sitting on his bunk. He tipped his head in her direction for Xavier to sit next to her.

Xavier sat down. 'Can we get on with it? I need some sleep.'

JJ took in the angry face of his brother, looking around the room in impatience. Then, after a couple of paces up and down the small space between the beds, he sat down on Richie's bunk opposite.

Xavier finally looked at him and waited for him to speak.

'Honestly, I don't know where to begin,' JJ said, letting his hands drop wearily into his lap.

'Then I'll say it for you,' Xavier said, completely deadpan. 'We're getting too involved. All of us.'

He was absolutely right. So right, that he still couldn't think what to say to it.

'But wasn't that what Dad wanted when he sent us here? To fit in. To assimilate?' Alexia said, beginning to raise her voice.

JJ understood how she must be feeling. It was always hardest on her to fit in. With two brothers, there weren't many boys who would dare give her any real chance. All he could do was bob his head at her for a very good point. However his mind shot to what had happened that night and the very first time he'd gotten close to Latitia. 'I'm not sure this was what they had in mind.'

Alexia looked confused and Xavier still looked moodily blank. 'I think we should put a case to him to leave now,' JJ said.

'Finally,' Xavier said, relaxing. 'Maybe you'll start listening to me now.'

Alexia jumped to her feet. 'Wait! No! I like it here. It's exciting. It's real. Do you want to go back to a school where all they're interested in is how rich we are or how royal? Or worse still, being schooled at home where all we get to mix with are cousins who always get on our nerves? Come on, guys. For the first time in my life, I feel like I'm living.' She flopped back down onto the bunk, deflated. 'I really like him.'

JJ watched her tirade and felt every moment of it with her. She was right in everything she said. He immediately dropped down on his knees in front of her and held her hands. 'I know, Lexie. It's the same for us all. Even Xav,' he said, flicking his eyes to his brother sitting silently, listening, next to her. 'But think about it. Nothing can possibly come of it. All that will happen is that we'll ruin their lives.'

She was already shaking her head while tears fell down her cheeks, knowing full well he spoke the truth and not wanting to hear it. 'I'm not leaving. I don't care what you say.' She bravely held in her sobs and glared at him.

JJ hated being the bad guy with her; he always managed to leave that job to Xavier. He knelt up and went to hug her when Xavier put out a hand to stop him. 'Stop crying and listen,' Xavier said, in his hard no-nonsense voice. 'You won't mean to, but you'll kill him. Is that what you want?'

JJ was so shocked that he'd put the thing he'd skirted around so concisely that he made Alexia look him in the eyes to prove he agreed. He had no idea things had moved so far along between Xavier and the girl he knew he liked. He simply nodded and said, 'He's right.'

When she stopped crying, he eased back onto his haunches and looked straight at his brother. 'What happened with you tonight?'

Xavier looked wretched. His eyes seemed wild and desolate like he'd never seen them. Not even in any of the times they'd been in danger as a child. 'Don't you feel it? Doesn't it happen to you?' He sprang to his feet, even though there was nowhere to go in the small space.

JJ eased into Xavier's place on the bed next to Alexia so he could see him more easily. Even Alexia had stopped crying to hear what was wrong. 'What do you mean, Xav?' JJ prompted, although he had a good idea. He felt it too. The flash of heat that seared through him whenever he got hot for a girl. Although he guessed it was worse for those with purer genes.

'The heat when you—' Xav flicked his eyes at Alexia uncomfortably, not wanting to finish in front of her.

She rolled her eyes. 'For God's sake, Xav. You don't think I feel it too?'

JJ had always been able to talk more freely with Alexia. For some reason, Xavier's protectiveness kept him aloof. 'It's worse with Latitia,' he said, to head off an argument between them. Alexia was growing up and would no longer be pushed around by them. He'd need to stress that to Xavier when he had him alone. 'What's it like for you?' he said, more gently, in the hope of coaxing her out.

'She won't have – she better not have,' Xavier said, turning and glaring at her squarely.

'Not helping, Xav,' JJ said, looking up through his eyebrows at him in warning.

He was a geyser about to blow. 'We need to leave, JJ. I kissed Paige and I ...'

JJ could see the turmoil about how to put it. He rarely confided with this kind of stuff. Then he got what he was driving at and couldn't stop the wide grin spreading across his face. 'Felt the bonding urge,' he finished for him, amazed. It was something he was yet to feel and with his watered-down genes, he wasn't sure he would feel it at all. He was suddenly envious of his brother, which wasn't logical.

Xavier rolled his eyes. 'You don't understand. I didn't do anything to her. I barely even know her. One minute we were doing homework and then I almost combusted with heat.'

The image made JJ let out a burst of laughter. Alexia giggled next to him.

Xavier scowled. 'If I go any further, and I will if I stay here much longer,' he said through tight lips, 'We'll need water and I'll kill her.'

JJ's eyes widened when he realized Xavier wasn't playing around. He was genuinely scared. It wasn't just the drowning part, either. A shower could cool him down; it was the exchange of breath. The part of a person breathed into another to share their spirit. It was the real marriage between Atlanteans and one never taken lightly. If Xavier was getting feelings like that, then this was more serious than he thought.

He turned immediately to Alexia. 'And you get this too?'

She shrugged and nodded. 'I think so. It gets stronger every day.'

JJ looked away to digest what he'd heard and let out a slow breath. It sounded like Alexia wasn't where Xavier was yet. Maybe it was stronger with males. He wasn't sure. Perhaps Dwayne wasn't 'the one' or maybe they just hadn't got intimate enough to spark it. It was very hard for him to gauge with his far more human genes. 'It may not be as bad as you think, Xav?' he said, in an attempt to calm him down a bit. My father is more human and is alive to tell the tale.'

Xavier shifted his weight in exasperation. 'That's as maybe, but are you willing to take that chance? He's in our world, JJ. He was fully aware of the risks and chose it.'

JJ sighed and nodded. Xavier was right. Even if Latitia survived being with him, she'd need to leave her world. Her dreams of being a dancer, life as she knew it, would be over.

Alexia broke him from his thoughts by getting up. 'So that's it. We give up on the people we've liked the best in our whole lives just because of tiny genetic differences?'

She was almost shouting, making Xavier look nervously at the door and patting the air in front of him for her to keep it down.

'That's just racist,' Alexia said, moodily flopping down on the bed opposite.

Her comment was so ludicrous it made JJ smile at her, which infuriated her as he knew it would.

'Don't be ridiculous, Alexia,' Xavier said. 'Tiny differences that could kill them.' Then he turned to JJ, a plea in his eyes.

'We need to pitch it to Father as a diplomatic minefield about to go off.'

'He'll only ask what the difference is here?' He couldn't fault Xavier's logic. 'What's different to the school in New Hampshire? Dad won't buy it. You know he won't.'

They were silent for a beat while they all absorbed the truth in that.

'Well, I'm not going, JJ. Not yet,' Alexia said, folding her arms like a full-stop.

'What about if we talk to Keenan?' Xavier said.

JJ nodded. 'What, get him to intercede for us? If we can convince him, he might be able to convince Dad.'

Xavier nodded.

Alexia got up and stomped to the door. 'You can talk to him all you like, but I'm telling you both now, I'm not going.' And with that she left them to it.

Now alone, a slow grin crept across JJ's face. 'You really like her, don't you? For a moment there, I thought we were going to have the usual fight, over Latitia.' His tone was playful and not at all accusatory. Despite the obvious problems, he was pleased for him.

Xavier shrugged moodily and looked away from him. 'So did I.'

'What is it about this one? Why is she so different from all the others?'

Xavier sighed deeply and slowly shook his head. 'Honestly, I don't know. Part of me wants to get as far away as possible from her.'

JJ nodded. He knew that feeling. Then he noticed the set of his brother's jaw. Most people made the mistake of thinking that because Xavier was often the voice of reason and tried to follow the rules, he was the placid, sensible one. And compared to him, he probably was. But Xavier had his father's volatile temper and much of his power. He knew it because they'd been butting heads since they were small children. They would come up against each other for the kingdom one day, a thought that gave him chills. Not just because he was more than a worthy opponent, but because he loved him and they would ultimately be ripped apart. They needed to safeguard this closeness between them as long as possible. 'And the other part?' he prompted, as he hadn't said anything.

Xavier let out a slow, weary breath. 'She's naturally beautiful, clever like you wouldn't believe, ambitious, driven and hasn't had the spirit sucked out of her by this god-awful place.'

JJ bobbed his head, absorbing everything he said, but he hadn't missed the glint of stubbornness in his brother's expression as he spoke, that he knew so well. 'But you can't set her free,' he added for him.

Then Xavier looked him in the eye, in that way where they always knew what the other was thinking. He looked defeated. His head was hung low and his hands were on his hips. JJ's heart hammered in his chest, dreading what he would say next.

'It's worse than that already, JJ. If we don't leave, I think I would tear anyone apart who got near her.'

JJ let out a single blast of uneasy laughter and his mind shot to how he felt earlier with Latitia dancing with another boy. He flopped back down on Richie's bed and Xavier resumed his seat opposite.

'Is it the same for you?' Xavier asked, his interest dissipating some of his anger.

JJ shrugged. 'I guess, a bit. I mean, I feel it there gnawing at the edge of my nerves, but I refuse to go there. I haven't allowed myself to.'

The anger had completely gone from Xavier's aura now. He was giving him one of his 'you can't kid me, remember' looks. 'But now?' He smiled for the first time in the whole evening. 'Something changed for you to call this meeting.'

He shrugged. 'She's interested. All the while she was hard to get …'

'It was the same old game,' Xavier finished for him.

JJ nodded. 'Now I can catch her.'

'You're scared to.' Xavier studied him for a long moment. 'You know, the law of averages says one of these days you'll catch more than you bargained for. It doesn't have to be some mystical, ordained meeting of the planets.'

'I could say the same to you,' JJ shot back. Although they both leaned forward with their elbows on their knees knowing full well the Fates didn't work like that.

'We're going to have to drag Alexia out of here kicking and screaming,' Xavier said. 'I don't understand why she doesn't get it?'

'She doesn't want to get it.' JJ got to his feet. Inactivity was killing him. 'Maybe she thinks she's ready to make that kind of connection.' He and Xavier sure as hell weren't. It made up his mind and he headed for the door.

'Where are you going?' Xavier said, getting up to follow him.

JJ yanked open the door and smiled at his brother over his shoulder. 'Vampire hunting.'

Xavier quickly caught up with him in the hallway. 'Do you think Keenan is around?'

'Only one way to find out.'

XAVIER SLIPPED QUIETLY OUT of the door with JJ so as not to draw attention from any of the others. Then they walked shoulder to shoulder, down the path, turning right, through the garages and into the road. He pushed his hands deeply into his pockets and tipped his head down into the drizzle. He should have grabbed a coat.

Strangely, the dumped car and rubbish blown everywhere by the wind, didn't bother him nearly as much as it used to. Something cleared his mind about the evening. They got a hundred yards or so from the flat when JJ held him back by his arm. At first, he thought he wanted to say something, then quickly realized it was for the necessary contact. 'On three, blast, OK?'

Xavier quickly caught on. They were going to call Keenan and the other guards with a powerful mental blast that would be picked up by any Atlantean within a mile radius around them. If they were nearby, Keenan would hear them.

JJ nodded.

One, two, three, Keenan! Xavier projected.

JJ did the same and it vibrated through their heads like a great bell. It was hard to believe anyone would be around. For London, it was fairly deserted. Just parked cars and a cat screeching somewhere, followed by the clank of a bin lid.

Then they heard it: a car approaching at speed. It turned into their road as if it was being chased by the police. It made them step back on the pavement, just in case.

The blacked-out SUV skidded to a halt at an angle in front of them. For a brief second, Xavier thought it was Trick returning for payback, but a window lowered and Keenan's face appeared. He ran his eyes over them quickly for damage, then flicked them behind him to the rear door. 'Get in.'

Xavier looked at JJ and together they stepped into the road and got into the back seat. The car immediately moved off, at a more sedate speed this time. Two guards had squashed up for them to fit on the back seat and Keenan turned to face them from the front, next to the driver. 'What's up, boys?'

The craziness of it lifted his spirits. For Keenan, being mentally summoned at one o'clock in the morning was the most normal thing in the world. A pang of homesickness hit Xavier hard. He missed the castle, his island home of Filfla, his younger brothers and his many cousins. Then JJ nudged him to start talking. 'We need to get a message to our fathers.'

Keenan looked thoughtful, then pointed to which direction to take. They were travelling at a much more leisurely pace but kept moving so as not to look too conspicuous. 'You're going to have to give me a bit more than that, boys,' he said.

Xavier looked at JJ and shifted uncomfortably in his seat. It was a hard subject to broach in a car full of alpha males. 'We've met someone. Er … both of us …'

JJ nudged him in the ribs to continue.

'Even Alexia,' he added, noticing the smile Keenan was trying to hide and how the others suddenly found what was out of their side windows extremely interesting. When JJ was no help either, he became infuriated. 'Oh come on, guys. Little help here,' Xavier said, throwing up his hands.

JJ turned his head back into the conversation. 'Look, Dante needs to get us out of there before we kill someone. OK? We've learned our lesson. This is serious.'

Keenan's smirk disappeared as he looked between them. 'The local faces threaten you again?' he asked, his face darkening.

They both shook their heads. 'No, nothing like that. It's a problem none of us has experienced before,' Xavier said, pleading with his eyes that Keenan wouldn't make this any more embarrassing for them than it already was.

'Not like this,' JJ added.

'We can't—' Xavier began.

'Not without water,' JJ finished for him.

Then understanding registered with the widening of eyes, followed by a slow nod by each of the men. 'Girls,' they said together with huge grins.

Keenan immediately relaxed and the driver laughed. 'Bite them and fuzz their memory,' he said. 'Works for us.'

Keenan gave him a warning look. 'I don't think that's the issue here.' Then he turned back to the boys. 'Is it?'

Xavier felt his cheeks blast red while they both shook their heads.

'We don't have the teeth. This isn't exactly our first rodeo, here, you know,' JJ said, which made the car erupt into laughter.

'We shouldn't have come,' Xavier said through gritted teeth. They were never taken seriously. He didn't know why he thought this time would be any different.

Keenan saw they weren't laughing and tried to restore order. 'He does have a point about their memories, though, boys.'

Xavier had had enough. He sat forward and looked Keenan squarely in the eye. He was done with this clowning around. 'It's not like that. Not here.' Then he glared at each of the men in the car so they were in no shadow of a doubt how serious he was. They may be young and not as worldly wise as present company, but they were bloody going to hear what he was saying. 'My father is investing heavily in the area for some reason known only to him, so if he doesn't want an international incident where two girls and possibly a boy end up dead, then I suggest he gets us out of here, pronto.' With every word, he got angrier and more emotional and desperately tried to keep the wobble out of his voice. 'Because I'm telling you, it's gonna happen, soon.'

The car went silent for a beat, while they all absorbed what he said. JJ was looking at him as if he'd grown another head. What he wouldn't have given to have had a window seat for somewhere else to look at that moment.

'He's definitely his father's son,' the driver said, followed by a mumble of agreement from one of the guards next to him.

When he met Keenan's eyes again, it was to a subtle nod of respect. 'OK, we hear you. Leave it with us. I'll speak to your dads in the morning and get straight back to you.'

Xavier felt a great wave of relief and nodded. By then they seemed to have arrived back where they started. They pulled up smoothly next to the curb. JJ immediately went for the door.

'You too, JJ?' Keenan asked as he went to step out.

JJ simply nodded and got out of the car. Xavier followed and they stood on the pavement while Keenan wound down his window. 'I'll contact you tomorrow with your father's answer.' Then the window whirred back up and the car pulled away.

The rain had stopped, but the air felt dank and heavy.

'Do you think they took us seriously?' JJ said as they turned and walked slowly back to their block. It was eerily quiet except for their footsteps echoing on the garages and the constant hum of traffic.

Xavier let out a long breath and shrugged. He honestly didn't know.

'He was right, you know. You did sound like Dante.'

Xavier's heart churned. JJ was paying him a huge compliment. His father was a loved and respected king, great at speaking and dealing with people, but he was under no illusions. He was also a wily statesman and hugely unconventional and unpredictable, which was why they were where they were in the first place. 'One thing I am sure of is, if we don't get a satisfactory answer, I'm done trying to fit in and

I'm done getting pushed around. If he leaves us here after this, then we do it our way. Then we'll see what he has to say about that!'

JJ looked at him, clearly intrigued, a smile creeping across his face. 'What did you have in mind?'

CHAPTER 15

*B*y the time they slipped quietly back into the flat, it was almost one-thirty in the morning and everyone was in bed. However, when they got in their room, Dwayne was leaning over the edge of his bunk in conversation with Richie. They immediately stopped what they were saying as the two of them entered the room.

JJ narrowed his eyes. They were plotting something. 'What's up?'

The two brothers looked at each other and Dwayne eased back into his bunk. 'Nothing. We were just thinking of a way of getting back at Trick for tonight,' Dwayne said.

'We can't let him get away with it or Dwayne's DJ career will be over. Where'd you two get to?' Richie asked.

JJ pulled out clean PJ bottoms from the bag stowed under his bed. 'Nowhere. We just had a family thing to discuss with our uncle.' Then, before they could question what that might be, he threw in, 'We'll help you … with Trick.' Then he stood squarely to look at them. 'If you agree to help us.'

Both Johnson brothers immediately sat up with interest.

. . .

THANK GOD IT WAS SATURDAY. Alexia lay in her bunk ruminating on last night's events, thankful that the young ones had got up at the crack of dawn to watch the big-screen TV, now firmly entrenched in the living room. Latitia was still asleep. She could hear the soft purr of her breathing in the bunk above her.

Her brothers were up to something big. Their conversation last night weighed heavily on her. She didn't want to leave Dwayne, but she knew what they'd said had been right. They weren't trying to control her; it came from a place of real fear. She needed to pay more attention. She'd been so wrapped up in getting to know Dwayne that she hadn't taken much notice of what was going on with them.

Alexia guessed JJ was scared of getting involved with Latitia, which was a worry, as she was Dwayne's sister. JJ had a coldness in him that had frightened her since she was a little girl. He could be ruthless. And Xavier, usually the more stable, sensible one, had become volatile and unpredictable since they'd arrived there. Now, she couldn't imagine him allowing himself to get close to anybody. Change made her uneasy. It could have dark and far-reaching consequences.

The honeymoon period was very definitely over.

JJ LOUNGED about with the others, all day, waiting for Keenan's call. He couldn't concentrate on the sci-fi film they were all watching, or any book. He even tried doing his homework, which was unheard of.

Nothing took his mind off the wait. It was driving him mad. Latitia had gone out and Dwayne and Richie were occupying their room, so when Alexia and Xavier had a ridiculous argument over who'd had the TV remote the longest, it forced him out to the kitchen.

Valarie was unpacking bags of shopping.

He felt sorry for her. On her one day off, before she started her shift pattern of nights, she'd spent her day cleaning the flat and shopping for a bunch of ungrateful teenagers. He'd never witnessed any of the females in his family have to work so hard on top of being a parent and, even that, they hadn't done that well.

JJ stooped and began to help unload the bags.

'Wow, you must be bored,' she said, but her smile was warm and friendly.

He shrugged and smiled a little, piling tins on the countertop, not sure where they went exactly. 'I'll set up a weekly delivery for you, the heavy stuff, so you don't have to struggle with all this,' JJ said.

She looked at him curiously, clearly wondering what planet he came from. It made him a little uncomfortable. 'Just to contribute, you know,' he added.

She nodded and carried on unpacking. 'So what's the matter with you all today? It's Saturday, it isn't raining, and you're helping me while your brother and sister are fighting in there like a pair of alley cats.'

He smiled to himself. It was kind of funny. 'We're waiting to hear from our uncle,' he said, opting for honesty. After all, whatever the answer was, they would be leaving this place.

She frowned and stood up straight and studied his face. She was an astute woman. 'You're going, aren't you,' she said flatly, as if she was disappointed. Then he hated that she looked around the kitchen as if she wasn't surprised they wanted to leave the poor accommodations. She seemed bitterly disappointed.

JJ felt instantly sorry. Her aura went from a soft green to the deepest, sorrowful purple and he instinctively knew it wasn't due to the loss of income.

He took a step closer into her personal space. To an outsider it would seem threatening. However, he looked down into her eyes and picked up her hand. *I don't want you to say anything to my father yet, OK?* he said, directly to her mind.

Any shock disappeared as he passed his thumb gently across her hand while he went through her mind, turning anxiety switches off as he went. *Just until my uncle gets back to us today with what is happening. Don't worry or be alarmed. I will see to it that your income stays the same.* They hadn't done a single thing so far to make her life easier; it was something he was determined to remedy.

He watched the internal struggle on her face. How she wanted to articulate what was happening to her, but couldn't because it sounded so outlandish. Until, in the end, all she could do was nod her head. *I'll continue to watch over you,* he said, slowly drifting out of her mind, like an echo on a breeze.

Valarie sagged, as if she was released back into her skin and was left out of breath. She grabbed hold of the corner of the counter as if the world was spinning. 'Don't do stuff like that, JJ. I mean it. A simple conversation would have done it.'

JJ grinned and picked up a packet of biscuits. 'Hobnob?' he said.

XAVIER HAD WATCHED three episodes of his favourite cop show after several arguments with Alexia, followed by one with Latitia for butting in in her defence, and having built a brick tower for the little ones. He'd even phoned his brother, Roman, for some undercover intel, but was none the wiser. If someone didn't get in touch with them soon, he'd be forced to kill.

In the end he flopped back into the sofa between Alexia and JJ, making her shout, 'Ow, you idiot!'

'Do you think we're being ignored?' he asked.

JJ didn't take his eyes off the TV and let out a long sigh. 'Maybe.'

A rap at the front door made them all collectively freeze.

'Is it them?' Alexia whispered

Xavier rolled his eyes and shot to his feet with JJ. The presence the other side of the door was definitely Atlantean, they both sensed it. They bolted for the door, but Valarie was already opening it, her eyes widening at the scale of the man in front of her.

Xavier felt Alexia's hand on his shoulder as Keenan smiled and addressed Valarie, with two cousins looming next to him like harbingers of doom. 'Good evening, Mrs Johnson. May we come in? We have something important to give the children.'

His voice was soft and lulling and holding her in his thrall. An effect many Atlanteans had over humans – particularly vampires. Then, without speaking, she took a step back.

They seemed even bigger and more imposing than ever inside the flat, making Latitia hitch a breath when she and the little ones came out to the hall and saw them. The two children scooted around the newcomers' legs before Valarie could stop them. Craning their little necks, their eyes open wide, one said. 'Whoa. Are you giants?'

Keenan grinned and knelt down. 'Hey, fellas.'

The smallest of the two poked out a finger to touch his large canine with eyes huge with wonder. 'Have you come to eat us up?'

Keenan grabbed him and tickled his stomach. 'Only naughty boys.'

The boy squealed into giggles.

'Are you good?'

'Yes!' the boy said, breathlessly.

Then as soon as he let him up for air, Valarie whisked him

out of his arms as if he were playing with the Devil himself. 'Cute kid,' Keenan said, getting back to his feet. Then, as soon as she'd ushered the others away, his smile faded and he faced the three of them.

'What did Father say?' Xavier prompted.

Keenan turned his head to his cousin and held out his hand. He reached into the breast pocket of his black bomber jacket and pulled out a package wrapped in brown paper. Keenan took it from him, opened it and held up a glass vial with clear liquid in it. 'Your father sent these.'

Xavier looked from the vial to Keenan and then to JJ in consternation. 'What, that's it?' A white-hot anger began to fill every cell in his body. All the hope, the waiting and discussion, for this. 'Elixir!' he spat. He knew exactly what it was.

JJ put out a calming hand to hold his arm and stop him exploding.

Reading his mood correctly, Keenan passed the package to JJ. 'There are nine vials. Give them to your—' He paused and frowned, clearly not knowing what to call them. 'Intended,' he said, eventually, and continued, 'Twelve hours apart and they should survive.'

Then, without another single word of explanation, he turned back towards the door. Xavier was too angry and flabbergasted for words. It was JJ who held out his arm. 'Wait. That's it? Father said nothing more?'

'Of course he didn't,' Xavier said through gritted teeth.

Alexia, always so tuned into everyone's emotions, began to cry. It was ridiculous because she was the one who wanted to stay. She was simply feeling the anger, disappointment and abandonment for them all.

Keenan was a nice guy and genuinely sorry he had no better news to give them. Even through the haze of his anger, Xavier realized that.

'You told him what we said?' JJ persisted.

Keenan nodded, his smile apologetic. Then he seemed to relent a little. 'Look, your dad just said that you have the elixir now, you have somewhere to live and go to school, access to unlimited funds if you need it and we're nearby. He doesn't see a problem. Sorry, guys.' He turned, dipped his head slightly to fit under the doorway and his fellow guards followed him.

Xavier felt so angry he wanted to fly out after them, but JJ spoke to his mind. *Wait! This doesn't change anything.*

The last guard closed the door after them and Xavier swung around on JJ. 'What? You're OK with that? Stuck here and palmed off with elixir?'

'Didn't you hear him? Unlimited funds,' JJ whispered, eyes wide with excitement.

Xavier frowned, struggling to make sense of what difference that made. Then his meaning sunk in. 'The royal account,' he whispered back.

They both went for their jackets, hanging on the hooks by the door and found their wallets in the breast pocket. Xavier pulled out the black plastic card and JJ did the same. They stared at the plain black credit card that now held so much more meaning. Simple and plain, with distinctive gold writing on one side, of which there were less than five hundred in the entire world, held their names, ID number and the letters CAB, which stood for the Central Atlantic Bank: their father's bank and now meant their complete freedom. 'Unlimited funds,' JJ repeated, waving the card in front of his face. 'We're as good as emancipated.'

Xavier smiled wryly. 'Not exactly. Only until he puts a stop on it.'

JJ shrugged. 'We'll be set up by then.'

Xavier studied his brother's face, poised and waiting for

the answer that he knew would be yes. *What did they have to lose?* 'Where to first?' Xavier said.

JJ laughed, something he rarely did.

Alexia stepped in and snatched the card out of Xavier's hand. 'You're mad. What on earth do you think Father is going to allow two underage boys to do?'

Xavier snatched it back. 'He won't know.'

'We're moving out,' JJ said.

Alexia laughed cynically. 'Where are we moving to? They don't even rent houses to minors, you know.'

Xavier simply looked deadpan at JJ. 'She has a valid point.'

JJ grinned his most evil grin. 'We're going to pay our local tough guy a visit.'

THAT EVENING it wasn't hard to find the two goons who'd attempted to collect money from Valarie at their flat. Early Saturday evening was a great time to catch unsuspecting people at home. The estate was full of struggling people, ripe to borrow money from the shark the two guys worked for.

JJ ordered Alexia to stay home and he and Xavier went for a walk, spreading their Atlantean senses wide.

'What do you think Father will do when he realizes what we've done?' Xavier asked as they walked leisurely along the pavement.

It was dusk, chilly, but not raining, and the streetlights were buzzing to life, casting down their gloomy light on the bins and old cars beneath them. JJ liked it, deciding that the yellow glow against the damp night air was something intrinsically English. It didn't look or feel the same anywhere else in the world. 'There's nothing they can do,' he said with a shrug. 'Not if we stick within the parameters of his orders.'

'*Your* dad won't exactly care about that,' Xavier said, ruefully.

JJ thought about his own, quietly confident, biological father, Jay Gardiner. Xavier was right. He would be an added complication if he decided enough was enough. It wouldn't matter to him what orders Dante, the king, had decreed. He'd turn up wherever they were and there would be trouble. Still, he'd never been afraid of his dad, and he wasn't about to start now. 'We'll just have to make such a good job of it that it simply can't be ignored.'

Their footsteps echoed as they kicked a can between them through an underpass. 'We'll stay in the area, go to the same school, mix with the humans and even learn to manage them. We could even give back a little. You know … improve the area. How can he complain when we're doing exactly what he asked?'

Xavier smiled sceptically, then laughed and pointed as they came up on the other side of the tunnel.

JJ followed his line of vision. The men they'd been looking for, including the one he'd fried, were pushing a bike along the balcony of the block of flats in front of them. Some poor guy was flailing his arms behind them, shouting, 'Hey! How am I supposed to get to work now, eh?'

'How do you want to play this?' Xavier asked.

JJ watched the two men struggling with the bike into the stairwell and down the stairs. One of them had to play the part of aggressive thug and the other the leader. That's the dynamic these humans understood and, after the last time they'd met, one they'd emulate. 'I'll do the talking,' JJ said. 'Then, if they underestimate you, they won't know what hit 'em.'

Xavier nodded but looked thoughtful. They'd always made a good team, just like their fathers before them, but for them, the rivalry went a little deeper, a little more intrinsic, somehow. The idea wasn't a stretch. Everyone always assumed JJ was the psycho out of the two of them and Xavier was the reasonable one. However, in Atlantean circles, no one quite knew who the ringleader was, exactly. JJ read Xavier's aura. It was simmering between purple, green and red. Undecided. But going along with him, anyway.

The two men were clear of the building and pushing the bike, past an abandoned sofa, towards them. They slowed to a halt when they caught sight of them. 'It's them kids,' the one he'd floored previously, pushing the bike, said.

'We just want to talk,' JJ called out, before they came to a stop a few feet in front of them.

'You've got some nerve,' the one pushing the bike said.

JJ bobbed his head, accepting it as a compliment. 'We want to talk to your boss.'

The two men looked at each other and laughed.

'Come on,' JJ persisted. 'What do you have to lose? At the very least it should give you a good laugh.'

The taller guy, not pushing the bike, narrowed his eyes. 'What would two youngsters like you want him for?'

'Tell him we want to talk business. We have a proposition for him,' JJ said.

The man rocked on his heels and took in a deep breath as if he was considering what he said. Then he looked at his friend and tipped his head in the direction of the road. 'Come with us to the van while we load this up.'

JJ faced Xavier and looked him in the eyes, while the two men swerved them with the bike and headed to their van.

Xavier shrugged and nodded, so JJ led the way, following the men. *So you do have it straight, what to say?* Xavier said directly to his mind.

Yes, don't worry, I know what I'm doing, he replied.

Xavier was a quiet presence behind him after that. He always understood. There was no one upmanship between them when there was a common goal. They were equally clever, equally strong, equally everything. That was the trouble. When you knew that, everything else was a game: girls, sport, fighting. Everything needed to be won and the need was getting stronger between them. They loved and respected each other, but ultimately only one would be king. This. The thing they were doing now. It was only the start. And judging by Xavier's simmering aura, he knew it as well as he did.

CHAPTER 16

The taller one made the call with Xavier and JJ waiting nearby. It was almost dark.

He put the phone to his shoulder and called over. 'He said, come to Trevor's Turf tomorrow at eleven. You know, the betting shop on the High Street? His office is at the back.'

'We're not old enough to go into a betting shop,' JJ shouted back.

'Then you got a problem, don't cha.' Both men laughed as they got into either side of the van.

Xavier stood with JJ and watched the men drive off.

'Come on,' JJ said and turned for home.

Xavier put his phone to his ear as they walked slowly back to the Johnsons' place.

'Who are you calling?' JJ asked.

'I'm calling a cab for the morning. It's our first test. If we can't negotiate this, then we aren't going to be able to operate at all around the humans,' Xavier said.

JJ nodded, knowing straight away he was right. Their plan was getting increasingly complicated.

· · ·

XAVIER HAD to wait with JJ till everyone went to bed to get any privacy. 'You're both mad, you know that, right?' Alexia said. She hugged both of them goodnight from behind their chairs at the living room table and kissed the top of their head.

At last, they were alone. Then Xavier and JJ spent most of the night going over their plan. They got to sleep around 4.30 and got up with their alarm around 10. Then they rushed around to get ready before the rest of the flat got up and their cab arrived at 10.50.

The journey was short and they reached the dingy old shop, with the dusty green sign, bang on time. Xavier got out looking up at the shabby gold lettering. 'I guess our guy is Trevor,' he said to JJ, getting out the other side of the cab. He zipped up his bomber jacket against the cold.

'So, I'll start with the talking, then you take over as if you're leading the show,' JJ said.

Xavier nodded. It was what they'd rehearsed. 'How are we going to get in, though?' That part, they knew, they'd have to wing on the day. Xavier looked up and down the High Street, busy, like any other ordinary day. There was nothing sleepy about this part of town on a Sunday.

'We could go around the back to see if there's a back way in, or we could go right in through the front door.' JJ looked him in the eyes and they both grinned.

Xavier nodded. No skulking for them. It was perfect; sending exactly the right message.

JJ led the way, parting the multicoloured PVC strip curtain, and walking inside. Xavier followed and was met with stares from leathery gentlemen, of varying shades and nationalities, perched at the ledges that ran the fifteen feet of either side of the shop, holding stubby little pens.

They both nodded at the suspicious faces as they walked through. The floors were bare floorboards, but the walls were covered with photos of racehorses, fighters and dogs. They came to a stop in front of the wooden counter, with an impressive bank of TVs above and a balding man in his thirties behind it. He held a phone to his shoulder and quickly sized them up. 'Come back in about five years, boys,' he said, immediately.

JJ did his thing and immediately met the guy's eyes. *Look at me,* he whispered straight to his mind. He carefully entered the surface of his cerebral cortex and gently suggested that Trevor was waiting to see them. 'We're not here to bet, Mr?' JJ said, smoothly.

'Mike! Mike Jones,' the guy said, doing a complete three sixty, now eager, as if he was meeting some kind of celebrity.

Xavier smirked. Humans were so easy.

Mike lifted part of the counter, built on a hinge and pointed to another doorway behind him. 'He's in the office right down the hall.'

'Thanks, Mike,' JJ said and they breezed through as easy as anything.

A narrow corridor was on the other side with peeling magnolia walls, covered by the now-familiar pictures of photo finishes and prize racehorses. They walked to the very end, where a dark-wooden door was closed to them.

JJ knocked.

'What?' a gruff voice shouted from the other side.

JJ tried the handle and then a bolt clanked the other side. The face of an older guy appeared with a cigarette hanging out of the corner of his mouth. 'Who are you?' he barked. 'How did you get back 'ere?'

'Who is it?' came from behind him.

'Some kids. Who let you in 'ere?'

'Mike,' JJ said, as if it was the most obvious thing in the world. 'We have a meeting with Trevor at eleven.'

A smile spread across the oily skin making an already

Roman nose look really hooked. He peered behind him. 'They have an appointment with Trevor,' he said, in a mocking aristocratic accent.

There was a chuckle behind him. 'Let 'em in,' the voice said. 'But they might 'ave a bit of a wait while I nip to the cemetery and dig him up.' Loud peals of laughter followed, but the guy pushed the door wide and the two of them walked cautiously into the room.

Four men, all smoking, were sitting at desks pushed together to make an oblong where two faced two on either side. Another desk was at the far end where a man with grey hair, in his late fifties or early sixties, sat on the other side. He was the one they'd come to see.

XAVIER HUNG BACK a little and observed. The four men were putting stacks of money through a money-counting machine. The guy behind the desk grinned and took a puff on a huge cigar. 'Boys? What can I do for you?'

'Trevor?' JJ said.

They all laughed again and the guy behind the desk narrowed his eyes and took a loud puff on his cigar. 'You taking the Michael, Son?'

The laughing suddenly stopped and there was an excruciating moment of silence. Xavier shifted uncomfortably, getting ready to run. However, the man grinned and the room collectively relaxed. 'I'm Trevor Junior, you could say. My ole man was the name over the door. Passed away three years ago, so you can call me Mr Cooney.'

The men all laughed at him again. He was clearly putting them in their place, but JJ didn't miss a beat. 'I'm JJ. This is my brother, Xavier.'

Mr Cooney put up his hand to stop him. 'I know who you

are. You been staying with the Johnsons. You had a bit of a run-in with my boys a couple of weeks back, I believe.'

Xavier watched as JJ's aura pulsed yellow as he furiously tried to hold the conversation together so as not to antagonize the situation. A troubling tingle was crawling up his spine that he didn't have time to analyse; he was forced to tamp it down. His pulse doubled, it felt stiflingly hot and he continually wanted to cough because of the smoke. He decided it was time he butted in to take the heat off JJ. 'What my brother is trying to say is that we are looking to branch out in business and we're here as a courtesy. We know you are a spokesman and somewhat of a public servant in the area. I thought we could help each other out.'

The men all laughed again, but a little more nervously this time, cautiously keeping their eye on Mr Cooney and how he would react. He looked wide-eyed from Xavier to them and back again as if he'd never heard anything like it. 'By all means. Let me know what it is I can do for you.' The regal wave of his hand suggested that he was treating it all as a joke, making it feel like a farce quickly becoming out of control.

JJ took another turn. 'Can we talk privately?' he said.

The guy looked amused like he was more than a little intrigued to see how it would play out. 'A minute, boys,' he said, nodding towards the door.

The men slowly stood with a scrape of their chairs and filed out of the room. A big guy came in and leaned against the wall. 'He stays, though,' Mr Cooney said.

When the door finally shut behind them, JJ launched right in. 'I need a space for my brother and I to live and run our operations from. It needs to be large, doesn't have to be domestic; we can remodel, but it has to be near enough to the school.'

Mr Cooney's eyes widened and changed expression with

every item on their list. By the time JJ finished with, 'That should do it for starters,' it was obvious the guy thought it was some sort of joke.

Then his eyelids lowered and his smile dropped. 'Right! Now you've had your fun, it's my turn to make demands. You can clear off, before I lose my patience and one of you gets 'urt. You're lucky it's a Sunday and I want to get off early today.'

Xavier immediately straightened and he felt JJ do the same. The feeling up his spine was becoming unbearable. The answer so obvious, it could no longer be ignored.

'I assure you, we are deadly serious. We can make each other a lot of money,' JJ persisted.

Mr Cooney looked at the pair of them as if he doubted that very much. 'I don't run drugs, Son. And, besides, you look like you should be asking your dad for help, not me.'

Xavier could feel JJ's growing frustration, however he held it together. Instead, he sliced the air with his hand in front of him and said, 'You're right, but we're done with our father. Let's just say we've reached a difference of opinion. Look, we came to you out of respect. You know the area and seem to get things done.'

Mr Cooney sniffed and straightened in his seat. JJ's massage to his ego was working.

'We're businessmen, just wanting our start. Think about it. We're at school. We have a whole new demographic to offer. A hitherto untapped source of business for you to reach.'

Mr Cooney looked at his friend, leaning with his back against the wall with a look on his face that was hard to decipher between amazed and disbelief at their sheer cheek. 'Can you believe these kids?'

His friend shook his head and let out a breath of laughter.

Mr Cooney studied them for a long moment as if he was making up his mind. 'Your brother don't say much, does he?'

'We're of the same mind,' JJ said.

'Is that right?'

'It is,' Xavier said, now looking around him for the source of the bad feeling.

'And what would Xavier here say if I was to get Charlie here to give you both a good slap and throw you out on your arses?' Mr Cooney said, raising an eyebrow.

'I'd say you could, but then you'd lose out on a great business opportunity of working with the Dubonnetti brothers. And that doesn't come up every day.'

Mr Cooney and Charlie really laughed at that.

'Is that so,' Mr Cooney said when he finally stopped laughing. 'I'll tell you what. Leave it with me. I'll have a think about what you can do for me.'

'And the property we need?' JJ prompted.

Mr Cooney narrowed his eyes as if they were really pushing it. 'I'll see what's around. But only because you've got guts. Not many grown men would have waltzed in here and do what you just did.'

Xavier's heart pounded as they turned and headed back for the door. It took every ounce of willpower not to run. His skin was literally screaming and it wasn't elation at what they'd just accomplished, it was dread. They had actually pulled it off and everything was really happening. For the first time in their lives, they were in control of their own futures and yet he wanted to grab JJ and run.

Frustratingly, JJ held him back. 'How long till we hear?' he said, before they went out.

'Give me till the end of the week and I'll have your answer for you by then.'

The door opened before they'd even touched it, proving they'd been watched the whole time.

However, with Mr Cooney's parting words of, 'You'll owe me,' Xavier had an even more uncomfortable feeling that all was not what it seemed. Maybe Mr Cooney just had excellent security, or maybe he wasn't the head honcho that everyone in the area thought he was.

They walked quickly along the hallway, through the counter – immediately raised by Mike and back out of the shop. It seemed both couldn't wait to get out of there. *Keep walking,* JJ projected, as soon as they were clear.

Xavier kept pace with him. *Did you feel it?*

JJ nodded. *There was definitely a very powerful Atlantean. Somewhere nearby. Did you see the mirror?*

Yeah, definitely two-way. You realize he'll own us, Xavier reminded him.

JJ nodded, slowing down to a normal walk.

Whoever that Atlantean was, if they're an enemy of father's, it puts us in a really dangerous position. He's not going to want to let us go.

JJ stopped at the corner of the High Street and nodded. *We don't have a choice. We'll use him to get our start, then we'll break away.*

CHAPTER 17

*K*eenan watched through the greyed glass, with three of his compadres, as the two boys came out of the seedy betting shop as if their ass was on fire. He clicked the camera on his phone several times as proof and sent them on to their father, Jay. Dante was on the other side of the world and would only be disturbed if their lives were at stake. Jay wanted detail. 'What are you little rascals up to?' he said, squinting his eye into his spy glass as they went further down the road looking like they'd seen a ghost.

'Are they gambling now?' one of his cousins asked from the back seat.

'I don't think so. It's owned by the shark who sent the goons round to the Johnson place.' Keenan slowly lowered his spyglass while he gave it some thought. 'No, they're up to something.'

As if on cue, JJ touched his brother's shoulder, pointed straight at them and waved.

'We've been made,' his cousin said, grinning.

Keenan was surprised it had taken them this long to sense

them. He tapped Jay's number and put the phone to his ear. 'What do you want me to do?'

'Keep on it,' Jay's voice said immediately, 'But hang back. I'm intrigued to see what they're doing.'

'And the king?' Keenan asked.

'I'll keep him up to speed. He's dealing with a crisis at the moment.'

'THEY'VE SEEN US,' Xavier said. The Uber stopped at the kerb, he scooted into the back seat and JJ got in quickly behind him. 'What shall we do?'

The taxi pulled gently away into the late morning traffic. 'Nothing. They were always going to keep an eye on us. They can only do one of two things: either take us home or leave us to it. Either way, we win.'

Xavier thought about it and guessed JJ was right. 'Who knew you spoke fluent gangsta?' he said smiling at his brother. 'You were great in there.'

'You played your part too,' JJ said, his face hardening. They'll completely underestimate us, then we'll be an unstoppable force.'

JJ was right, but he couldn't shake the feeling he'd had back at the shop. 'Do you think it could have been the guards we sensed back there?' But as he said the words, he didn't really believe it. Whoever it was had an aura darker and more powerful than any they'd ever felt.

'No, this was someone else. There was only one other guy I ever felt like that and he's long dead. I watched him die when I was small. This guy feels like that.'

It made Xavier shiver. He knew who JJ was talking about. Malleven. He'd taken the crown from their father for a few short weeks when they were children. A Florianna prince with dark powers learned from the ancient order of Magi. He hoped to God it wasn't someone with power like him.

'Don't worry. We're powerful too. And when we get going, Mr Cooney, the school, Keenan or even Dad won't be able to do a single thing to stop us.'

JJ SLIPPED BACK into the flat with Xavier. Alexia caught them and eyed them suspiciously, but because she'd made it clear she didn't want to go, she couldn't exactly push to find out what happened.

Latitia was a different story. 'Hey!' she said, as JJ went to go into his room.

Xavier seized his chance to escape and darted into the bathroom.

'Where have you two been?'

'Nowhere. Just woke up,' he said, pausing with his hand on the doorknob.

'No you haven't. Richie said you'd both gone when he got up.'

JJ closed his eyes, let out a breath and slowly turned around. He was going to have to face the inevitable conversation with Latitia head on. He looked at her blankly as if he had no idea what she could want.

'What, so we're going to ignore everything that happened last night?'

'I didn't think you wanted reminding that you turned up at the dance drunk.' The barb flew and hit her so squarely it made him inwardly flinch. He fought the urge to immediately comfort her and apologize. She was just too damn easy to read, which was why he needed to get away from her. He saw the exact moment she understood and the injury spread through the neurons of her brain, every nerve receptor, then out through her aura, pulsing in shades of purple and red as her anger replaced it.

Then she did something completely unexpected. She stepped in closer to him. It was a provocative move that would have meant a fight between two males. Nose to nose, if they'd been equal in height.

Her hot breath switched up his temperature.

'So that's how you wanna play it, is it?' she said, so only he could hear.

She'd so exceeded his expectations, he waited; intrigued, excited at what she would do next. 'I assure you, I don't play around at anything. I go hard or go home,' he said, continuing to glare into her eyes, but really beginning to enjoy himself.

Her eyes dilated, then narrowed as she tried to disguise how his threat made her feel. He found himself imagining everything he wanted to do to her. Her open challenge had ignited something primal deep within him.

After a beat, she countered with, 'Well go home, little boy, because we both know what's going on here is fear. You let your guard down and now you're terrified.'

He almost laughed in shock. It was a gross oversimplification, but she was right to an extent and no one had ever spoken to him like that before. He fought the urge to kiss her and attempted to keep his distance.

Latitia lifted her hand to touch the side of his cheek, but he grabbed her wrist and pulled her quickly into his room behind him. After looking around quickly to check it was empty, he did something he hated doing. He entered the edges of her mind, overtly, so she knew exactly what he was doing. The usual aim was to be undetected, but this time he wanted her to know. It was a deliberate show of his capabilities, done to make her feel helpless and in no doubt who was the more dominant between them.

He didn't want to inflict pain, but venture enough to speak directly to her mind. *Stop this goading, Latitia. You think you know who I am, but you don't. You will get hurt and that's the last thing I want. Xavier, Alexia and I will be leaving here soon and you can get on with your life.*

Her eyes widened with every sentence as the realization of what was happening hit her frontal lobe in blows. He hated himself for the fear that replaced her initial shock and then the resignation that what he was communicating was happening and was the truth. He wasn't some mafioso's son that she'd somehow romanticized in her mind, he was something far more sinister and scary.

When the fight had completely left her body, he slowly released her wrist and left her mind.

She absently rubbed where he'd held her but still looked up at him warily, now seeming so fragile and small. He felt instantly sorry he'd been so rough with her.

'What are you?' she whispered, her eyes darting like a terrified rabbit, desperately searching for a way out with a cosy, plausible explanation.

'Your worst nightmare,' JJ said, fixing her with a direct stare to show how deadly serious he was.

'And Xavier and Alexia are the same?' she said, frowning.

He rolled his eyes and bent down to pull his case out from under the bed. He finally answered, 'I told you, we share a mother.'

'And your fathers. They're like you?'

'More so … well, one of them.' He stood up and sat heavily on his bed in exasperation. 'Enough now, Latitia. The more I tell you, the more of your memory I will have to take.' He looked wearily at her confused expression and tried to soften his tone. 'And I'd rather not have to do that.'

She took a step back and sat down on her brother's bed opposite. She just sat there, staring at him. Running her eyes all over him as if some weird difference would make itself known to her. He had to admit she was stronger with the information than he'd expected. In fact, all he could think about was how adorable she looked, facing her fears bravely. 'So what you're saying is, you don't trust me.'

JJ smiled a little. She had guts, he'd give her that. 'I do trust you, but it's not safe for you to have that kind of information. The less you know, the better.'

'I can handle it. Tell me. Please, JJ. You owe me that, at least, don't you?'

She was adorable and infuriating, all at the same time. Ignoring that he fully meant to wipe her memories, he got to his feet and walked up and down on the mat between the beds, pushing his hand through his hair in frustration. 'I can't.'

'You can! So we kissed. Big deal. We're both still here. Aren't we?' she said, standing as well.

She had a point, he guessed. He looked up at the ceiling for strength, turned and faced her. He took in the warm caramel of her skin, the perfect heart-shaped face and the imploring eyes. The cute braids scooped into a ponytail making her look so young. The dimples he knew appeared easily every time she smiled. He could remember clearly how she'd smelled in the crook of her neck. The now-familiar bonding pain stirred in his chest as a stark reminder. It hit him then that he might be able to move where he lived, but he would never be able to set her free. Not completely. It was too late for that. He smiled haplessly. 'I don't think you'd believe me anyway.'

'Try me.'

He wanted to scream at her that it was the last thing he should do. But selfishly, he wanted her to remember him when they passed each other in the corridors at school. In the end, all he said was, 'Maybe one day.'

'One day soon.'

He laughed then. She was a dog with a bone and had completely overlooked that he'd only just invaded her brain, something never done in Atlantean polite society.

Instead, she got up and stood right in his personal space again. She looked up into his eyes and at his lips. It reminded him of a timid deer he'd once met on his father's estate, determined to make friends in order to be fed titbits.

Then it hit him that it wasn't her who was vulnerable. She would always be his weakness. He did the worst possible thing and caved. He bowed his head and brushed his lips against hers.

'But one day,' she whispered against them.

Her hot breath undid any distance he'd held between them and he was kissing her passionately. Lifting her until she clasped her legs around him. Tasting, swirling his tongue until he knew moving house, staying apart or being cruel would never be enough to keep her away from him. The heavy pain began to rise in his chest.

Then, like a bucket of cold water, he heard a cough behind him. He turned his head sharply and slowly released her down his body to her feet. Xavier was standing just inside the room.

There was no amusement on his face, only a lack of patience as he rolled his eyes. 'I see you remained as emotionally detached as planned,' he said, striding over, stooping and pulling his bag out from under the bed next to JJ.

JJ was forced to step out of the way, still in shock at how much he'd lost control. Another minute and heaven knew what Xavier would have walked in on.

Xavier put his hand into the side zipper and pulled out one of the vials Keenan had given them. He held it out to him as he straightened up. 'Before you kill her.' He flicked his eyes at Latitia, but there was no warmth in them.

JJ caught her lost, bewildered expression at what was happening between him and Xavier. JJ himself wasn't all that sure. He took the vial from Xavier's hand as if it was a grenade that would explode any minute. Not because of what it did, but what it represented. It was the symbol of who he was and what he must become. He knew it, and he was sure as hell Xavier knew it. He made sure he gripped the vial for a moment too long before he let it go. *And so it begins, Brother,* Xavier said, confirming it in his mind.

It was the biggest cold shower to his senses. 'There's no need,' he said, but his voice came out gruff and barely audible.

'Give it to her anyway. Remember what Keenan said: twelve hours apart and make sure she has all three.'

JJ looked his brother in the eye and they stood in some weird stand-off for a full minute, both assessing the other to question if they both registered the importance of that exact moment. It was where they both let go of being kids and became men and took up the mantle of their destiny. Neither could fight it. It was always going to come and there would be casualties. Many.

'Is someone going to tell me what's going on?' Latitia said, finally making him swallow and break his stare.

For a moment, JJ thought Xavier would open his mouth to speak, but then he read the unspoken no in his eyes. He merely nodded and left them to it.

JJ waited until he'd completely left the room and felt weirdly bereft. As if the brother he'd grown up and known his whole life had just walked out of his life, never to return. It was the strangest, gut-wrenching feeling. He wished he could have had at least one of his fathers there to talk to about it.

Latitia touched his arm and he looked down into her searching eyes. She was oblivious to what just went on between them but knew something had happened. He snapped himself out of it and handed her the vial. 'Take it,' he said.

She looked at it and pulled a face as if it was contaminated or something. 'I'm not drinking that. What is it, anyway?'

He let out a deep sigh and looked up at the ceiling for more strength. This wasn't going to go away without some real answers. He stared into her face hoping some inspiration would come to him, but all he saw was the curve of her soft cheek and her rosebud lips, swollen from kissing. He ran his finger along them.

Xavier was right. He wasn't ever going to be able to keep his hands off her. The pain in his chest was there as a nagging reminder. The one he never thought his blood was strong enough to get and was a time bomb complication to his life. It proved he and Xavier were very definitely equals. 'Drink it and I'll promise to answer any of your questions,' he said, knowing the offer was too much for her to resist. He figured she was too naive to ask anything too sensitive.

Latitia shifted her eyes reluctantly to the vial he still held in his hand and took it from him as if it would burn her. She uncorked it and sniffed the contents, immediately pulling a face. He didn't think it smelled of much; maybe vodka with slightly cabbagy undertones. Not great but not disgusting.

She eyed him suspiciously. 'What will it do to me? Take my memories?'

He smiled sardonically. 'I don't need potions for that. It won't do anything immediately. It will protect you in case we —' He didn't finish. It would only spark an avalanche of questions. 'Drink. I promise it won't hurt you. Then you get to ask me anything.'

She shot him a scathing look for the obvious blackmail, then tipped back the contents and emptied the vial into her mouth. Then she swallowed, pulled a face and poked out her tongue to prove it had gone.

'Good,' he said, then went over and sprawled out on his bed.

Latitia was left standing there. 'Well?'

'Well, what?' he said, checking his watch then resting his forearm across his eyes. 'Ask away. You have precisely five minutes.'

'Hey! You never said anything about a time limit.'

JJ smiled to himself. 'You're wasting time.' He couldn't resist taking a peek. Her cute face went from indignation to frustration and then her eyes darted about while she scrambled to think of the best thing to ask. She really hadn't thought this through. It was what he'd banked on.

'So, who are you, really?' she said, clearly relieved to find her opening question.

'You know my name. Jason Gardiner Junior.'

'No, your real name. I know it must be something else because it's so different to Xavier and Alexia's.'

He dropped his arm to look at her. It was really quite astute. He decided to reward her and leaned up on an elbow while he delivered the mouthful: 'Jason Themistius Enil Gardiner Bonaci Santalini Florianna Dubonnetti.' Then he flopped back down and put his arm back over his eyes, feeling the burn of her stare. 'Time's ticking,' he reminded her.

'That doesn't sound like a mafia family name?'

'I never said it was.'

'It's Italian, though.'

'Kind of.'

'Well, what is it, then?'

At first he thought she was wasting time on ridiculous

semantics, then he changed his mind. *Wasn't it the crux of everything?* 'Royal.' He said it bluntly and felt his heart sink right into the bed. The admission was the kiss of death to any budding relationship between them.

'What kind of royal? Her voice had already gone small and tight in her throat as if it was the last thing she'd been expecting.

'An Atlantean one.'

'Atlantean,' she repeated.

He rolled onto his stomach and rested his cheek on his folded arms while he watched her trying to rack her brains to think exactly where that was. 'So, your father is—?'

'King – well, Xavier's is. Mine was … used to be … It's complicated. Now he's just his right-hand man.'

She was frowning as if she was finding it hard to follow. 'I don't get it. What's that got to do with wiping my mind and giving me potions because we kissed?'

JJ slowly sat up and smiled. 'Nothing. Nothing at all,' he said more to himself. She was beautiful and clever and it was sad to watch the scales fall from her eyes, only to know they would have to go back up, permanently. 'And everything,' he added dryly.

A solitary tear rolled onto her cheek as she recognized the brush off when she saw it. He hated that he had to go through with it to make her stay away from him enough to keep her safe.

'Relax, Latitia. Deep down, I think you've known it all along.'

'Known what?' she said, shifting her feet irritably.

'That we're different. Something completely different to you.' He let her work through the implications of what he was saying, then continued, 'We're here to learn to fit in, to an extent, but we were never here to stay.'

Tears were streaming down her face now. He knew she

was grabbing hold of the slightest logical, romanticized straw and he allowed her that.

'And the kiss at the dance ... everything?'

JJ sat up with his feet on the floor. 'Shouldn't have happened.' He shrugged and leaned forward with his elbows on his knees. 'I'm weak around you. My brother was right to interrupt. I would kill you and I have no wish to do that.'

When she didn't say a word, he looked up at her through his eyebrows. He was expecting her to rant and call him all the names in her vocabulary. She didn't even bombard him with any more questions. She appeared to shrink and turn into a very fragile little girl and that, he realized, was much worse. She'd listened and heard what he'd said and now he'd said it, he wished he could take it all back. The only thing she said was, 'When will you go?' in a cracked and broken voice.

'In the next few days, probably.' They'd gone from kissing to robotic and awkward in a matter of minutes. His heart that always hurt around her now felt like an open wound. He'd never experienced anything like it. It wasn't what he'd had to do that got to him, he guessed it was simply her complete resignation.

'Well, OK then,' she said, turning on her heel, but stopping and turning her head before she left the room. 'I don't think you'll need to wipe my memory for that, JJ.' Then she disappeared.

Shocked, JJ jumped to his feet as if to stop her, but suddenly felt like there was nowhere to go. He went to walk forward, stopped, and went back. He felt confused and wanted to scream and smash things. He'd broken the only thing pure and good in his life. Now all he felt was empty, with a medicine ball hole where his heart should be.

Xavier came in, took one look at his face and nodded. 'You've done the right thing.' Then he flopped heavily on Richie's bed. 'We've got to get out of here.'

Alexia was feeling increasingly isolated. It was new and painful; something she'd never had to endure in her life before. She'd tried calling her younger brothers, Roman and Zander and even her Borge cousins, but they were either in the water or busy with their lives. She and JJ had always been the closest confidants and they had always been surrounded by a large family. Now, their cousins were thousands of miles away and JJ was distant, constantly meeting and whispering with Xavier.

Her logic told her it was for her own good. They were determined to defy their father and the less she knew the less she'd have to lie about, but it didn't make it hurt any less.

Now it was laughable.

Her goody-two-shoes stand not to go was not because she was passing judgement on what they were doing, but because she wanted to stay with Dwayne. And he was so eaten up with getting even with Trick, that she may as well not exist. He was too preoccupied by hatching something with his brother, Richie, to notice anything was wrong with her. It began with staying to practice after school in the music room and then, lately, hanging out in a local drinking club, Rhythm and Booze. Even she knew it was a place owned, run and frequented by shady characters. She would have gone with him, but he never asked.

Nowadays, the six of them walked to school in silence, scurrying off in opposite directions as soon as they had the chance. Leaving her alone and making her want to cry. It seemed like the lump in her throat was always so close to the surface that she battled tears all the time. She was almost at the point of ringing her mother and crying for her to take her home, when she noticed she wasn't the only one in the Johnson family getting frozen out.

Latitia was as quiet and alone as she was. She'd been so wrapped up in herself that she hadn't noticed that the formerly happy, lively girl seemed to have become completely withdrawn. She walked with her head down, sat alone in the canteen, just scrolling on her phone, not talking to anyone and even sat with her in class on occasion and she'd never done that before. It meant only one thing: *JJ*. He could be heartless when he needed to be.

She caught Latitia looking at her curiously a few times, like she wanted to say something but thought better of it. Then, when they found themselves partnered up for Geography, she could no longer keep silent. 'So what did JJ do?' Alexia said, measuring out a spoonful of their soil sample into a tube.

Latitia didn't look her in the eye. 'Nothing.' She continued to defuse her soil in cold water and swirl it around.

In the end, Alexia had to take it from her hands so she was forced to look sulkily up at her. She looked so unhappy that an awful thought suddenly struck her. 'He didn't—?' Neither of her brothers could be described as being gentlemen with girls.

Latitia shook her head. 'No, nothing like that.'

The flood of relief made Alexia sit heavily on the stool next to her. Although that didn't explain why Latitia had dark circles under her eyes, like she hadn't slept for a week. 'Then what is it?'

She began to pick at her nails. 'He told me who you were and gave me this weird stuff to drink. Now he won't talk to me at all.'

Alexia's heart constricted and then plummeted, all at the same time. All she could think was, *how could he?* No wonder the poor girl was confused. It was the worst possible thing he could have done. She knew there had been some kind of connection between the two of them and now he was plotting to get away from their father with Xavier and leaving Latitia in a mess he created.

JJ was usually the most closed-mouthed out of all of them and would never divulge anything about them to anyone. That meant this was serious. More than she first realized.

She immediately put up her hand. 'Go along with me,' she whispered.

'What is it, Alexia?' Mr Reece, the Geography teacher, said.

'Sorry, sir, but Latitia feels sick. Shall I go with her to the office?'

My Reece rolled his eyes at the go-to excuse for most girls – that and 'time of the month' – and nodded a little angrily. 'OK. Come straight back. No dallying in the hallways.'

Latitia looked a little in shock as they both took off their protective glasses and got down off their stools to take off their lab coats. However, she followed Alexia quickly from the room. 'Where are we going?' Latitia said, as soon as they were outside.

'PE block. Changing rooms,' Alexia said, half walking, half running down the corridor and out across the car park.

The Phys Ed block was empty as suspected when they entered through the double doors. Shouts and squeaks from trainers came from the sports hall next door, as she pulled Latitia into the girls' changing room to sit on one of the many benches. Clothes hung, hiding them, from the hooks above their heads. They didn't have long. 'Right, now tell me what's going on and don't say nothing,' Alexia said, fixing Latitia with a hard glare.

Latitia shrugged sulkily. 'It is nothing. That's just it.'

Alexia looked around her furtively and hushed to a whisper. 'What exactly did JJ tell you?' Her heart began to pump knowing this was more complicated than a simple brush-off.

Latitia shifted uncomfortably making Alexia want to shake her to hurry up and speak, but she dug her nails into her palms and her restraint paid off.

'I get it. I do. You're royal and everything and he can't be with the likes of me—'

Alexia drew her eyebrows together, astounded. It was the last thing she expected to hear. 'What, he said that?'

'More or less. He got all weird. Said he couldn't tell me anything else otherwise he'd have to take my memories. Then he gave me disgusting medicine to drink and said he could kill me. Honestly, Alexia, all he had to say was he wasn't into me and I would have understood. He didn't have to be all like that.' Latitia looked at her imploringly, desperate for her to understand and believe her.

Alexia did believe her. It had too much of a ring of truth about it for her not to. She felt sorry for the hash JJ had made of it. Her aura was sad, with tones of green and brown, showing just how bewildered she was. She let out a weary sigh and sank back against the clothes behind her. 'I kind of feel the same way about Dwayne. He's so obsessed with getting back at Trick, it's like I don't exist.'

Latitia picked up her hand and gave it a squeeze. Alexia

felt instantly guilty that she couldn't reveal that JJ's actions meant he liked her very much and it was more than anything he'd ever done for any other girl – human or otherwise.

'I just wanted to know a little about him,' Latitia said, continuing to hold her hand.

Even holding her hand, however innocent, felt like a betrayal, as it meant Alexia could get a surface read on everything she felt. 'And he left you hanging,' she said, feeling the worst friend ever.

Latitia nodded, sadly and looked at the fingers of her other hand in her lap.

'Boys are such shits. The minute something enters their heads, everything else gets dropped,' Alexia murmured, thinking selfishly of her own situation. However, it helped her make up her mind. No more moping around. She rummaged in her bag and pulled out her backup phone, hidden in the lining and hit one of the only three numbers in it. Her mother. She put it to her ear and looked into Latitia's light-brown, inquisitive eyes. She picked up on the second ring. 'Mum? Can I come home for a few days? Can I bring a friend?'

The soft, lulling voice of her mother calmed her instantly, just like she knew it would. 'Of course, darling. What's the matter?'

'Nothing major. Just need some TLC. You know, boy trouble.'

Latitia's eyes went wide at that.

Alexia nodded animatedly, even though her mother couldn't see her. 'OK. We'll be ready.' She clicked off the phone and jumped to her feet. 'Come on, you're going home, sick.'

Latitia got to her feet more slowly, bewildered. 'What now? What about the others? 'Where are we going, anyway?'

Alexia was already pulling her towards the door, which

was just as well as the doors to the gym burst open and kids began to pour out into the changing room. 'That's why we're going now. JJ and Xavier mustn't know.'

'What about my mum?' Latitia said, almost running next to her.

'My mum will square it with her and the school.' Her heart was beating with excitement; the most alive she'd felt in days. 'It's a good job she's in Ireland, otherwise we wouldn't be able to go.'

'Ireland? Wait!' Latitia said, suddenly dragging her feet to a standstill. 'I can't go all the way there, I don't have a passport.'

'Don't worry, I'll text her. She'll sort it.' Then she walked on even faster than before.

'Wait, Alexia,' Latitia said, stopping again. 'So that means your father is pretty powerful.' Her eyes widened. 'It's all true, isn't it?'

'More than you know,' Alexia muttered under her breath and kept walking.

She kept the pace up all the way home with Latitia half jogging next to her, firing all the reasons why it was impossible for her to leave at the drop of her hat. But they bounced off her as simply based on fear of the unknown. The fact was, Valarie was doing her afternoon shift at the hospital and the younger ones were at nursery, so there was nothing to get in their way.

She put her key in the door, burst in like a whirlwind and marched straight to the bedroom they shared. 'Pack!' she ordered, already pulling her bag out from under the bed.

Latitia did as she was told, mechanically, clearly not convinced it was something she should be doing at all, until a text pinged on her phone.

Alexia picked it up to read it, when an alert pinged at the same time from Dwayne on her Twitter feed, about some DJ battle. *Great.* She pushed down the instant pain that hit her chest. 'Come on,' she prompted, more to herself. She didn't want to leave anything to chance and for any of the boys to come home and talk Latitia out of it. She touched her shoulder. 'Look. Keenan is outside. It's an adventure. JJ's always saying how you're ballsy and everything. Let's see it,' she said, not waiting for her reaction. She bent down, grabbed her bag and headed for the door.

'Who's Keenan again?' Latitia said from right behind her.

Alexia didn't let it show how relieved she actually was that Latitia had finally given in and gone with the idea. 'My uncle. One of the big guys that came here that day. He's one of my father's elite guards.'

They went out through the front door and Alexia remembered to double-lock it. All the while she could hear Latitia saying, 'Oh my god, this is really happening,' to herself, over and over.

Alexia ignored it, extended the handle on her pull-along case and said, 'Come on, we have a plane to catch.'

THE SUN WAS ACTUALLY SHINING, and Alexia had never been so excited to go home. It hadn't dawned on her till then, how weighed down she'd been. It felt like a weight was lifted off her. The blacked-out SUV and her Uncle Keenan getting out to open the back door for them reminded her who she was and seemed to power her excitement like rocket fuel. Her bags were spirited away and she scooted into the back seat, where she smiled at the guard already there. Latitia got in more slowly next to her.

Keenan got back into the passenger seat and the car immediately moved off. Latitia looked nervously at the three huge guards and out the window in the direction they'd come as if she'd jump out at any minute.

'Don't be scared,' Alexia whispered. 'You wanted to find out about JJ's world, well, this is your chance.'

Latitia looked intently at her and gave her a small nod. JJ was right. She was ballsy. All this would scare anyone, let alone a sixteen-year-old girl.

Keenan turned and smiled at them from the front passenger seat. 'Weekend getaway, girls?' he said.

Alexia nodded. 'This is Latitia Johnson, everyone. She's coming home with me for the weekend. Has Mum organized her passport?'

Keenan looked at the driver, who looked back at him guiltily. He was Keenan's cousin, Reeve. 'There's been a change of plan,' Keenan said, finally looking back at her. 'We're taking you to Soho.'

Alexia sagged dramatically in her seat. 'No, not the Bluebell. Mum promised. She said it'd be fine,' she whined. 'Did Dad put a stop to it?' she said, anger suddenly shooting through her.

'What's in Soho,' Latitia said, fearfully.

Keenan looked impatiently at Alexia, who was clearly scaring Latitia. 'It's OK, it's JJ's dad's hotel,' she said sulkily. 'It's just not what I was expecting that's all … It's been weeks, Keenan,' she said, resuming her whining. 'I demand to speak to her!' she said, trying to bully her uncle, even though she knew it was futile.

They were zipping along, making good progress in the midday traffic. Keenan twisted in his chair to face her more squarely, no humour on his face at all. She braced herself for the telling off. 'It would take a lot more notice than an hour to take a hu— A friend,' he amended. 'Out of the country. Your dad is tied up in Russia at the moment. Your mum just thought it'd be easier for her to come and meet you here at Jay's hotel. And Jay thought …' His eyes flicked to Latitia, listening avidly. 'Things need to be broached a little more gently before throwing her in the deep end at the castle.'

'Castle?' Latitia repeated, snapping her head around to face her.

Alexia knew by that reaction alone that Jay had been right. However, it was still infuriating the way he always butted in like a second father and even more so because that was exactly what he was. Instead, she flipped it back on Keenan. 'She knows some things. She's not stupid.'

Keenan simply tipped his head in Latitia's direction, to her alarmed expression and looked at Alexia sardonically. 'Not enough,' he said.

Alexia threw herself back in her seat like a bratty child. She knew they were all right and Latitia was scared, but all she wanted was to go home for one stupid weekend. Two days to be herself, with her own stuff. Doing the things *she* wanted to do for a change. But *oh no,* that was too simple. 'It's not up to Jay to vet my friends,' was all she could say, moodily.

Keenan conceded with a small bob of his head. 'Maybe not.' Then he gave her a small wink. 'But maybe JJ's?'

She scowled and shut up after that. She shouldn't be surprised they were so well informed. Her father or Jay would insist they knew everything. She glared angrily out of the window and projected so only Atlantean minds could hear. *This is all crap. You know that, right?*

Keenan faced front and they crossed the river in silence after that. The blue sky had clouded over.

CHAPTER 19

It didn't take long for Xavier to catch on that both girls were missing after school. He and JJ waited twenty minutes at the gate, checking their various social media platforms for any clue where they might have gone, before they eventually walked home. 'We're going to have to ring the number,' Xavier said, eventually.

JJ shook his head. 'Not yet.

Xavier shrugged. He was worried, but it was bad to cave this soon into their self-emancipation plan. The whole point was to stand on their own.

'Dwayne didn't seem that concerned,' JJ said, his face a blank canvas. As usual, he gave nothing away, but Xavier knew he felt exactly the same as he did. A mixture of relief and anger that neither Dwayne nor Richie showed any interest that either of the girls were missing before they shot off to practice their DJ set straight after school. They were single-minded where DJing was concerned, since the night of the party. Richie just called back over his shoulder, 'They've probably skived off together and forgot the time.'

It was plausible, Xavier supposed. Plus, it would be

189

foolish to post anything the school could see during school time. Although Alexia was always such a goody-two-shoes and would have at least messaged JJ.

Finally, JJ voiced what they both were thinking. 'She's nowhere around here.'

Xavier nodded. They would have felt her. She'd simply disappeared.

They bounded up the steps to the flat, two at a time, along the landing, until Xavier put the key in the door, hoping their instincts had been wrong. He pushed into the flat, JJ closely behind him, and checked each room frantically. He was in such a panic he almost missed the note that fluttered off the living room table. *Gone home* was scribbled in Alexia's handwriting. With the little heart she always put on everything.

JJ was about to snatch it from Xavier's hands when his phone rang. He looked at the screen, then back at Xavier. 'It's Valarie Johnson.'

'Answer it,' Xavier said.

JJ looked at him as he tapped it and put it on speaker. 'JJ?' the clear female voice said.

'Valarie,' JJ answered, immediately.

'Just wanted to let you know that I had a call from the girls, just now, and they've gone to Jay's for the weekend. Latitia said that Alexia was homesick and wanted to go home to see her mother, but they've gone there instead.'

Xavier relaxed a little. He was still a bit angry that Alexia had swanned off without telling anyone, but Jay was more than capable of doing any damage limitation with Latitia.

JJ was a different story. He ended the call, thanking Valarie, but looked troubled. No doubt he was worried what Latitia would find out about him. 'I think we should go there,' JJ said.

Xavier frowned. It was the last thing they should do. It was obvious JJ was feeling vulnerable with Latitia so far out of his control. Alexia could be literally telling her anything. It almost made him smile to see JJ so on the back foot over something. In the end, he relented, feeling a little sorry for him. 'Your father is far from stupid, JJ. He's hardly going to divulge official secrets to her.' It was an annoying fact that he was always too discreet about everything.

JJ let out a sigh and eventually nodded. Xavier couldn't blame him. He was probably more nervous about what annoying secrets *Alexia* would be divulging. Possibly making the inevitable mind wipe dangerous or even impossible.

Just then, something rattled at the front door. JJ looked at Xavier and they both rushed out into the hallway to see what it was. A folded piece of paper was lying on the mat.

JJ scooped it up and read it out loud: *Top floor, The Old Papermill, The Wharf, 6 p.m. Don't be late. C.*

All of a sudden, the girls being out of the way, the boys practising and Valarie at work was the most perfect thing in the world.

WITHOUT ANY FURTHER CONVERSATION, Xavier and JJ showered and changed and met an Uber out on the street. They'd wasted a lot of time waiting for Alexia at school, so time would be tight. Xavier didn't get the impression Mr Cooney would wait.

In no time at all, they were inching through the early evening traffic. 'We should have walked,' JJ said.

'How much further?' Xavier said, leaning forward in his seat to speak to the driver.

'Five minutes,' the heavily accented man said, surrounded by brightly coloured religious relics hanging off his dashboard and sun visor.

The driver was right. Once they'd cleared the queue for the lights, they were there in no time at all. Xavier thanked him and they both slid out of the back seat and looked up at the building.

It was an old warehouse; red brick with windows divided into small squares, painted with light-green paint. Steps led up to a set of double doors in the same colour that had a new-looking entry phone system next to them. A chimney towered over it, at least a hundred feet, with the numbers 1806 raised in the brickwork. It had definitely been a paper-mill at some point in its previous life.

Xavier looked around as they mounted the steps. It had been an unusually nice day and the unseasonal warmth had infused the air with the smell of stale water. A canal was no more than a hundred feet away. Once a place for effectively transporting goods, it was now dotted with houseboats and small weekend cabin boats, moored at the edge.

'This is it,' JJ said, pointing at a gold plaque next to the entry phone.

Xavier skimmed over the numbers, one to ten, with *Top Floor* written out in full. 'Penthouse,' he said, smiling at JJ as he pushed the buzzer.

''Bout time,' JJ said, grabbing the door as soon as it clicked open.

'Should we have a plan or something?' Xavier said, following JJ, closely, in through the door. Xavier's mind was racing through a list of possible scenarios, not least of which was an ambush, where the pair of them ended up dead.

JJ looked up at the concrete stairs and green railing, going up out of sight and then sidestepped to a lift and pulled open the cage. He pushed the button and smiled wickedly at Xavier. 'I don't think we've done enough to piss him off yet.'

The lift whined as it got closer and eventually opened, meaning it had probably come from the top. They locked eyes and both stepped in, Xavier pushing the top-floor button. Everything seemed perfect for what they'd asked for, but he couldn't shake his unease. It seemed the longest lift ride of their life, when, in truth, it was probably only about six floors.

The lift juddered to a stop, pinged and the doors opened. There was just a small area of corridor and only one door, with a guy they recognized from the betting shop stationed just outside. He nodded once and tipped his head to the side to indicate for them to go straight in.

Xavier tried to look nonchalant and relaxed, but inside his nerves were taut and screaming, ready to run. JJ's aura seemed better, with tiny flecks of red that could be nerves. He didn't know how he did it; must get it from his father.

Suddenly they were inside and all thoughts of running disappeared. The space was superb. Just a simple empty shell, but it was perfect for what they wanted. Completely open-plan, with exposed brick and visible metal heating ducts and a floor of polished concrete. He could just imagine it filled with simple but tasteful furniture. Screened-off bedrooms, a jukebox, pool table, couple of expensive rugs. Maybe even a couple of good paintings.

Both boys ventured in further, taking it all in and imagining what could be. Xavier wandered past the L-shaped kitchen complete with American fridge, large professional hob, high-end oven and countertop, all in a matt silver and clearly never used.

Xavier couldn't resist a peek at the view. 'Roof terrace is just down there,' Mr Cooney said, coming up to his shoulder and pointing to some large glass doors to the right.

Xavier turned his head and nodded in appreciation at the large area about the size of an average house covered in plants and ferns and a few lanterns. The place really was fabulous.

'What do you think?' Mr Cooney said.

JJ joined them and wolf whistled his appreciation. 'What's not to like?'

'The catch,' Xavier said, sardonically, turning to face them and flashing a look to JJ.

Mr Cooney laughed. 'I knew I liked you boys.' He put his hands in his pockets and studied them as if he was making up his mind and not the other way around. 'I have to be honest, it ain't cheap, boys.'

'Whose is it?' Xavier said. Mr Cooney was a local shark; a development like this was way out of his league.

Mr Cooney offered a forced smile. 'Shrewd,' he said, pointing at Xavier, and clearly registering the insult. 'It belongs to a partner of mine. One I have certain dealings with. When I told him about the two of you, he offered you this place at a nominal rent, providing you work for him from time to time.'

Xavier's hackles began to rise, reminding him of the uneasy feeling they'd both had back at the shop. He would bet his whole fortune on it being the same guy. 'What if we'd rather pay full price and not owe him?' Xavier said. 'We're good for it.'

Mr Cooney laughed and tipped his head in deference. 'I'm sure you are. But that's just not an option in this case.'

Xavier flashed JJ another look and they both went to turn towards the door. The last thing they wanted was to be owned.

'Hey, hey! Don't be hasty, boys. You won't find anything like this in the area you want. And the favours he'd ask would be small.'

'What are they? Let's meet him, then,' JJ said, clearly getting impatient.

Mr Cooney wandered back over to the large window, made up of small panes of glass. 'That's not possible, I'm afraid. He's not in the country much. He's what you might call a silent partner.'

Xavier and JJ swapped a look again and turned to face him so that their arms touched. *What do you think?* Xavier projected.

It must be the Atlantean.

I agree. It throws up a whole load of complications. Are we sure we want to get into bed with this guy?

Or opportunities, JJ said, then he moved away closer to Mr Cooney. 'What kind of things do you think he'll want from us?'

Mr Cooney whirled around and smiled. 'Oh, nothing much. Not sure he's made up his mind yet. I think he's interested to see how you do by yourselves, first.' Then the smile dropped from his face, and the real shark in him showed through. 'I'd like to know too. This is my area, boys. No treading on toes. No trouble with gangs or bringing any trouble to my door. Otherwise you'll be dealing with me. Clear?'

Xavier wasn't sure what to say. They'd had a few ideas, but nothing you could describe as a plan yet. Thankfully, JJ spoke up. 'We told you, most of our business will be going through the school. That doesn't affect you. You'll get your cut.'

Cooney laughed loudly at that. 'Well OK, then. Fifty percent it is. Take it or leave it.'

Everything in Xavier screamed for him to protest, but the sudden change in JJ's aura told him he was on it. JJ stepped forward to shake on it and Xavier turned to distract Cooney's bodyguard with the time.

JJ didn't disappoint. As soon as he made skin contact, he quickly entered his consciousness and flicked a few switches in his brain. 'Twenty percent, then, boys. OK?'

'Twenty percent,' JJ repeated.

The guard looked over and frowned. But Xavier said, 'Do you have six-fifteen? My watch is fast.'

The guard nodded absently and looked back at him, confused; as if he'd never seen anything like it.

'Looks like they get on,' Xavier said, smiling at him. 'He's the father figure he never had.'

The guard nodded, still distracted.

'JJ?' Xavier called, not wanting any more questions between the two men while they were still there. JJ nodded, seeing what he meant straight away.

'Boys?' Cooney called just as they thought they were getting away. They looked at each other and slowly turned. Cooney threw them the keys. 'Get the feel of the place.'

'Aren't you going to at least tell us the name of our mystery benefactor?' JJ asked, catching the keys easily.

'They just call him Rasputin.'

'Russian?' Xavier said, surprised. His mind quickly working through what Atlantean family out of the five the powerful male could possibly be from.

'You've heard of him?' Cooney said, sounding equally surprised.

'Only his namesake, at school.' The implications were hitting Xavier one by one. Atlanteans lived long lives. This could be an actual Rasputin descendant, or simply an alias that grew from the folklore surrounding his power. This was much more disturbing than he first thought. 'Send him our thanks and our regards,' Xavier said to smooth over how disturbed he felt.

'I'll tell him you'll be moving in right away,' Cooney said, looking at his guard and tipping his head in the direction of the door.

'Thanks,' JJ said, putting a hand up. Then the two of them watched them go before either of them spoke.

Xavier immediately turned to JJ. 'Twenty percent? I thought we agreed five?'

JJ put his hands in his pockets and frowned.

'What's the matter?' Xavier asked.

'Twenty percent was the figure already fixed in his mind by someone else.'

Xavier let the disturbing thought sink in. Their new Atlantean benefactor was controlling Cooney quite closely – and particularly his dealings with them. He was obviously a very shrewd male. One who operated in the shadows and grey areas of the law, making sure he never implicated himself. 'We need to go careful,' Xavier said, feeling a wave of fear. Suddenly they were in a hostile, adult world where everyone played for keeps.

'If this guy is Atlantean and we know that he is, the chances are high that he knows who we are.'

'What if he is one of Father's enemies?'

JJ shrugged. 'Friend or foe, we'll use him to our advantage.'

Xavier came up to his shoulder to see what he was looking at. 'What are you doing?'

'I was thinking brown leather corner unit over there. Pool table there,' JJ said, nodding his head to the largest space.

Xavier laughed. It let out some of the tension and they needed it. They were really doing this. Separating from their father and making a little kingdom of their own.

$\mathscr{A}$lexia fumed all the way to Jay's hotel. It wasn't that it wasn't a nice place to take Latitia, it was fabulous: a tasteful, small boutique hotel, off a cute little side street in Soho. The small oak door on the street had a hand-painted sign above it with gold cursive, *The Bluebell,* on a powder blue background. Somehow it managed to look classy and quaint, all at the same time.

Friendly staff greeted them in the dark-wood-panelled entrance hall and a cute bellboy whisked them up to the top floor which was always reserved for members of her family.

Latitia's eyes were wide with excitement as she bounded about, checking out the stocked minibar, the enormous plunge tub and throwing herself on the super-king bed. Despite all that, Alexia recognized the weekend for what it was – a fob-off.

She'd stayed in Jay's hotel many times growing up. It was one of her parents' favourite places in the world. It was where her mother first met Jay and where he'd proved himself as a formidable businessman after her late grandfather had given it to him when he was a penniless orphan. It had a lot of history.

However her heart sank further when Jay was not able to see them until later that evening. His time was always taken up with business matters. The only good news was that her mother was flying over to join them.

'So this was yours all the time and you're staying at our dump?' Latitia said, arms held wide.

Alexia rolled her eyes and went to pour them both some iced cucumber water Jay had sent up. 'No, I told you. This is JJ's dad's hotel.'

'But this is your lifestyle, right?'

Alexia looked at Latitia wearily, holding back that this was quite low-key for her family, but she kept quiet, not wanting to totally blow her mind. It was made worse by a maid arriving to tell her that the pool in the basement had been emptied for them.

Alexia picked up her towel and pulled her bathing suit out of her bag. 'Come on, let's go to the pool. We've got ages to kill.'

'I thought they said the pool was emptied?' Latitia said, grabbing hers and following.

'Of people, der-brain.'

'Oh,' Latitia said, thankfully remaining quiet all the way down in the lift.

The maid was right. The spa was completely empty of guests when they got there. It had a beautiful pool reminiscent of a Roman bath, with pillars, plinths and potted plants on pedestals.

Latitia threw her towel down on a yellow-striped upholstered lounger and Alexia sat on the one next to her. 'Ah, this is the life,' Latitia said, lying back scrolling on her phone.

Alexia let her settle for a few minutes before she broached

the subject she'd been dying to ask. 'So what has JJ told you about us so far?'

The contented smile disappeared from Latitia's face and she seemed to drag her eyes from her phone to look at her. As if there was something infinitely more interesting there. 'Only that you're from a royal family, from somewhere I've never heard of and he can't be with me because of his duty to it one day.'

Alexia bobbed her head, still watching Latitia's behaviour closely. She guessed he'd kept it vague but true. Latitia probably assumed it was just some small principality somewhere. But there was something else – something she wasn't saying. She'd gone straight to looking intently at her phone. 'What is it?' she asked, her heart already speeding up.

'Nothing,' she said, quickly clicking it off and putting it back in her bag.

Alexia frowned; now alarmed at what it could be and held out her hand. 'Show me!'

Latitia reluctantly rummaged in her bag, pulled out the phone and passed it to her. 'It's just Dwayne challenging Trick to some battle. I didn't want to put you on a downer.'

Alexia re-played the short video shot behind his decks, posturing and pointing, with Richie chiming in next to him. He was challenging him to some kind of face-off in a couple of weeks' time. At least she knew what all the practising had been for.

'It's all over social media,' Latitia said.

Alexia swallowed back the hurt that he hadn't mentioned a thing and handed her phone back to her.

Thankfully, a hot young waiter came in in his cute uniform of black shirt and trousers and broke the awkward moment. 'Excuse me, Miss Dubonnetti, Mr Gardiner told me to let you know that he will see you now, privately.'

Alexia smiled a thanks at the guy, probably fresh out of

college. Then, as soon as he'd disappeared, she got to her feet, determined not to dwell on what couldn't be changed. She'd been summoned and she wouldn't put it past Jay to embarrass her and come and get her, if she ignored it. 'I'd better go.'

Latitia was still studying her with a look of concern. She smiled brightly to show it was forgotten and threw her the key card. 'Stay a while, then go up and start getting ready if I'm not back.'

Latitia nodded, looking a little relieved. 'No problem,' she said, easing back into her lounger, her mood quickly switching back to enjoying herself in what she thought was the height of luxury. 'Beats school.'

Alexia smiled and made her way back to the lift. Suddenly it no longer felt like a light-hearted trip away with a friend. She had to forget Dwayne and gather her thoughts. There was no fooling Jay; he was one of the shrewdest people she knew. She made her way to the ground floor and towards the back of the hotel. Then she tried to calm her beating heart outside his office door. She rapped on it with her knuckle.

'Come in, Alexia,' came from the other side.

ALEXIA CLOSED the door quietly behind her and faced Jay. He was sitting behind his desk working, as expected, and looking as suave and impeccably dressed as ever. She didn't think she'd ever come across anyone more handsome or more groomed than Jay. Today his hair was perfectly razored, strategically falling over one eye, and his pale-pink cotton shirt was perfectly teamed with a pale grey tie, striped in an identical shade.

He looked up, beaming a perfect smile that lit up a face that was already impossibly handsome. The corners of his bright-blue eyes creased and added to the room lighting effect. To someone who didn't know him, he could have been an actor or a model; the overall package was that stunning. Only those, like her, who knew him personally, or in business, knew how driven and ruthless he could be. He was a complete contradiction. His induction into the Santalini soldier family, and a body covered in warrior tattoos, attested to that.

She looked around. It always surprised people how small and unassuming his hotel office was. A throwback from when he was a simple hotel manager. He always said he was OK with it, and she knew that was true. There was nothing showy about Jay. If anything, there was always more hidden away. He joked that if he wanted to boost his ego, all he had to do was go over to the Bonaci Corps building across town, to his large corner office, where he oversaw the huge business for her great-uncle and grandfather.

Jay pressed a button and asked the desk to hold his calls and to send a pot of coffee. Then he stood and walked around the desk to greet her; his grey pants fell into perfectly tailored place over the smart Italian shoes she knew he always wore.

He pulled her in and kissed her cheek. He did it stiffly, as he always did, finding shows of affection like that extremely difficult. Her mum always said it was just the way he was, but that he loved them all fiercely. So Alexia accepted it as the most demonstrative he ever got and felt flattered that he only ever reserved it for her and her brothers.

'Take a seat,' Jay said, leading her towards the chair next to his desk. She took it and he walked back round to his side of the desk. 'Shall I order you a snack or something?'

Alexia shook her head. 'No thanks.' She tried to rekindle her anger for his hijacking of her weekend, but it was very hard when the warmth of his kiss was still on her cheek, his gorgeous cologne wrapped around her like a hug and his smile lit his perfectly chiselled face. His gaze was direct and blue, waiting for her to speak. So annoyingly direct, straightforward and gorgeous, she wanted to throw something at him.

'Say what you want to say, Alexia,' he said. 'Is everything OK with your brothers? Is that why you're here?'

She went to open her mouth when there was a knock at the door. A young blonde girl she didn't know brought in the coffee and set it down on Jay's desk. She scurried away with a red face at Jay's smile of thanks. Jay affected everyone like that. He poured and pushed a cup her way, then sat back and studied her, holding his cup.

'I wanted to go home, Jay,' Alexia blurted, moodily.

He dipped his head in agreement, proving he knew full well what her plan had been and made no apology. 'So your friend – Valarie's girl, isn't it? She likes the hotel?'

'Of course she likes it. You know who she is. I'm almost seventeen, Jay. Please stop treating me like a kid.'

Jay took a sip of his drink and eyed her shrewdly, giving nothing away of what he was thinking. Then he set his coffee down as if he'd come to some sort of decision. 'Your father put a lot of trust in the three of you, placing you there, Lexie. He knew it would be hard, but there is always a method to his madness, you know that. You just have to rise to the challenge.'

'And we have!' Alexia said, beginning to raise her voice as her anger rose inside her. 'We've done everything Dad asked. I just wanted to go home for the weekend, Jay.'

'Taking a friend – a human – someone JJ is particularly close to?' Jay kept his usual soft tone, but fixed her with his gaze.

Alexia felt her anger rise higher. 'Not anymore. They broke up.'

Jay's expression didn't change, so it was hard to work out if he was sorry, angry or misinformed. He simply answered,

'It doesn't matter, Alexia. You must understand that, once you enter our world, you never get to leave. It's a choice you shouldn't make for a person without real forethought.'

Alexia shrank a little under his steely gaze. She'd never thought about it like that. It was clear he was partly talking about himself, spending his life with them, but she'd always taken for granted that it was something he chose because he loved them. It never occurred to her that it was something he would have done differently.

Then she thought about Latitia. She was hardly moving her in. 'It's not the same, at all, Jay. Kids go home and take friends for sleepovers all the time.'

'Not to castles, Alexia, with underground chambers, where water-breathing relatives come and go all the time. What were you thinking? Your father has enemies. Do you want your friend exposed to that? Do you think so little of her?' His face looked hard and she saw the anger in the glint in his eyes and the set of his jaw.

Alexia was angry too now and rolled her eyes. 'She's the same age as me, Jay. What's she gonna do, sell secrets to the Russians?'

She was gratified by the small smile that played on Jay's lips before he banished it. 'I understand, I do, Alexia, but this one means a lot to JJ, doesn't she?'

Alexia shrugged moodily. She should have guessed Jay would take JJ's side.

'And he recently finished it—' Jay continued.

'So it means he doesn't get a say—'

'Because, perhaps, he was trying to save her from that kind of decision?' Jay said, as if she hadn't butted in at all. His eyebrows were drawn together in a way that said surely she could understand that.

She went to argue because she hated being wrong. Instead, she sank heavily back in her chair. If JJ had wanted

Latitia in their world, then *he* would be making this trip with her right now. Jay had made her see perfectly what had happened. JJ hadn't turned his back on Latitia because he didn't care, but because he did. He didn't want to rob her of an ordinary life; the life he'd love to have in a heartbeat.

Alexia put her hands over her eyes to cover her welling tears. She was sorry for all the trouble she'd caused. But, most of all, she was sorry for herself. Dwayne didn't have JJ's excuses. He hadn't left her alone for some higher reason. Her choosing to go there with Latitia had come from a good place of two girlfriends supporting each other. She hadn't intended to hurt JJ. In the end, she looked at Jay, utterly defeated. 'Does that mean I can never have friends?'

His smile was kind when he shook his head. 'Not at all. But we need to arrange it so that you seem a little more—'

'Normal,' she said for him.

His smile was dazzling then. He was a brilliant negotiator. No wonder he did so well for her family in business. Now his mission was accomplished, he immediately changed the subject to lighter things. 'So we'll eat at seven. Your mum will arrive at around nine and she wants to take you both out.'

Alexia's eyes went wide with excitement. She knew she'd see her mother, but she'd assumed that she'd want to spend time with Jay. She always did. 'What, us both out out?'

Jay actually laughed, then nodded. 'Yes, she said you're old enough to see a few of her old haunts.'

Alexia sat forward, suddenly alive. All the serious issues of earlier were quickly forgotten; the weekend had revived itself. 'Latitia loves dancing,' she squealed, clapping her hands together.

'So I understand,' Jay smiled indulgently.

Alexia was already on her feet. 'Are you coming?'

Jay nodded. 'Of course. I'll be part of your guard.' He

tipped his head towards the door. 'Now go. I guess you'll want to get ready.'

LATITIA SQUEALED with excitement and jumped up and down with Alexia when she told her what was happening. 'That's so brilliant,' Latitia said. 'Mum said your mum was some superstar DJ when she was younger?'

Alexia glowed with pride. She guessed her mum really was pretty cool. 'Come on then. Let's get ready.'

Alexia showered and the two of them chatted excitedly about music and dancing and places they'd seen. There was a moment when she thought how much Dwayne would have loved this evening, but she immediately sobered and told herself that he'd made his own choices and it was his own fault he'd missed it.

LATITIA DECIDED that literally everything in Alexia's life was jet-set and exciting. She must have posted a hundred pictures already. If it wasn't too weird, she'd be snapping as she walked through the tasteful restaurant. Instead, she followed Alexia and listened to the soft chatter, the clink of glasses and the burst of sophisticated laughter here and there. By the time they reached the table, she was sure Alexia must be the luckiest girl in the world. Right down to having the most handsome stepdad she'd ever laid eyes on. He was already seated and she couldn't stop staring while Alexia introduced her. The resemblance to JJ was astonishing, except JJ's eyes were greener, and he was a younger, edgier, less intimidating version. But that could purely be because she knew him.

His father did have style. Like she didn't know much about older men's fashion, but he oozed a sophistication and good taste that only came with money and years. When he stood and kissed her cheek, she was immediately hit by his fabulous smell. In just a moment, she'd clocked his indigo loose-fitting shirt over dark grey trousers that perfectly showcased the super-fit body underneath. JJ had no worries if it was true kids someday transformed into their parents. She screwed her nose up when her mind shot to her mother.

He locked brilliant-blue eyes with her curiously, as if he hadn't missed a thing. He was clean-shaven and perfect-looking, however any leanings she may have had to describe him as angelically beautiful were immediately offset by the angles of his jaw and the don't-mess-with-me impression he exuded. In fact, she was positive he commanded any situation. It made her swallow when she remembered JJ was his son and she realized she couldn't hope to ever stand a chance to hold him.

Then he disarmed her by giving her the smallest hint of a smile. It was in the slight curve of his lips and a glint in his arctic eyes. In the micro gesture, he conveyed everything was OK and that she could relax. It was remarkable. He was remarkable. She'd never met a more affecting person in her life. 'Sit down, girls.' His voice was soft and perfect too. Something inside her sighed and she could do nothing but obey.

'What can I get you to drink?'

Latitia must have been gawping at him shamelessly because Alexia nudged her. She frowned and looked blankly: what that was for. In the end Alexia answered him, 'Two cokes,' she said, rolling her eyes.

Latitia surveyed the small restaurant in a kind of daze. It was such a far cry from Camberwell. Everything was perfect, from the wood-panelled walls to the white tablecloths and napkins on the tables of beautiful trendy people. It was definitely one of those 'it' places she'd read about.

Jay had seen to it that they were in a quiet corner where a

row of plants gave them a level of privacy but the ability to still 'people watch' and not miss anything. The tables were filling up, even though it was still early. Especially the bar at the far end, where people wandered in off the street before they went off to some interesting club or theatre somewhere. Dinner jazz added to a wonderful avant-garde atmosphere that she vowed she would be a part of one day. The whole place made her inwardly sigh.

Jay issued some indiscernible orders to his waiting staff and sat down at the table. Latitia got another waft of his lovely cologne. 'Thank you for joining me, ladies, I seldom get the honour these days.'

Latitia smiled, but she doubted that very much. She imagined him beating supermodels off with a stick.

'It's always lovely to see you, Lexie. And Latitia. It's great to finally meet one of my children's friends.'

It felt like an odd thing to say about kids in their teens – especially as he was JJ's biological father, but when she thought about it, she couldn't imagine JJ bringing kids home to tea at any age. It made her smile. 'Thanks for having me, I love your hotel.'

When she looked up, Jay was watching her closely. It felt like he always saw more than he said. She'd caught JJ with that same look. 'How is Valarie? I haven't seen her in such a long time.'

It was still difficult to imagine her ordinary mother ever running in the same circles as this unbelievably beautiful guy. She'd be working her hospital shift still, wearing her navy-blue tunic, edged in purple, over the standard-issue trousers of the same colour. It just didn't compute. Yet he was asking after her like an old friend. 'She's fine,' she found herself saying. 'You know, busy working, running after my brothers and everything.'

He nodded, thoughtfully, seeming genuinely interested.

'Well please send her my warmest regards and tell her if she ever needs anything, or a break from all that work, there is always a room for her here, OK?' The smile that followed was dazzling. It transformed an already handsome face into film star beautiful.

She nodded. 'Thank you. She'd love that.'

Their food came. Jay had ordered some sort of seafood pasta, salad and crusty bread that tasted great. However, she was too excited to do anything but pick. She watched closely as Jay did the same; she wondered what his stomach was in knots about. He drained the contents of his heavy-bottomed glass, then asked for a refill.

Jay smiled his knockout smile again, then asked a few run-of-the-mill questions about school and class. He was a good listener; an expert in getting Alexia to open up and talk. He still kept an eye on the workings of the restaurant, but whenever Alexia asked a question, however small, he was there, on the button, to answer right away. His answers were quick and to the point and proved he'd followed every word. Latitia sighed again. She could watch the two of them all day and not leave that table.

By the end of the meal, Latitia was in absolute awe of Jay. She decided that if she hadn't already met JJ, she would have a huge crush on Jay. In fact, she probably still did.

'Does Pedro still do those amazing sorbets, Jay?' Alexia asked.

Jay smiled and took a sip of his drink. His eyes rested curiously on Latitia as he said, 'Why don't you go and find him? Ask him to do you one of his specials and one for Latitia,' he said, smiling, still holding her with his eyes.

Alexia was straight on her feet. 'Coming?'

For some unknown reason, Latitia looked to Jay for permission. 'Let her digest her food for a moment,' he answered with another reassuring smile.

She knew then that he wanted her on her own and she shifted uncomfortably in her seat. She wasn't exactly scared of him; it was more trepidation at being alone with such an older, sophisticated man. One who distinctly gave her the impression that he wanted it that way.

CHAPTER 21

'Drink?' Jay said, as soon as they were alone.

'No thanks.' She had to take a breath so she didn't come off as weird.

He smiled as he sipped his drink and studied her face. It made her blush and sip the dregs of what was left in her own glass. 'Maybe I will have that drink,' she said with a nervous giggle.

'Relax. This isn't the third degree. You're a beautiful girl. I can see what my son sees in you. My sources tell me you're a dancer.'

His look was so intense she found she had to look away. She had no idea he knew so much about her. 'Thanks,' she said, feeling heat go to her cheeks. 'I hope to be, one day.' Her mind scattered all over the place; this really *was* the third degree. 'We're not actually together, though ... me and JJ,' she felt like she had to tack on.

Jay was studying her closely, running a finger around the rim of his drink. 'I have a feeling we'll be seeing more of you.'

Something lit in Latitia's chest. Without any effort at all, he made her feel great. Everything was fluid and easy about this man and she found herself saying, 'I hope so.'

As if saved in the nick of time, she spotted Alexia coming towards them, with a dark man in a white tunic and a tall white hat, carrying two of the biggest iced creations she'd ever seen. There was a lit sparkler in each one. She looked at Jay and he almost laughed, then he rolled his eyes and shook his head indulgently. 'She has asked for one of those since she was a small girl,' he explained.

It put Latitia at ease more than any other thing. It gave him a softer family side that he was lacking before in her estimations. Now he was simply perfect. It was obvious that this stunning, no-nonsense man loved his stepchildren as well as his own. You couldn't get better than that. A pain twisted in her chest at the thought of her own father, out there somewhere. Not that she really knew him. Alexia had two and one was as perfect as this and wasn't even blood. She was such a lucky girl.

Alexia arrived like a whirlwind, pointing at a place on the table where the chef should put them down. 'This is Latitia, who I told you about. This is Pedro, Latitia. The best chef in the world,' she said, clapping her hands together.

He laughed, a little embarrassed, and muttered a 'Pleased to meet you, young lady' in a Spanish-sounding accent.

Alexia threw her arms around his neck and kissed him loudly on the cheek and he hugged her back indulgently. She had so many people to love her.

'Enjoy the ices,' Pedro said, nodding at Jay. Then he pulled Alexia to him and kissed the top of her head. 'I must work, or you'll get me the sack.'

'Daaaad,' Alexia whined. 'You're such a slave driver.'

Jay didn't bother to answer as Pedro put up a hand of goodbye and hurried back to the kitchen.

Alexia immediately forgot her complaint and told her to dig in. 'Isn't it the best thing you've ever tasted?'

Latitia dug her long spoon through the swirl of raspberry sorbet, berries and vanilla ice cream and grinned. It definitely was. They both 'Mmmmd,' several times, making Jay actually laugh.

'So when is Mum getting here?' Alexia asked with her mouth full.

Jay looked at his expensive-looking watch. 'Soon. I've sent a car to the airfield.'

The word choice struck Latitia for a moment. *Airfield and not airport?* That must mean a *private plane.* It was the last thing in a very long list to blow her mind that day.

'Are we going straight out?' Alexia said, bouncing in her seat. 'I can't wait.'

LATITIA FLOATED through the meal in a beautiful dream. The tasteful hotel, the stunning people, their chic clothes, great food. Then Jay rose from the table. Latitia turned her head to follow his line of vision and stopped breathing as a stunning woman glided in on a soft breeze.

She'd heard her own mother use the term gobsmacked and until that moment she'd never really understood what that meant, but she literally froze with her mouth open. The perfect blonde apparition cleared a path through the bar, turning heads as she went. Two of the biggest men, similar to the ones who'd visited her flat, flanked her. *Bodyguards,* she remembered someone calling them.

Alexia jumped to her feet and her mother swept her into a tight hug, swathing the area in her expensive perfume. Then, after kissing her, she turned her head to Jay and the look she gave him then would stay with her for ever. If she achieved nothing else in life, she wanted to love someone like that and judging by the smoulder in the one Jay returned, it was mutual. It was the look any girl longed for.

Latitia had to remind herself: this wasn't the guy Alexia's mother was married to. However, it was clear what these two meant to each other. It made her wonder about her marriage and what Alexia's biological father was like. Whatever it was, it was clear that JJ was no accident from any kind of fling.

Then, while she was still carried away on her romantic daydream, the two of them turned and faced her. Alexia's mother immediately smiled. 'Hi, I'm Tia. You must be Latitia. I've heard so much about you.' She came right around the table to pull her into a tight hug, ending with a kiss to her cheek.

She felt slim, small-boned and smelled gorgeous. Pulling apart, Latitia stuttered, 'Thank you … you too.' She couldn't stop staring at the enigmatic woman. She had to be in her late thirties to have had Alexia, but looked at least ten years younger. Her hair was blonde and in two braids down her back. Her skin had a light golden tan and her eyes, when she pushed her sunglasses up on her head, were large and dark green, giving her an elfin look. In fact, her whole figure was petite, like that of a teen. Her clothes were perfect for a night on the town. Nothing blingy or over the top. Just boot-legged blue jeans over brown boots and a tank top in black silk with several tribal bangles at her wrists. There was no other word for it. She was so cool.

'It's so lovely to meet one of my children's friends,' Tia said, looking sincerely at her with those big saucer-like eyes.

Latitia couldn't stop staring at her. 'You too,' she said, backtracking wildly. 'My friend's parents, I mean.' She felt her cheeks burn like a furnace. 'Alexia said you're a great DJ?' she said, trying to recover herself.

Tia bowed her head, graciously. 'That's kind of you. Used

to be. I don't really play out these days, but I still keep a toe in where I can.'

Jay looked at her adoringly. 'She's too modest. She still does the best mixes I've ever heard.'

Latitia found their dynamic fascinating; she longed for the full story about them. She found herself imagining Alexia's father as some evil, unloving prince who kept her locked up in a tower, driving her to escape into her lover's arms. She was sure it had to be something like that.

Tia cut through her daydream with, 'Shall we get going?'

Alexia squealed with delight and dragged her to the lift to go quickly up to their room while Jay showed Tia to hers. The ride up with the four of them was so charged with electricity that it left Latitia wondering what would happen behind closed doors as soon as they separated on the same floor.

She found herself sighing over Alexia's exciting life for the umpteenth time. Everything was so perfect and completely opposite to her own.

It didn't take long for them to be ready. Alexia had changed into a dress so short that she had to wear shorts underneath it because you could clearly see her knickers. She'd opted for black jeans, ripped at the knees and a sleeveless red shirt. She felt dull in comparison, like a moth to a butterfly.

They knocked on their mother's door and it immediately opened. Tia hadn't changed – just added a jacket with silver sequined flowers sewn into it and loosened her hair. She should have guessed. Alexia's mum couldn't look any cooler than she already did. She was perfect. Just subtle pink lip gloss and her amber wraparound shades and she looked like a superstar. Out of this world.

Alexia had been watching her the whole time. 'Sorry,'

Latitia found herself saying as she went red. Again. 'I didn't mean to stare. Your mum is just so stunningly beautiful.'

Alexia just smiled knowingly. Guess she was used to people being bowled over by her mum. Jay slipped his arm into his black leather jacket and flashed Tia one of his secretive smiles. 'Come on, let's get out of here,' he said.

Latitia was thrilled he was escorting them, not totally sure whether Jay was there to spend time with them or Alexia's mother. Her money was on the latter. Either way, they were fascinating to watch.

They went down in the lift to the underground garage where they got into a blacked-out SUV. Jay got into the back with the girls and Tia. The two huge guards got in the front. Then they pulled away on a squeal of tires.

Latitia's heart thumped with excitement. It felt like she'd entered some Netflix universe. Especially when a second squeal of tires made her look out of the back window to spot a second SUV following them. *Who were these people?* she thought yet again. JJ had not been exaggerating. This was a security detail to rival the Prime Minister.

They pulled up at the first club remarkably quickly. In fact, so quickly they could have walked. Guess it drew fractionally less attention than turning up with eight Special Ops guards. This way they pulled up right outside, Jay got out, the doorman nodded – obviously knowing him – and they poured out of the car and into the club. Latitia was surrounded by so much testosterone that she couldn't even see the envious line that she knew went down the street.

It made up her mind that these people were definitely royalty – and not the low-key, bicycle-riding kind. Her heart hitched in her chest at what she'd gotten herself into. These people weren't like Kate and William on TV all the time and yet doormen knew them; they were surrounded by guards and were undoubtedly wealthy.

They were whisked by the payment booth, down a narrow stairwell of red painted walls and thumping bass, until they came out into the small underground club. Alexia was ecstatic and so should Latitia have been, but a cautious reserve began to creep over her like a sixth sense. Jay, she realized, always stayed with Tia, talking intently about god knows what. She smiled graciously at everyone and accepted drinks appearing regularly from waitresses as if from nowhere. She even danced. But all the while, she kept her wits about her, looking around. Something was off. Something in this whole situation didn't feel right or add up. Her hackles told her she was into something far bigger and scarier than a film plot where a poor girl meets a prince.

In the end, she had to shake herself out of it. Alexia was beginning to look at her curiously and ask if she was OK. She just had to calm down and ride it out. One good thing about being brought up in Camberwell was that it taught her survival 101 from an early age.

They moved on to a second and a third club, where everyone treated her with nothing but kindness and respect. In fact, everyone had, the whole time she'd been there. She had to remind herself of that, over and over, but she couldn't shake her feeling of doom.

Maybe JJ had been right to try to protect her from all this. It was completely overwhelming; it got to the point where there seemed like no air. She began to feel dizzy and sick. She snuck away and went over and sat at the bar. Then, out of nowhere, Tia was there. 'Are you OK, darling?' she said, putting out a delicate hand on her arm.

Then Alexia was there too, with a look of concern.

'You haven't been sneaking alcohol, have you?' Tia said, looking mildly annoyed at her daughter.

'No, Mum. I swear we haven't.'

Then Jay was there and all Latitia wanted to do was disappear. 'They haven't, I've been watching,' Jay said.

Great. She'd spouted off about wanting to be a dancer and her she was, at her first proper West End clubs, flaking like some sort of lightweight.

Jay stood in front of her and looked intently into her eyes. It made her annoyed to think he was assessing her for drugs, but before she had time, he looked at Tia, tipped his head to the exit and said, 'Come on, it's one o'clock. Let's go back.'

And, just like that, the evening was over. Latitia deflated with a weird wash of relief, tinged with disappointment. She needed to go back to process it all, but it still felt like she'd let herself down in some way.

Back in the car, she began to feel like a foolish little girl who'd got out of her depth. They'd been nothing but fun; exhilarating company. Maybe she was coming down with something. It would certainly explain the dizzy spell.

They were back in the underground garage in no time at all. Tia took charge and whisked them into the lift and straight up to the top floor.

'Are you OK?' Alexia asked, several times.

Latitia nodded. 'I'm sorry to ruin the night. I was just a bit dizzy, that's all.'

'You do look a bit drained,' Tia said. 'Drink some water and get some rest. You'll feel better in the morning.'

Jay put the key card in the door and pushed it open for her to go inside. 'We'll leave you two to it,' he said, his eyes already on Tia's.

'We're just next door if you need anything,' Tia said, locking hers with his.

Latitia's head was already buzzing with overload and couldn't even begin to imagine what was going to happen between them. The chemistry between them had crackled all evening. She wondered why Alexia didn't seem to see it. 'It's

OK, I'll be fine. Thank you … for tonight,' Latitia said, willing them to go.

Alexia went to go ahead, then stopped abruptly. I'm just going to go down and see if Pedro will do us a couple of his frothy hot chocolates.'

Latitia frowned at the suddenness of the decision, but thought nothing more of it. Alexia pushed past her, back out into the corridor and Latitia headed on into the main room of their suite, relieved to be back. The moment she reached it she froze, feeling like her feet had taken root in the shagpile.

There, sitting on the edge of the king-sized bed, with his elbows on his knees, was JJ. He smiled wanly. 'Welcome to my humble abode.'

Latitia swallowed at the intensity of that look. It held an accusation, disappointment and curiosity at how she would react, all rolled into one. 'How did you know I was here?'

'It's all over your Instagram … not exactly hard for me to recognise. And your mum told me.'

She instantly felt stupid and uncomfortable. He, on the other hand, was a powder keg of something, that was for sure. She felt guilty. She'd gone behind his back. And while she knew what she'd done had been Alexia's idea and been innocent enough, she'd known full well he wouldn't like her doing it without his knowledge, probably because he'd have put a stop to it. He'd come all the way across London to catch her out with his own parents. That did seem bad. She gulped and swallowed again. 'Sorry,' she whispered, not thinking of a single thing worthy to say.

JJ's MIND was all over her aura. It seemed beaten down and splattered with confusion. Fear was there too. But not of him. Nothing had happened. Alexia would have blabbed as soon as he'd slammed her mind with a *piss off* and *leave us alone* as soon as the door opened. *No,* this was purely coming from Latitia. She'd sensed something significant enough to unsettle her.

'What are you doing here?' Latitia said, trying to gain some sort of control of the situation. He admired her for it. She was a tough girl but way out of her depth, and she knew it. She was just buying time to regroup.

Well, he couldn't allow it. 'What am *I* doing here?' he repeated with a sardonic smile.

It was a little gratifying to see the blush enter her cheeks. 'Your sister wanted to go home for the weekend and she invited me. What was I supposed to say?' she blabbered, knowing it was just an excuse.

He got slowly to his feet and stalked deliberately towards her, not stopping until he looked down into her eyes. 'In case you hadn't realized it yet, this isn't home, Latitia. It's one of my father's businesses.'

She was so incredibly easy to read, even without a scan. A rainbow of hurt, foolishness and then anger spread over her face until she scowled up at him, determined not to let him intimidate her. His anger disappeared and was replaced with the urgent need to kiss her. She was so fiery and ruled by her impulses. So opposite to all things Atlantean; always calculated and premeditated, at least eight moves ahead.

Her aura showed anger as well as shame, proving she knew what she did was wrong on some level but also fury that he was pulling her up on it. She really was an intriguing creature. Then his righteous anger switched to love when she shoved him in the chest and pointed her finger at him. 'Now look, you! I'm really sorry that I upset you because you feel I went behind your back, but your sister is my friend too. And she was upset with my brother, which kind of made me feel responsible, and she asked me to go home with her. That's it. She didn't even know we were coming here. It got changed at the last minute, or something. I promise you. I had no idea.' Then she scowled as if she'd just renewed her anger with a certain thought. 'And to be honest, JJ, I thought you'd made it clear what you thought about us …'

Then it hit him. The nagging futility. 'There is no us,' he said, quietly, stepping into her again, with all the pointlessness he felt. She was right. What *was* he doing there? She would have had a slightly weird weekend that would have piqued her interest for a while, but she would have forgotten it and eventually moved on. But *he* couldn't let it go.

Then she shocked him. She jabbed him in the chest again. 'Don't you dare try to bully me to scare me. It's you who's scared. You!' she shouted.

His eyebrows rose at that. He tried to keep the smile off his face, but he couldn't help it. 'Scared of a little girl like you?'

Her eyes dropped immediately to his lips as he fought in vain to keep the smile out of them. She completely intrigued him. So much, that he couldn't help toying with her. Like a cat with a little mouse. 'What do you suppose I might be scared of?' he said, narrowing his eyes, playfully.

'You're scared of letting me in. That I might actually get to know the real you … Oh, I don't know.' She threw up her hands and went to turn away from him.

He stood there, stunned, watching the way her shoulders hunched over as if with the huge weight of it all.

'Maybe because you don't want to care about me.'

It was clear she didn't want to look at him, but he'd been too quiet for too long and she was forced to. He studied her features, feeling somewhere between being slapped and amazed. No one had been that honest with him before. And because he didn't speak right away, it seemed to give her the courage to carry on. 'I think you're used to getting your own way.'

His mouth eased into a small smile at that. Then it fell away as soon as it came. 'Your life is so simple, Latitia,' he said, shaking his head.

'Well of course it is, in comparison to yours,' she said, going to turn away again, angrily.

He took another step closer and put out a hand to stop her. 'No, please, Latitia. Listen. Your life is going to school, doing homework, dreaming of being a dancer; that you will probably one day be. But if not that, you'll train for something else that *you* want to do. If I was like that …' He trailed off before he bothered to finish and the strength drained out of him.

Her eyebrows drew together as she took the words he'd tried to say and made them add up all wrong. 'So you think I'm lucky, do you?' she said, her voice almost a shriek.

He shifted his feet uncomfortably. This wasn't how he wanted it to go down at all, but it seemed they were on target for a showdown anyway. 'Well, yeah,' he said, looking her provocatively in the eye.

She took a step into him and poked him in the chest yet again. He made a note to cut that fingernail in her sleep. 'Lucky,' she repeated as if she still didn't believe he'd used that actual word. 'I'm lucky going to that dump of a school, living in that tiny flat with too many kids and a mum I hardly see because she has to work long shifts and is too knackered to do anything with us, in an area that's too rough. Sometimes I don't know if she's caught late at work or whether something's happened to her on the way home.' She was crying now but he let her continue, figuring it was something she needed to get out for herself. 'I'm a second mum to my little brothers and I don't want to be. I'll do crap in school because our school is rubbish, which means dancing is my only ticket out of there. I have no fancy, quiet environment to do my homework like you, Mr Fancy Pants. I could go and do it at my dad's but, oh, wait? My dad disappeared off the face of the earth not long after I was born,' she ended shouting in his face.

In the end, he had to catch her index finger in his hand as it was beginning to hurt with the jabbing. She dissolved into tears and he pulled her into his body, wrapping his arms around her. He kissed the top of her head. He'd never thought how tough her life might actually be on her. He could escape if he wanted but she couldn't. It made him think of his own fathers and what they were trying to teach him about everyday people. He had two who cared for him a great deal, and she didn't even have one. And the fact that she brought it up at a time like this meant it was a big deal to her that she normally kept bottled up. 'I'm sorry, Latitia,' he whispered into her hair.

She pulled away a little to look up at him. Her eyes were red and surrounded by a smudge of black from her mascara.

'But Mr Fancy Pants?' he said, raising an eyebrow, resting his weight on a hip.

She let out a blast of laughter and he pulled her back into his chest. 'You don't think so, but you *are* lucky, JJ.' He felt her wipe her nose on the back of her hand. He bent down and pulled a tissue from a box by the bed and handed it to her. She blew it loudly. 'You have parents who love you and all this,' she said, holding out her hand to encompass the room. Then she let it drop as if the energy had gone right out of her. 'Maybe you're right. Maybe we are just poles apart.'

He stiffened. She'd only echoed what he'd just thought anyway, but it suddenly struck him what his miserable options actually were: to carry on in the way he was going; to remain single. Keeping girls at a distance. Eventually getting together with one of the daughters of the five Atlantean families to bring strength to his family by tying them to the crown.

That thought actually made him shudder and shift immediately to the last school full of bratty, entitled humans. Titled Atlanteans were even worse. They knew exactly who he was and what came with him. That would be lonelier than being single.

He became conscious of Latitia, small and trembling in his arms.

She seemed to sense his reticence and looked up at him with those trusting light-brown eyes.

Or he could take a chance on a human – much of which was in his genetic mix anyway. His mind churned. He could protect and care for her. Maybe help the school. Give her and her family all the things they were lacking, but then his mind switched back to all the restrictions and expectations of his station. 'You think all this is great, Latitia, but it's nothing more than a gilded cage.'

She frowned slightly, as if she was thinking about what he'd said. Then she surprised him. 'All of us are trapped, JJ. We're all just trying to find the best way to deal with the hand life dealt us. Just feeling our way through,' she said, searching his eyes as if it was a fundamental truth he should already know.

Then something just switched in his brain. He let her go and reached down for her hand.

'Where are we going?' she said, as he led her to the door. 'Can I at least clean my face?'

'You won't need to where we're going.' JJ had a single thought in his mind that he now knew he wouldn't waver from. Nothing had ever been clearer in his head.

'Where are you taking me?' she said with more than a trace of fear.

JJ pulled her into the lift and pressed the button to the basement. Then, as the doors clanked closed, he stared purposefully ahead of him. 'To the pool.'

Xavier was initially stunned that the usually calm and calculating JJ had dropped the ball in this way. However he soon snapped out of it and seized the weakness. After all, such a gift from the Fates could not be ignored. It was exactly what JJ would have done. So while JJ was chasing his baser instincts, he, Xavier, true Prince of Atlantis, would take the reins of their budding empire and assert himself at the helm. Early impressions were everything and he would be making them way before JJ.

The first thing he did was to order all their furnishings for their new loft space. With the amounts he was spending, it wasn't difficult to insist on next-day delivery or he'd take his business elsewhere. Besides, it was also a good test of how closely his father was keeping an eye on their spending. He hadn't revoked their cards yet and that was a good sign.

The feeling of absolute freedom was thrilling. He bought the largest, most expensive bed and placed it in the optimum place, close to the walkway to the roof terrace. He ordered foosball, pool and air hockey tables, a jukebox filled with the music he liked, a professional basketball basket and a fully stocked bar for parties. Several deep-pile rugs followed, in various shades of blue and green and one white and one black three-seater sofa, purely because he couldn't make up his mind. Then, finally, the pièce de résistance, a nine-foot aquarium filled with his favourite tropical Discus and Angelfish to remind him of home.

By the end of Saturday afternoon, all that was left was a large food delivery and some tasteful garden furniture for their terrace. In twenty-four hours he'd spent big and spent quickly and everything had gone through on the Central Atlantic Bank credit card, like a dream.

'Thank you,' he said, into his mobile phone. 'Don't bother to come up. I'll come down now.' The final thing on his order had just been delivered to the car park beneath the building. It was still light and he wanted to show Paige everything while he was on a roll. He turned and surveyed his handiwork and chuckled. It was good – very good. Then he called out, 'Lights off!'

He was weirdly nervous getting into his new silver Mazda MX5. It had been a deliberate choice. Expensive enough to be taken seriously, but not so over the top that his father would make him send it back. It was fast, fun and flashy, but modest compared to what he could have chosen. Just the antidote for the weeks of deprivation. However it wasn't the sleek little tease that was really at the bottom of his cause for concern, it was Paige. He literally had no idea how she would react. Normal girls would love it, but he was acutely aware that Paige was not an ordinary girl – or rather she was and that was way out of his usual realm of experience. She was the first regular human girl he'd ever wanted to know, and his instincts told him she didn't even conform to that. So with his heart pumping, he gripped the steering wheel, breathed in the wonderful New Car smell and screeched out of the car park. The garage door lowered behind him and so did his roof as he set off into the buzz of the London dusk.

The air was cool and dry, the sky clear. He immediately cranked the heating, put his phone into the cradle and turned up some XXXTentacion. The soft voice over great beats soothed the edges of his ragged nerves. London seemed to be alive at this time of the evening. People coming home or venturing out to discover what the night had to offer. Excitement prickled in his veins and, just for a moment, he felt like king of all he surveyed.

He had his loft apartment, kitted out like a dream for any boy their age. He had the car and now all he had to do was impress the girl. The one he'd singled out from the beginning. Then tomorrow, before JJ got back, he would make inroads to show his face to the people he'd do business with.

He eased back and relaxed in his seat. Life was good. He'd allow himself one night to enjoy himself. He'd overrun Paige's senses, so all she could do was give in and be his.

JJ GRIPPED Latitia's hand and led her out of the lift to the pool area of the spa. It was deserted at this time and had a soft hue from the emergency lighting. They wouldn't be disturbed. Staff at the Bluebell were used to letting the Dubonnettis' nocturnal use of the pool go unchallenged. However, for Latitia's benefit, he let go of her hand and put a broom through the door handles. Then he went and pushed two of the yellow and white striped sun loungers together to make a bed.

As he pulled his t-shirt up over his head and pushed his hair back in place with his fingers, he gazed out at the pool looking eerie – like a lake in early morning – with steam rising as it hit the cooler air of night.

'Won't somebody come?'

JJ saw she hadn't moved and was hugging her bag to her chest. He shook his head, moving slowly towards her, until he was looking down into her eyes. 'We'll be perfectly safe here. He couldn't resist running his thumb across her cheek The pool heat was making a perfect glow on her skin, now dewy with perspiration. Her eyes seemed large and dilated as they looked up at him a little fearfully. He almost wavered in what he was about to do, but her eyes slowly skated down to take in his chest and abs, covered in the tattoos of his people.

'Why are we here?' she asked, swallowing hard, her eyes still on his midriff.

'Privacy,' he said simply, bringing them back up to his. He gently took her bag from her iron grip and let it fall on the sun lounger next to him.

'Don't you want to lose some clothes? It's so hot in here,' he said, letting a small devilish smile creep over his lips.

She frowned. 'I've been swimming today,' she said, suddenly alarmed, which made him laugh.

Everything she thought was always so perfectly spelled out over her face. At another time he would remind her never to play poker. He pulled her into his body and noted how snugly she fitted. Her face on his bare skin almost made him moan as his mind went to how it would feel with the rest of her. Particularly as he felt her breathe in to sample his scent.

He forced himself to put her away from him before he got too carried away. 'You asked for answers and I'm going to give them to you.' He held the tops of her shoulders and for a second he let his mind wander to all the delicious things he'd like to do. 'I came here to lay myself wide open to you, to come clean for one night for you to choose. Then the opportunity will be gone for ever.'

For a moment she looked up at him, shocked, searching

his face to gauge if he was serious. 'I don't understand. What will?' Her expressive brows pulled together with worry.

'I'm giving you something I never had: the chance to choose.'

She half laughed and then schooled herself again when his expression didn't change.

He was deadly serious, more than any other time in his life before. Because, honestly, he didn't know which way she would go – or even if she should accept him. Part of him wanted to tell her to run and never look back. And the other, the selfish part, wanted her to stay and walk with him; through hell if need be.

'What's going on, JJ? You're scaring me,' she said, taking a step back out of his grip.

His heart was thrashing in his chest. He was losing her, but it was too late to go back. 'You want to know about me. You want the truth? Well, I'm going to give it to you. The power. The money. Who my family is? The secrecy. I'm going to give you one shot at the answers, but by morning, you're going to have to choose whether you want my life or not. Because there're no half measures. You're either all in, or all out.'

She grinned, her eyes skating over his face looking for the joke and then frowned in alarm when he continued to look intensely at her. He had to. She had to understand she couldn't treat this lightly. It was huge. Life-changing. He was breaking every rule he'd learned since he was a kid and he was doing it for her. *Was he, though?*

When he took in the perfect curve of her cheek, he recognized that he was doing this as much for him. So he was no longer completely alone. He needed someone. Her. To be by his side to face what was ahead. Then, with a voice gone totally hoarse, 'I'll show you.' He turned and went to walk towards the pool.

She was soon behind him. 'What? Panic was making her voice high-pitched and squeaky.

He looked over his shoulder before he jumped in. 'Or it will be like we never met. You'll never see me or my family again because you won't know us.'

Then he stepped out of his pants and took a perfect dive into the water.

LATITIA MOVED to the edge of the pool, stunned. The dive took him almost to the far side of the pool. Then he swam gracefully back in an arc and came to a stop a few feet in front of her. The way he swam reminded her of the sealions she'd once seen at the zoo. He was obviously an excellent swimmer. But he didn't come up. He held himself a few inches under the water. His eyes were wide, dark and held hers the whole time. The blue-green in them seemed to disappear to be replaced by wide pupils.

A tingle went up her spine, ridiculous in the current heat. She wanted to call him and tell him to stop messing about, but something stopped her. The mist, the temperature, the glow from the lighting; it all made him look so strange – almost otherworldly. His skin lightened. Even his tattoos looked weird, taking on a striped, almost animal skin look. *Don't be scared.*

She looked around her in fright. It was his voice, but impossible as he was still under the water. 'Stop it, JJ. Get out now. Please.' She knelt and reached down a hand, as if to pull him out. He'd been down there ages and must be running out of breath. But she almost recoiled at how different he looked. His arms gently circled to keep him beneath the surface. There were no bubbles and he seemed perfectly at ease as he eased back a little more out of reach. 'OK … enough now, JJ.' The time for joking had way passed. Her heart was beating and sweat was running down her face. Then, as she pulled her hand back and sat on her lower legs, she understood. It was fear. JJ was showing her something way beyond her understanding and she didn't want to face it. She didn't like it. 'Get out!' she shouted in what sounded like desperation. It echoed around the walls, making her struggle back to her feet and take a step back.

Finally JJ swam to the side and, with a slosh of water, hauled himself up the chrome steps.

She took another step back at the sight of him. It was him, but it wasn't. It felt like he'd grown as he towered over her. His skin was pale, almost grey, and the tattoos that were always there were punctuated with grey tiger-like stripes – even his face.

His arm moved out and grabbed her arm before she could scream. *Stop!* he said, but it entered her mind and his lips never moved.

She cowered and looked up at him, petrified, but he held onto her firmly. It was JJ but not JJ. He was different. His unusual aquamarine eyes seemed larger somehow and his face looked fierce, slashed in Vs on his forehead and cheeks. The stripes licked down his neck and onto his chest. Her scream seemed to die in her throat in absolute terror as she took the whole of him in. Ribcage. Legs. Stripes everywhere. He looked primal and dangerous, like nothing she'd ever seen before.

She stood rigid; in shock. His words – *you can choose whether you want to know or not,* – reverberated around her brain. Anything rather than face the one word she knew lurked there, in front of her.

This is me, JJ said, straight to her mind again.

She closed her eyes, willing him to go away. Let her go to bed and wake up and this all be a dream. But when she opened them he was still there, looking soulfully at her. Waiting patiently for her to acclimatize.

Please don't be scared. Calm down and we'll talk. Remember, I can make it all go away ... if you want, he said, with large, sad eyes.

Her heart thundered in her chest. Her first instinct was to run if her legs would actually move, but they were frozen. Until she finally let in the word she'd been too terrified to face. *Alien.*

And then she screamed. 'Make it go away!'

CHAPTER 23

Xavier phoned ahead and got Paige to meet him on the corner of her road. He didn't want to waste valuable time getting caught up with her mother or brother and sister. And, of course, he wanted her to get the full impact of his new car.

It was almost dark as he went to turn into her road. The streetlights were coming on and it felt like his blood buzzed through his veins. The roof was down and the great sounds of Lil Skies was pumping out of the state-of-the-art sound system he'd insisted was installed before it left the forecourt.

There she was. Bathed in the orange beam from a street-light, looking paler, younger and more fragile than he remembered. His heart wobbled for an instant as he took in her blue skinny jeans and the short fake-fur jacket. Then she saw him. The small, insecure smile reminded him why he liked her and he forgot any misgivings as he pulled into the kerb. 'Get in,' he said, with a huge grin. He leaned over the passenger seat and opened the door for her.

She got in eagerly, eyes wide with admiration, mouthing

'wow' as she settled into her seat. 'Oh my god, Xavier. Where did you get this?'

He leaned over and she met him with a small peck on the lips. Then he grinned and pulled away. 'It's mine. It came today.'

When she didn't say anything, he glanced across at her. 'Did you bring a bag?' His eyes had already dropped to the small rucksack she clutched in her lap. She nodded, looking really nervous. 'I said I was staying at Jade's.'

Xavier nodded and watched the road. He kept an eye on her in small glances though. She looked as though she'd bolt at any minute. 'Relax. It'll be fine, I promise. We'll talk, OK? No big deal.'

She dragged in a ragged breath and gave him that small, unsure smile again. He could tell she was trying really hard to hide her nerves, but when she wasn't gripping her bag hard enough to turn her knuckles white, she kept pushing her hair back behind her ear with a slightly shaking hand. All tells, even if her aura wasn't flashing indigo and purple.

They reached the wharf in no time at all. He was grateful as he was sure she wouldn't have made it through a longer journey without making him turn around. As it was, her eyes widened in terror as he hit the key fob and the garage door opened for them to descend into the darkness under his building. The lights bloomed and he pulled into his designated parking space.

She looked terrified as the roof slowly rose behind her. He would have teased her if he wasn't so worried she'd run. 'Come on. I can't wait to show you my new place.'

She forced a smile and unclipped her seat belt. Xavier jumped out and ran round to open the door for her. He helped her out and felt how much she was shaking. He couldn't help himself, he pulled her in for a hug. She froze in his arms, but she didn't pull away. In the end he kissed her cheek and let her go, stealing a breath of her wonderful clean soap and shampoo smell. She did look up at him and smile genuinely then. 'OK?' he asked.

She nodded and let out a little of her tension, so he took her hand and led her to the cage lift at the far side of the car park. He pulled it open and closed it when they were both inside with a noisy scrape and crunch of metal. 'Shall I carry that for you?' he said, pointing at the bag she still had clutched to her chest.

'It's OK,' she said, shaking her head a little manically. He got the impression it was comforting her in some way, like a barrier between them or something.

'OK, then.' He pushed the button and the lift moved up with a judder.

She looked straight ahead of her, watching the five floors come and go until they got to the sixth. He stole sneaky peeks at her cute profile the whole way. 'You don't have to stay over if you don't want to. I'll take you home at any time.' The lift came to a stop and he smiled as he pulled the cage across.

'Thank you,' she said, looking truly grateful. It made him mildly ashamed that, deep down, he had every intention of making her stay. She didn't understand that she was literally the only person he wanted to celebrate his new circum-stances with. He kept it to himself, though, and held out an arm for her to leave the lift.

'JJ isn't home,' he said, overtaking her and putting his key in the door. He looked down into her eyes before he pushed it open. 'I just thought it would be nice to talk, drink a little alcohol and not have to worry about driving.'

He took in her aura as she looked up, listening to him carefully. She was assessing whether she believed him or not. The red tinge of worry around her became speckled in orange. She did that when she was considering something she wasn't sure of. She was carefully gauging him for any hint of sleazebag. He applauded her for it. Humans were too trusting. A young girl couldn't be too careful.

He smiled a little, giving her the strong hint that he knew and she visibly relaxed. Then he pushed open the door with a, 'Ta-dah!' and all nerves seemed forgotten.

Paige wandered into the apartment, looking around her. The bag she had been clutching was soon being dragged along the polished concrete floor.

Xavier quietly closed the door and followed her, smiling, taking in every nuance of her reaction. She seemed awestruck. It was exactly what he was going for.

She looked up at the vaulted ceiling, threaded with silver industrial air ducts. Then her eyes went straight to the aquarium – you couldn't miss it – and the expensive art pieces along the far wall of exposed brick. She ran her hand along the burnished-metal countertop of the industrial style kitchen. She almost ran to the window to check out the view – which was pretty spectacular over London and the canal below. She pointed at his huge bed, soft and inviting with its throw in autumn russets and browns, and hitched a breath at the glass door next to it, calling you to venture out to the terrace. Everything rolled perfectly from one to the other. 'It's like one of those huge lofts single guys always have in the films,' she said, whirling around to him, eyes sparkling with excitement.

Xavier was grinning widely.

'Alexa, play some Russ!' he called out.

'Playing Russ,' the female voice replied immediately.

'It's amazing, Xavier.'

'Make yourself comfortable,' he said, going to the fridge and taking out the bottle of champagne he'd stashed to cool earlier. He watched her pick up a few of the small sculptures and books he'd bought, examine them and put them back down. She seemed genuinely interested in them. In her day-to-day life she was a diamond in a yard of coal that nobody noticed because she was still in the rough. Both he and JJ had been brought up to appreciate beautiful things and to honour what separated a species like Atlanteans and humans from the animals. He could see it would grow in Paige too, with the encouragement he planned to give her. 'How do you afford all this?' she said, holding a Philip Jackson that probably cost more than her mother earned in a month.

He smiled ruefully and passed her a glass of champagne. 'Drink … then we'll talk.'

She took the flute and took a sip. Her face brightened. 'Fizzy,' she said with a giggle. 'I've had this at my cousin's wedding.'

He smiled, hiding his sadness. It was Dom Pérignon, so he doubted that very much. Her eyes stayed rooted to his, watching his reaction. Looking for the slightest hint he was mocking her, trying to work out just how rich and powerful his family was. All the while he calculated how near the truth he wanted to go with her.

He held out an arm for her to join him on the black leather sofa while he checked off a list in his head. Did he want to have sex with her? *Yes.* Did he intend to carry on seeing her after? *Probably.* Did he want to get to know her? *Yes.* Then, as he took his seat, the most poignant question of all: did he want her to get close to him? *Maybe. Possibly.* Which led him to the killer, real issue: did he want her to trust him? He leaned back and let out a long breath, because he knew the answer to that was yes. He wanted her to know and like him no matter who he was. For some reason that was extremely important to him. Maybe parts of JJ were rubbing off on him. He got sick of playing a part because of duty.

However, despite all of the above being true, he would

have to take his time and reveal little truths in increments. He didn't want to scare her off or put her in any kind of danger. The less she knew, the safer it was for her. He'd need to walk a fine line.

She sat at the far end of the sofa, turning her body to face him so her lower leg was across the cushion. She was sipping her drink and still looking around her. He leaned forward and topped up her glass and sat back, mirroring her position with a creak of expensive leather. He waved her on with a hand. 'Ask me your questions and I'll do my best to answer them honestly.' It felt fairly safe. She couldn't possibly touch on the truth; it was too far out of her experience.

Her eyes widened with excitement as if they were playing a game, then darted about as if she was scrambling in her mind for just the right question before the small window of opportunity closed.

'It's OK,' he said, laughing. 'We have all night. There isn't a time limit on them.'

She nodded and relaxed back into her seat. Then she took a large gulp of her drink. 'OK,' she said as if gathering her thoughts. 'Tell me who you really are.'

He paused for a beat and frowned a little. She was waiting on his words, excitedly, but it struck him how truly knowing her question was and that it was now or never for honesty. What he said then would set the tone for their whole relationship. She seemed so vulnerable and small he convinced himself he just wanted to protect her, so he cautiously gave her his full name. 'Xavier Michelangelo Sebastian Dubonnetti, eldest son of Dante Dubonnetti and Tia Bonaci Storm.' He was watching her closely while he debated whether to continue. She seemed undaunted and nodded in encouragement for him to continue. So he did. 'King and Queen of the Atlantean nation.'

For a moment she looked at him and blinked in absolute

silence. It went on for so long he felt an overwhelming urge to say, 'gotcha'. But he kept quiet, held eye contact and kept the gravity of the situation. He wanted her to get it, he really did.

Understanding entered her face slowly, like the filling of a cup. Until it was full and she had to preserve it from spilling over and losing valuable drops. Her perfectly arched eyebrows drew together. 'You're serious,' she said flatly. 'And JJ?'

He nodded, grateful she wasn't freaking out. It was a good question – a great question, in fact. The one at the nub of it all. 'Eldest son of Jay Gardiner – adopted son of the Dubonnetti, Bonaci, Santalini and Florianna royal families, former king and lover of Tia Bonaci Storm. My half-brother and equal heir to the crown.'

Her eyes widened with every damning detail and the dawning realization that he wasn't joking. 'Oh my god. You are.'

He searched her face, mapping the honesty of it. She had no guile or game. What you saw was truly what you got. Then he frowned as a smile crept across it.

'So where is your nemesis now?'

He burst out laughing. He couldn't help himself and she joined him. It was pretty funny, with the champagne helping, of course. 'Chasing Latitia Johnson, I expect.'

It seemed to fuel their laughter and suddenly everything was hysterically funny, like the lid suddenly blown off a pressure cooker. His stomach hurt from laughing so much.

'So why are you here, in this dump?' she said, rolling her eyes exaggeratedly at their opulent surroundings, and they laughed hard again.

It wasn't going at all how he imagined. As he held his sides, trying to get sensible, he thought how much he was enjoying himself with her. He thought she'd get upset and then he'd have to comfort her and sneak his way into her affections that way. Instead, he looked at her in semi-amazement and appreciated she'd be a much harder nut to crack. 'Punishment,' he said, simply. 'To teach us how the other half live.'

She sobered instantly, realizing he was serious.

'We got kicked out of our exclusive New Hampshire school. It was the last straw.'

Suddenly her face had transformed to real concern. 'What for?'

'Fighting.' Then he couldn't help the slow grin. 'Womanizing – JJ, was, anyway.'

She laughed a little. 'Of course,' she mimicked. 'So let me get this straight,' she said, looking up at the ceiling. 'You're supposed to be slumming it with the Johnsons – wait! How do you even know the Johnsons? Doesn't matter,' she said, dismissing it with a hand. 'So you moved out and spent your dad's money on this place?'

He smiled and tipped his head. She was a clever girl and he knew exactly where her mind was going. 'That's right. Temporarily. We plan on getting our own revenue source, eventually.'

She looked concerned again. 'Doesn't living here kind of fly in the face of what your dad's trying to teach you?'

He tipped his head again, smiling wider. He shouldn't be surprised that she wasn't like most girls, gushing that they were there with a prince. Paige immediately got that it wasn't as important as why he was there in the first place. 'Or you could argue that this is exactly what my father was going for. Reaching our potential and dealing with loads of the people we will one day oversee.' As the last of his words left his mouth, he saw that he'd fallen right into her clever little trap. He grinned and his eyes dropped to her mouth. She was frighteningly brilliant and he imagined all the delicious things he'd like to do with her.

'Then what are you hoping to achieve with me?' She said it sadly, as if she totally knew the answer to that.

Words disappeared. Patter was never going to cut it. Xavier slid across the leather in one fluid move. She was warm and in his arms in a single second and he was kissing her. Long, deep and glorious; it was what he'd been thinking of doing all along. One hand tangled in her hair and the other pulling her backside closer so she was forced to climb into his lap and he relished it. The taste, the softness; all that encased the fiercely sexy, diamond-sharp mind. She drove him wild. Actions were the way to communicate with this girl. She would see straight through bullshit and he loved that.

When he finally pulled apart for air, her eyes looked bewildered and desolate. 'What's the matter?' he said, panicking he'd read it all wrong and at the same time knowing he hadn't because her aura was pulsing the rainbow.

'What's the matter?' she said, nonplussed. 'It's great you like me, Xavier, but don't you think it's a kind of given that you're on a time limit here? I'm a one night, one week, maybe a month tops, event in your otherwise busy life.'

Her eyes were accusing him and he understood.

'I'm just a placeholder, Xavier,' she said sadly as a final full stop to his libido. 'Even I know that.'

He frowned, suddenly angry with her. 'Even you?' he repeated, putting her away from him and standing up abruptly from his seat. He looked around at all the ridiculous, pointless things he'd bought that weekend. It was partly to anger his father in his usual competition with JJ, but a lot of it was to impress Paige. It had seemed imperative to take the opportunity while JJ was away. He pushed his hand up through his hair in frustration, because in a lot of ways she was right.

'You'll soon have a new pet project.' She stood up too and began to search around until her eyes landed on her bag that she'd let go of a few feet away.

In that moment he understood how completely self-centred he'd been. He half laughed to himself at how right his father had been to send them there. It wasn't a game to people like Paige. This was her life and he had no right to toy with it. 'I'm sorry,' he said, watching her bend to retrieve her bag. 'You're right and I didn't get it, but I do now.' He held out a hand for her to take.

She looked at it, unsure, then allowed him to lead her back to the sofa. 'Can I get a glass of water, please?'

'Sure,' he said, going to the kitchen area, filling a tumbler and bringing it back to her.

He watched her drink the whole glass down in unladylike gulps and he wondered if it was to give herself time to think or to clear her head from the champagne. He decided there and then that to salvage this he'd need to let her know how he felt, maybe for the first time in his life. 'I genuinely like you, Paige. I admire your ambition. You're clever – much cleverer than me.'

She stopped drinking and openly stared at him.

'You're beautiful – not in a contrived way, like lots of girls, but in a way that makes me continually want to know what you're thinking … how you're feeling.' He was looking directly into her completely trusting eyes, becoming moist and filling with tears. He was torn between wanting to grab her to him and taking refuge in anger and blaming her for this in some way. Like how was he supposed to know she wasn't interested in his money or his title, but he knew the idea was preposterous the moment he thought it. She might even laugh at that, which rankled because he loved her all the more for it. *Love.* Then the words tumbled out before he could stop them. 'Just give me a chance, Paige. Let me show you that I can make your life better and not worse.' Even he frowned. *What a lame plea and non-declaration of how he felt that was.*

'And then what?' Paige said with an exaggerated shrug. 'So you prove you can be a regular person to your dad. Then what?'

He went to expound with some big speech to put her in her place, but it died on his lips. In the end he sagged in defeat. 'No, Paige,' he said, shaking his head. 'You don't get it. I have to prove to my dad I'm a king.'

Paige sat staring at him, stunned. That made two of them. Xavier had never understood his own motivations so clearly and it had taken knowing Paige to do that. In a moment she understood the gravity of it all and what he'd just admitted to himself. He wanted to be king and he wanted to beat JJ. In the end he flopped down into the sofa next to her. Then he sat forward, picked up her hand and held it in both of his. 'Look, I promise you that I won't push you or make you do anything you don't want to do. I don't know how long it will last between us, but does anybody, Paige?' He searched her eyes and she continued to weigh what he was saying to her. He took it as a positive response and continued, 'JJ and I plan on making the school ours – not just for us, but better for everyone that goes there. And if you allow me to get to know you, I promise you that by the Christmas holidays, if we're still together, I'll take you home with me and you'll know everything about me … if you choose to, that is.'

She visibly softened, gratifyingly before his eyes. She turned their hands over and stroked the back of his. 'OK,' she said, with a croaky voice. 'But if I need space to process any of this, then you have to give it to me.'

'Done!' he said, as his chest ached and his heart soared. He pulled her into his body in a tight hug to hide his emotion, then kissed her hard in a moment-long outpouring and finally let her come up for air. 'Tell me what you want. Anything. I want to give you a gift to seal our agreement. Tell me and it will be yours.'

She stared at him, half laughing and then widening her eyes when she realized he was serious. She shook her head. 'I dunno, a new top … a keepsake or something? I don't know at the drop of a hat … you don't need—'

Xavier rolled his eyes, knowing that she would think of something practical and sensible. It was the thing he loved most about her. She was completely un-superficial. 'No Paige. There will be many gifts. Think of the thing that will bring you the most joy.'

The look she gave him then made him want to kiss her all over again. It was full of feeling, as though she was truly seeing him for the first time. But he could tell she was still trying to think of something modest. 'Come on, Paige,' he said in a whisper and with a wicked smile. 'Be bold. Think of me as the granter of wishes,' he said unable to stop himself laughing.

She laughed along with him. 'What, like a genie?'

'Yes!' he said, pointing at her. 'That's exactly it. Tell me the thing that would make you most happy.'

*P*aige felt really put on the spot. She could immediately think what her best friend Jade would ask for. It would be blingy and expensive, like jewellery or designer clothes. The new jumpsuit she'd seen in the High Street, in Retro-Jean's window or concert tickets to see Stormzy next month. A million things a girl of her age should want. But none of those things would make a real difference to her life or make her happy for longer than a day.

Then it came to her. Totally ridiculous because there was nothing Xavier could realistically do, but it was the single most useful thing that would help her mother and in turn make her life easier and therefore happier. 'Someone to help out with my brother and sister,' she said with a shrug. 'You asked and that's what would make me most happy. My mum works three jobs and I have to take care of them, which makes me miss school and the study time I need.'

The look Xavier gave her surprised her. Like she knew it was a silly thing to ask for and there was nothing he could do about it, but she at least expected him to roll his eyes and tell her to think again so he could give her the grand gesture he was after for her. Instead, his eyes kind of glowed like he was choked up or something. Then he got up, making her jump, and went over to the kitchen counter to retrieve his phone.

His eyes stayed on hers as he spoke. 'Max?… It's Xavier… Yes, I know I've spent a lot. We'll talk about that another time. Right now I need you to find me a nanny for two small children.' He put the phone to his shoulder. 'What are their ages?' he asked Paige.

Suddenly panicking that things were moving so fast, she blurted, 'Boy and a girl. Two and four.'

Xavier repeated it into the phone. 'Let me know when you have one and I'll text you the address. They must be ready to start on Monday.'

Paige watched him in a state of shock as he clicked off his phone. She'd said the thing that would make her the happiest. She didn't expect him to get it for her. 'We can't afford that,' she said, suddenly exasperated with him.

'I can.'

'My mum probably won't go for it. She won't know them.'

'I'll get them to send her the three top candidates and she can pick one. Then if she's still not comfortable in a few weeks, I can speak to JJ about opening a crèche at the school. I'm sure there are other families in your position or young mothers who are forced to leave school.' He batted away every excuse it wouldn't work, until, in the end, she had to look at him amazed. He looked adorable then, waiting for some hint of her approval. All she could do was jump up, run to him and fling her arms around his neck. She didn't know why she felt like crying, but she did. 'No one has ever done anything like that for me,' she said into his collar bone.

She stayed there for a long moment and he held her without saying a word, until Xavier said, with an equally broken voice, 'How are you at Foosball?'

She laughed loudly and pulled apart, to look up at him. And, just like that, they were teenagers again, messing around without a care in the world. But as he grinned down at her and took her hand, something had shifted in her chest.

ALEXIA HEADED BACK to the Johnsons the next day, after breakfast. There didn't seem much point hanging around. She was still angry with JJ for gate-crashing her weekend. Latitia hadn't been the same since. He'd arrived like a whirlwind and was gone before they got up – *like, what was the point in all that?*

Latitia had gone to bed with a headache after an otherwise great evening had fallen flat on its face. *Thanks a bunch, JJ.* So there seemed little point hanging around. Her mother had already flown out and Jay had a business to run, so had left them to it.

She put up a hand to say goodbye to Jay's driver and the two of them pulled their cases along the cracked pavement in silence. Just as she rummaged in her bag for her keys at the Johnsons' doorway, a text pinged on her phone. An address for an apartment by the canal.

So they'd actually gone ahead and done it. JJ and Xavier had moved out and left her. Suddenly the Johnsons' felt a lonely, desolate place. Dwayne was out or asleep and Latitia hadn't spoken all the way back. *What about me?* she texted back, trying to appeal to a grain of sympathy. Then she almost crushed her phone at the reply of *Hang tight* from Xavier. JJ hadn't even bothered to reply. She wanted to scream.

She seldom got involved between her brothers and their constant stream of girls, but when JJ stayed quiet, her anger and disappointment got the better of her. Her fingers tapped quickly, *What happened with Latitia last night? She hasn't said a word.*

His one-word answer stopped her heart: *Wiped.* Then a sad face emoji.

She stopped to think about that. It was the last thing she expected. JJ seemed to really like her. Maybe he liked her more than she thought. Her heart sank for him. The only reason had to be he'd opened up about who he was and she'd rejected him. It was the curse of all their lives. Maybe her brothers were right to be angry. Their father wanted them to fit in and it was impossible. They would always remain apart. Her answer was equally cryptic: *Everything?* It was important she knew how much Latitia still had.

Most, he sent straight back.

Alexia let out a long, sad sigh. The bare minimum, she guessed. Enough to get by. Like his name and who he was to her, nothing personal. She'd get the details when she saw him. She felt an overwhelming wave of sadness, for him, Latitia and herself. It was the curse of who they were. Her own situation wasn't much better. Worse, in fact. Dwayne had rejected her before he'd learned anything about who she was.

Latitia had disappeared back to bed so she made tea and ran a bath. The Johnsons' place had never been so quiet. Everyone must be asleep or out. Her question was answered soon after, when Dwayne wandered out from his room bleary-eyed, his hair bobbly, wearing only his boxer shorts.

'Hey, JJ and Xavier have moved out,' she said, to make conversation. She couldn't help raking her eyes over the ripped top half of his body. Every contour of his chest and abs were defined. He'd clearly been working out. It gave her another pang of pain that she didn't know that about him.

'Yeah, Mum said.' His voice was a croak.

'Haven't seen much of you lately?' she said to his back, walking into the kitchen.

She heard the ring of a cup being stirred and he wandered

out sipping tea. He shrugged a little. 'Been busy at the club. Practising and that.' He pulled the cup away from his mouth as if he'd had a great idea. 'You know, you should come to the club tonight. I've got my own set and in a couple of weeks, they've billed a battle between me and Trick. It's gonna be epic.'

Alexia smiled wanly, remembering the video Latitia had shown her. 'I thought you hated Trick,' she said, lowering her eyes to hide the accusation.

Dwayne seemed oblivious. 'We're never gonna be mates, but I'm gonna prove I'm better than him … and rivalry sells, you know?' he said with a shrug like nothing was a big deal.

Well, it had clearly been a bigger deal to her. A huge weight settled over her heart when she was forced to acknowledge how far apart they'd gotten. It was like they didn't know each other. 'I'll see if Latitia or my brothers are going.' It was a deliberate cue for him to invite her with him, but he missed it.

Instead, he went on about the new direction he was taking his music in and how much edgier it was. 'Trick did me a favour really. I've stepped up my game.'

It washed over her. She watched his mouth move, but the sound faded into the background. It was really quite hurtful to have been dropped so brutally. They had been getting on so well and now it was like he had no feelings for her at all.

Then her hand shot to her mouth and her heart stopped beating in her chest, as if she'd been struck by a bolt of lightning.

'What is it?' Dwayne said, frowning.

Bile rose in her throat. Scared she'd throw up, she waved a hand and ran for the bathroom to think. She locked the door and stared down the loo at the water. The sickness passed and her vision cleared. *Latitia … memories … taken.* But JJ would never do that, not without explaining why and what he was doing first. He just wouldn't be that cruel. Her mind shot to Xavier. *Xavier definitely would.* He'd hated her getting close to Dwayne from the start. He'd have justified it as better for her, good for him and best for the crown. *Bastard.* It all made sense now. The more she thought about it, the more convinced she became that Xavier had done some sort of selective memory wipe and it had happened right after the disastrous school party. Everything had been perfect until then. Now fortified by her anger, she came out of the bathroom and caught Dwayne about to go back into his room. 'Can I just ask you whether you've spent any time with my brother, Xavier, lately?'

He turned around and looked at her strangely.

'Only, I haven't seen much of him,' she said quickly, so as not to come off too weird.

He looked up at the ceiling and pulled a face while he thought about it. 'Not really. At school and he might have come into the club a couple of times.'

'OK.' She gave him a small nod of thanks, but her eyes had already lowered with the 'gotcha' she said under her breath. Xavier had sabotaged her relationship with Dwayne and she vowed to get him back.

MEANWHILE, JJ put his key in the new apartment lock. He'd barely slept and was bone tired – not to mention the open wound in his chest cavity. There was no way he could go back to the Johnsons now, not only because it would rip out what was left of his heart to see Latitia, but it could affect the memory wipe and be quite painful for her. Spending time with a subject, particularly one he had an emotional tie to, risked memories breaking through. There had even been recorded cases of psychosis or other mental illnesses in some instances. He'd only redirected neural pathways and not taken the memories completely. A little foolish, he knew. He'd told himself it was less dangerous for her, but the truth was he was a sap. He just couldn't bring himself to do it. So for now, he'd just close down any thoughts of Latitia and crash on the floor of his loft. He'd organize getting his stuff later and maybe a bed, when his head was on straight.

Then, as JJ put a foot in the door, he heard noises. Music. Beats. Too close to be coming from another floor. He pushed the door wide open and was immediately hit by warmth and the smell of fresh coffee. He edged his way in, slowly, with his mind racing, preparing scenarios. Squatters. Cooney and his goons. He was already confused by what looked like the corner of a huge sage-green, deep-pile rug. Then a double-take at the Jackson Pollock on the far wall, identical to the original that hung in their family's hideaway of Filfla.

By the time he reached the stainless-steel kitchen island, it was clear who'd been hard at work while he'd been away. And there he was. On the huge black leather sofa – unmistakable black curly hair and long, athletic body – with a pale blond girl draped over him with a throw. *Xavier*, sleeping like a baby, with the socially awkward boffiny girl from school.

He'd be lying if he said he wasn't envious. *Why had he felt the need to get all noble and honest?* Xavier seemed to be doing OK. In fact, he reminded him of a lounging cat. He should have known the moment his back was turned he'd seize the advantage and do exactly what suited him. It left a bitter taste in his mouth. He had to give it to him, though. The apartment looked great and he'd made a darn sight more headway with his girl.

JJ coughed, loudly.

Xavier blinked and the girl jumped awake. As expected, Xavier put up a lazy hand of hello and grinned. 'How do you like what I've done with the place?' he said, sleepily. The girl – Paige – snatched the throw to her chest as if she had no clothes on, which she definitely did. In fact, they still looked dressed in yesterday's wrinkled clothes.

Paige struggled to get up and ran a hand through her hair.

'You've been busy,' JJ said, trying to keep the bitter edge from his voice, dumping his bag down on the floor and putting his keys on the countertop. He began a slow meander, noting all the new furnishings.

Xavier watched him closely, clearly keen for his reaction and not at all bothered by poor Paige's discomfort.

The first thing JJ noticed was the prime bed position, next to the roof terrace. It was exactly where he would have chosen for himself. Then he glanced around and looked at Xavier wryly. 'You could have got me a bed, Xav.'

Paige was now on her feet, frantically looking for her bag. JJ saw it under the coffee table and pointed at it for her.

She flashed him the briefest smile of embarrassment and turned to Xavier. 'I'll go.'

'Don't go on my account,' JJ said, but his eyes were on Xavier. His smirk had suddenly disappeared and his focus was on Paige. It surprised him just how much Xavier cared for her. Somehow that hurt the most. Yet another blow, that Xavier seemed to have managed what he couldn't.

'Don't rush off. Give me a minute and I'll take you,' Xavier said, sitting up and reaching for his shoes under the coffee table.

Take you? Xavier had even managed to get himself a car. He couldn't wait to see what it was.

Paige's eyes flashed to JJ with guilt. 'No, it's OK. I can see you've got lots to talk about.'

Clever girl, JJ thought and gave her a flat smile of agreement. He had to remind himself that none of this was her fault.

'Bye, I'll see you Monday,' she said, putting a hand up to Xavier and almost running to the door.

JJ just stood there glaring at Xavier until he heard the open and shut of the door. 'You're on my bed, I believe,' he said, nodding at the sofa Xavier was still sitting on.

Xavier stood up, grinning widely and holding out an arm of invitation dramatically. JJ swore under his breath, shoved him out of the way and lay down, making sure he pulled the throw over him as he went.

Xavier was laughing at his bad mood. 'I didn't order you a bed because I knew you'd want to choose your own.'

JJ closed his eyes to rest them. He knew he was right, but that wasn't the point. He'd done all this without him, which was something they didn't do. He grunted in response. He was just too raw, too tired and too angry to deal with Xavier at that moment. Deep down, he knew it was more than just the flat that irked him, he just didn't want to examine any of his jumbled feelings now.

'Do you want coffee? It's a super-fandango barista that cost the best part of a grand.'

'No!' JJ said, knowing Xavier knew he was angry and was enjoying poking him nonetheless.

He felt Xavier nudge his leg. 'I take it things didn't go well with the sultry Latitia.'

JJ's eyes opened at that in a silent dare. He was clearly goading him for a fight. Like when he was bored when they were kids. He did it for the real excitement of danger that only a kid with anger issues and telepathic abilities could inflict. His eyes were bloodshot from lack of sleep and alcohol and he wore a smirk to prove he was right.

However, instead of taking the bait, JJ was hit by a wave of sadness. He didn't know why he hadn't seen it. It wasn't really him furnishing the flat, or even Latitia. The day the two of them always knew would come was already here. They were no longer kids scrapping. The trip had changed something subtly between them. Maybe their fathers knew it would. Without even realizing it, they'd taken up their prophesied mantles as rivals. With all his extra sensory perception and he'd still missed it; he'd been too preoccupied. 'I took her memories,' he said, in numb resignation, as the final piece of his heart felt like it was ripped from his chest.

Xavier's eyebrows rose at that.

It was a confession in a last-ditch offering of vulnerability between brothers. Xavier would understand that there was only one reason he would do that: he liked her enough to reveal his true self to her.

A flicker of guilt ran across Xavier's face as he registered it and then it disappeared. JJ kept his eyes on him as he walked over to the expensive coffee maker and made one for himself. 'Talking of mind wipes, Alexia is on the war path because of Dwayne,' Xavier said, stirring sugar into his cup.

Something inside JJ's chest shrank, if that were possible. *Poor Alexia.* It had made such complete sense at the time and now he was on the receiving end he felt hollow with guilt. She would have fallen in one day. Latitia had simply been the nudge. Dwayne's indifference, his preoccupation with Trick, hardly being home; Alexia had every right to be angry. He wanted to reach out to console her as he'd always done as a child, but she wouldn't thank him and he needed to be careful with Latitia. He was too tired to give it the serious thought it deserved and Xavier was clearly in a volatile mood. In the end, before he succumbed to sleep, he said, 'You're gonna regret that, Xav.'

Then Xavier's laughter and, 'I don't think so,' drifted far away.

*a*lexia was relieved that Valarie Johnson was working lates all over the weekend as she was dragging Latitia to Rhythm and Booze to see Dwayne. Not only had it been plastered all over social media and conspicuous to miss, but she had to see if she could get through Xavier's mind wipe. She'd heard stories of how strong emotion and being near a subject could sometimes make cracks appear. She just had to try. The idea appealed to her romantic side.

The notion had occurred to her to go into Dwayne's mind and throw a few switches herself, but she was inexperienced and it was dangerous. She didn't want Dwayne to end up a vegetable in the hospital. *God,* it suited Xavier either way. Her blood simmered every time she thought of Xavier's smug face. Heaven knew what kind of suggestions and fail-safes he'd left behind. Xavier hadn't even picked up his phone when she'd phoned to have a go at him. In the end, she'd texted *How could you?* And cried frustrated tears.

Eventually the reply came: *I will not let my sister get dragged into street battles with local thugs over DJing. You'll thank me one day. X.* She ended up throwing her phone and cracking the screen.

So now, as she gave their names to the bouncer to check the guest list, it was with a smugness to spite Xavier as well.

Latitia was still quiet and subdued. She'd normally be hopping with excitement to get out and do her favourite thing in the world: dance. Instead, she shuffled her feet as if she was cold or nervous and it was unseasonably warm for October.

Inside was a brightly lit cocktail bar, with the club name in yellow neon over the optics and photos of R&B singers through the ages around the walls. The place was small, with high stools around little pillar tables, encouraging people to cluster with their drinks around them and a stairwell in its centre, leading down to the music and club below.

Alexia felt a strange tingle in her chest and the hairs prickled on the back of her neck. It was unusual for her to feel nerves.

Latitia yanked her arm. 'Let's get a drink,' she said, pulling her towards the bar.

Alexia couldn't help keeping an eye on her; snatching sideways glances when she thought she wasn't seen.

In the end, Latitia turned to her squarely and said, 'What? Is my eye makeup smudged?'

The sudden aggressive way she said it almost threw her off balance, but she quickly recovered. 'Just an eyelash,' she said, flicking the imaginary object from the top of her cheek. It worried her given her plan for the evening. Latitia was clearly unstable. When the young, smiling barman came and leaned forward to hear them, she quickly ordered: 'Two virgin daiquiris, please.' She daren't allow Latitia alcohol in her current state.

He nodded and they both watched as he threw the ingredients into his blender, shook them and threw the contents into two tall long-stemmed glasses, with a slice of strawberry on the side.

They both took a long sip in silence. Latitia was unusually quiet. 'Are you OK?' Alexia said eventually. Latitia led the way to one of the perching tables. 'Only, you haven't said much since we got back.'

Latitia climbed onto her stool and sipped her drink again. 'Honestly, I feel hungover, but I know I didn't drink last night.' Then she pulled a face. 'Do you think someone could have spiked my drink?'

Alexia mirrored her position on the stool opposite and took a bite from her strawberry. 'I don't know, but Jay was watching over us like a hawk, so it's unlikely.' She felt her cheeks go pink with guilt. 'Did you see JJ last night?' she asked, not able to look her in the eye. It was still unclear how deep JJ's mind wipe went and how it affected a person after.

Latitia pulled her 'no-clue-what-she-was-on-about' face again. 'No, why would he have been there?' As she said the words, her hand went to her forehead again. She was clearly in pain.

Alexia tried to laugh it off. 'It is his dad's hotel.'

'Oh, yeah. I forgot.' But she'd gone a grey colour like she was going to be sick.

'Are you sure you're OK?' Alexia said, feeling terrible. None of it was her fault, but she felt responsible in some way. She wanted to text JJ, but she was still too angry with Xavier and didn't want him getting involved.

'I don't feel so good. I think I might just go to the ladies,' Latitia said, sliding down from her stool.

Alexia went to go with her, but Latitia put up a hand. 'It's OK. You stay and look after the drinks. I won't be long.'

Alexia didn't like letting her go alone at all, but she reluctantly eased back onto her stool. She watched Latitia pick her way quickly through the growing crowd feeling the worst kind of friend. Was she really any better than Xavier, being a party to this? She was quick to blame Xavier, but this had been JJ; her beloved brother, the one she'd been closest to since birth. She felt wretched and confused. Everything was turning to crap as it always did around them. She delved into her small clutch bag for a tissue and dabbed the corner of her eyes.

Two more virgin daiquiris appeared on the table in front of her from the same young handsome barman. Then he went to move on to a new customer. She immediately held up her hand to get his attention. 'Excuse me? Sorry! I didn't order these.'

The barman smiled a broad, friendly smile. 'No charge,' he said, with a dismissive wave. 'He told me to say they're from an admirer.'

Alexia looked around her to see if she could spot anyone looking at her, secretly hoping it was Dwayne. 'Can't you give me a clue?'

The barman laughed, making him very handsome. 'It's more than my job's worth.' He went back behind the bar, clearing some glasses as he went. She hadn't heard of a secrecy code of conduct between barmen. It occurred to her that maybe he had bought them himself, but then dismissed it as he'd paid no extra attention to her. She sipped her drink through a straw, churning over who it might be, until she felt a familiar presence next to her and her heart sank. *Oh you,* she projected.

JJ was right next to her with the rat-bag, Xavier, right behind him. She wanted to scream, but instead put down her drink and held her head in her hands. She was too upset and angry to deal with the pair of them right now.

'We need to talk,' JJ said in her ear.

She whirled around on him, angrily, on her stool. 'Well, we don't always get what we want, do we?' she said, flashing

Xavier an angry look over his shoulder. 'You shouldn't even be here. Latitia is in the Ladies, probably throwing up because her head hurts so much and you'll make it worse.' She glared at JJ. Then her eyes narrowed on Xavier. 'And you! I'm not even talking to you.' She looked at JJ again. 'Did you know he was going to do that to Dwayne?'

JJ put up both his hands to calm her down. 'That isn't the point, Alexia.'

Alexia tutted and gave them her back.

'You should take Latitia home,' JJ said.

She just couldn't believe it. She hated her brothers sometimes. They ruined everything. 'We were here first!' she said through gritted teeth. She picked up her drink and drank it fast until the air rattled through the straw loudly. Then she picked up the other, regretting the brain freeze.

'Please, Lexie,' JJ said, using the pet name in the soft voice he had reserved for her since they were small. 'We'll talk soon, I promise. We have to meet someone here tonight to talk business and it's dangerous for Latitia to see me.'

Alexia huffed and rolled her eyes. Then she slammed down her drink and said, 'You may as well have those,' and slid off her stool. 'Some stranger brought them,' she said spitefully to Xavier. He registered her meaning as she elbowed through the pair of them and flashed him an image of her dating another faceless boy. They'd want to know who it was and it would irritate them. Even if she knew, she wouldn't tell them.

She found Latitia holding the sides of the sink in the ladies. 'Sorry,' she said, splashing a face that looked pasty and miserable.

'Come on, let's go home,' Alexia said, grabbing her some paper towels. 'It was a bad idea, coming here. You're obviously not well. We'll go outside and I'll call an Uber. The air might do you some good.'

Latitia nodded and allowed her to lead her. They pushed their way up the stairs and made it out to the street. She was right. A wave of relief flooded her with the fresh air. It was dark and there was no wind and only the slightest bite of cold. It was a nice evening for a walk. So they sauntered in the direction of home, Alexia figuring she'd call an Uber as soon as they got too tired or cold.

'I'm sorry, Alexia. I don't know what's the matter with me.'

Alexia put an arm around Latitia's hunched shoulders. 'It's OK. No need to apologize. There's loads going around,' she said, flinching slightly at her shameless lie.

They hadn't gone that far when a sleek black car slowed down next to them and the driver rolled down the window. 'Alexia?' he asked.

Alexia looked around them for someone they knew and nodded with a frown.

'Get in!'

She hesitated. They hadn't ordered a taxi and certainly nothing as upmarket as this one. This was more like an executive car.

'Everything is OK, Alexia. We know who you are.'

Latitia was foolishly reaching for the handle having had enough of their walk. Obviously not registering how strange this was, even for her. 'Did my father send you?' she asked, praying it was as her feet were now aching.

'One of your people,' he said, cryptically.

Latitia was already in the back seat, so Alexia felt pressured to get in behind her. She rested a little easier when the driver pulled away, talking into a phone instead of a radio. Stuff like that was familiar territory – especially when he took them straight home without even asking their address.

Still, she hadn't been able to relax. Something felt off. She gave Latitia an unfriendly shove and got out with a huge sense of relief onto the pavement. She'd been stupid to blindly get in and she would pull her up on it. It could have literally been anyone. It was probably just her brothers, making sure they got home, but she vowed to have a serious word about communication.

Then, as she turned away, the driver called, 'Wait!' He got out, walked around the car and handed her a card. She took it gingerly and immediately examined it for clues. It had a simple eleven digit number on one side and four familiar symbols on the other. 'What's this?'

The driver was already walking back to the driver's side when he said, 'Your admirer sends his regards.' Then he turned and flashed her a smile as he opened his door. 'And he said if you ever need him, for anything at all, call the number and someone will come.'

She stood frozen in shock as the man got back into the car and it glided off. Latitia was fidgeting next to her. 'Can we go inside? I'm freezing.'

Alexia nodded absently, her mind still on the mysterious message. She slipped the card into her bag and watched the tail-lights disappear into the distance.

The symbols were arranged like a logo, but it was clear what they were to anyone who knew them. They were recognizable to any Atlantean. Four consonants from the Old Language, but she had no idea what they meant. She hadn't exactly been a model student in Atlantean Antiquities Studies with Max.

Still, as she walked back to the apartment, a vice gripped her heart with the realization. Her admirer – the one buying her drinks and sending expensive cars – wasn't someone her age. He was rich and powerful and very definitely Atlantean.

Latitia put her key in the door and, for the first time in days, Alexia had butterflies. Imagining who it might be was just the distraction to take her mind off Dwayne.

CHAPTER 26

JJ nudged his way through the crowd of the downstairs part of the club. An empty space with wooden floors and simple red uplighters in the walls that made it darker and more conducive for dancing.

Why are we even here? Xavier projected, leaning in from behind him.

JJ spotted Dwayne behind the decks, completely oblivious to what had been done to him. He felt a pang of guilt. He hadn't exactly told Alexia the truth. Xavier wasn't flying solo on this one. *To be faces, we need to be seen* was his reply over his shoulder.

Xavier rolled his eyes.

He couldn't deny that night clubs attracted people, provided fronts for illicit money, which attracted more villains and villains marked turf. And wasn't it a coincidence that they were here to see their favourite turf accountant.

Dwayne dropped a heavy tune and everyone started to chant and bounce. JJ had to hand it to him, he was really quite good. He'd come on leaps and bounds since the last time he'd heard him.

JJ felt a tug on his arm. 'Mr Cooney will see you in the back.'

That was fast. They hadn't even had to announce themselves; proved they had good CCTV and spotters out in the club.

He turned his head to Xavier, who raised his eyebrows and gave him the universal look for *here we go*. Then they followed the huge guy to the furthest point and through a black painted door at the back of the club.

The narrow hallway was painted red and veered off to the right before they came to a stop in front of another black door and huge bouncer standing in front of it. JJ noted they were all human, worked out and were built for strength and not speed. Despite their size, they would be easy to take down.

The two men nodded at each other and the doorman stepped out of the way, allowing them in. JJ and Xavier followed cautiously. They were immediately hit by a cloud of cigar smoke. There was a large circular table with about six men around it involved in a serious game of cards. There was already a pile of money in the centre.

Two girls in pink heels and short sequined dresses were serving them drinks. It put JJ in mind of a speakeasy of the 1930s.

'Ah, there's my boys,' Mr Cooney said, from the far side of the table while gripping a large cigar with his teeth. 'These are the lads I was talking about, fellas. Pull up some seats for 'em. What's a matter wiv ya,' he said to the hangers-on, perching on stools nearby.

Two chairs were immediately squeezed in at the table. JJ shot Xavier a look and the two of them sat – a greasy man in a sharp suit and bad teeth grinning between them. 'Breakfast,' he said, looking over at Cooney and making the whole table laugh.

JJ let the slant go. It worked in their favour to be underestimated. *Don't win too soon or too big,* JJ projected. Their opponents' auras alone would give them away, even without the ability of entering their minds.

Got it, Xavier replied, splaying his hand of cards.

'Cigar?' Cooney said, making the table laugh again.

'No thanks,' JJ said. 'It stunts your growth.'

Cooney and the table laughed at that. 'See what I mean, lads. Clever sods.' He took a few short puffs, still holding his cigar in his teeth, and blew the smoke over the table, making JJ want to cough. 'Settled in the wharf, OK?' Cooney asked, while the game proceeded.

'Nearly,' JJ said, shooting Xavier a scathing look. 'Just got a get a few things. It's great, though. Thanks for setting us up.'

Cooney nodded, accepting the respect, and took his turn taking a card.

'I'm not sure we have the kind of money needed for a hand,' JJ said, looking warily at the huge pile of money already in the middle.

'Don't worry. The house will sub ya. You can owe me,' Cooney said, slyly, to low chuckles around the table.

JJ had to school his face. Xavier would be thinking the same thing: Cooney sought to trap them into debt to him. The evening would be tricky. They'd need to win enough to pay back the house and not too big as to anger him. He had to keep face.

'Deal,' JJ said, with his most brilliant fake grin. A guy next to Cooney counted them each out a thousand pounds. He took the money and put a couple of hundred into the pot. 'When will we get a chance to thank Mr Rasputin personally?' JJ said.

'How do you know he's not here already?' Cooney said with a sly smile.

JJ's heart missed a beat at his obvious blunder. He absolutely knew there was no other Atlantean in the room, but Cooney didn't know that. *Does he know?* he quickly threw at Xavier.

I don't think so, Xavier flipped back. *I think he's just trying to unsettle us.*

JJ relaxed a little. 'Just a hunch,' he said, looking at the idiots around the table and not hiding it.

Cooney chuckled, proving he was much cleverer than he looked.

'I mean, no one looks particularly Russian,' he added, just to cover himself.

Cooney studied him shrewdly.

'You're the quiet one,' Cooney said, directly to Xavier.

'Not always. Just observing,' Xavier said.

'The clever one,' Cooney said, with a devilish look towards JJ.

JJ smirked. The divide-and-conquer routine would never work on them, they were too close. They would fight to the death for the crown, but that was their personal business and no paltry human would ever come between that.

The game wore on. JJ made sure he lost bigger than he won and Xavier followed suit. All the while, Cooney was making jibes at their expense. JJ had become used to it in the human world. Men with fragile egos, seeing him as some rich, entitled kid who needed taking down a peg or two, to make themselves feel better.

However, after totting up in his head that they owed the house around three thousand pounds, he made sure he won the last hand. Then both he and Xavier stood up, leaving the pile of money on the table. 'I believe that makes us square,' he said, tipping his head towards it.

Cooney narrowed his eyes at being outwitted. His mind was already whirring on a much cleverer opponent than he first realized. Then he pointed and clicked his fingers over his shoulder. 'I almost forgot.'

One of his men handed him a square, manilla-wrapped package. He threw it towards him on the table. 'Your first job … Rasputin asked me to give you this.'

'What is it?' JJ asked, picking up the box about the size and shape of a book.

Cooney shrugged dramatically, protruding his bottom lip. 'Dunno. He was just clear he didn't want anyone else opening it.'

'Who's it for, then?' JJ asked, turning it over in his hands in an attempt to guess what it could be.

'Your father.'

JJ and Xavier immediately froze and locked eyes. Even though they had two of them, it could mean only one thing. This Rasputin was definitely the Atlantean they'd been sensing and they finally knew what he was after: he wanted contact with the king.

'He stressed it was for nobody else's hands but his.'

'WHAT DO YOU THINK IT IS?' Xavier said, as he and JJ stared down at it on the kitchen counter.

JJ shook his head. 'I have no idea. It's too light for a book.'

'What if it's explosives?' Xavier said, the idea suddenly occurring to him. Their father was under constant threat from people who'd like to topple the Atlantean monarchy.

JJ looked at him sardonically. 'I think our mystery crime lord is too clever and too greedy to be a terrorist. No, he'll want something from him.'

Xavier relaxed a little. JJ was right, although it was unsettling that the guy had managed to sniff out the royal children for his line of communication. So whatever it was, it was Atlantean-specific. 'I say we open it,' Xavier said, looking JJ straight in the eye and seeing his greed and desire reflected there. He laughed. There was no way they weren't going to open it.

'Go on then,' JJ said, pushing the brown package closer to him.

Xavier rolled his eyes, gingerly picked up the parcel and began to untie the string. 'Will we still deliver it?'

JJ frowned. 'Depends what it is.' He nodded towards it to hurry him along. 'All the while this guy is waiting for us to do it, we have the upper hand.'

JJ was right. He ripped off the last of the paper to reveal an old green and burgundy, patterned wooden box. On closer inspection, it had been painstakingly painted with fern leaves edged in deep red. A work of art in itself.

'Open it,' JJ urged, nudging his arm.

Xavier clumsily lifted the lid off the box. The whole thing felt very old and flimsy. Inside was a yellowed envelope with a blood-red wax seal. 'Now what do we do?' Xavier said, knowing full well if they opened it, they'd need to crack the wax and there would be no way of recreating the seal. It would have been pressed from a ring or a stamp somewhere and was exactly why the method was created, i.e., their father would know it had been opened.

'To hell with it,' JJ said, walking away and then back again in frustration.

Xavier lifted it up to his eyeline to look closely at the wax.

'What is it?' JJ said.

'This was sealed a very long time ago. The wax is crumbling slightly, see?' Xavier held it up so JJ could move in closer to see it.

Xavier wasted no more time. He passed JJ the envelope, took out his keys from his pocket, found the small penknife and opened it quickly. Then he took the envelope and, placing it on the kitchen side, very carefully and painstakingly slid the blade under the thick wax. It took no time at all to separate it from the paper underneath. The triangle opened, temptingly. 'Go ahead,' Xavier said, not wanting to be the one who actually looked at it first. 'It might be cursed.'

JJ tutted, opened the leaf and pulled out the folded piece of delicate, browned paper.

'What does it say?' Xavier said, bumping his shoulder to see.

There was a green and red crest, with similar leaves to the design on the box, and symbols in rows going from top to bottom that looked like stick men and circles. His heart began to slowly sink. He'd seen this type of writing before, in the library at home. Neither of them had been good students of Atlantean Antiquities, which meant that they couldn't read it. And to enlist someone who could, would immediately expose what they'd done. 'What shall we do?' Xavier said, wanting to throw it at the wall in frustration.

JJ shook his head, looking as disappointed as he was. He went to the drawer and took out a candle.

'What are you going to do with that?' Xavier said, alarmed.

JJ lit the burner on the stove and put the candle under the flame. 'Put the letter back in the envelope.

Xavier, seeing where he was going with it, slipped the paper back inside. JJ placed it back on the countertop and very carefully dripped two small drops of wax in the place where the seal had joined to the envelope. It was clear to see as it had left a red stained ring. Then he pushed it down and held it for a full minute.

It worked. He held it up to his eyeline with a grin. 'See? Good as new. We can deliver it and no one will know it was opened.'

Xavier smiled, unconvinced. He felt a gnawing pain in the bottom of his stomach. There was something far deeper going on here than organized crime.

JJ WORKED with Xavier on their proposal to the Department for Education after that. It had to be watertight to convince Dr Henry. It was long and complicated and had to include a good business plan to fund it through a dummy corporation. Then they had to work out how to make real money after that. There was only so long before their father would demand to know where huge sums of his money were being syphoned off to.

After many after-hours hypothetical questions to their father's legal team and accountants, and working way into the night, they finally emailed their proposal to Dr Henry and eventually slept. In fact, they stayed in bed for most of the next day. JJ's eyes strayed to the re-wrapped package a few times from his makeshift bed on the sofa. 'Do you think Dad will know him?' he said, when he sensed Xavier was awake too.

'Hard to say,' he replied, straight away. Proving it was on his mind as well. 'He might have heard of him.'

'We don't even know what that is,' JJ said. Still not believing the guy was sponsoring their new lifestyle and they had no idea who he really was.

JJ's new bed came later that day and he placed it at the opposite end of the loft to Xavier. It was in the next best place. Partitioned off, behind a wall of glass bricks, close to the large walk-in shower and dressing room. He went back to bed after that and went into a heavy sleep, where a faceless male watched from the shadows and moved just out of his reach.

· · ·

By THE TIME Monday came and they rode the short distance to school in Xavier's shiny new car, they were ready to make their pitch to the headmaster. He would have studied their business plan, which, long term, meant changing the school to opt into the independent system and they arrived thirty minutes before school for their appointment with Dr Henry.

They parked just around the corner which still raised a few eyebrows. JJ had insisted on not parking in the teachers' car park. Students just didn't drive to school at all and teachers drove small, sensible hatchbacks with miles on the clock.

'Way to be conspicuous,' JJ said, getting out and trying not to catch anyone's eye. Xavier laughed. 'Oh chill out, JJ. It's time we came out of our shell.'

CHAPTER 27

'Ah, boys. Sit down.' Dr Henry stood and held out his arm to indicate the two chairs facing him on the other side of the desk. JJ had forgotten just how tall and rotund he was.

While he spoke, he appeared to be searching behind them for someone else. 'I read your proposal. Very interesting indeed. I was hoping your father would be with you, given what you said you wanted to discuss. Finance can be tricky waters to navigate,' he said with a nervous laugh that didn't sound promising. Like they were about to get the 'come-see-me-in-ten-years' conversation.

JJ and Xavier exchanged a look. 'We've come up with some ideas to help the school ourselves, sir,' JJ said, turning and facing him directly, crossing his leg over his knee as he'd seen his father, Jay, do all the time, when he wanted to show he was relaxed and confident.

Dr Henry caught it and any discomfort at letting them down gently changed to mildly amused. 'Well, I'm all ears,' he said, leaning back in his chair, clearly humouring them.

JJ hid his rising frustration and went for painting a

picture of their overall vision. He was hoping to light an ember in Dr Henry that, with minimal powers of suggestion, would get him on their side. 'We want to create a school in the heart of South London, where children young and old, from parents, no matter how poor, can enjoy good facilities, great teaching, school trips, books … everything they need to go on and become anything they want.'

Dr Henry let out an exasperated breath and couldn't hide his impatience. 'Yes, that's all well and good, but this is the real world, boys. Camberwell. What you propose will take money.'

JJ wanted to build it up slowly, logically, so their takeover happened naturally. They needed to not only get it past Dr Henry, but also win over the parents and not alert the governors and authorities overseeing the school, so mind control on its own would never work. Funding had to appear to have a watertight business front from seemingly genuine companies. His father's legal team were already on it, moonlighting for them at a profit, with client confidentiality, of course. So while JJ very carefully entered Dr Henry's mind creating positive responses, he laid out their very feasible plan aloud. 'After the initial cash injection from some of my father's companies, we have a number of ideas we'd like to introduce over time, but we thought we'd start with a shop. One that sells everything a kid needs to go here: uniform, stationery and even snacks.'

'And a crèche,' Xavier added. 'For mothers connected with the school who work, older siblings, even some who go here, you know.'

JJ looked at him, feeling like he'd seen him for the first time. They'd lightly tossed the idea between them, but it was obvious Xavier had given it a lot more thought and it was clear who it was for. *Paige.* Another painful twist in his chest.

He faced Dr Henry again as he was speaking, but his mind was still on Xavier.

'Well. I have to say, I'm impressed. I applaud your industriousness. But tuck shops have been tried before and rarely turn over the kind of revenue you're talking about.'

'Not like this, sir. It could go in the old gym store, sir. It would be a lot bigger than any school as ever seen. Eventually, it could be like a small mall. Employing parents. Giving back to the community.'

Dr Henry looked impressed, but, JJ could tell, he still thought it was all a pipe dream. 'And the crèche. There are strict laws governing that type of thing.'

'And we will learn them,' Xavier said, making JJ stare at him again. 'The old drama block has been out of use for some time. It's single story, separate from the school for the noise. Instead of being demolished, it could be easily renovated, fenced-off, gated and kid-proofed to all the specifications.'

JJ watched his brother, amazed as Xavier got out some papers from a folder he was carrying, obviously prepared. 'I took the trouble of having these plans drawn up, sir. There isn't too much structural work needed. A lot of it is superficial.'

JJ was literally gobsmacked, but so impressed. This was what love could do for a person. He'd never seen Xavier so enthused and interested in anything, let alone kids. He was moved and happy for him. Still, as he turned and faced Dr Henry again, JJ hardened. Kids, love and a happy ever after, were not in the story for him, so he refused to give it head space. It was much more productive to think of how perfect a crèche would be to pave the way for some of the more dubious things they had planned down the line – ideas they wouldn't be telling Dr Henry about. Then, by the time he found out, they'd be in too deep to change anything.

'Tell me honestly though, boys, how far is your father backing you in all this?' Dr Henry asked, narrowing his eyes.

Xavier jumped in again, just as JJ was about to open his mouth. 'This is our venture, our ideas, but our father's initial capital through several of his companies, so you have no worries there. He is keen for us to show him our business acumen.'

JJ faced Dr Henry again, raising his eyebrows as if to say, 'like he said'. The truth was, he felt bewildered and unprepared in comparison. As if he didn't know his own brother at all right then. They'd clearly grown further apart than he thought.

Dr Henry's chair creaked as he hoisted up his weight and began a slow stroll around the room with his hands behind his back. He went over to his window and watched the lines of children filtering into the school. 'I just don't know, boys. Your ideas are admirable—'

'Don't you want to be the headmaster who really makes a difference around here?' Xavier said, turning in his seat to watch him.

JJ was still in a daze at his brother's behaviour, but shook himself out of it to speak up. 'It's a big step, Dr Henry, we know. But we promise you that if you put the application in, the money will come, one way or another.'

'Our father would never allow the school to flounder,' Xavier added.

JJ looked from his brother back to the headmaster and nodded. It was true, their father wouldn't, but they'd never let it get to the point where their father had to take over. Then he gave Dr Henry the final mental nudge he needed.

The effect on Dr Henry was immediate and obvious. He came back around to his side of the desk, took a piece of paper and began scribbling numbers, doing the math.

'It can really work, sir,' JJ added while he wrote.

He finally stopped writing and looked up and studied them both, staring at him expectantly. Then he let out a long breath and shook his head. 'I'm going to say, maybe. Let's send in the application to change the school's status, and if you can get me some more solid information about the finance from your father – better still, a meeting with him, himself, then we'll go from there. OK?'

JJ and Xavier both laughed delightedly, got to their feet and shook Dr Henry's hand. They could iron out those wrinkles later.

Dr Henry's loud laughter boomed along with them. He was a true educator. JJ already knew from his little venture into his mind that there was no self-aggrandisement here. This was all for the good of the kids and the school to him. What can I say, boys, I'm so impressed. How did you come up with it all? What inspired you?'

JJ relaxed a little. He prided himself on being a good judge of character and Dr Henry was one of the good ones. He'd know it even without the soft pulsing tones in his aura. It was the way he hadn't once mentioned profit, only what could be done. 'We came from a very privileged school before here, sir.'

'We decided we want to improve the school environment for everyone,' Xavier added.

JJ studied his brother as he went on about the disparity between the classes and what he was saying wasn't wrong. And it was true, their father was trying to teach them something, only it wasn't to carve out their kingdom just yet, in South London.

'Very well,' Dr Henry said, hauling his weight out of the chair again. He came out from behind his desk, walked to the door and opened it for them. 'Let me look into it. Make a few enquiries about permits and the legalities of it. And if your father's people can contact me, hopefully I'll have more answers for you by the end of the week. Then he shook both their hands jovially as they left. JJ wasn't sure if he felt happy or not.

XAVIER'S BRAIN was buzzing with spin-off ideas all the while he walked. Some legal, some not, but all put through the shop. The meeting with their father would be a simple mental implant. By the end of the week, Dr Henry would remember it as a business meeting that went extremely well and all misgivings would be squashed.

JJ was brooding and split off quickly to make a call, which was a relief, because he spotted Paige walking quickly towards him. 'Hey!' he said, smiling and kissing her on the cheek. Then he frowned at how flustered she looked. 'What's the matter?' He was used to her carrying the weight of the world on her shoulders, but this seemed different.

Paige shook her head, hopelessly. 'Nothing. I just got in so much trouble over Friday night. Jade's mum phoned my mum and blew my cover and now she's on the warpath.'

'What about the nanny interviews, didn't they soften her up?'

She looked at him then as if he had no clue about anything at all, which stung a little. 'Well, no, actually. She wants to see you. She's not comfortable with it.' Then she seemed to soften and reached out to touch his hair and the side of his face. 'It was a lovely, generous idea, but I just don't think it's going to work.'

Xavier pulled her into his body, then kissed her shamelessly on the lips. Several wolf whistles came from passersby. He steered her away from the onlookers, behind the cover of a wall, and cupped her face gently with his hand. 'Don't worry. I'll come after school and see if I can talk her round … Oh, and I want you to get your geeky science club friends together.'

'Why?' she said, her face lighting up immediately.

'I have a proposition for you for some clinical trials.'

JJ WANTED to speak to one of his father's tech team about an idea of his own. Now he'd seen how serious Xavier was he needed to immerse himself in something too, and tuck shops and crèches were not going to generate the kind of money they needed. For them to be free of their father, they had to make enough money to fund themselves and make the school independent, without making parents pay fees. Parents had to know they were onto a good thing to accept the takeover. *They* had to hold the power and not the Department for Education and certainly not his father's council. They had to have complete autonomy and for that, they needed to separate from his father's purse strings with a high level of technical know-how. Possibly to rival Silicon Valley. Neither of them was voicing it yet, but in short, they had to rule.

A couple of phone calls and he'd set up a video call with someone who could help him do just that after school. Then, putting his phone back in his pocket, he turned back for the building and spotted Latitia sitting all on her own on a bench. A stab of pain twisted his gut. He'd never seen her so lost and alone. This was the back-end part of the school, where the generators, cleaning and storage areas were. No place for her to be, not like this. Her hair was flat and her face pale and bare. Her eyes were cast down as if her thoughts were miles away. He couldn't leave her like this, so he carefully approached, calling out, 'Latitia,' quietly, so he didn't startle her.

She looked up at him, bleary-eyed.

'Budge up,' he said, forcing her to shuffle along the bench as he sat down with her. He inwardly flinched as she touched her head in obvious pain. He shouldn't be there. His presence would play havoc with her troubled mind. Intense emotion would threaten to expose the memories buried deep inside her psyche like a raw nerve. 'What are you doing all the way out here. First period has started,' he said, trying to distract her.

'Has it?' she said, looking utterly confused. 'You're Alexia's brother, aren't you?' She was now squinting with the pain from the light.

He nodded, his brain racing; hating himself for his treatment of her. He wasn't sure if he could keep this up. It was cruel. 'What's wrong?' he said, closing his eyes, despising himself. He'd entered many minds and he'd learned neural pathways, thinking of it as a game as a child. He'd toyed with mental switches to learn what they did, like preferences on a computer. Most of the time it had been to get his own way, to get served alcohol by weak-minded humans, or let off homework, but he'd never conducted a complete sweep of someone so close, who had such deep feelings for him. He felt ashamed. It was foolhardy at best and, looking at her now, it was downright dangerous.

'Oh nothing,' she said, listlessly. 'Just tired, you know? And I keep forgetting things, like why am I here?' she said laughing and holding out her hands. 'I feel so silly.' She frowned as if she only just realized how much. 'I'm like an old person,' she said with a nervous laugh.

JJ smiled at her, wanting to kiss away all the badness and worry, but he knew if he did, the shock of her memory would come back and possibly kill her. However, she was on a roll and determined to talk.

'Like I walk into a room and forget why I'm there. I'm looking for something and I don't know what it is. I'm late for school because I keep going round and round in the flat looking for it, but I don't know what it is.'

JJ felt terrible. She was looking for him and didn't even know it. Someone would think she was losing her mind. He had to get away from her to think. 'Why don't you go home? I can tell the office for you.'

She stood up and shook her head. 'No, it's better to be here. I have to find it.' She got hold of his jacket and began to shake him. 'Can you help me? Can you help me look?' Her pupils looked wild and dilated.

His pulse began hammering in panic; he had to do something. He looked around him frantically and saw a group of girls who had congregated to smoke. 'They're in your class, aren't they? Go with them. I'll help you later, after school. I promise.'

She looked where he was pointing, muddled and confused. Luckily, one of them spotted her, waved and called out, 'Latitia, come here.' It did the trick and she wandered slowly in their direction.

JJ shot behind a wall before she could see him go. He peered around to watch her and she continued to turn and look for where he'd been. He closed his eyes, despising himself and swore. He couldn't leave her like that. Those girls had witnessed their chemistry for weeks. Any comments would only add to her current confusion and he didn't want to get into any more damage limitation with friends. That could get really complicated. No, he had to admit he was in over his head and get professional advice.

He went out of sight to where the large council dumpsters and bicycle sheds were kept. Only the stoners hung around here. He took out his phone and tapped the best person he could think of and prayed they were currently out of the water. There were a few options. His Uncles Vionne and Darres had the strongest mental abilities, being from part of the Borge family that lived permanently under water. They had the purest DNA; no vocal cords and communicated totally with their minds. The mess he'd made of Latitia would be a simple fix for them, but they weren't so easy to call long distance over the phone. His Aunt Isla, married to Darres, was his best bet.

She picked up after three rings and he finally breathed, not realizing he'd been holding it.

'Good morning, nephew,' she said in her usual soft voice. 'You caught me. I was just returning to Murrtaine.'

He could picture that so easily. Her on the edge of the fountain, in his father's beautiful hideaway retreat of Filfla, just off the island of Malta. His chest hurt with longing to be there.

'Is everything OK?' Isla asked, when he hadn't spoken for a beat.

Then it all came out. 'I've done something really stupid. I panicked.' He laid out the whole sorry story for her. How much he realized he must have liked Latitia to reveal who he was, but that she hadn't reacted well, which had made him hide her memory of him instead of scrubbing it and how he longed to go back in time and handle it differently, but he couldn't. 'She couldn't accept me,' he said, almost choking up.

Isla listened to it all in her quiet, understated way. 'I just don't know what to do, Isla, to put it right.' He slid down a wall to sit on his haunches when a caretaker walked by.

Isla sighed. 'You know, the deeper feelings go, the harder and more unpleasant it is for the subject when you take them,' she scolded.

JJ did know that, but all he'd wanted to do was to take the look of horror from Latitia's face. He couldn't feel any more wretched than he did right then. 'What can I do?' he said in misery.

'You say you hid them rather than take them completely,

JJ? Because what you've done is dangerous and a grave viola-tion. They aren't yours to take.'

He was pulling at the roots of his hair, his face burning red as the strain of it all wracked his body. 'Yes, they're hidden,' he said, quickly, before his emotion came out in a tidal wave and a single sob escaped him. He guessed, deep down, he'd hoped he wouldn't need to hide them for ever.

She remained quiet, letting him get a hold on his emotions. She was a gentle soul but with a core of steel. His father had always said never to let her gentleness fool you. She was the most ruthless of all his mother's sisters. He'd told him she'd once been a government assassin. It blew his mind when he thought of the gentle, unassuming woman. 'Then you have only two choices. You must restore her memories and live with the consequences or get out of her life completely. Only then will the damage be limited and she be able to heal.'

It was the answer he already knew. He guessed he hoped she would say something different because both options seemed impossible to him. 'Or what will happen?' he asked, closing his eyes, dreading the answer.

'Latitia's mind will crack and split with the strain. If you continue to stay in her life, the strongest memories will break through, possibly causing lasting damage and she will hate you for what you've done.'

It was what he expected her to say. He nodded, emotion-ally exhausted. 'Thank you, Isla.'

'I have to tell you, I'm disappointed in you, JJ. That you would treat a human girl so poorly.'

He closed his eyes and nodded again. She was right. He knew what he had to do. 'Bye Isla.'

'One more thing, JJ.'

He waited.

'If you choose to restore her, and she doesn't handle it

well and it threatens the race, she will be brought in for conditioning.'

JJ understood. It rarely happened. Most humans had no idea of their existence. And those that did were in the highest levels of government and the absolute last thing they wanted was knowledge of an alien race getting out into the general population. So it suited them to keep their secret. Atlanteans mostly kept separate. In this situation, her mind would be wiped, professionally, and he would never see her again. But that just wasn't an option here, without going to his father, and ultimately the king, admitting the whole sorry mess and his failure. So if relocation wasn't an option and if Latitita couldn't keep a secret, then there was nothing left to do but silence her once and for all.

He didn't know what terrified him more: that the result would be permanent, or that it would be done in a lab by a Murr. Either scenario scared the life out of him.

'I love you, JJ,' his aunt said. 'I know you'll do the right thing.'

He ended the call with a heavy heart, but grateful that she'd given it to him straight. He knew she would keep his confidence and be there if he needed her. He got up slowly with lead feet and walked back into the main building, churning it over in his now aching head. Latitia on one side and what he and Xavier were trying to achieve on the other. *Wasn't it to decide who would be king? Which one of them had it in them? Who was the one with the strongest will?* Right then, it felt like Xavier was winning hands down.

He remembered his second father, Dante, the current king. How the Fates had favoured him and yet he never followed the rules. He'd had the gumption to follow his own beliefs, despite how crazy they sometimes seemed. In the end he overcame all the obstacles, all his enemies and gained the love and respect of his people.

He could do that. He could totally do that.

With every step in the direction of the school office, he became stronger with renewed purpose. He couldn't restore Latitia's memories and he couldn't leave. So still preoccupied with his revelation, he spoke to the school secretary and removed himself from all of Latitia's classes. Today she'd be left with a slight headache, but it was done and he prayed it was enough. Now he must see to it that he and Latitia never crossed paths.

CHAPTER 28

lexia went from class to class, often sitting alone or with someone she never usually spoke to. The subjects went over her head, the teachers' voices a constant drone. There was no sign of her brothers. They weren't at school and the flat seemed like a quiet and lonely place, which was ridiculous considering it was always full of people. Her one ally, Latitia, was a changed person and had refused to get up that morning and didn't even care if she was late for school. She was normally so alive and bubbly. And Dwayne, the one that hurt the most of all, had left for school early. He was no longer interested in her and barely spoke, and if he did all he could talk about was DJing and beating Trick, Trick's music and *more bloody Trick*. Then, at lunch, she even recklessly dropped hints of memories that only pertained to her, like the time they went to the noodle bar, and got no reaction at all. She guessed Xavier's mind wipe had been more effective than JJ's, probably because he'd just added suggestion and trigger associations, rather than wiping it all. Judging by how quickly Dwayne tried to get out of her presence, he'd just linked her with something unpleasant. She'd kill Xavier when she found out what that was.

Even in Chemistry, when they were forced to be lab partners, he sat as far away on the bench as possible to her. 'I don't see you at all these days,' she whispered, almost crying.

'Busy, you know,' Dwayne said, not even able to look at her.

It was always the same excuse, over and over. She was sick of it. 'Don't you miss doing stuff together? Remember the school party?' It had been the best night of her life and been the last night they'd spent any real time together.

She soon wished she'd never mentioned it. His face clouded and he began to look angry. 'Yeah, well, I have to concentrate on my career if I want to get somewhere. No offence, but I can't waste my time on girls who want to know where I am every second of the day. You need to live a little.'

Aaaand there it was. Clingy? How dare he. The axe blow to her heart shrivelled it down to fury and she narrowed her eyes. 'Offence taken.' She had to remind herself she was talking to Xavier through Dwayne's lips. It was clear he'd filled Dwayne's head with ideas of stardom and beating Trick to be king-pin and that she was the thing holding him back. It was clever as it allowed her to be around him. It didn't affect Dwayne badly, it only served to compound his repulsion of her. She never thought she'd say it, but he'd been a whole lot cleverer than JJ in that regard. JJ and Latitia were in tatters and so were she and Dwayne. Only Xavier was free to swan about without a care in the world. She had to hand it to him.

The school day finally limped to an end and she loitered at the school gate for Latitia. Kids burst out of every doorway in every direction in their rush to get out of school. Some huddled in lively groups of chatter and others cut a purposeful path through the hordes to an after-school appointment or simply for the gate to get home. Wherever they were heading, they all shared one thing: a place to be.

She spotted Latitia walking towards her, oblivious to the lively conversation her friends were having around her. Dwayne bashed out of the doors just behind her, his long strides catching up with her quickly. He said something to her, then Richie joined him and together they went out through the gate, neither bothering to acknowledge Alexia. To compound the kick in the teeth, one of Latitia's friends remarked, 'Your brothers are so fit, Latitia.'

'Yeah … and talented,' said another.

Alexia couldn't bring herself to say anything at all and simply walked in step with Latitia and her friends as they passed her for the short walk home. The only good thing was that Latitia seemed a little better – at least she began chatting with the other girls. 'I heard your brothers and Trick are playing at the same club now,' one of her friends said.

'Yeah, at that Rhythm and Booze place,' said another.

Alexia's ears pricked up. Everyone knew, which meant everyone would go. Latitia replied with a shrug, 'It's all they do at the moment.'

Alexia watched with an empty feeling of detachment as they linked arms with Latitia in front of her, until, one by one, they all peeled off, to go to their separate homes.

They'd dwindled down to just the two of them and were almost home when Alexia spotted the same executive car that had taken them home from the club the other night. It was by her building with the engine running. Her heart sped up; more from anticipation than fear, which, even to her, seemed foolish. A stalker was hardly something to get excited about. *Or was that a sign of how sad her life had become?*

She decided to ignore it and went to turn with Latitia down the pathway to her block. Then, not sure what made her, she changed her mind and stopped dead. 'I'll be up in a minute.'

Latitia just shrugged and quickened her pace towards their building. Alexia watched her go in, sadly. She hadn't even noticed the car or was even curious to find out where she was going. She had changed so much.

Alexia sighed and turned back and retraced her steps towards the car. All the while telling herself that she was losing her mind. The nearer she got, the more scared she became. Her blood was tingling in her veins and her hackles were rising – and not in a good way. It felt like she was being lured by something she couldn't resist and yet a little voice on her shoulder was warning her to run. It was the sixth sense you got when you knew something was lying in wait.

Alexia hoped it was just the driver when she saw his bright smile through the half-opened window. However her heart hammered when he got out and opened the back door for her to get in. 'We've been waiting. I have someone who wants to meet you.'

She slowed to a halt, unsure what she'd find. The car was dark inside. A wonderful smell of musky cologne permeated from it and warmth brushed her skin as if she was next to a fire. She looked back at her building and actually thought about running, but something made her legs heavy and refuse to move.

'Please, Alexia. No harm will come to you, I promise,' the driver said with a smile.

He'd used her name in the way it should be pronounced, which she was sure she'd never told him, and he had spoken in an accent she recognized. She walked haltingly forward, ducking her head to get inside. It took enormous strain to ignore her instinct to run, but, at the same time, every muscle in her body felt out of control, like there was no way she wasn't getting in that car. The feeling was bizarre. In the end, she just had to tell herself that if they were going to hurt her or kidnap her, they could have done it the other night. The alternative was another lonely night in front of the TV, doing homework that she'd covered ages ago.

She held her breath and got inside in one quick move. Then, before she had time for her eyes to focus in the poor light, the door was closed, the driver was in the driver's seat and the car pulled smoothly away.

A tall man was in the back seat with her. At least she first thought he was a man. The prickle that travelled up her spine making her heart thrash, made her amend that thought to male.

He was Atlantean and a powerful one, but like no other she'd ever seen.

There were just five pure families in the Atlantean nation that could be traced back to Atlantis. There were the Dubonnetti, of which her father belonged, the underwater branch of Borge that lived in Murrtaine and the Santalini soldier vampires like Keenan. That left just the Bonaci, her grandfather's line, and the mystical Florianna. And while this male's aura was probably the closest to the latter, he seemed like none of them, really.

He seemed to emanate power and yet sucked the light from the car. It was as though he was sick. His face was mostly hidden by a black Fedora hat, pulled low over his forehead, and, as if that wasn't enough, he had on strange black wraparound sunglasses. The little of his face left uncovered was deathly white. He wore a black trench coat with the lapels turned up to cover his neck, even though the heat was stifling and the weather unseasonably warm. She took a final visual sweep at the black slacks that rode up to reveal black socks in black leather shoes, where his legs were relaxed and crossed at the knee. She couldn't suppress the overwhelming feeling that he exuded danger and that he repelled the light, heat and all that was good. It was a ridiculous way to feel about a person she didn't know, but she couldn't help it. His clothes were black, his aura was black and he was undoubtedly the darkest soul she'd ever met.

He watched her, coolly, as the car eased into traffic. She noticed the inside of the windows were covered in a light-cancelling film – something she hadn't noticed the other night in the dark.

Then he spoke for the first time and his voice shocked her with its softness. It was the complete opposite to how he looked. 'Hello, Alexia,' he said, in a deeply accented voice that sounded Eastern European. 'Forgive the intrusion on your day but I have been wanting to meet with you.'

She watched his red lips move in stark contrast to the paleness of his face. From what she could see, his skin was clear, clean-shaven, with a straight nose and strong jawline. If he didn't look so much like he'd been drawn by a manga illustrator, she would think he was quite handsome. Without the get-up, of course, which made him look severe and harsh. Or maybe that was just how he projected. Even his manicured aristocratic hands and long white fingers were curiously inked with small black symbols right down to the edge of the nailbeds. A golden eagle on a large black ring adorned the pinky finger of his left hand. She had to admit, he was utterly fascinating, even though he was downright terrifying at the same time.

'You're Atlantean,' came out before she could stop herself. She hated coming across as childlike when all she wanted to do was seem grown up and sophisticated.

'I am,' he said simply, in that calm and lulling voice she found hypnotic.

'Who are you?' He was no commoner; she was sure of that. 'I've never seen you at the king's court.' She was sure she would have remembered somebody as striking and powerful as him.

He tipped his head in a small bow. 'You are perceptive and correct. My name is Yaroslav Anatoly Demidov and it is a long and tiresome story that I will not bore you with right now. Let us suffice to say, there is a long and ancient reason why we have never met. As is often the case in Atlantean tradition, is it not?'

He made her feel all kinds of uncomfortable like he was avoiding telling her something important. She glanced out at the shops drifting by and thought how overcast and stormy the world looked because of the tinted windows. 'I thought we were the only ones here,' she said, quickly, trying to salvage the conversation. Commoners were everywhere, she knew. Her father had once explained that there were many with such watered-down genes that they didn't even know what they were. But when she peeked across at the male watching her, she doubted his genes were watered down much at all. He had that eerie stillness the underwater Borge family had and yet the slow red slash of a smile put her in mind of blood and made her think of the Santalinis. 'What family are you from?'

His smile thinned, proving she was right. He was avoiding something. Although it was hard to tell with the dark glasses and everything being so covered up. Then he completely shocked her by saying the absolute last thing she expected him to say.

'I promise to tell you anything you want to know if you agree to let me take you to dinner.'

Suddenly the heat in the car was unbearable. She didn't know how he stood it in his huge coat. For a moment, her mind raced for an excuse. Dangerous stranger, unvetted by any of her family and all that. He seemed so much older than her for a start, and yet there was something youthful about his face. She sagged in defeat. It wasn't as if her diary was full. 'Do I get to see you without the Inspector Gadget outfit?'

He suddenly laughed loudly; a surprisingly deep and beautiful sound.

The driver looked at her in the rear-view mirror, as surprised by it as she was. She averted her eyes, quickly, feeling a weird sense of disloyalty, which was ludicrous. For all the male's obvious power, she sensed something fragile and breakable. It was the strangest feeling. JJ had always said she had the greatest gift out of all of them; being able to sense the heart of people. And the mystery guy wasn't unattractive. She was certainly intrigued enough to want to see what he looked like and maybe hear him laugh without all the garb.

Then, before she knew it, the car came to a stop. She went to get the door while she could, but his soft, lulling voice stopped her panic. 'We are back where we started, have no fear.'

She breathed easier when she recognised the graffiti on the Johnsons' building and a car that had been dumped and left. Then, while she was still processing that the meeting was over so quickly, the driver got out to open her door. She automatically put her hand on the door handle, but the driver appeared to be waiting. As if he was giving them privacy. When he didn't open it, she looked over her shoulder at the stranger again. He was holding something out to her, so she eased back into her seat.

She took the small plastic object from him. 'An old person's phone?' she said, wrinkling her nose.

He laughed again, long enough to distract her while he took her hand.

She hitched a breath because he caught it and held it firmly. His skin was soft but deathly cold, and his grip like iron. She'd never felt a touch like it. A shiver climbed her arm like an icy tentacle. Shocked. She couldn't read him. Not one little bit. She was forced to look into the blackness of his wraparounds and saw nothing there to help her.

His blackened, slightly yellowed nails threatened to break the skin like a bird's talons. He released his hold slightly. 'It's a burner phone containing just one number. No one can trace it and you can contact me on it any time, day or night, and I'll know it's you.'

It would seem really romantic if she wasn't still looking down at his ghostly hands and felt the uncomfortable shiver again. She might not be able to read him, but he was reading her. She'd put money on it. 'You make it sound like something bad might happen to me.' Her cheeks felt hot from more than the balmy temperature of the car. She knew now that he needed it because his body ran so cold.

'The world can be a very dangerous place for any girl, particularly a young princess.'

She looked at him suddenly at that. His aura pulsed purple and went back to black. It was so scary it made her almost recoil, but he stroked the inside of her wrist to calm her. And, strangely, it did; making her wonder what powers he was hiding. He was calming her, lulling, luring, attracting, all softly and unobtrusively with the simple back of an index finger. However she couldn't ignore that he knew exactly who she was and that was the most ominous thing of all. Being there was meant to be a closely guarded secret.

She was about to turn to get out of the car when he held out another object. It was a small black velvet box. 'My gift to you … For spending some time with me today.'

She took it gingerly, checking his expression. The little of it she could see seemed coy, almost embarrassed. 'But I've done nothing to deserve it,' she said, feeling equally awkward.

'Open it,' he said with a nudge, finally releasing her hand.

She checked his face again and stopped. A small smile was playing on his lips and prompted her to ask. 'Can I at least see your eyes?' Something told her they wouldn't be ordinary, like many in her race.

He bowed his head regally. 'Believe me, I would like nothing more. But, as you can see, I have a condition that afflicts me in the light. If you agree to see me after dark, then indeed, I will reveal myself to you.'

His accent and the softness of his voice gave her butterflies in the pit of her stomach. His smile was full and took her breath for a moment. There, in the row of impossibly white teeth, were the prominent canines of the Santalini. She wanted to shout ah-hah! That she'd guessed his family, but then she thought about it. He might have the teeth of her Uncle Keenan, but he also had the build of the Borge and the power of the Florianna. He was no ordinary male. There was more to his story. More to him.

Then, before she could formulate another question, the door opened, as if her mystery man had willed it and the driver said, 'Goodbye, Your Highness.'

She got out stiffly, not sure whether she was ready to go or not. Before the driver could close the door behind her, she turned and stooped, suddenly needing to check he was real. 'The mysterious male seemed already absorbed by the darkness and her eyes blind from the light. 'Use the phone. You may call me Yaro. Until we meet again,' he said, pre-empting all her questions.

The driver gently pulled her away and closed the door. She stood and watched him walk all the way around the car to get in on the other side. He got in and the car slowly eased away. She was left dazed, wondering what the hell had just happened, when a blacked-out SUV pulled up in its place.

Dwayne and Richie got out, still laughing about something and slammed the doors. They put up a hand and the car screeched away, blaring thumping bass as it went. 'What are you doing standing out here?' Dwayne said, walking past her, laughing at an in-joke with Richie.

The normality of it shook her out of her thoughts and she walked back to their block behind them. She felt strange. Changed. Dwayne seemed an immature, annoying boy after her encounter. Nothing like the older, sophisticated male she'd just met. 'Just saying goodbye to a friend,' she said, thoughtfully, hiding his gifts from view.

CHAPTER 29

Xavier left school with Paige and JJ squashed in his car, with the top up because of the drizzle, thankfully dropping JJ off at the wharf on the way. His car choice was not feeling quite so inspired when he had to leave it unattended on Paige's estate.

He approached a group of youngsters congregating on the street corner and offered them a tenner to watch it. After handing over a twenty, they agreed and sniggered as if he was soft. He resisted the urge to squish their doughy little minds.

Paige was calling him away, looking nervous. However, they did stay near his car when he kept an eye on them as he walked along the balcony to Paige's front door.

'Oh, bloody hell!' her mum's voice said from the kitchen just as they got inside. 'I forgot the milk. I knew there was something.'

'We can go,' Paige called out.

Xavier pounced on the opportunity. He caught her wrist and said quietly, 'You go. I'll talk to your mother.'

She nodded after holding his gaze with a meaningful look. 'OK,' she mouthed.

He gave her a fiver and she went straight out of the door.

Xavier gathered himself together and followed the clattering sounds to the kitchen, where he found Paige's mum, Linda, unpacking groceries.

One of the little ones threw himself into his legs, clearly delighted to see him. He found himself picking him up and tickling his stomach before realizing how out of character it was. He never took notice of kids as a rule. The younger little girl jumped up to be treated the same and he swung her up on his back, like a little monkey.

Paige's mum smiled at him and shook her head indulgently. She looked more tired than ever today.

'Why did you turn down the nanny?' Xavier said, adjusting the girl from her neck strangling grip.

Linda immediately stopped what she was doing and straightened up to look at him. It was exactly what he needed. He wasn't about to waste valuable time on pointless conversation. Paige would be back any minute. He quickly latched onto the edge of Linda's conscious mind and carefully ventured inside.

'I didn't want strangers in the house,' she said, squinting as if the light suddenly became too bright.

Xavier paused from racing through her neural pathways. She was speaking the truth, but it was tinged with shame. What she'd omitted to say was that she didn't want strangers seeing how they lived; how poor they were. It explained a lot and something that would have never occurred to him before. He continued on, but a little more slowly this time, looking for the avenues and switches he needed, while he considered alternatives. All the while, he talked to her softly. 'It only needs to be short term. And we're opening up a crèche at the school. You can use that when it opens and, in the meantime, maybe accept a babysitter. Possibly someone you already know. It's not as starchy as a nanny and more acceptable to you. I will text you a number if you don't have one. But it won't be Paige. Paige's life must take priority. Do you understand? Paige must be free to study.'

She frowned as if she knew something was not quite right with what was happening to her, but could not make out exactly what it was because the logic seemed sound.

Xavier tried to tone down his impatience because he now understood why, but he wouldn't be moved on this. This was for Paige. 'Please text me your weekly schedule and your bank details and I will set up an allowance to cover your childcare. Do you understand?'

His eyes bore into hers, dispelling any negative thoughts as soon as they arose, making it clear that it came from a place of concern and care for Paige. There was nothing she could do but acquiesce. The logic was watertight. She simply swallowed, nodded and rubbed the centre of her forehead. In the end, all she could do was nod and smile. 'Thank you. It's very kind.'

Xavier felt no shame in bending her will to his. He'd adjusted his plan and taken her feelings into account, so she should be grateful. Without knowing it, she was now connected to the most powerful family in the world and must accept the benefits that entailed. Humans were so intent on free will that they seldom understood what was good for them.

He felt her smoothly relax into his will and he eased from her mind, just as the front door clicked and opened in the hallway behind him. 'You'll be pleased to know that your mum and I have come to an agreement,' he said, smiling, as Paige entered the kitchen and put the milk straight in the fridge. He was genuinely surprised that they kind of had. He hadn't bulldozed through her feelings to assert what he wanted, which was his original plan. He was proud of himself.

He grinned at Linda, who was still blinking and trying to smile as if she wasn't completely sure what she'd just agreed to.

'That's great!' Paige said, flinging her arms around her mother's neck.

A warmth entered Xavier's chest that he'd never felt before. It was selfless joy. This was what someone got out of helping people. *Who knew?* 'Yes, your mum agreed to a crèche and a babysitter. It was the nanny thing she didn't like.' He looked back at her to back him up.

Linda just said, 'Mm,' and nodded like she was completely out of her depth.

Paige looked at him lovingly. 'I can't believe it. It's the nicest thing anyone's ever done for me … us,' she amended, hugging her mum again. 'It's amazing,' she said, making his heart swell again with the smouldering look she gave him. 'What changed your mind?' she said, looking at her mother curiously.

Xavier had a flash of nerves as he recognized that changing her mind was rare for her mother. He quickly prayed that his suggestions had taken. It was curiously evident that Paige's happiness was not solely dependent on what he did for her, but what he did for everyone she loved. He made a mental note to look into a way to improve her mother's situation, so she didn't have to work three soul-destroying jobs. Maybe one where she could be there for the kids and not have to leave them with anyone at all if she didn't want to.

'Xavier explained that you needed time to study and he could help; what with what an important year it is this year. I'm sorry, love. It just wasn't an option before with money tight and everything.'

Her mother hugged her tightly and Paige looked at him with awe from her mother's arms. 'That's so brilliant.' Her eyes seemed to glass over and for a moment he thought she would cry. The warm glow swelled in his chest. He never knew he could feel so good from making another person happy – scratch that, Paige happy. 'Are you stopping for tea?' she said, breaking away from her mother's arms.

He'd been in South London long enough to know that she meant supper and not the drink, so he shook his head. 'No, I have stuff to do, but I'll call you later, before you go to sleep.' He leaned forward and kissed her on the cheek.

Linda looked on a little bleary-eyed.

'Don't forget to let me know of anyone you know, otherwise I'll call you early in the morning with a sitter's name. She'll be here for eight o'clock.' Then he left with one last penetrating look.

JJ SAT down at the impressive bank of monitors he'd had installed in his part of the loft. Xavier was out, as planned, when he dialled into the video call scheduled with one of the tech experts his fathers had on permanent retainer. It hadn't been easy. He couldn't exactly go through the front door with guys like these. Not only because he didn't want his father to know, but these guys were ghosts. He'd had to go through several forums, text communications called relay chats and dropping key words in certain places that would act like a call sign to make them get in touch. Then eventually, when they'd checked out who he was, he was able to make real contact through a safe server somewhere in Northern California. Not that he would ever know who they really were. 'Chris!' JJ said when the handsome, tanned face filled his screen. He didn't exactly fit the geek cliché. *That was the life*: surfer by day, mysterious hacker by night. A lifestyle that totally appealed to him.

'Hey, JJ, how's it goin'?' Chris said in his lazy laid-back way that gave away nothing of the dangerous clandestine life he and his little band of tech warriors led. They were totally bad ass.

JJ had always wondered what they did for his fathers, exactly. Anything, he guessed. Social media. Election strategy. Re-routing money to offshore accounts. Absolutely anything a secret, powerful king would want to fly under the radar. 'I'm fine thanks, Chris. Thanks for getting up so early to speak to me. It means a lot.'

'No problem. Tell me what I can do for you?'

'Social media,' JJ said, watching the micro expression of confusion flash across Chris's brows. 'Not just any old social media. I want a platform designed from scratch. Just for us, down here in my area. It needs to generate money and it needs to start fast.'

A slow grin was spreading over Chris's face as he spoke, which was incredibly infectious.

'How long do I have?'

'As soon as you can. I'd like to be up and testing by Christmas.'

Chris let out a single blast of laughter that totally said he didn't want much, and bobbed his head. 'Can I bring on board my team?'

JJ hesitated. He would have liked Chris to have worked alone. They were less likely to get leaks to his fathers that way. 'I want it dark though, separate from my fathers. OK, Chris? I'm going lone wolf on this one.'

Chris tipped his head as if it was a given. He would understand. His father, Jay, had told him the story once of how a small group of hackers brought down a corporation, plummeting shares that rocked the world's financial markets in response to a pension scandal. It was the last in a string of daring Robin Hood-like hacks that inevitably led to their arrest. It was typical that his fathers saw an opportunity and rather than see them rotting in some American jail, he, alongside Dante, the king, had bartered with the authorities to release them onto their payroll. With the prospect of facing over a hundred years of jail time and realizing the scope and the funds available to them, Chris and his little band had jumped at the chance.

It was a masterstroke, on his fathers' part and wouldn't have come cheaply. Now the hackers worked for them and still kept their anonymity. Something JJ found exciting and fascinating and could only look up to with awe. They went by the name of Wolfpack and had a wolf's head as their logo. He had no idea if they had Atlantean blood. He didn't care. Everything about them was cool. With a simple click of their fingers, they could affect elections and even bring down governments, if they wanted. The average Joe was oblivious to every advert, every news item and story being completely tailored to their interests and views. Through something as simple as their news feed, anyone can affect opinion. People like these guys were the real influencers. So they could easily help him to bring in a revenue stream to help one small South London school.

'No problem. The guys do stuff like this for entertainment. I take it we're not just doing the usual teen, crap-chat type platform?'

That made JJ laugh. Then he laid it all out on the line. It did have to be kind of like that, but with a little extra. Something he could totally control. The kids of Camberwell had to feel it was theirs and yet exclusive. Like a society not everyone could join. A place where you felt at home, but where anyone who was anyone was on there. An 'it' place for keeping in touch, but for meeting people as well.

'Kind of a cool dating app for kids,' Chris said, following perfectly.

'Yeah,' JJ said, thoughtfully. 'But more. I want the algorithm designed to drive opinion, to sell products and drive aspirations. You name it and I want to control it.' It was a big ask for someone his age. But Chris took it all in as just another job.

'Meta-heaven it is, then,' Chris said, making them both laugh again.

JJ guessed it was kind of reinventing the wheel and maybe Chris might have been hoping for something a little more taxing. The difference was it was never in the hands of a seventeen-year-old boy before, let alone one with designs on south London domination.

'I get you,' Chris said, getting suddenly serious. 'Small scale that only you can control,' Chris repeated. 'But tell me, is Xavier in on this with you?'

It was a good question and no surprise that Chris was up to speed. They were together in most things, but it was an eye-opener that even in the furthest reaches of their father's kingdom, their people knew how things would have to go. That despite their closeness, they would be opponents one day. JJ smiled wanly and nodded. 'Don't worry. It's my baby but we're together on this.'

Chris didn't hide his obvious relief. He guessed no one had any idea whose side they'd ultimately have to come down on. 'And the king?'

JJ scratched his head and laughed a little nervously. 'Er, not so much.'

Chris laughed. 'Well, OK then. I'm on it. I'll have some ideas for you by the end of the week. That just leaves the name. Any idea what you want to call it?'

JJ had thought about that a lot. It couldn't point too much

to its origins. It had to be cool but at the same time blend in. 'I was thinking B2H.'

Chris nodded, looking genuinely impressed. 'Business To Human. Nice. Great tech term. I like it.'

'But with the logo having triple Xs in a row, with a line through the middle, above it—'

'Like a crown,' Chris finished for him cautiously, seeming unsure about the last part.

JJ wasn't surprised. ~~XXX~~ were the symbols for the elite or highest class of Atlanteans in the old language.

'Don't you think it's kind of an arrow pointed at your head?' Chris said.

JJ had thought of that, but there was also plausible deniability in that XXX could also mean the obvious, explicit, three kisses, or even just street slang for clean or a straight edge. 'I think we can take that chance.'

Neither of his fathers were going to like it, but after cheekily using his father's resources to get going, he'd soon be on his own. They were seventeen, which ruled out banks and they weren't about to go to the local crime lord for it. It wasn't ideal, but south London was just the start. This was his stake in the ground for the battle everyone knew was coming.

Chris drew in a deep breath as if he knew it too, and wasn't so sure of the shitstorm he'd be helping create. 'Well, OK then. If you're sure?'

JJ was. He really was.

Xavier had been busy too. Except his contact had been a cousin of the water-breathing Borge family. He figured why mess around with production when you could simply go for the best out there. The human world lagged far behind Atlanteans in this kind of thing.

Using his brother Roman as a go-between, he'd already ordered a trial batch of what he needed to be couriered from the underwater city of Murrtaine. Secrecy was paramount, so his father didn't get wind of what he'd be exporting. Now he strode purposely with Paige, who'd done as promised, and scheduled an after-school meeting with her Advanced Science Club. Her geekiness proved sexier by the day.

There were six students assembled, waiting for them in a cluster of high stools at one of the long wooden benches. The air smelled of gas and chemicals, not surprising with valves of burning Bunsen burners arranged every six feet or so. Their animated chatter died as soon as he followed Paige into the room. He felt as in place as a prize fighter at a tea party for old ladies.

Paige introduced him awkwardly, pausing at the word 'boy' before friend, to wide eyes; as if the group had just witnessed something truly outlandish. He guessed it was. Beautiful people like him rarely mixed with geeks unless they absolutely needed to. They generally had little need for anyone else. It made him feel a pang of sad detachment that he hadn't felt before.

He allowed Paige to speak for him, explaining that he had a proposition for them and making them laugh with some geeky in-joke about how they wouldn't be disturbed, as absolutely no one ever came anywhere near the science block.

When she finally nodded for him to take centre stage, he looked each of them in the face, one by one. There was one girl and five boys and they all looked younger than their years. If he passed them in the street, he'd assume they were about thirteen or fourteen, not in their last year of school. They had poor dress sense, hair that ruled itself and particularly bad skin. *What was it with nerds, spots and specs?* Four out of the six wore glasses. The group made Paige look like a cheerleader in comparison.

She did make brief introductions, but Xavier forgot their names as soon as she said them.

'What's he doing here?' Dark, curly-haired, spotty boy number one said.

Xavier would have spoken up if he hadn't been so affronted at the assumption that he must be thick, looking the way he did. Atlanteans almost always had both looks and intelligence. But hadn't he been guilty of doing the exact same thing? He relaxed a little and decided to play the one card they wouldn't be able to resist: flattery to their own vanity – *their brains.* 'I'm not sure if you know me yet from around school, but my name is Xavier. I haven't been here for that long. My brother and I are seeking to improve the school by making it self-funding.'

The group were looking at him as if he was a Martian speaking in a foreign language. He looked at Paige as if he'd said the wrong thing, then one of them spoke up.

'Won't that need initial capital?' A surprisingly well-spoken, scruffy, ginger boy said.

Xavier appreciated the intelligent question to kick off the conversation. He tipped his head at him. 'You're right. We will be supplying the initial funding.'

'How will it benefit us? Something like this almost always means a new gym or something showy to make the school popular.'

Xavier bobbed his head again. Athletes did always win out in these kinds of things. 'And, outwardly, that will still be the case. But if you don't mind not being in the forefront, I'm looking for a think tank of ministers, who could work behind the scenes to help me with more, shall we say, radical money-generating ideas.'

Bingo. Their eyes glinted with excitement as they looked

at each other to gauge they were thinking the same thing. Then the dark curly-haired one looked over at Paige hovering at the edge of the room, 'And you know and are OK with this?'

She stepped forward. 'Mostly. Yes. We're waiting for your ideas, but we want to begin with some clinical trials.'

There seemed to be a collective intake of breath as if it was the last thing they were expecting. 'What kind of clinical trials?' the girl with long, lank, mousy-brown hair said, looking a little appalled.

Xavier let them have it straight; both barrels. He hoped their analytical brains won out. 'First in human – or, more accurately, first in teenager.'

'Drugs,' Ginger said, flatly.

'Yes and no. One is an odourless, undetectable gas that relaxes and heightens the senses.'

'Like Entonox,' the height challenged Asian boy said.

Xavier pointed at him, 'Exactly, but this is something different. It's new to the world. We call it Breathe and it's harmless to humans.'

'If it's harmless, what do you need the clinical trials for?' Mousy girl said.

Xavier conceded a nod her way. It was a good question and one he was expecting from kids as sharp as this. He looked at Paige and she nodded a little to urge him on. The faith she showed him then, so clearly in her eyes, was the exact moment he fell for her completely. He knew he wanted her to always look at him like that. A look he'd never had in his whole life before. Not from his parents or any of his siblings and not even from any of his many cousins. Only her and he loved her for it. She knew without any shadow of doubt that what he was trying to do was for the good of the school. 'Word of mouth,' he said, facing back to his little gallery of faces. 'We will hand-pick the subjects most likely to want it.'

'The stoners,' Ginger said, dryly.

'The connoisseurs, yes,' Xavier said, nodding in his direction. 'They will be the ones to try it and they will tell their friends. When word gets around, more and more people will want it and we will be well on our way to funding bigger projects in the school.' When he finished, Paige's eyes shone with admiration. A look that he would keep with him for ever.

The rest of the kids looked at each other, a little in shock. They weren't as unworldly not to know just how close they'd be flying to the wind legally on this one, but they still couldn't hide their excitement at the possibilities of it. 'And we can study the effects?' the taller, Nigerian boy said.

'Of course. I insist on it.'

'And what about the other drug?' Dark and curly said.

Xavier paused to take a breath because he knew this one would be a little harder to pitch. 'That one is a little more serious. It's something called Focus and I suppose its nearest comparable drug would be Adderall.'

'An ADHD drug?' Dark and curly said, frowning and looking worried at Mouse, next to him.

Xavier wobbled for an instant, until Paige urged him to continue with her eyes. This was always going to be the sticking point. 'Only in that it can be used as a study drug. It actually comes from a type of seaweed and works by building connections between neurons, making the recipient more efficient in cognitive function, concentration and even building higher IQ.'

All their eyes widened at that, as they imagined how it could benefit an already sharp mind, like their own.

'So it's completely natural, then,' Ginger said. 'How does it affect a person physically?'

Xavier tipped his head at another very good question. 'That's what we're not so sure about and where an arm of your clinical trials should go. I suggest we take five small samples, of say, five groups. Starting with super boffiny like you, then athletic, midrange nondescript, introvert and maybe even popular underachiever.'

'Six, with a control group of some of each,' Ginger added.

Xavier grinned, knowing they were already onboard. 'Yes, exactly,' he said, pointing at him. Then he added the clincher. 'That includes yourselves,' he said, watching the doubt and indecision spreading over their faces, knowing they were absolutely dying to try it. 'You can't all be on the drug. Half must be part of the control group. As for the others, the whole bloody school is your control, but I'll leave that up to you.'

As he watched them turn and squabble between themselves, he knew he had them. The chance to study and be part of something that could possibly improve their superior brains was too much to say no to. He pulled Paige into his arms and she grinned into a kiss. 'Putty in your hands,' she whispered.

Xavier gazed intensely into her eyes, already imagining what he would do when he was alone with her, but he turned to face the heated debate before he got too carried away. 'So, are we clear on our objectives?' he said loudly over their chatter.

He caught the eye of the girl he now called Mouse. 'If you can guarantee it's not going to kill anyone, we're in,' she said, nodding.

Xavier smiled and nodded once in thanks. 'It's not going to kill anyone.' He picked up Paige's hand and led her towards the door, knowing that his work there was done. Their geeky, excited little minds were already talking trial arms and activities to test when they closed the door behind them.

He kissed Paige in a corridor that smelled remotely of farts because of some chemical or other. She melded straight into him as if she'd always been his. His mind whirred onto the shiny silver cylinders that could be sold discreetly for the Breathe gas and maybe capsules of the ground powder for Focus. He'd get straight onto his Murr supplier when he was alone. He smoothed back Paige's hair from her face and decided, wherever life took him, he would never let her go.

CHAPTER 30

*A*lexia wasn't really any happier after her encounter with Yaro. Even with their assignation still buzzing in her memory and his perfect gift of a golden fern pendant, tucked beneath the neckline of her clothes. Whatever JJ had done to Latitia had changed and infected their friendship and Dwayne and Richie now acted like she didn't exist. Valarie was polite, of course, but most of the time, if she wasn't working, she was exhausted. That left her completely alone. A social pariah.

The more time she had to mull it over, the more it came down to Xavier. *She* had been the happy one in the beginning. There was no escaping that Xavier had ruined it for her. Again.

Frustrated tears stained her face. She hated the flat, hated the area, hated the school and all the people in it. In short, she was miserable and hated her life.

Alexia looked at her watch. It was eight o'clock on a very dark evening. Perhaps the darkest of her life, figuratively speaking.

Valarie was bathing the two little ones, Latitia was in her room and Dwayne and Richie hadn't even come home.

It was the final straw. She jumped up from the sofa, grabbed her phone and keys and ordered an Uber. Then, without telling a soul where she was going, she stepped out into the crisp night air. She paced a few feet up and down until her Uber arrived.

She didn't see why Xavier got to breeze through life after doing this kind of thing, scot-free. *No.* This time, he was going to pay. She was winging it, but she was going to have it out with him once and for all and if he didn't show the right amount of remorse, she'd have nothing more to do with him. Someone had to stand up to him.

The fact that JJ was seldom squeaky clean in these things escaped her. She only had enough room for hatred of one brother at that moment. She soon got to the wharf, pressed all the buzzers so someone let her in and fumed all the way up in the lift.

The door was left ajar for her when she got there. *Of course* they would have sensed her coming. Even that fuelled her anger. Like she would actually want to pay a social call. Then there was the massive step up in accommodation. That was rocket fuel. *No more bloody slumming it for them.*

Alexia did not see JJ as she marched in. Only Xavier, watching her smugly from the huge leather sofa placed strategically under the huge Pollock print she knew and recognized. As the lump wedged itself firmly in her throat, Xavier held his arms open wide. 'Welcome, Sis … you like?'

The world dropped an octave as her last nerve broke. 'No, I don't bloody like. In fact, I frickin' hate! How dare you meddle in my personal life and then leave me all alone without a care of how I'm feeling. Every place we've ever gone, it's the same old story. Well, I'm sick of it. Sick of it!'

she screamed, catching him twice with her fists in his face before he could stand up and grab them.

She struggled and wailed as Xavier shouted at her to quit. Then a second pair of hands touched her gently on her shoulders and JJ's voice went to her mind like a soft caress. *Calm down, Lexie. Surely it can't be that bad?* She hadn't realized he was home.

She continued to scream, 'I hate you!' at Xavier until her voice cracked and he shoved her away with a final 'Get off!'

Then she was turned and her nose buried in the soft fibres of JJ's sweater, swathing her in the familiar smell she associated with home, childhood and safety. It calmed her instantly.

'All this over a stupid boy? A boy that didn't need much persuading, I might add,' Xavier said angrily, now that his initial shock had subsided.

'Go easy,' JJ's voice rumbled from beneath her cheek. 'Imagine how you'd feel.'

'No, I won't,' Xavier snapped. 'She needs to understand her station and that she can't throw herself away on some low-life hoodlum who will never be able to take care of her and will never be worthy of her in a million years.'

Xavier's anger only served to recharge her own. Her temper rose and she turned to face him like a spitting Cobra. 'How dare you? It's not up to you who I see.' Her voice shocked her how low it sounded. She didn't sound anything like herself. As if she'd changed into a different person. 'I can date Genghis Bloody Khan if I want to. You're not my bloody king.'

Then Xavier stepped into her face, making her hitch a breath at the sudden ferociousness of it. 'Oh, but I can. In this world where our father saw fit to dump us, I am king and don't you forget it.'

Alexia was so shocked at his statement that she turned to look at JJ. He was staring at his brother as shocked as she was. Then he said just one word: 'Stop!' It wasn't shouted or even demanded, just said flatly, but somehow held all the threat and venom that was required.

She looked back at Xavier, who'd registered the same thing and seemed to gather himself. It was as though she was witnessing something huge, like something was changing between them and, despite her anger before, she didn't like it.

'No, I won't bloody stop,' Xavier said, renewing his momentum. 'My whole life, it's been you two ganging up on me. Well, I won't have it. Not anymore.' He reached out and grabbed Alexia's chin, painfully. 'You think I was alone when I had my little mind walk with our local boy, Dwayne?'

'Xav!' JJ warned.

It was said so suddenly and so fearfully that Alexia took her eyes off Xavier for a moment to look at JJ. The expression on his face was like nothing she'd ever seen on him before. Panic. He was literally imploring Xavier not to go on. But, of course, it was Xavier, so he did and dropped the bomb on the last vestige of brotherly respect she had left in her. For the brothers she'd followed blindly, worshipped and adored, the blinkers were ripped off, but instead of allowing her to see, the light scalded her eyes and blinded her to reason. A noose wrapped itself around her neck and tightened as she said the words, 'Well go on, Xav, you know you want to.'

Xavier roughly pushed her away.

JJ narrowed his eyes in an unsaid dare. *Correction*, he was threatening Xavier in his head.

Alexia's blood pressure rose to a thumping in her temples and her mouth felt sawdust dry. 'Why don't you just say what you're dying to say?'

'Don't!' JJ said, with an earnest plea on his face that hit her in the gut and settled like a medicine ball.

A weight of dread pulled her heart downwards into her bowel and she was already shaking her head, no longer wanting to hear what she knew Xavier would say.

'It was straight after the dance,' Xavier went on, reflectively. As if he was trying to get the order of memories straight in his head. 'The Johnson brothers were in their bunks, plotting on how to get back at Trick. JJ and I just gave them the push they needed to do it and, we both decided, it wasn't a safe place for you.'

And there it was. The wretched, caught-out, guilty as hell look on JJ's face. In that one moment, everything she thought she knew, her whole belief system in her family, fell away to leave a smouldering pile of ashes.

She'd never had much security as a kid, with her mother not exactly stable with either of her fathers, but she'd always had her brothers – particularly JJ. He had been the constant in her life. 'How could you?' she whispered, barely able to get the words out, her throat was so closed up.

You have to listen to the context, JJ said in her head. He turned his murderous look on Xavier and they were quickly locked in a psychic argument that didn't include her.

Typical. Even then, they excluded her.

Acid filled the cavity where her stomach should be and she headed for the door. She had no idea where she was going. Anywhere from there.

Not home.

Not the Johnsons.

'Come back,' Xavier called, with mock contrition. 'We did it for you. We really did. Don't you understand, Alexia?'

When she didn't turn around and a great blackness settled around her heart, his final words were not so diplomatic. 'One of us will be your king, Alexia.'

'Not mine,' she said, under her breath. Then, as soon as she breathed again in the lift, she pulled the card out of her pocket.

CHAPTER 31

*J*J was left staring at Xavier, aghast. He couldn't believe he'd just cut off the only line of communication with their sister out of spite. 'Who will keep an eye on her now?' he said, nonplussed. *How would he keep tabs on Latitia?* He really would have punched the 'what have I done?' look right off Xavier's face if he wasn't so completely left-fielded.

Xavier was already struggling to smooth over the fact that his big mouth had run away with him. 'She'll be OK. Give her some time. She'll come around.'

JJ shook his head. 'I seriously doubt that.' All the while, he was searching his brother's face for any semblance of the boy he'd loved and grown up with and saw only a stranger. He rubbed his head wearily. 'What has happened to us all?'

Instead of being sorry, Xavier's face darkened and he walked away in disgust. 'We grew up, JJ. We just grew up.'

ALEXIA HAD WALKED in the drizzle for what felt like hours after she'd left Xavier and JJ at the wharf. Finally, after cold began to seep through to her bones, she took out the small old-fashioned phone Yaro had given her. It had taken her so long because it was such a monumental decision. To ring the number on the card was to ask for a lift, but to use his phone was to change her life. She instinctively knew it. It was a precipice jump, because despite Yaro's promises, there would definitely be strings and he was still a stranger. Albeit an intriguing, terrifying one.

She didn't know why she was so surprised when it was his voice that answered immediately. 'Alexia?' his heavily accented voice said immediately. 'Is everything alright with you?'

It took her a moment to breathe and then cough to answer. Then, despite her best efforts to hold it in, a sob escaped her and the whole sorry mess came out with her tears. 'No … I'm not alright, Yaro. I'm not alright at all.'

His voice changed and became stern. 'Stay exactly where you are. My car will come for you.'

She looked around her, blinking back her tears. 'But I don't know where I am,' she said, wailing again. She had stomped off in her anger and then wandered in misery and hadn't taken notice of where she was going.

'Do not worry,' he said, sounding completely unperturbed. 'We can track your phone. Simply text me.'

She sniffed back the tears and the first, distant alarm bells. 'OK. Thank you so much.'

'It's OK. Everything will be fine; you do not need to worry about anything. I will look after you now.'

She felt immediate relief that she'd finally called him; he'd played on her mind for days. And it did solve her immediate problems. But she was a bright girl, despite what her brothers thought of her. She felt uneasy. He was a powerful male who'd probably been alive a long time and he was interested in a girl like her. Even she knew that didn't add up.

Maybe she'd given in to him a little too easily. Perhaps she'd relinquished too much control. It was those disturbing thoughts that prickled the back of her mind until the car pulled up next to her. Then the butterflies at seeing him again completely blew them away.

The driver came round the car and opened the door for her. The drizzle had turned to rain. For a moment, she paused and looked behind her at the shiny streets reflecting the lights from the shop fronts. For a split second, she considered running back. To her old life, her childhood, her brothers … but it was only fleeting. Too much had happened for that.

'Miss?' the driver said, to hurry her along.

She looked up into the handsome, clearly Atlantean face. 'Sorry.' She got in. The car was empty this time, but Yaro was there in the balmy warmth and aroma of Eastern spices, she'd begun to associate with him. It calmed her instantly and made her relax into her seat. 'OK, miss?' the driver asked from his seat.

Alexia nodded, heart pounding. 'Where are we going?' she asked in sudden panic.

'Prince Demidov has requested I bring you to his private residence, Your Highness.'

Prince. She swallowed. *There was nothing to fear. So, he was royal. Big deal. Everything was exactly what he said over the phone.* She tried to breathe and slow her heart. Staring out of the tinted window, she could barely see the lights anymore. They were shrinking away and she prayed to the five moons and whatever deity was out there that she'd made the right decision. Then she snapped herself out of it. Her mother should be proud. She'd become her own woman; she was branching out on her own.

· · ·

ALEXIA'S MIND went from terror to excitement throughout the journey to Yaro's. It felt achingly long. She tried to figure out where she was going, but it was hopeless. The most she could work out was they'd gone west, as they hadn't crossed the river until the streets became greener and lined with trees and the houses much larger. 'What's he like?' she said to the driver, instantly feeling silly. He wasn't exactly going to reveal he was an ogre.

The driver smiled at her in the rear-view mirror. 'Have no fear, Your Highness. He is a great prince.'

She smiled back at him; her mind not put at rest at all. She still wasn't entirely sure whether he was a genuine prince in the Atlantean sense, or if it was an alias or simply that his character put him above the humans he managed. She had no way of knowing. It only added weight to the already niggling voice at the back of her mind that told her she didn't really know him.

At last, they pulled into a treelined street of huge manses, each one different and more imposing than the last, to a pair of impressive-looking wrought-iron gates. She wasn't that worldly wise, but even she knew a house this size, located in the capital, had to belong to someone super-rich. Real nerves began to disperse her butterflies. She was beginning to see Yaro was more powerful than she could have ever imagined.

The gates opened slowly and the car glided onto a shingle driveway. The house loomed through the trees, made of red brick, with huge chimneys and diamond-shaped lead in the windows. It was obviously Tudor and not the mock kind. It seemed to go on forever. Tiny lights lined the drive, illuminating the imposing building like a fairy tale and the large, manicured gardens with perfectly maintained topiaries.

The car swung around a wide circular fountain with a crunch and came to a stop in front of a large overhanging porch with two tall lanterns on either side. It gave a friendly glow to a house that appeared to be in complete darkness. 'We're here, miss,' the driver said.

Part of Alexia couldn't wait to get out of the car and another was dreading what she'd find inside. However, she had no choice when the driver opened the door for her and the huge door to the house opened wide. A lone dark figure stood behind the light of the lanterns, making it impossible to see his face.

'The butler will show you in, miss,' the driver said, answering her question but making her long to cling to him a bit longer.

'Sorry, thank you. I don't even know your name.'

'Anton,' he said, with a friendly smile, showing neat square teeth. He nodded once and got back into his car.

She was left feeling cold and alone. The wind whipped around her still-damp clothes and she was forced to face the dark figure of the butler or die of exposure. 'This way, Your Highness,' the butler said with a bow.

It was a shock that he knew who she was. Her father had many staff, but he always insisted that they were never as formal as this. She put her first foot onto the red-tiled step and slowly entered the house, hesitating on the threshold.

The butler noticed and turned. 'You may enter. All privileges have been extended to you.'

It was a really peculiar thing to say, but she put it down to cultural differences and the traditions of an ancient family. *That must be it,* she reassured her clanging alarm bells going off all over the place.

The hall was wood-panelled as she would have imagined, and the red tile became chequered with black in an intricate design. It swept your eye up to the grand staircase and huge painting midway of a fierce-looking knight on a foaming black horse. The banisters were richly carved and swept up in two directions either side of it. The walls were a deep red but the lighting was low as if lit by candles alone.

The light was kind of cosy, if not a little creepy. No wonder you couldn't see in from outside.

Eventually, they came to a halt in front of a door that the butler pushed wide open. 'The prince will be with you short-ly,' he said.

Her eyebrows rose at the confirmation of his status. She was learning more about Yaro by the minute, but she smiled and walked in, taking in more of the opulence of the house. He was obviously a collector of expensive and beautiful things.

The theme of candlelight continued into the room of rich reds and russets. The walls were covered in red flock, golden paintings and lined with cabinets of collectables and glass-ware. A rich rug swallowed her feet as she inched towards the red sofas, facing each other next to the open mouth of a fire. It blazed like a furnace, already warming her face and hands, until she felt an icy draught behind her.

'Welcome, Alexia.'

CHAPTER 32

The familiar voice was sudden and came from right behind her. It made her jump and put her hands to her chest.

'Please don't turn and look at me yet.'

At first her Atlantean senses were overwhelmed, firing off all at once at his proximity. No one had ever crept up on her like that before. It was either the speed of his arrival, or he'd cloaked himself in some way. All Atlanteans sensed each other, but she was gifted, even with humans. Then, as the feelings subsided, she became excited at finally meeting her rescuer, tinged with a little apprehension when he seemed so reluctant for her to see him.

Alexia had relived their meeting in his car a hundred times, until he'd become a hero from a romance novel. His red lips and pale skin that needed to be shielded from the light. The tattoos on his long fingers, hinting at Atlantean royalty. Everything about him was so exciting. *How bad could he be?* 'Thank you for coming to my rescue tonight,' she said in a cracked voice.

'It is my pleasure to assist, just as I promised,' he said, sounding more Russian than ever.

Her heart was pumping hard in her chest. 'Why don't you want me to see you?' she said, trying to turn her head, but he was just out of sight. Deliberately.

'Because I'm not your conventional man, or even Atlantean,' he said.

Alexia frowned, finding it hard put to think of a single conventional Atlantean. They were all so extraordinary in their own way. But instinct prickled the hairs on the back of her neck that he wasn't joking around and so she humoured him. 'So does that mean you're going to stand behind me for ever?' she said, laughing lightly.

'I only ask that you bear with me and trust me for a while.'

She swallowed, wondering what difference a delay made. 'OK,' she said, when she realized he was waiting for permission for something. Her chest tightened at what the hell it could be.

Alexia hitched her breath as soft black silk came down over her eyes and was tightened behind her head. She breathed a little easier when it wasn't total blackout. The light from the fire and small candles around the walls were still easily visible.

A dark figure loomed, towering a head and shoulders taller in front of her. It was him, merely touching distance away. The instinct to pull away the blindfold was almost irresistible. 'Are we playing a game?' she said, a little disappointed. 'I thought we were going to meet properly.'

Then the wonderful aroma she recalled from their first meeting began to reach her. It was so heady she couldn't get enough, breathing in deeply. She'd never smelled anything like it.

Alexia hadn't even realized she'd swayed, but he seemed to catch her and lower her down into a seat behind her.

'That's it. Just relax,' his voice said, softly, next to her cheek. Even his breath smelled divine, but it felt cold, like a draught in winter. 'The blindfold is simply to show you what it is to be me. What I see in the light.'

Sudden understanding sent her into freefall. He was demonstrating his lack of sight. She got it, but she was reeling as if she was drunk.

'Only in the light,' he reiterated, 'strangely.'

It shocked her into silence. So this was what he saw all of the time. 'You're blind,' she said, sadly. Finally understanding what he was trying to say. 'But surely seeing you won't scare me all that much?' But her words came out breathily, as she was already anticipating the worst. The extent of his illness was beginning to sink in.

However, as her thoughts all clicked into place, something intangible felt like it was winding itself around her. Soft, like a feather boa, barely there and yet making her want to open herself up to caress it. Along with the luxurious cologne and his gentle voice, she felt the most relaxed in a long while. 'If you're an Atlantean, surely you can't be that different to others?' she said, bringing her knees up under her chin and snuggling up in a ball. 'I mean, is it just you, or is everyone like you in your family?' She felt so comfortable, as if she was in a warm bath.

Somewhere at the back of her mind, she knew how she was feeling was out of place and some external force must be making her feel that way. But it was simply too strong to fight and, frankly, like stopping a good massage, she wasn't sure she wanted to.

'You are very astute, as I knew you would be. Traits very often occur in families,' Yaro's soft, melodious voice replied. Even that seemed to make her inwardly sigh.

'Let me see you,' she whined. 'You can see, I'm not scared of you now.'

She heard his light chuckle – the one that livened her butterflies.

'Remember, I can barely see you either. In order for me to see you perfectly, I must dowse the lights.'

The sudden grasp of what he was saying pulled her from her stupor. 'Night vision,' she whispered. Realizing he wasn't blind at all.

As if he willed it, her world plunged into darkness. The fine silk over her face now made her sweat as it captured her breath and stifled her. Just as she was about to panic, his presence was in front of her. She felt it in a rush of cool air and the blindfold loosened until it fell from her eyes.

She blinked and saw him for the first time.

As an Atlantean, her vision was good at night, but he was beautiful.

He was so much, she couldn't take him all in. His aura was what captured her attention at first. It shone brightly in a white, yellow and orange starburst, like angels' feathers. Lighting him in a halo against the darkness.

It almost blinded her.

Then, gradually, as her eyes adjusted, she could see his hair was black and curled gently to the collar of his white shirt. His skin didn't seem that pale now in contrast to the light that surrounded him, but it was threaded with delicate blue veins on his forehead and under his eyes. Eyes that were deep carmine and dilated with pupils that seemed to narrow and open like a camera, adjusting to the light.

He was tall, as she expected, but not stooped or deformed. In fact, he was well proportioned, even athletic in build. The thought suddenly struck her that he wasn't ugly at all. 'You're an angel,' she said, before she could stop herself.

He laughed. 'Hardly,' he said, tilting his head regretfully.

'I mean, beautiful like one.' It all made perfect sense then. Someone as iridescent as him couldn't function in the human world at all in the open, and so he had to hide himself away. During the day, anyway. 'I understand now. But why were you worried about me seeing you?'

Then suddenly, just as all the wonder came, the lights returned and everything dimmed to mute. The contrast was staggering. Her eyes took a moment to adjust as if she'd been looking at the sun and couldn't get its image out of her eyes.

A dark figure began to materialize in front of her. The whiteness of his shirt seemed grey, tucked into his black, well-tailored pants but there was nothing diminished about him. Now with the light gone, she understood why he hid with a deep feeling of dread. His visage was fearsome and harsh. His black hair contrasted with his blue-veined face and looked severe and cruel and, the worst of all, his eyes were a deep ruby red. 'Because we live in a world of light, and this is how it sees my kind.'

Alexia took a moment to take him all in. Strangely, she wasn't repulsed. It was simply that he was two people. Twins in the same person. One light and one dark and not the way round you'd think. In the dark he was an angel, with a glorious aura that was so dense it sucked all the light from around him. Then, in the light, when you'd expect to feel relieved, he became this demon of death with eyes that pierced you through the heart. He was right. This was the version of him she found the scariest.

He was slim and well dressed, but his eyes, though unseeing, remained fixed on her with a predator's focus, reading her reaction and whether she would run. He was the real live Dracula, in the flesh. She found herself skating her eyes down his taut body, right down his excellently tailored legs and shiny dress shoes.

When she finally made her way back to his face, he

looked puzzled. 'Well you're different, I'll give you that, but you don't scare me.' That wasn't strictly true, however, she was more afraid of the sheer power he held in that super-fit body of his. 'So when the light is on, you're blind?'

'That is correct,' he said, looking at her.

She shifted a little to her left and his eyes followed her like an eagle. It sent shivers down her back. He might not be able to see, but his other senses were cut-throat sharp. He was terrifying.

'So turn them off again,' she said in a strangled whisper.

This time, before she could marvel that he turned them off with his mind, she was standing and he was right in front of her, breathing down her neck with his magnificent light all around him. He moved, shifting his red eyes fixated on her vein to track back to hers. 'You are the most beautiful Atlantean girl I have ever seen.' After he spoke, he breathed in deeply, making her shiver. His scent wound itself around her so she couldn't move if she wanted to.

Suddenly she realized just how vulnerable she was. A little mouse being toyed with by the most dangerous predator alive. She was forced to take huge breaths to calm herself down and the more she did it, the more his power took hold of her. 'My mother is a Siren,' she managed, breathily.

An icy finger trailed down the side of her cheek and he nodded slightly, still reminding her of a bird of prey, sizing up whether she was ready to eat. 'Only a great beauty could have borne such a rare jewel.'

This close, she could follow every threaded vein that crossed his brow. They seemed to emphasize his intense eyes that showed he meant every word. It wasn't empty flattery. It was then she became aware that he was holding her in his arms and she had no idea he'd moved. It took her breath and her eyes went wide in panic. He made no further move, but continued to look deeply into her eyes. 'Stunning,' he whispered.

She shivered under his touch. 'You're so cold.'

He passed an icy finger over her slightly parted lips. 'Atlanteans are colder than humans, Murrs are colder than Atlanteans, Ambragio are colder still.' His words came out as steam on a frosty day.

Her fascination overtook her fear. He was ridiculously cold and it explained a lot. He was no blood-sucking vulture, he was simply from a different and rare blood line. Plus, he was completely beguiling.

Then, just as suddenly as he came, the lights returned and he stalked slowly away.

He turned back to face her, now brooding and dark again.

'Please, just tell me who you are,' she said, still reeling from how it felt to be held by him.

Now his eyes pierced her right through. Like he was a walking contradiction who warred within himself, whether he was good or bad and whether or not he wanted to eat her.

However, his expression changed to perplexed. Then amazed, even. 'And you really have no fear of me?' he said, tilting his head like a puzzled dog.

Alexia knew he was testing her and that one of the things that terrified her most about him was the scope of his power. So she decided to go with the truth. 'You scare me half to death, but …' She frowned when she realized exactly what it was. 'But it's more like when you approach a dangerous beast. One that could kill you in an instant, but you want to make contact because you know, deep down, it wants to make friends. As long as you make no sudden movements, it won't hurt you. I just know you won't hurt me. Does that make sense?'

His piercing gaze changed to one of wonder, of admiration even. As if no one had ever spoken to him like that. 'And you plan to stay in this house with me, all alone?' he said in amazement, sounding as if he was getting his facts completely straight in his head.

She thought about it for a moment. He was perfectly right of course; she just hadn't given it much thought at all before she came. There was no way she could go back. The Johnsons no longer trusted her, she was furious with her brothers and there was no way she'd go back home. 'Well, can I?'

His eyes widened in surprise and a single blast of laughter escaped him. He looked devilishly handsome then. The laughter creased the corners of his eyes and transformed his face and she caught a glimpse of sharp teeth. Then he seemed startled, as if he knew.

She straightened too and her heart plummeted. 'You can read thoughts,' she accused with narrowed eyes.

His red lips curled into a small smile, neither admitting nor denying it. 'A skill not unknown for many,' he said with a non-committal shrug.

'Well stop it, if I'm going to live here.'

His eyebrows rose but then he frowned, and for a moment she thought she'd gone too far and angered him.

Instead, he pulled his feet together, bowed dramatically and then straightened. 'I will certainly try.'

With the stirrings of something she didn't fully understand in her chest, Alexia couldn't help but stare at him. Such a powerful male, used to getting his own way in all things, was genuinely trying to please her. No one had ever done that before. It was the biggest compliment, better than diamonds or clothes. She swallowed down a painful lump.

He saved her by coughing and pointing at the chair she'd left, behind her. 'I will order some tea and explain who I am.'

She nodded gratefully and sat, glad of the distraction and eager to learn of his ancestors. He sat opposite, leg crossed at the knee, and regarded her closely.

Thankfully, the silence was broken by the butler bringing in the tea. He poured and she settled back in her seat and waited with anticipation. 'How old are you?' she blurted. Suddenly it seemed very important to know; he seemed far more worldly wise than her.

Her heart stopped when his red piercing eyes seemed to penetrate hers and he replied, 'Two hundred and seventy-two.' Then he waited.

She couldn't help feeling disappointed. He looked so young. Atlanteans lived long lives, she knew. Some even into the hundreds, but they still physically aged along the way. Yaro looked in his twenties.

'We live longer than the other families and do not age until right at the end of our lives.'

'Other families?' she repeated. 'Other *royal* families?' It didn't make sense. She'd never once met anyone like him. 'You have to explain now, Yaro, I'm more confused than ever.'

Yaro bowed his head as if it was no less than he expected. Then he fixed her with his piercing, non-seeing stare. 'You have to understand that you are the first person to hear my story. None have lived to tell the tale. I'm revealing myself as a mark of my regard for you and the comfort I wish for you to have around me. There must be no secrets between us.'

Again, Alexia felt that pain in her chest. It hurt, but it was him doing it and she wanted more. She swallowed and nodded for him to continue.

He began with the story she'd heard since birth ...

'NO DOUBT you know the party line of our existence here on earth. How we came from the planet of Atlas ten thousand years ago, colonized earth, built Atlantis and overran the world. Then Atlas came again and destroyed all semblance of our civilization, until the five royal families learned to grow again in secret. They flourished, as you know, until Atlas was forced to return again, recently, and finally gave your father their blessing to rule over us all.'

Alexia nodded. That was it in a nutshell. The story she'd heard a thousand times. The same thing all Atlantean children were taught.

It was then she truly saw the male sitting there. A quiet storm. Not emitting light in his glory as in the dark, but the real him simmering, brimming under the surface. Perfectly contained, about to erupt any minute. Brewing with a fury so intense that she finally understood what it meant to see him in the dark. It wasn't his glory like some angel, it was anger literally leaching out of him like a burning out star.

Now she saw it all. Saw him. It was there in the set of his jaw wound too tight, in the furrows of his veined brow, pulled together and creased just above his perfectly straight nose. It made her tense just to watch. 'So I take it, it didn't really happen like that?' she said softly, not wanting to anger him but doubting that six million Atlanteans could have it so wrong.

'Have you never questioned how an underwater race was able to make the leap from water to land?'

He waited for her to answer, not seeming outwardly angry, but wanting her to reason it out.

She shrugged. 'It's no secret. It was the Santalinis, my uncle's family. My father's honourable guard. They were the soldiers who ventured out first. Living on a diet of blood. It's why they have a dispensation from the crown to drink blood now. Everyone knows the story,' she said.

Yaro exhaled wearily, as if he expected nothing less. 'And, in part, you would be right. But an intricate operation like that was not carried out by the ham-fisted branch of the family you see today.'

Alexia began to feel the first real tentacles of fear as a chill made its way up her spine. 'So you're saying it wasn't the Santalinis,' she said flatly. If he was going to go against everything she knew, then he was going to have to explain himself. She got the impression that the next part was more difficult to say. 'Then tell me what really happened,' she said more softly. 'What happened when we left the water?'

CHAPTER 33

*A*lexia waited as Yaro took a moment to gauge her, then he continued …

'Before we left Atlas, the five royal families were not as distinct as you see them here on Earth today. There were cross overs and sub-sections, sub-sets and sects that they never saw fit to represent in the new colony. They were intent on keeping the families pure.

'Many such off-shoots had gifts and practices long lost in the annals of time to what would become the Atlantean race.'

The cold chill became a shot of adrenaline to Alexia's heart. 'And you are one of these?' she said, breathlessly. Pieces of his story were starting to fall into place.

Yaro tipped his head and he smiled a little. Something she was coming to realize was rare on his severe and intense face. 'There were great cities under the great expanse of water of Atlas. Built like nothing you've ever seen here. Great structures that grew vertically, up to the light of the five moons. Elite light-seekers, rose to the top, leaving those who adopted the darkness below. Happy to remain unseeing and unseen at the very bottom: the base dwellers.'

It made perfect sense. His aversion to light, the coldness of his body, his eyes. It explained his anger. He belonged to a lower class of Atlas. It seemed irrelevant when she looked at him now. Then he upended everything she'd just thought.

'However, there was one such family – a distant relative of the Santalinis. They were famed for coming from the greatest depths, from beneath the founding rock of the oldest city, itself. They had enormous strength and speed to withstand such pressure. They could swim to the deepest trough in the ocean and even breathe air between the pockets of rock. Their skin saw no light and felt no heat and so they were pale and their sight only developed to see in the furthest reaches and therefore held no pigment. The red you see in my eyes is simply blood flowing through clear irises. So you see, we could stand much harsher conditions than any creature alive. A secretive people the humans later referred to as demons. We were the demigods, which morphed into the name, Demidov. Smaller-framed and yet stronger than our more surface dwelling Santalini cousins. We were not chosen as a lesser people, but as the elite of the elite. If the Santalini were the Special Ops, then we were the Secret Service. Sent to Earth to be the first out of water and infiltrate the native species. We were the ones sent to stake our claim.'

Yaro was passionate and angry by the time he finished speaking and Alexia's heart was beating wildly. His story was amazing and scary and totally appealed to her teenage sense of romance and adventure. 'But that's great, isn't it? Your people basically founded the world as we know it.'

Yaro narrowed his eyes and his look darkened, making her shrink back into her chair. 'And you'd be right. But unable to blend in with humans, we became feared and reviled. Driven into the shadows, called demons and shunned. Stories spread, calling us Strigoi: undead spirits who took nourishment from the blood of their children. There was no longer anywhere for us to go, so their stories became true. The new Atlantean kings turned their backs on us and we were taken out of the history books, only to appear in human folklore to scare children. Known from then on as Vampires and monsters, we went below ground again, in order to survive.'

Every sinew on his body was taut as he spoke through a clenched jaw. Every syllable was dripping with hatred, making his eyes shine redder than ever. He looked terrifying.

Then he looked straight at her, making her jump. 'We are Demidovs. A royal family of Ambragio. Famed immortals of our race, because of our longevity. Driven to hide in the underworld, below even the humans. Unable to show our face.'

Despite his fierceness, Alexia had an unbelievable urge to go and hug him. To comfort him and tell him everything would be OK, but she stopped herself just in time. 'We'll go to my father. Explain. He's a great king who has righted many wrongs already. I promise he'll help.'

Yaro smiled menacingly, showing an impressive set of dentures for the first time. She was sure it was deliberate; she could see it in the glint of his red eyes. Then he seemed to switch and sank back into his chair wearily, as if he'd had enough of the whole subject. 'Enough of such dreary things. It is far too serious for a young girl to dwell on. We should speak of lighter things. It is a long time since I had feminine company.'

Alexia's heart plummeted. She didn't care how big and powerful he was. 'Don't! Don't do that!' she spat.

There she was, sitting across from the genuine version of Count Dracula and he actually looked startled at the way she'd spoken to him. 'Don't diminish me into an empty headed little girl.'

His eyebrows rose and he inclined his head. 'I apologize. It was rude of me.' But when he finished speaking, he was smiling as if he was pleased.

'So, can I stay with you then, or what?' she said, immediately to press her advantage.

His mouth dropped open for a second and then he laughed loudly.

She was forced to laugh along with him. It was a lovely melodious sound and she was sure it didn't happen that often. Then it slowed and his expression morphed into something else, something darker that turned her insides to liquid.

She had to remind herself that this wasn't a foolish teenage boy with raging hormones, he was an experienced male several times the age of her father and very definitely on the wrong side of the law. 'So what's your connection with the Rhythm and Booze club?' she asked, to change the subject from the charged pause in conversation.

'I own it, as I do much on this side of London.'

It was another notch on the list of reasons she shouldn't be attracted to him. Bloodsucking vampire aside, if he couldn't operate in the open, then it was quickly becoming apparent that he was some sort of crime lord. 'So you know the DJs they have playing there.' She was trying to think of Dwayne and how holding hands on the way to school had been enough for her.

Yaro's eyes softened as if he knew. 'The ones your brothers use to their advantage?' he said, seeming mildly amused.

Her cheeks infused with anger and embarrassment. 'Oh, you know.'

'You still miss him?'

Her eyes shot to his, still vacant and unseeing. The depth of his knowledge was unsettling. But she guessed mental scans were an easy habit for an Atlantean as powerful as him.

'It is simple to reverse, if you want him?' It was posed as a question, like a test.

She had absolutely no doubt he could do what he said. It came as no surprise, but what did surprise her was the small part of her that was disappointed. Yaro was offering her a boy he knew she was once romantically involved with and that suggested a lack of interest in her like that. She guessed she should have jumped at the chance, but she didn't.

He was waiting, gauging her reaction. *God, he was clever.* He was forcing her to face the truth.

She inwardly smiled. Her interfering brothers could never say he was weak and couldn't look after her. 'So you know my brothers, too?' she said, deflecting.

He smiled knowingly again. It always felt like he held back so much more than he said. As if he enjoyed knowing things and indulging her. 'The budding entrepreneurs,' he said with a chuckle. 'Of course. Their apartment is mine.'

Her eyes widened at that. The extent of his reach was staggering. She was completely out of her depth with an experienced male she couldn't read. Reading people was usually her gift – particularly emotions. In the light, he had no aura at all and she was sure that was the point. 'Are you a bad guy?'

She found it very hard to look him in the eye, even though she knew he was unseeing. The intense look they gave her always felt like they drew something from her. His expression seemed as relaxed as it could be while he nodded slowly. 'I expect so, … in the human world I'm as bad as it gets.'

Her throat felt like it was closing up and she found it hard to swallow. 'And as an Atlantean?'

He shrugged, exhaling wearily. 'I stay in character.'

Alexia thought about that for a moment. That maybe he'd woven a trap they'd all neatly fallen into, like a funnel spider.

His eyes glinted as if he was intrigued and had followed her every thought.

Maybe he had.

He smiled, proving she was probably right.

'Am I a prisoner? she asked, barely able to speak.

He laughed loudly and appraised her appreciatively for a beat. 'As much as I love having you here and haven't had so much fun in decades, you are free to go as you please, Alexia.'

She let out a breath she hadn't realized she'd been holding and the veins at her temples thumped. Her emotions were yo-yoing all over the place. Now she felt disappointed and wanted to ask him why not. *Wasn't she good enough, old enough, sexy enough?* Freefalling into self-loathing and questioning whether he actually liked her at all. *Did he have some other agenda or would he be just a friend like some benevolent uncle?*

His grin widened again, no longer scaring her with his impressive canines. Now he was just making fun of her. 'Stop doing that,' she said, scowling.

He burst into laughter, but before she could respond, his face suddenly dropped. 'You must understand that to stay here, I must sample your blood.'

CHAPTER 34

Alexia's eyes shot straight from Yaro's alluring physique to his hypnotic gaze, not believing her ears. 'You're joking, right?'

He tilted his head to the side, in his cute, puzzled way, like he was enjoying scrutinising her immensely.

She had to keep pinching herself as a reminder that there was nothing cute and cuddly about the creature in front of her. He was an apex predator.

'Is that such a hard notion for you to accept? Doesn't your own uncle drink from your aunt?'

He seemed to know everything. She guessed she shouldn't be that surprised that he knew her Uncle Keenan was a Santalini. Yaro was Atlantean after all and powerful enough to have feelers everywhere. 'Yes, but that's a private dispensation only allowed between mates of that family,' she answered cautiously.

Yaro tipped his head slightly. 'And am I not one of that same royal family?' His smile seemed vicious through thin red lips and deliberate show of fangs, that didn't quite reach his eyes. Now he more resembled a wolf. 'Some might even argue I come from far purer stock.'

Alexia's blood pumped so hard she could feel it throbbing in her temples. If what he'd told her was true and he was a Santalini, then he was right. He was fully entitled to drink blood and, judging by his dental work, fully equipped.

In an instant, like a whip of a cane, air whooshed in her face and he was right there in front of her. Without even seeing him move, she was on her feet, he was holding her head and exposing her throat. She hadn't even had time to scream. In one bewildering second, he'd demonstrated he could have ripped it open.

For what felt like a long moment, they were perfectly still. Then, as he slowly released her, he kissed her neck, reverently, with surprisingly soft lips.

She was shaking uncontrollably.

He narrowed his eyes. 'You are afraid,' he said as a statement, as if he wasn't surprised at all.

It was weird because, after everything, that was what annoyed her the most. She didn't want him to look at her like a silly little girl. 'A bit. What do you expect?'

He tilted his head again, smiling as if he'd been toying with her the whole time. 'And yet you yourself called me and put yourself at my mercy for my protection.'

She studied him, trying to fathom whether there was any real kindness in those blood-filled eyes.

He seemed to soften. 'Don't be afraid, Alexia. I give you my word that I will not harm you.'

While he enunciated his words in his strong Russian accent, her spirits lifted a little, as she felt she'd won him over in some way. She decided he was devilishly handsome. He was fierce and severe and far too pale, but somehow, because he was so serious and contained, he became all the more attractive to her.

Then he seemed regretful. Even a little sad, when he said, 'You must know also, that I will not lie to you. It is true, while I am of your species, I am not Atlantean, not like any you've ever known. We are pure, like the Murr, Borge family, rarely taking a mate, living long and not tamed by this world. We take what we need and we follow our own laws. It has always been this way.' His eyes bore into hers, meaningfully. 'We answer to no one.'

She knew he was coiled and ready to ignite. He was talking about her father and watching her for her response. 'Except for my father,' she ventured, bravely, now testing him. 'I don't think you're such a bad guy,' she said. Then, with her heart thrashing hard, she went on tiptoes and put her lips to his cool cheek and kissed him. 'Thank you.'

His arms felt like granite as he stiffened while she held them a moment too long. A low growling sound vibrated through his throat, making her draw back in alarm.

Her eyes widened at the change in his face. His lips had thinned back from his teeth and his eyes had darkened as he zeroed in on her neck.

Then, breathing through her fear to calm down her heart, she began to understand. By leaning into him, she had exposed the blood pulsing through her neck, now at rapid speed due to fear and put it tantalizingly close to his mouth. 'I'm sorry,' she said quickly. Covering her neck with her hand. 'I didn't realize.'

It occurred to her then that blood drinking, for him, must be much more of an instinct. A survival thing for nourishment and much less a bonding thing than it was for her Uncle Keenan and the Santalinis she knew. 'Do you eat human food at all?' she asked to distract him.

His eyes shifted back to hers and he blinked, reminding her again of a bird of prey. He took a moment to register what she was saying. He swallowed, shook his head in answer and regained some of his composure. He was utterly fascinating. 'We drink only blood and a little water if we're sick.'

The myths, legends, night-walking, drinking blood, all buzzed through her mind. 'So the stories about vampires hunting humans are all true,' she said, amazed.

He bobbed his head. 'In part. Most of the time we have regular, willing donors. People who have been with us for years.'

'I see,' she whispered. Thinking of the many films about vampires. 'Are they human?'

He shrugged. 'Mainly.'

'And female?' She found she couldn't look him in the eye at that. Somehow it seemed really important.

When she stole a furtive glance at him, his expression had softened. As if her childlike questions surprised and pleased him a little. The image of him intertwined with a beautiful, waif-like damsel stung her like a barb to the heart. It really hurt. She was stabbed with jealousy, completely illogical given what she knew of him.

His eyelids lowered and the intense look he gave her melted her insides.

'Does it hurt?' she found herself asking and swallowing hard.

He shook his head slowly, still eying her speculatively. 'Most find the experience exquisite,' he said, a slow smile spreading over his lips.

It was then she smelled his wonderful cologne. Dark, musky and wrapping itself around her. She found she wanted to take huge lungfuls of it and get even closer to him than she was standing already. Her head was clouding and she almost offered herself over to him completely, when she hitched a breath and stepped back.

His grin widened.

'You spelled me!' she said, outraged, holding her neck again.

He laughed and sobered. 'Simple pheromones that attract and act like a basic anaesthetic. Our subjects find it quite enjoyable.'

It was shocking and she found her mouth had gone completely dry. 'Do you kill them?' she asked, with an image of him slowly draining his victim while they died in ecstasy.

Yaro smiled and shook his head, looking so gorgeous then with his tousled hair falling onto his forehead that she was sure his hormones must still be working on her. 'Draining people would make no sense – unless we wanted to kill them,' he said, recovering his smile. 'We would soon be detected and would simply be diminishing our food source.'

It made a lot of sense and she nodded cautiously, a little relieved.

'I myself retain a handful of subjects that have fed me for years. Trustworthy friends, belonging to the same family, who have been loyal to me for generations. They are paid handsomely and work for me in all kinds of ways.'

It gave her a strange feeling. He was such a powerful being. Like no one she'd ever known. He drank blood and was much older and cleverer than her. A hunter. Someone, she was sure, who could be ruthless and yet, somehow, she knew he wouldn't hurt her and was interested in her on a level far deeper than food. 'So you want to drink from me?' she asked, quickly, before she could stop herself. It felt desperately important to know.

He snatched her to him, making her yelp in shock. He held her tightly but didn't crush her while he stared down into her wide, frightened eyes. His eyes became gorged with blood. A hunger reflex, she realized, trying to shrink away from him. 'I make a point of rarely drinking from Atlanteans and never from a female – particularly a royal one.'

'Why?' she said in more of a whimper, then squealed in reflex as he put his nose to the crook of her neck and inhaled deeply.

Alexia's heart was thrashing painfully, while she waited, not daring to move a muscle.

His grin widened and he gently put her away from him at a safe distance. He always managed to make her feel young and foolish. Her cheeks burned and she felt like crying.

Yaro looked speculative. Then, just like that, he straightened, like he'd made up his mind. 'You will stay with me from this night. I will not drink from you, nor will I touch you.' However he took a terrifying step to loom over her again. 'Until your eighteenth birthday,' he said like a promise, intensely, boring into her eyes.

Lines of light whisked past her and a gust of wind that took her breath and she was left alone. Not fully understanding what had just happened, she flopped back down into the armchair as if the energy had just been sucked out of her. Her eyes darted, unseeing, trying to make sense of it all. *Did he like her? Didn't he? Did he find her attractive? Didn't he?*

In the end, she just had to satisfy herself that she was the daughter of a king and Yaro had to tread very carefully around her. He'd said it himself. He was respecting her station. But when she was eighteen, his words echoed through her mind like a promise. She remembered those long, tattooed fingers on her burning skin. The ache she felt as his magical scent wrapped its arms around her. The slash of that severe mouth and those teeth and what it might feel like to have them pierce her.

Fourteen long months until her eighteenth birthday. She wasn't sure whether he was counting too, or whether he planned on driving her away long before then, but he'd done something irreversible to her tonight. She felt changed. No longer a child. She wouldn't wait fourteen months; she was sure of that. She'd ingratiate herself, make herself wanted and indispensable to him. Then after a while, the big bad hunter wouldn't need his pet humans anymore. He would only want her. Then, her brothers, or even her powerful fathers, would be able to pull them apart.

CHAPTER 35

For JJ, all the days were dark after that. And it wasn't just that winter seemed to have set in early, with day after day of freezing rain; the three of them led separate lives.

Xavier spent his time with Paige and the science club. *God only knew what he was up to there.* While JJ worked with Chris on his social media network, Alexia, worryingly, avoided them completely. She didn't go back to the Johnsons and skipped school. They had to constantly cover for her with the teachers and Valarie so they didn't call their father. However, JJ knew they couldn't keep it up forever. She was spiting them and he hated how she must be feeling, but how was he supposed to prove he was sorry if she never picked up her phone?

Then there was Latitia. The only way he could keep tabs on Latitia now was to support her brothers in any way he could. He made sure he got behind their promotions whenever they DJ'd at the club. It also helped the school and would be a celebrity pull for his social media platform. It meant he'd be the first to hear when Alexia finally contacted anyone. That was what he told himself, anyway. B2H would launch any day now and he had to concentrate on that.

XAVIER HAD NEVER BEEN HAPPIER. He left the mooning over Alexia's hissy fit to JJ. She was only acting out and always had to be so dramatic.

His group of geeks had formed a cabinet around him, as was the general idea, leaving him and Paige to review the clinical trials that were proving more successful by the day. It was now the time to schedule a meeting to reveal what he'd been doing.

JJ answered his summons and sauntered into the science block after school. Xavier held Paige's hand and it wasn't just to show JJ, he honestly didn't know what he would have done without her in the last few weeks. Now he understood what his father had meant when he said it was lonely at the top. His eyes fell on JJ again, thinking he was so right about that.

Xavier straightened up when Alexia strode in confidently. She looked ordered and smart. Her uniform was pressed and her hair neatly tied in a bun at her nape. She seemed surprisingly together. Good, even. His eyes shot to JJ's; who looked as surprised as he was. He tried not to feel so pleased about that, but he was. He felt triumphant at how the tables were turned. 'Take a seat,' he said to both JJ and Alexia, pointing at two vacant seats facing the white screen set up at the front of the classroom.

Xavier watched JJ sit moodily after Alexia ignored him and the geeks shifted in their chairs so she could sit nearer to them and further away from JJ. JJ continued to look at Alexia while she faced front and projected, *Get on with it, for god's sake,* straight to Xavier's head.

Xavier took a step closer to the screen. 'As you know,

we've been working on ways to generate cash for the funding of the school. Dr Henry confirmed to me this morning that the necessary applications for the change have been submitted.'

JJ paid attention to that. He sat forward in his seat, pausing whatever he'd been communicating to Alexia, and began to listen. 'Thanks for telling me,' JJ snapped.

Ginger edged his chair away. Xavier he'd grown used to, but his tattooed and volatile brother was way out of his skill set.

'Let's begin,' Xavier said, taking a step back as a succession of short films began, each showing one of the arms of their clinical trials. 'The athletes,' he announced. Then he watched JJ closely as he watched the film of basketball players making baskets, high jumpers clearing bars and runners sprinting way ahead of the field. It soon became obvious that he registered the subjects performing way ahead of their peers.

The next section went on to spelling tests, maths, science and general knowledge. All the things the school usually tanked on, being performed by average students not usually renowned for top marks.

'What is this?' JJ asked, eventually. He looked up at the ceiling and slumped back in his chair.

'What? What is it?' Alexia said, finally talking to JJ for the answer.

'We said no drugs. We agreed,' JJ said, clearly annoyed.

The rest of the science club looked at each other, nervously. However they were not so scared as to miss the show and remove themselves from danger completely.

'Meh!' Xavier said, shrugging at the semantics. 'These are harmless.'

. . .

IT WAS a long moment before JJ tuned in to Alexia tugging on his arm, forgetting she wasn't talking to him to ask over and over, 'What is it? What's happening?'

JJ stood up as he said to no one in particular, 'Murr drugs.'

In a single step, Xavier was there in his face. 'This is my project and it works. You're just sour you didn't think of it first. It's the fastest way of generating cash and you know it,' Xavier said through gritted teeth.

The geeks had scattered to a circle around them and Alexia was already marching for the door. JJ was too at a loss to even respond to him. 'I'm out of here,' he said, turning, knocking a chair over in his haste.

As Alexia looked back at the doorway, JJ called out, 'Wait!' He quickly caught up when she disappeared into the corridor. 'Alexia,' he called after her. 'Are you OK? Where are you living?'

She tutted and continued to walk, so he had to run to catch up with her. 'So now you're interested, after all this time?' She laughed derisively. 'Tell Mum sorry, but I don't think I'll be home for Christmas.'

JJ's heart was racing now. He was guilty for neglecting her in his competition with Xavier for the school, but she was his favourite person in the whole world and he loved her. 'I miss you, Lexie. Talk to me, please. I'll make it up to you. Promise. Don't leave.' He stopped walking and waited in the middle of the corridor.

Alexia finally turned with a roll of her eyes. 'What for, JJ? For you all to control my life, then forget I exist? If any of you took any notice, you'd know I've been feeling shit, JJ. Shit!' With that she shook her head and stepped out of the exit.

JJ was forced to run after her again, stopping at the doorway. 'I'm having a big launch at the club,' he called after her. 'It's this Saturday, come!'

Just before she disappeared across the quadrangle, she turned, but continued to walk, backwards. Just for a moment, JJ saw the expression of love and regret he remembered. The one she reserved only for him when he was hurting and then it was gone.

'Can I bring a plus one?' It was as if she was issuing a challenge.

It took JJ aback. For the first time he was forced to no longer see Alexia as a little girl. It was clear she'd left the Johnsons and didn't care about school. They'd been so locked in their battles that he'd believed Xavier when he said their father would watch her. *Had he, though?*

She was living with someone. His favourite sibling had grown into a woman. *Be careful, Lexie,* he projected straight to her mind.

No one calls me Lexie anymore, she replied, before she disappeared from view, leaving JJ with a hole in his chest.

ALEXIA RAN and ran until she'd cleared the school gates. She shouldn't have come. It had taken all her willpower not to run to JJ, cling to him and ask him to make her a little girl again.

But she was no longer a little girl. She was a grown woman living with a mature male and she should have stayed in the bubble she and Yaro had created. She had no doubts, then. He made her feel beautiful and made sure she had everything she needed.

A delicious pain hit her lower abdomen when she thought of the bed she now shared with him. It had happened quickly, as you would expect from a male of his years and experience. The night she'd met him, she was broken and he'd rebuilt her, smoothing her fears and making the petty power struggles of her brothers a million miles away. The love she thought she'd had for Dwayne had shrunk to nothing more than a memory of a teenage crush. He was a skilled lover who obliterated anyone else in her life, overrunning her senses like an attack on all fronts, until there was nothing else but him. He had charm, wealth, great intellect and brute force sex appeal, like nothing she'd ever experienced. He was a real male. An Atlantean, royal and of standing, from a lineage as pure as her own. He was simply perfect and no one could dispute his eligibility for her. She loved him and he had declared that he loved her.

They would never understand. Even her mother, who'd pleaded with her that very morning to come home. They had to allow her to be herself.

Her father was just worried because he couldn't control her anymore. They were all the same – her parents, her brothers. They just couldn't let her go. That's why Yaro was so perfect. Because he was as powerful as them. Not even the king's Santalini guardsmen had been able to find her.

The blacked-out SUV pulled up next to her and she got in, saying, 'Home,' a little sadly, wishing they could all understand how meeting Yaro changed everything.

ALEXIA HADN'T RESURFACED and Xavier finally had to admit that she was missing. JJ had called his father, Jay, who would undoubtedly tell their father, the king. Deep down, Xavier still believed she was acting out, but even he had to concede this was the longest she'd ever kept it up and he was a little worried. It was clear by his reaction that JJ hadn't seen her, the Johnsons kept asking after her and she hadn't been back to school. He'd been so busy with his plans to beat JJ that he hadn't really paid much attention to her. She'd turned up to the reveal of his clinical trials and then disappeared. At least she'd seen fit to prove she was alive, he supposed, *but who with?*

'This is your fault,' JJ said, pressing the buzzer to let Keenan and his men in downstairs. 'If you'd kept quiet, she would at least be talking to one of us.'

That was so typical. 'Why should I, JJ? You were as much a part of controlling the Johnson brothers as I was, and I'm not going to let you continually label me as the bad guy.'

Xavier knew JJ better than he knew himself and that he was panicking on a level far deeper than he showed. JJ also knew he was right. Alexia was the one person he loved more than anyone and Xavier had ruined that for him, but he remained unrepentant. It was about time Alexia knew that JJ was as devious as he was.

'Sometimes it's more important to do the right thing than win, Xav,' JJ said, his temper evident in the firelit aura bursting out of him.

Xavier would have pointed out that he was just as ambitious for the crown, but the lift clanked, meaning Keenan had reached their floor.

'Our fathers will get involved now, they'll have to,' JJ said, shaking his head. 'Not cool, Xav.'

Xavier ignored him and, smiling sweetly, turned ready to greet Keenan. However, he was concerned. For JJ to make that call, meant he was seriously worried. For a moment his confidence in her being OK wavered. He reminded himself that it was salvageable. They'd done the right thing – albeit a little late. They'd called their fathers, she'd be reprimanded, then they'd all go back to their usual petty arguments.

JJ did have a point, though; they should have sorted this

out if they were proving they could rule. Family intervention was the last thing they needed. There was no way he wanted their fathers hijacking their plans. 'Maybe we should call Cooney. He will know everything that goes on around here.'

JJ came and stood next to him to offer a united front and nodded. 'If she's still around here, he'll know.'

Men's boots and voices sounded from the hallway. 'Nice digs,' Keenan said with a wolfwhistle.

He and his three cousins came in and seemed to fill the large open space. 'I've contacted your father, he'll be here this evening.'

'Which one?' both Xavier and JJ said at the same time.

'Jay! If she doesn't turn up by morning, then the king will travel here himself from Malta.'

Those final words hit Xavier the most. For the king to come himself, it was serious. The niggling feeling that Alexia could be in real danger was becoming harder to squash. This was the first trial of their so- called 'going-it-alone' phase. They'd managed to fail in the most fundamental responsibility of a king: keeping people safe. They'd neglected their own sister. If they didn't come up with something quick, their father, the king, would come crashing in, blame them and smash everything they'd built. 'We have one thing we'd like to try first?'

Keenan's eyebrows rose as he waited to hear what that was, exactly.

Xavier was already tapping his phone and put it to his ear. 'Cooney?'

Two rings. 'Yes, Son?'

'My sister, do you know where she is?'

There was a low chuckle as Cooney played to his usual gallery of onlookers. 'Took your time, didn't ya?'

Fury reared up in Xavier so fast he almost crushed his

phone. To think he could have saved them all this shitstorm and worry. Keenan stiffened and JJ took a step closer to listen. 'Don't get your knickers in a twist. I'll make a few enquiries.'

WHILE XAVIER ENDED the call and Keenan questioned him closely, JJ took a moment to step away. He tapped a text into his own phone: *Alexia. I'm sorry, we were genuinely trying to keep you out of something to keep you safe. Please come back or message to let us know you're OK. If you don't, our dads are coming and they'll ruin everything for us all.*

He played a hunch that she was perfectly safe, stewing somewhere and prayed to the five moons that nothing had happened to her. If that was the case, then she wouldn't want to be dragged home any more than they did.

A final flash of inspiration made him add: *It's Dwayne's battle with Trick tonight at the club. Come?* He hit Send and joined the conversation between Keenan and Xavier which was becoming quite heated on Xavier's part. Keenan remained in his usual state of calm. The kind of confidence a male has when nothing much scared him. All the Santalinis had it. Although Xavier was trying him. There was a stiffness to his jaw, a tension in his brow that showed he was showing extraordinary restraint. Anyone else wouldn't dare talk to him like that.

'Can I make a suggestion?' JJ said, trying to defuse the situation.

Xavier glared at him as if he'd thrown mud in his face and Keenan raised an eyebrow that totally said, *Yes please*, before he squashed him.

'Tell everyone to hold off until after tonight. We've got something going on at the club; she might turn up to.'

Xavier's eyes lit up and he nodded animatedly. 'That's

true. She fancies one of the Johnsons. He's DJing, she'll definitely turn up.'

Keenan rolled his eyes and looked at his cousin Reeve, who shrugged.

Xavier leapt on it as a yes, but before he could get too excited, Keenan poked him in the chest. 'That's if nothing's happened to her in the meantime.'

Xavier scowled at him. There wasn't really anything either of them could say to that. Keenan was right. They'd taken their eyes off the ball on this one.

'She'll turn up. I know she will.' Then JJ sent up a silent prayer that she did.

RHYTHM AND BOOZE was decorated everywhere with B2H launch night banners and balloons. It added a real excitement buzz to the evening and thanks to the standard social media jungle drums, was filling up early. The battle between Dwayne and Trick was scheduled for ten and the resident DJ was keeping the growing crowd hyped with old favourites.

JJ was watching Xavier closely. He'd changed. They both had since they'd arrived. Tonight was important and he was bricking it as much as he was. They were both now in it for the long haul.

Paige was noticeably absent. Meaning he'd left her at home on purpose. That was another way Xavier had changed. He was in a real relationship that meant something. Her not here meant he didn't want her to see what might happen.

JJ's stomach churned at that thought. He had no such control over Latitia. She was here with her friends to support her brother, so he had to constantly watch her to make sure he stayed off her radar.

A doorman tapped him on the shoulder. 'Cooney wants you out back.'

JJ looked around and seeing Xavier busy talking to someone, he followed him to the door next to the downstairs bar that took them to the manager's office.

He tapped the chest of his jacket to make sure the mysterious box was still safely in the inside breast pocket and relaxed at the hollow thud. He'd sneaked it out past Xavier.

Cooney was as sarcastically jovial as ever, dressed in what he thought was a sharp suit. He'd thrown a lot of money at it, but you couldn't make a good frame out of an old clothes horse and he'd ended up looking like a dressed chimp. JJ nodded at his greeting in his usual piss-taking way.

'Tonight's the night. Exciting, eh?'

JJ smiled. 'Any news on my sister?'

'Yes!' Cooney said, as if it had totally slipped his mind. 'As a matter of fact, there is. She's safe and staying with my partner, Rasputin. Remember the guy I told you about? She'll be here later. He said 'e's proud of ya and wished ya luck, 'e did.'

The rest melted into blah, blah, blah. All JJ could think of was getting the hell out of there to tell Xavier that their sister was being held by the worst possible person he could think of.

'Who?... What?' Xavier spluttered, incandescent with rage.

JJ had to grab his arm before he went and did something they'd both regret. 'Stop! All we have to do is wait. He said she'll be here later.'

Xavier pulled the roots of his hair and screamed; he was so angry. A couple of people looked over, but most of it was drowned out by the noise. 'It's him. That Atlantean. He has her ... leverage. I should have known. That box. We didn't deliver it.' His eyes were wild and darting.

JJ had never seen him so agitated. Seeing him like that

made him calm his own nerves. One of them had to keep their head. Xavier was right about one thing and he reached into his breast pocket and pulled out the box. 'I planned on giving it to my dad tonight.'

Xavier looked so relieved; he completely missed the fact he'd gone behind his back.

'I didn't know if I was going to give it to him or not,' JJ said in all honesty.

'Well, we have to now,' Xavier said, appearing calmer by the minute. 'He'll take it back to father.'

JJ nodded. It was all they could do. It made him wonder what the hell was in it that was so important.

'I hate that we don't know who he is, JJ,' Xavier said, reminding him of the little boy he once was.

JJ nodded. 'Me too. And, right now, he owns us.'

XAVIER HAD NEVER FELT this way. It was the helplessness and frustration at Alexia's sheer stupidity. He was so scared and angry for her he couldn't think straight. Dark and dangerous was normally JJ's department. Until today, he'd felt confident and ahead of JJ in the rivalry to be king. Calmer, more level-headed and driven. Now Alexia flouted him at every turn, putting herself in danger just to spite him. This Rasputin guy had disrespected them and Jay was forced to come in over their heads and put him in his place. Just like when they were little boys. They could have handled it. *They could have.*

Breathe was flying off the figurative shelves and was already living up to expectations and making them a fortune. Focus, was set to go on sale on Monday. Pre-orders were already through the roof.

He had to tell himself that Alexia was alive and kicking – albeit stupid, so he shouldn't let some low-life Atlantean or even JJ's dad take that success away from him, however close to him he was. The one thing his father had taught him was that it was the crown that mattered. He understood that now. You couldn't take control of a situation like this without it. He had to win it and keep it at any cost. Alexia didn't care. JJ didn't really want it. He'd never hidden the fact. He always had to be the rebel without a cause, character. The brooding anti-hero, always in cahoots with Alexia, against him.

His rambling thoughts were halted when the easy-to-spot Santalini guards started to filter through the packed crowd towards him. They were a good head and shoulders taller than anybody else. Jay would be somewhere among that lot. As an ex-king himself, he would always be a VIP in Atlantean circles and had almost as much security as his father. Tonight, he guessed, he was on official business.

The music went off, drawing Xavier's attention straight to the DJ booth to see what had happened. JJ tapped the mic as if he was making an announcement.

Xavier frowned and turned to face him. He felt Jay and the others gather to form a group around him to watch too.

'Welcome, everyone,' JJ said. 'Thanks for coming. I just wanted to make a small announcement before we kick off the battle.'

There were a few cheers as JJ nodded his head towards the DJs already crowded onto the small stage, organizing themselves for their sets.

'I guess you've been noticing the banners here and around the school for B2H. It's been a hard slog and many nights of burning the midnight oil, but tonight is the night that we finally get to launch the app. After twelve, tonight, you can download it for free from all the usual places. It's the new platform for everything a kid needs in South London. So raise your glasses and let's take control of what matters most in our area. To us!'

JJ looked straight at Xavier when he held up his glass and

everyone cheered. It was a look that said, 'it's on'. Time slowed to something completely apart from all the drama with Rasputin and Alexia. Both understood it as a moment between them.

Then, after what was probably no more than about three seconds, JJ focussed on the two DJs in front of him. He tossed a coin, Trick won to go first and the place erupted into thunderous cheers and stamping of feet. The loud music dropped, and the room moved on. However, JJ's message still reverberated in Xavier's mind. The full extent and the brilliance of what JJ had been working on began to hit him. He assumed it would be something confined to the school, but this was so much more. It was genius. He should have thought of it himself. The only thing more potent than drugs to control the hordes of stupid humans was the control of public opinion and social media. It was a megaphone straight into the homes of willing listeners.

He tipped his head to his brother in respect; credit due to a master stroke.

JJ DIDN'T MISS the look returned in Xavier's eyes. It was the vengeful kind that said, 'OK, so I underestimated you' and stayed with you a long time. The battle was very definitely on. Trick was behind the decks and JJ stepped down off the stage feeling raw and hollow. Yes, he'd won the evening, but as he went towards Xavier and the clan of testosterone grouped around him, it was with a heavy heart. He spotted his father and surprised him by pulling him into a rare hug. He clung to him for a moment as if he was clutching the last vestige of his childhood. Jay looked at him curiously as he let him go, knowing displays of emotion didn't come easy to either of them and that something must have brought it on.

The crowd began to jump to the beat already vibrating

the walls, making conversation impossible, so JJ nodded towards the staircase to the quieter bar upstairs. He breathed, grateful to escape Jay's enquiring gaze.

They congregated around the bar as he called out to get a round on his tab to the busy barman. Keenan and his men drank beer as they kept a keen eye on everything around them. He and Xavier did the same with a coke.

'You both organized this?' his father, Jay, asked.

JJ glanced at Xavier's sullen face and they both nodded. They still didn't know the extent of the trouble they were in.

'Impressive,' Jay said, giving nothing away on his face.

However, JJ knew his father. He was there on official business for the king, not a social call. Scouting out the land and whether it was safe. Ready for the king to arrive and sort out the mess of their missing sister. JJ prayed he'd predicted correctly and the idea of the battle between Dwayne and Trick would be too much for Alexia to miss. *If he could just see her. Talk to her.*

Xavier widened his eyes and tipped his head towards Jay to remind him of what they still had to do. 'Oh, I almost forgot. We have this for the king. Someone – an Atlantean – asked us to give it to him.' JJ flashed a glance of 'here goes' to Xavier and pulled the box Cooney had given him out of his breast pocket and handed it to Jay.

'What is it?' his dad said, frowning.

JJ shook his head. 'Some old Atlantean letter, or something. I think Dante will want Max to take a look at it.'

Jay put it on the bar, took out his phone and photographed the box. Then he opened it and took out the envelope and using the box to hold it up, took a photo of it as well.

JJ watched intensely as he didn't open it. He simply put it back in the box and handed it back to him. 'You can give it to Dante yourself when he gets here. If I don't see for myself that your sister is fit and well by the close of play today, he'll be here first thing in the morning.'

JJ swore under his breath, put the box back in his pocket and threw a look at Xavier. He looked as pissed about it as he was.

It was then the strange tingle curled its way up his spine and made him turn around. It was her. *Alexia.* The world around him seemed to stop and became muted. The two bouncers on the front doors immediately stepped aside as six of the meanest-looking Atlantean men he'd ever seen outside the Santalini royal family marched in like they owned the place with Alexia between them.

JJ felt Keenan and his men straighten and saw Jay tracking the scene intensely as well. As if he was quickly gauging whether she was being held against her will.

JJ wasn't registering that. He was glued to Alexia. It was Alexia, but not Alexia. She was a version of her he'd never seen before. Wearing a slate-grey glittering cocktail dress and with her dark hair in a single curl over her shoulder, she looked a confident, sophisticated woman. Heads were turning as she went.

The men with her seemed strange and everything about them was black. They wore long black coats, their wrap-around sunglasses were black, even their overlong hair. They radiated something, or repelled it, he couldn't make up his mind. It was the strangest feeling. Even from where JJ was standing, he could tell they were like no other Atlantean he'd ever seen before. They exuded darkness. The temperature in the room dropped a good five degrees and the lights flickered.

They went through as a unit with purpose, making for the stairway down. JJ spotted a guy with Alexia, holding her hand. He seemed more covered than the rest. His collar was pulled up and he wore a hat pulled down over his forehead. It was obvious the guy didn't want to be seen.

That was their guy, he flashed to Xavier.

He didn't have a chance to register a reply, as they suddenly paused at the top of the staircase. Rasputin leaned down and whispered something in Alexia's ear. She nodded and he disappeared down the stairs, leaving Alexia and two men stationed at the top.

Alexia started towards them and, turning her head over her shoulder, she ordered the two men to stay where they were. They looked at each other, a little unsure, but seemed satisfied eventually that she was still in sight.

JJ watched, perplexed, as she swayed over to them in her expensive heels. He wanted to grab her, shake her and shout in her face. He'd never felt so unravelled in his entire life.

Xavier was already pointing and shouting, 'You're a selfish bitch!' and all the other names he reserved for her since they were children. 'Thanks for ruining everything for us, idiot.'

Keenan threw an arm between them, while Alexia simply rolled her eyes. 'It's not all about you,' she said on a weary breath.

The two guards looked unsettled, not sure whether they should intervene.

Thankfully, Jay stopped the tirade by hugging her and kissing her cheek. 'Are you OK?' he said in a soft voice.

She nodded.

JJ was speechless. It was obvious that she was with that guy. The weirdo – whoever he was. She'd moved out and gone and grown up without him. *How could she?* It felt bad, not good and he couldn't shake off the feeling. He didn't like it one bit.

'Who is he?' JJ managed to say at last, when her eyes finally landed on him.

She looked at him sadly as if she understood and he hated that too. 'Is that all you have to say to me, JJ?'

JJ closed his eyes and counted, before he said what he really thought. Xavier had said quite enough for the both of them.

Thankfully, his dad butted in. 'You know you're still under eighteen, Alexia. You can't just go off without telling someone, like that. You have a responsibility to your family,' Jay said, in his calm, reasonable tone.

JJ wondered how often he'd said similar words to his mother, during their turbulent life together. He guessed he was well practised.

Alexia took a step back from them as if it was the reception she'd been expecting. 'You know, none of you can tell me what to do. For the first time, someone is taking me seriously and I'm happy. Is that too hard for you to take?... For me to be happy?'

'What, that guy?' JJ said, before he could help himself.

As Xavier shouted in her face. 'He's a local hood, Alexia. You're a princess. How stupid can you get?'

JJ finally put his finger on why he was so hurt. He was no longer her 'best brother' as she'd always called him. He was no longer her 'go-to' favourite in the world. The mystery guy had taken his place. That was what hurt like hell.

Jay silenced Xavier with a hand and Keenan went to pull Xavier away. But Alexia was too quick and bit back. 'Make up your mind, Xavier. He's not a teenage boy who can't look after me. Look around,' she said, holding an arm out to the two bodyguards watching the situation closely. 'I'm in a relationship with a powerful Atlantean. That should please all of you.'

As she went to turn and flounce off, Jay grabbed her arm to wait. JJ wanted to pull her aside and do something – anything. To tell her how sorry he was for neglecting her. He was desperately sorry that their relationship was slipping away. But he didn't get the chance.

'Your father is going to want to see that you're safe and he will want to meet him, at the very least,' Jay said.

She seemed to gather herself together and stand even taller. Then she looked straight at JJ and said the words that froze his heart. 'Give Father the box and then text me. Yaro will meet him on neutral ground.'

She gave Jay one last glance, scowled at Xavier, turned and strode away.

JJ's heart sank a little more if that was possible. Because it was clear now what this was all about: that box and getting an audience with the king. It was so obvious and his naïve sister couldn't even see it.

When she reached the top of the stairs, *he* was waiting there. No one had seen him appear. The coat was done up to his chin, revealing a strong pale-skinned jaw and a slow smile, as he tipped his head in a greeting that was reserved just for him. Everything around JJ seemed to zone in to just the two of them.

Then the Santilinis went to take a step forward and they were gone. Whisked out on a gust of wind, they disappeared out of the doors completely. No one had ever seen anyone move so fast. 'What the—' Keenan said.

While loud chatter and consternation broke out between them all, JJ turned back to the barman. 'Who was that? Do you know?'

The young man threw him a 'where have you been' glance as he wiped the counter. 'That's the guy who owns the place.'

JJ's heart was thumping against the walls of his chest, making it very hard to breathe. He looked over at Jay and Xavier, speechless.

Xavier looked at him knowingly and Jay clocked the exchange. 'What is it?' Jay said.

'You'd better make sure Dante gets that box and not just a photo,' JJ said.

Jay frowned as if he didn't know what difference that made.

'He asked us to deliver it into Father's hands. That's the guy everyone around here calls Rasputin.'

'He owns everything,' Xavier chimed in.

'He owns us,' JJ corrected, straight at Xavier.

CHAPTER 36

*B*attle night was a resounding success. Cooney was ecstatic as he'd taken a ton of money on the door and at the bars.

JJ shook his head in disbelief that Dwayne, Richie and Trick now appeared to be friends. It seemed they stayed in character to create the hype and sell tickets, but underneath, they understood they were a springboard for each other's success. Without which, they would probably disappear into obscurity. And so, at evening's end, there were many man hugs and back-patting and letting bygones be bygones.

Everyone couldn't get enough Breathe so they'd sold out and a sufficient buzz had been created surrounding B2H. It was downloaded from the virtual shelves by the hundreds, where people couldn't wait until the morning to get the app.

All of which meant neither JJ nor Xavier slept. They got home around 3.30 a.m. and they didn't even discuss the success of the evening that much. They just sprawled out on each of the sofas in a numbed state of shock.

'It's all about the box?' JJ said aloud. 'What could it possibly be to go to so much trouble to get it to the king?'

'I dunno,' Xavier said on a sigh. 'Trust Alexia to get sucked in by him. She's going to get hurt, bawl her eyes out and who's going to have to pick up the pieces? ... Me! As usual.'

JJ didn't bother to reply. Xavier's inability to put himself in his sister's shoes just robbed him of speech sometimes. She would probably get hurt though, and for that, he felt sorry. The guy definitely had an agenda and despite dying to know what that was, he couldn't shake the image of Alexia, the sophisticated woman, out of his head. She looked very far from the victim. The little sister they knew and loved had been replaced by a strong, assertive woman.

Deep down, JJ knew he should be proud of her, but instead, he felt fearful. Scared that she'd got into bed with a monster; one that couldn't be controlled.

By 10 A.M., the small car park below the wharf was filled up with shiny black SUVs. Santalinis began to pour out, taking charge of the area for the king's arrival.

'Here we go,' JJ said, standing with Xavier, looking over the wall of the roof terrace. They watched closely as Jay and Dante got out of separate cars and embraced warmly.

They disappeared into the building and JJ turned to his brother and touched him on his shoulder. 'Whatever happens, we must stick with what we started, OK?'

Xavier nodded, solemnly.

It was a relief to know they were together on this. 'Otherwise, it's all been for nothing.'

They went back inside just as JJ's second father, Dante, the king, sauntered in. He looked as handsome as ever, dressed in his customary rock star black, in slacks and an expensive leather jacket. He was looking around and taking in the home they'd built for themselves. Jay walked a little behind him, doing the same but less obtrusively, in his usual watchful mode.

Dante was far more at home with his feelings and grabbed both boys and hugged them fiercely. 'So this is where you've been hiding,' he said in his rich Irish lilt.

'Coffee?' One of the Santalini guards said, already pressing buttons on their impressive-looking barista.

JJ curbed his annoyance at the total invasion of their space. Dante put up a hand as he wandered over to the bank of windows to check out the view. 'So let me get this straight,' he said, turning around to face them. 'I put you in a perfectly adequate home, with a nice family, and the pair of you not only snub it and walk out, but you abandon your sister. You're selling drugs and have all but taken over the school that I was set to control, myself. Tell me, have I missed anything out?' he said, looking at Jay for help, who was reaching for a cup of coffee.

Jay shrugged and shook his head, then took a sip of coffee. However, JJ wasn't fooled by the double act. They were seasoned pros at it. Jay was the angriest he'd seen in a very long while. 'Don't forget becoming indebted to the local money lender who happens to work for an Atlantean crime boss.'

Dante's face brightened as he pointed at his oldest friend. 'Ah yes. Correct. How could I forget. The very same one your abandoned sister ran to in her time of need and now resides with.'

JJ looked furtively at Xavier. It did sound bad. Xavier flashed a look back a little less repentantly. 'It didn't happen like that,' Xavier said, moodily.

Dante whirled around to face him with his hands in his pockets. 'Yeah? Tell me then. What might I have wrong?' He stalked up to his son so closely, he was looking down on his face.

'Did you open the box?' JJ said, trying to steer the conversation away from the point of probable violence.

It did the trick. Dante snapped out of his fixation on Xavier and took the cup of coffee one of the guards offered him. 'I did.'

'Do you know what it means?' JJ asked.

'Not right away. Max did though.'

JJ felt the uneasy tingle in his spine whenever he thought of the mystery Atlantean. His father's advisor, Max, walked in, obviously telepathically summoned, with a tall Murr he didn't recognize gliding in beside him. JJ was used to being with Murrs his whole life at home, his grandmother was one, but it always struck him how strange they looked in the human world. He looked ridiculously tall, in a long tunic-like suit, with albino white hair and overlarge black eyes that seemed penetrating and yet unseeing.

'Why is he here?' Xavier said, looking just as nervous as JJ.

'He's here to sort your mess out,' Dante snapped at him. 'He's going to correct the hash you made of your mind control on the Johnson kids.'

JJ's heart banged in his chest. He knew what that meant. Dante didn't know the whole story. Latitia knew what he was and the moment she came to her senses, she'd not only hate him, she'd be terrified of him. But he kept silent while his mind raced over what he could do.

'So?' Xavier prompted, not in the least bit bothered about what could possibly happen with the Johnsons. 'Who is the guy and what's in the box?'

Dante flopped down into the large leather sofa and felt the softness of the leather with his hand. 'Turns out your sister is mixed up with a Demidov – the so-called demons of the race.'

'They thought they were extinct on Earth,' Jay added.

JJ looked at Xavier, shocked. It was the last thing he'd

been expecting. A chancer from a lesser branch using his sister as leverage seemed the much more likely scenario. He seemed as bewildered as he was. 'I don't get it. What does he want?'

Max rummaged in his briefcase and took out his papers. 'We don't know much. It seems the family has been written out of many of the history books – hence the importance of the letter to him, I suspect. It dates back to the time of the destruction of Atlantis. What we are left with is mainly rumour and hearsay and a few wildly inaccurate human films and books. The only irrefutable proof we have left of their existence can be found in the Tome of Justice, containing the catalogue of Atlantean laws. It travelled to Earth from Atlas and survived the destruction of Atlantis.'

'This book actually exists?' Xavier said, turning to his father as if he didn't really believe it.

Dante inclined his head as if he thought that way once too. 'Actually, it does. It contains all our regulations from the home planet and is so valuable that it was held in a Swiss bank vault and moved recently to the vaults beneath Filfla.'

JJ had no idea. 'And you've seen it?' he said looking at Dante, then Max.

'It lists the five royal families that left Atlas and their crests and one other, beneath the Santalini,' Max explained.

'They worked on the pictures I sent and then I handed over the box this morning,' Jay added.

Max was gushing in his element of expertise. 'I scarcely believed it when I saw the seal.'

'What is it?' JJ said, feeling increasingly nervous and not understanding much at all.

'It seems upon leaving Atlas, the secret Demidov clan, known as the Ambragio – the immortals, were included in the number sent to colonize Earth. They were to be the first on land and act as the Secret Service of the race here. The proclamation was in the tome and signed by Artaxertses the great, himself, as was your letter, written in the same hand,' Max said over the rim of his glasses. 'He was the king in power at the time they left Atlas, around 8500 BC.'

JJ's mind was completely blown as he tried to get a handle on what it all meant to them and their sister.

Jay, now wearing white gloves, carefully took the box out of its new wrapping of tissue paper and put it down on the kitchen counter. JJ and Xavier gathered around it with everyone else.

'The box is decorated in the ferns dipped in blood – symbol of the Demidov family,' Max explained.

'What does the letter say?' JJ asked. 'We couldn't read any of it.'

'It's in the most ancient dialect I've ever seen,' Max said, wistfully, slipping his hands into his own pair of soft white gloves. He seemed to hold his breath as he carefully opened the box and took out the envelope containing the fragile document.

JJ looked at Xavier guiltily. He didn't meet his eyes. They had woefully manhandled something that was basically priceless. They were lucky no harm had come to it.

JJ faced Max again, who was skimming the contents of the letter. His hand went to his mouth as he was stifling a sob or laughter. JJ couldn't decide which.

'My goodness,' Max said.

'What?' Everyone seemed to say at the same time.

Max began to read aloud.

I, Artaxerxes the Great, king of the fourth quadrant of Atlas and second moon of Aquillo, son of Maxim, do grant elite status to the Ambragio, the immortal branch of the Santalini family, to accompany the mission to colonize the planet known as Earth. To act as agents for the crown and secure for his people a great kingdom satellite. To gain knowledge and riches and subdue its people, by any means necessary.

It is decreed that the family of Ambragio should never again be looked upon as base dwellers and should henceforth be revered as great pillars, as the strength and backbone of our people.

MAX CONTINUED to skim the page. 'Then it goes on to say the usual threats in such communications … *Any person tampering with this parchment or its purpose therein, shall be cursed, abandoned by the five moons, the chi and its graces sent forth in its stones, the Orb and its peoples.'*

'Ah, here we have the crux of it:

From this day forward, our gratitude and prayers go with the Ambragio, known as the sixth and final family of Atlas. I, Artaxerxes, decree it. Therefore, it shall be so.'

When Max looked up, it was with tears in his eyes. JJ understood the shock, but not the emotion. 'It is astounding and humbling to me, that these words, from a great king, on the other side of the solar system, have not been heard for ten thousand years. I can scarcely comprehend it,' Max said, now making perfect sense.

JJ was still sifting through what it actually meant for them and, more importantly, their sister.

'So what you're saying is, there is another unacknowledged royal family,' Dante said, exchanging a glance with Jay.

Max nodded, still in a state of amazement. 'And one, it seems, that despite what it says here, has been taken from the rest of the history books and ignored.'

That sounded bad. JJ looked at Dante while his eyes focused and he thought through the ramifications.

Jay stepped forward to take a look, even though JJ was

sure it would tell him no more than the rest of them. 'So, the real question is, what does this guy want?'

'Well, he ain't happy – assuming he knows what this says,' Dante said.

'And he has Alexia,' JJ said, steering them back to what really mattered. He couldn't bear to think of what could be happening to her.

Dante looked at the ceiling, clearly in anguish. JJ felt instantly guilty. He must be worried sick too. 'It has to be leverage,' he said for them all.

'I'll take a unit and just get her back,' Keenan said as if it was the easiest thing in the world.

Dante shook his head.

'You saw the speed of them. We need to know what we're dealing with before we charge in,' Jay said.

'No!' Dante said emphatically. 'As much as it goes against the grain, we need to treat this diplomatically.'

'He owns everything around here,' JJ added.

'And we'll drive Alexia further into him if we try to pull them apart,' Xavier added, looking the most contrite he'd ever seen him. 'She's infuriating like that.'

Dante tapped his hand on the arm of the sofa and got to his feet. 'That settles it then. We'll agree to meet this guy on neutral ground just as he requested, but we'll stipulate that Alexia must go back to school and must be at the meeting.'

JJ felt relieved. It was a good plan. At least he'd be able to see her and talk.

'You're caving to his demands,' Xavier said, throwing up his hands and walking off angrily.

However, Dante wouldn't let him and pulled him back by the arm into a hug. He held him tightly and spoke to him closely to his ear. 'I know it's frustrating; such things take patience.' Then he looked over his son's shoulder at Jay, who was watching the scene sadly. 'Sometimes, being a king means taking the course of action that safeguards the most amount of people.'

JJ recognized the deeper meaning between his two fathers but had no patience for it right then.

Dante kissed his son's cheek and put him away from him, holding the tops of his arms. 'You've done brilliantly here, both of you,' he said, glancing at JJ too. 'I'm so proud of you. But this is serious. It affects your sister's life and possibly the royal family system here on Earth.'

'Can't we just bury it like it never happened and just get Alexia back?' Xavier said, almost on the verge of tears. He was appealing to his father's sometimes volatile nature and the plan was not without merit. It had crossed JJ's mind too.

Dante let him go, nodded at Jay and together they made for the door. Both JJ and Xavier watched them, thinking he simply wasn't going to answer. Even the Santalinis began to fall in behind them.

However, he stopped just before they disappeared. 'I think burying it is the problem. I'm hoping that all this guy really wants is recognition and vindication for his family, he sees as wronged. I'll keep you posted.' With that, he turned and the whole party followed him out.

'He still needs teaching a lesson,' Keenan muttered to his cousin at the back.

JJ and Xavier were left staring at each other. After thinking they were saving Alexia from Dwayne and the dangers of the South London streets, they'd managed to push her into the arms of a creature who was possibly the most powerful and scary ever to walk amongst them. 'Bloody typical,' Xavier said.

B2H WENT LIVE the next day and spread like a forest fire. Kids were clambering so fast that a postcode had to be coded in it at join-up, just to keep it within the boundaries of south London. Not only did JJ want to keep the VIP vibe for its members, but his reach of control had to be limited so as not to get himself noticed and make waves with the human authorities. Then his father would need to get involved more than he already was.

JJ wasn't the only one with a success on his hands. Breathe was selling faster than they could stock it and Focus had pre-sold its first three shipments – and no one apart from their test subjects had even tried it. It felt like now they had their platform of B2H, they could sell cow dung to farmers.

Now Dante knew what they were up to, rather than being angry, which they kind of expected, he loaned them his full team of hotshot lawyers to secure the school as a self-funding, independent entity – as long as he was on the board of governors. They decided it was a good trade and accepted.

That meant work on renovating the gym store for their school shop and the drama block for the crèche could start right away. The sports wing was scheduled for the new year and Dr Henry was courted by local radio and newspapers as the best head teacher to ever grace Camberwell's streets. He was walking on clouds and they were actually doing it. Neither JJ nor Xavier could quite believe it. Since the whole Alexia thing, they were working together and making a success of it.

Then Alexia came back to school.

CHAPTER 37

Xavier knocked loudly on Paige's door and waited. The TV was always on far too loud. Even at 8.30 in the morning, when they should all be ready for work or school. It was like living in chaos. Some public-spirited soul had even left a fridge in the gangway overnight. However, he resisted the urge to move Paige into his loft with him. Not only would JJ think he'd lost his mind, but he didn't want to deal with why he was getting urges like that. Paige was happier with her family and the childminder was working out well. Besides, the crèche at the school would be ready soon and they'd all be travelling to school with him.

JJ would be right; he was losing it. Paige had actually started joking about swapping his car for a family hatchback. 'Never!' he'd snapped and she'd laughed. But that wasn't the scary part. It was that it didn't scare him nearly as much as it should have. The truth was he loved having her around. Even with all her noisy, snotty-nosed family.

It was true, he didn't want her permanently living in his loft; she needed to study and he had to take care of business. He had to be single-minded and didn't want her becoming clingy, as girls often did and the rot setting in. Paige was beautiful, clever, driven and completely naive to any silly love games. She was perfect. That was the real reason he kept her at arm's length. He had to be absolutely sure he was ready and they were so young. Because the moment they spent the night together, it was game over with life as he knew it, with the added aspect that could kill her. Not only would she be permanently linked to him in the Atlantean world, with all the dangers that entailed, but he, being typically him, could break her heart. She was so wonderfully trusting in him that he wanted to be a better man – a better king.

The door finally opened at the second round of knocking and the kids, squealing 'Zavi-yay!', swarmed around his legs, clearly delighted to see him as if they hadn't seen him for a year. 'When can we ride in your fast car again?' the taller one, Luke, shouted, jumping up and down.

'Soon!' Xavier said, his attention already on Paige, who pulled him in for a kiss on the lips.

Paige hauled her brother and sister off his legs and dumped them roughly back inside the door. They instantly giggled and ran back. She caught them struggling by the arms, ignoring their complaints. 'When the crèche is finished at school. Then you can come,' she said, answering their question.

'No, now!' they both said over and over, until Linda, their mother, came out.

'Morning, Xav,' she said, relieving Paige of the two kids, still kicking and screaming like a pair of captured turkeys, and dragged them back inside.

The door closed with a loud slam, muffling the noise until it disappeared completely. It didn't bother Xavier. He was now used to it and kind of liked it. He was reminded again that it was the domesticity he'd never known, having grown up in huge palaces and hideaway bunkers. It felt perfect. Paige was perfect.

He picked up Paige's hand and led her along the balcony, down the steps and back to the car. He opened the door for her as he always did, but before she got in she looked at him curiously. 'What is it?' she said, looking concerned.

He hadn't realized his thoughts had made him frown. He quickly rectified it with a smile. 'It's nothing. Alexia is supposed to be coming back to school today, that's all. I'm not looking forward to it.' It was the truth. They were never going to see eye to eye on the ridiculous choices she was making.

Paige nodded, understanding immediately. He kissed her and she got in the car. He got in the driver's side, plugged in his seat belt and switched on the engine.

'Latitia is coming back today as well,' Paige said. 'Jade told me. It's so weird how all three Johnsons have been off sick since the battle.'

Xavier indicated and pulled out, looking out of the side window to avoid Paige's gaze.

'I really thought Latitia would end up with JJ, and Alexia with Dwayne, didn't you? They all got on so well.'

Xavier made a concerted effort not to roll his eyes. 'Dwayne was a ridiculous choice,' he said, trying to keep the snark out of his voice. 'He could never be enough for my sister.' He released his foot off the gas pedal, realizing he was driving too fast.

'Really?' Paige said, sounding surprised. 'He seemed nice. So this guy she's with now, He's a lot older than her, isn't he? And she really likes him ... I guess she must do if she's living with him.'

Xavier felt his face burn with sudden panic, as if he'd almost fallen off the edge of a cliff. He was getting it a lot lately whenever the subject of his sister was raised. Paige chatted on, oblivious to him controlling his breathing. He wanted to rant and shout and say it was all some pathetic idea of a joke. The Atlantean was obviously using Alexia to get to their father and she was too stupid to see it. Or, worse still, enjoying annoying him with it. 'She's acting out, that's all,' he said through tight lips.

Paige didn't notice. She was watching all the kids swarming the pavements and filing into school. They pulled into the car park to the usual envious looks. 'Oh look! There's Latitia,' Paige said, pointing. 'I think JJ still likes her more than he lets on.'

Xavier followed where she was pointing just as Latitia looked over, straight into his eyes. He knew it because the colour drained right out of her face.

She knew.

The Murr had done his job and she had full cognition. 'Today should be interesting,' he said and got out of the car. By the time he turned and looked again, she was gone.

JJ WAS TWITCHY AS HELL, which was totally out of character for him. He had to face Alexia and try to salvage their relationship, after what she saw as a betrayal and navigate around the Johnsons, with at least one of them knowing he was from another species. It was not going to be a good day.

He hovered, fidgeting, nervously near the front of the building and then froze when he saw Xavier pull into the car park. Then he saw the long black limo pull up at the gate. *Alexia.* Neither appearing to give a damn about how conspicuous they were being. The driver got out and opened the rear door for her. JJ watched transfixed as his sister got out and thanked him. She was dressed the same as ever, in the navy-blue school uniform, but she seemed different, taller, more grown up somehow. It could be that she wore her hair a bit differently. More like a 1950s film star, but she'd always been well groomed. He had to admit to himself that while he and Xavier had been bickering like a pair of kids, their sister had gone and grown up. It probably hadn't happened over night. They just didn't notice. His cheeks pricked with shame and then his stomach churned when his imagination kicked in with what she was probably doing with a much older guy.

Alexia adjusted her bag on her shoulder and hurried towards the building, just as he spotted Latitia coming from the other way. Their trajectory meant they were going to cross. He held his breath as the two girls stopped dead in front of each other.

Alexia went to put out a hand to touch Latitia's arm and Latitia looked down at it as if it held a spider, swerved it and hurried towards the building.

Something painful shifted in his chest as he witnessed his sister left hanging and the terror on Latitia's face. The weight of responsibility felt heavy as it sank in that the day was going to be a lot harder than he thought.

With a deep sigh, he walked slowly towards the entrance to the school, making sure he would intercept Alexia as she reached it. 'Alexia!' he called, coming alongside her and matching her steps.

'JJ,' she said, evenly and continued to walk.

'Can we talk for a minute and clear the air. I'm sorry about everything. Can I explain?' *Please?* he finished, directly in her head.

'Or what?' she said, stopping and turning to him abruptly so the stream of kids were forced to go around them like a boulder.

JJ yanked her to the side of the corridor, out of the way. 'Nothing,' he said, trying to get her to look at him. 'I miss you. I want to—'

'Want to what? Go back to letting you and Xavier boss me

around? Go back to telling me who I can and can't see?' Her eyes were wide and lips tight, waiting for his answer.

JJ didn't rise to her anger, but his heart broke. The hurt underneath the anger was so clear to see. It was all over her face. 'I'm so sorry,' he said again. 'Really sorry. If I could go back and change it, I would.' He'd go back and change how he reacted to a lot of things, he thought, as Latitia entered his head too. 'If you want to date Dwayne, I won't stand in your way. It was just that night, it was so dangerous and you were our responsibility. I couldn't stand the thought of you vulnerable like that.'

She seemed to thaw a little and he thought he was getting through to her. 'Look, I do forgive you, JJ, you're my brother. And I know you thought you were doing the right thing, but I won't be going back to Dwayne. She shook her head quickly as if the thought was ridiculous to her. 'I'm with Yaro Demidov now. It's him. He's the one.'

JJ went to open his mouth, not even sure what he was going to say, just as the bell sounded. They were literally saved by that bell because he sure as hell wouldn't have said anything constructive.

Alexia smiled as if she knew and went to move off. JJ grabbed her wrist in reflex. 'The one. Can you hear yourself? You're not even seventeen yet, Alexia. A baby. How can you know that?' All the while he spoke, his inner voice was telling him to shut the hell up. To make it worse, Latitia passed them and their conversation died while they all looked at each other.

Then, just like the sound being switched back on to a movie, Alexia leaned into his ear. 'Not long and I'll be eighteen,' she whispered. 'I should say you have far bigger problems than my love life.' And she pulled out of his grip and moved away.

JJ let her go. His line of vision was still on Latitia's

progress down the corridor, looking over her shoulder at him several times as she went.

FIRST PERIOD WAS SCIENCE. Alexia dropped her canvas bag on the floor and got up onto her stool at her usual bench. It felt a lifetime ago that she was last there.

Her face heated when Xavier sauntered in and got into the seat behind her. 'Sister,' he said, simply, with no explanation, apology, or anything. She didn't know why she still expected it. Paige smiled kindly and took her seat next to him. Xavier must have pulled strings to have orchestrated that.

JJ turned up and took his seat at the back, now preoccupied with his own worries. The teacher would insist Latitia was in the seat next to him.

Talk of the Devil, and there she was. All three Johnsons walked in together. Richie touched Latitia on the shoulder as a gesture of moral support and then left them for his own class. She smiled weakly and headed towards JJ with her eyes downcast and Dwayne sidestepped between the benches to the seat next to her. It all felt really awkward.

Alexia avoided eye contact by deliberately leaning down to pull her books out of her bag, but Dwayne's presence burned like an open fire as soon as he sat down next to her. She was dying to move further away but couldn't without making it obvious. Instead, she faced front and neither of them said a word. The first time in the history of the world a girl wanted class to start on time and the teacher was late.

'Alexia,' Dwayne said, quietly.

When she pretended not to hear, he said it again, turning on his stool to look directly at her, making it impossible to ignore. 'Please, Alexia,' he pleaded.

She was forced to look up into his face. Her cheeks

heated and her heart sank at the obvious anguish in his eyes. She would have rather been anywhere else in the world right then.

'I don't understand what I did. I thought we were good. The school party and everything after, I get that. I do … I'm so sorry, I really am.'

The more he spoke, the more ashamed she felt. None of this was his fault.

'I know I've been working a lot. Everything just feels kind of a blur after that. Mum said we've all been ill with a weird flu or something. Next thing I know, weeks have passed and you've all moved out.'

She coughed to disguise how uncomfortable she felt. It was an obvious cover story for the blanks in his memory, but everything was more complicated for her. For him, he was in a time warp, where his feelings were exactly the same as the night her brothers had changed things. For her, a lifetime had passed, since. The Murr had now left it to her to be brutally honest with him.

He was waiting patiently for her to say something, his eyes still holding out hope. Pain and longing were literally leaching out of him, making her feel wretched. It was no good, the band-aid simply had to come off.

'A lot's happened since then, Dwayne.'

'You couldn't wait a few weeks?'

'It wasn't like that.' This was awful. She'd never had to let anyone down like this before. All the sweet things they'd said to each other and done suddenly came back to her in a rush. She understood now why her brothers were such cowards with this sort of thing. She almost wavered. But then the image of Yaro came to her mind: severe, powerful and dangerous and there was no longer any contest.

Hope died in Dwayne's eyes. 'So you're into older guys,' he said, quietly.

She studied him closely for the accusation in his words and there was none. Just hurt. 'Isn't just that. He's from the same place as me.'

He faced front again and she watched his Adam's apple move as he swallowed, getting a hold on his emotion. The conversation was over. Enough had been said. The teacher had arrived.

Alexia didn't say any more but continued to watch his profile as he pretended to listen to what the teacher said. That was what a broken heart looked like, she thought, sadly, suddenly wanting to cry.

JJ's first encounter with Latitia wasn't going great. It seemed all his efforts in distancing himself had been in vain. One of the conditions in taking over the school was letting Dr Henry still hold the reins. They'd initially done it for independence. Now he could see it was for so much more. They were young lions from the same pride fighting for dominance. Their father, the king, had always known that. Instead of being angry, he'd applauded them for taking the initiative. They were simply carving out a small kingdom where they could benefit those they would govern. Good training, he'd said. However, he'd also stipulated there could be no ripples or undue attention drawn. The transfer had to be seamless. In short, Dr Henry was a good educator and the school still had to function as a school and not end up like some kind of youth club, where teenage boys got to call the shots. That meant in Dr Henry's words, 'not dictating lessons and cherry-picking which ones he attended'. So here he was, in his seat back next to Latitia. He could have used mind control, like Xavier had obviously done to sit with Paige, but he'd learned his lesson and steered clear. Besides, there was a huge part of him that welcomed it. 'Everything

OK?' he said as she pulled her chair further apart from his, moodily.

At any other time, it would have made him smile, but he had no idea what memories had been restored and what hadn't. Cover stories could have been implanted and he would have no idea what they were. All he'd been told was that it would be as near the truth as possible for her sanity.

Latitia flashed him an angry look that troubled him even more. 'Are you feeling better?' he asked.

All she did was shake her head and laugh derisively.

His stomach churned with nerves. He'd never felt so out of control. 'What?' he hissed, losing patience at last. 'Tell me?'

The teacher walked in with the worst timing ever and Latitia attempted to get out her books. He slammed his hand down on them, making a few heads turn around. Her face reddened and he continued to glare at her until she was forced to return it.

The teacher called out; 'Everything OK back there?'

'Yes, sir,' she said, still holding his furious gaze. 'JJ has forgotten his work.' The words were deliberate, dripping with irony. The last thing this was was some lovers' tiff.

JJ frowned, his brain scrambling, trying to decipher where she was in her mind. *Did she care, didn't she?*

The teacher began to address the class with the day's lesson and Latitia leaned over so only he could hear. 'I was in bits, JJ, and you just left me.'

His mind went into freefall. He had no idea what page she was on, real or otherwise. 'Come outside, we need to talk.'

'I'm not going anywhere with you,' she spat.

'Please,' he said a little too loudly. 'At least let me explain.' He had no idea what that was because he had no idea what she thought he'd done. All he could think of was getting her alone to find out.

A weird, reckless excitement gripped his heart that

maybe, just maybe, this was salvageable. Perhaps she was still in the era of the time before he'd made the mistake of revealing his true form.

She got up from her stool abruptly, making it scrape. 'I need the toilet,' she said, loudly. Then she turned and marched for the door.

JJ said, 'So do I,' and followed her, leaving the teacher standing there, mouth wide open.

CHAPTER 38

J didn't hear what the teacher said after that. 'Latitia, wait!' She was striding off down the corridor. He ran to catch up with her, grabbed her and pushed her into a storage cupboard. He yanked on the light cord and put a hand over her mouth.

'JJ!' she squealed into his hand.

He snatched her to him and held her tight. 'Please, Latitia. One minute, that's all.'

Her protestations were muffled into his shoulder and her breath felt warm and damp. She struggled for a moment before her arms went around him and she relaxed.

JJ breathed in relief. 'I'm glad you're OK,' he said, his mouth in her hair, revelling in just how good she smelled and felt.

'But I'm not OK, JJ, I'm not.'

He put her apart from him slightly to look at her face. Her eyes looked hurt and angry. 'I've been ill, JJ. Really ill. I thought I was losing my mind and you weren't anywhere.'

The hurt on her face burned intensely, but he couldn't help the sense of relief that tumbled into his stomach that she appeared to have no memory of anything. 'Do you remember Soho? My dad's hotel?' His heart thumped, knowing it was dangerous steering her in that direction, but he had to know.

'Yes,' she frowned. 'But everything has been so hazy since then. 'I've had such horrible dreams, JJ. You're drowning in them and I can't save you. Then I'm drowning and I can't breathe.' She broke down into sobs and he hugged her tightly again.

'I'm here. I'm here. Don't worry, baby. I'm here now. They're just dreams.'

She seemed mollified and stopped crying, allowing him to stroke the side of her face. Eventually, she pulled apart to look at him. 'But you all moved out and just left us,' she said, hurt returning to her eyes.

He bobbed his head, unsure what he should say about that. 'That's true. But not because of what you think,' he rushed to say as she went to pull out of his grip. He gently moved her chin so she had to look at him again. 'Listen to me, Latitia, because I am telling you the absolute truth. Everything became a mess. We were put in your house by our fathers and you got ill because of us.'

She went to open her mouth to argue, but he shook his head. 'Listen to me. We had to take control of our lives, so we rebelled. That's all it's been about. Nothing to do with you, or how I feel about you or anything you've done. We've just taken control.' As she searched his face for the truth, he worried the Murr might have taken the memory of how she felt about him. However he decided that she wouldn't feel abandoned like this if she didn't care. It was a massive lesson learned, even if his fathers hadn't intended it that way. You just didn't meddle in things that didn't need meddling with. He understood then that the Murr had simply restored her reality with the mildest of adjustment. So subtle and precise, she would never know. They were the absolute masters at it. 'My sister has moved in with this much older guy,' he said, steering the conversation to more comfortable territory.

Latitia's eyes widened. 'I know. I heard. Isn't he the scary rich guy who owns the club?'

The Johnsons must have been talking between themselves and still knew they worked there, which was handy. JJ picked up her hands and rubbed his thumbs over the back of them. 'Listen, do you think we might carry on where we left off?' JJ said, with his heart beating wildly. He'd absolutely never put himself out there like this.

She looked down at what he was doing to her hands, then up to his face. There was a definite sparkle in her eye that he hadn't seen there for weeks. He felt a rush of relief, like she was actually back. Her gaze dropped to his lips and it was all the permission he needed. His mouth crashed into hers and they were kissing wildly. They fell against the rows of shelves, sending cans and broom sticks clanging to the floor. The lower half of him pinned her against them and she responded, clawing his neck and back with her nails. Nothing had ever felt so needed in all his life.

Then the familiar weight slammed into his chest and he remembered the vials. She'd only had one of them. He was forced to pull apart from her before he did something reckless.

She looked beautiful. Her eyes were still closed as she caught her breath. 'Wow,' she said, slowly opening them.

He laughed. 'We'd better get back before old Benson sends out a search party and we end up in detention.'

She nodded, but seemed reluctant and that made his chest hurt again. She took his hand and led him from the stock room and he was sure she was just as bewildered at the turnaround as he was. His mind was swirling with all kinds of thoughts and emotions, primarily relief. Relief that he had her again and she appeared to want him in the same way, and that look of revulsion that would haunt him for ever, seemed to have gone. However there was an underlying feeling of unease. A feeling of dread, that memories would come back and, worse still, that he could never be himself around her. He dismissed the thought instantly, ignoring that trust and honesty were essential to a successful relationship, but he couldn't give her up. For now, they would have to live a lie and be like any other teenagers. For her he would be human. Normal. It was the least he could do for dragging her into all this. His heart sank further. If she could never accept him for who he was, then their relationship was doomed. With or without Elixir, how could he bind someone to him who was repulsed by who he was?

They walked hand in hand back to class. She hadn't noticed his turmoil and smiled up at him, trustingly.

IT WAS A WEIRD SUMMONS. Valarie Johnson, of all people, had told them to come round. No excuses.

'Who does she think she is?' Xavier said, looking across at JJ in the passenger seat of his car. JJ should be happy now he appeared to be back with Latitia, but he was his usual moody self. 'What have you done to Latitia?' Xavier said, already bored. They'd been all over each other since the Murr had tidied up their messy mind wipes. 'I bet this is your fault,' he said tutting.

JJ threw his hands up and looked out of the passenger window.

They were all going to get roped into an excruciating safe sex conversation now. Particularly with Valarie's nursing specialty.

'I've no more of an idea what this is about than you have,

Xav,' JJ said, shooting him a scathing look. 'I've probably done a lot less than you have with Paige.'

They turned into the estate. 'Why?' Xavier asked, now genuinely intrigued.

'Probably for the same reason that you haven't, I guess,' JJ said with narrowed eyes. Then he shook his head and continued to seem troubled about something.

Xavier felt his own heart speed up. Even though he'd made Paige drink Elixir and he no longer thought he might kill her, JJ was right. The thought of breathing himself into her, sharing himself completely with another person and the permanence of it, scared him half to death. He nodded, sobering instantly.

'Hey, we should be celebrating,' JJ said.

Xavier smiled at the deliberate change of subject. He pulled up right outside the Johnsons' building and looked up at it as he switched off the engine. New graffiti: 'Free the Camberwell six', (whoever they were), had been spray painted just below the roof line.

JJ did the same. 'Feels like a lifetime ago, doesn't it?' JJ said with a deep sigh. 'It worked. Our fathers really did make us grow up.'

Xavier conceded with a small, thoughtful nod of his head. 'I guess we did.' He chuckled. 'In style, though.' With their father now on board, the school seemed to have been fast-tracked and just granted independent status for the end of December, and with a building contractor already hard at work, the crèche and the shop were due to open in the new year too. 'We've come a long way,' he said, pleased with himself.

'The Johnsons can't grumble too much. The boys are local celebrities, thanks to us,' JJ said.

'No, of course not,' Xavier said, unable to keep the laughter out of his voice. 'And you're dating their sister.

What more could they ask for?' He couldn't help finding the whole thing highly amusing.

JJ rolled his eyes. 'Come on,' he said, getting out of the car.

Xavier did the same, still grinning. They ambled into the building and up the stairs to find out what it was all about.

Xavier thought he'd never feel so at home in his new life. It was the happiest any of them had ever been. He hoped JJ realized it before he ruined things like he always did.

JJ knocked the door and they both waited. Valarie opened it immediately. 'Great! You're here. Come on in, boys,' she said, holding out her arm as if they didn't know their way.

Xavier followed JJ into the living room which had remained unchanged. The TV system still dominated, with the two kids sitting right in front of it. They both cheered and jumped up to say hello and ask what they'd bought them. Xavier produced two bars of chocolate. JJ looked at him strangely. 'What?' Xavier said, irritably.

JJ just shook his head as if the world had gone mad. Xavier nodded to all the other Johnsons sitting around the room. He was surprised to see Alexia already there. *So they'd all been summoned.* His theory of it all being JJ's fault was quickly evaporating. There were no seats left so he perched on the arm of the sofa, while JJ sat on the floor between Latitia's knees. It was very telling. It meant JJ, who never showed how he felt about anything, didn't care who knew. But he couldn't dwell on how mad that was. Valarie looked decidedly nervous and that worried him the most of all. She was fidgeting and biting her lip like she had something to say that she didn't want to deliver. 'Spit it out, Val. We're all grown-ups,' JJ said, with his cheeky smile that always won women over. It worked as she smiled and one of the kids jumped on his legs. 'Yeah … I'm a grown up,' little Marcus said.

Xavier looked back at Valarie in the hope she'd just say whatever it was.

'OK, I'm just going to say it. Sorry, baby,' she said, looking straight at Latitia.

Everyone looked at her and she went bright red. Xavier dropped his eyes to JJ's, who looked suddenly alarmed.

'I had to contact your dads in the night. I'm sorry, but I had to.'

'Mum!' Latitia barked.

Xavier and JJ exchanged a startled look. 'Why?' they both said at the same time.

Valarie didn't seem to be able to look them in the eye, which was worrying.

'Now I don't want you to think that I don't think you're good kids, because I do. It's just well … we all know there is something different/special about you.' She flashed a look at Latitia again and she put her face in her hands. 'Mum, don't,' she groaned into them.

'Sorry, baby, I can't not tell them the reason.' She straightened and seemed to get taller as she renewed her purpose in speaking. Then she looked both JJ and then Xavier in the eyes, which made Xavier raise his eyebrows in shock.

This couldn't possibly be anything to do with him; he'd had barely anything to do with any of them since he'd left.

'My kids haven't been the same since you all came here. They've been fighting, distant, moody and, recently, Latitia has been getting the most awful night terrors.'

Xavier looked at JJ, who looked increasingly uncomfortable.

'What did our father say?' Xavier said for them all.

'I'm sorry, you can't stay here anymore. He's taking you home.'

All three of them jumped to their feet.

'No! Alexia shrieked as if someone had died.

Xavier looked up at the ceiling, already running ways they could stay through his mind to get around this.

'I'm so sorry. Your dad asked me to be honest and so I have. I no longer think you're a good influence for my kids to be around.'

JJ shuffled his feet, struck dumb and Alexia ran out crying.

JJ DIDN'T KNOW what to say. He knew it was his fault. It was always his fault. All he could do was look at them all watching him closely and just shrug. To their credit, they weren't gloating. They all looked either sad or ashamed. They'd been brought up well by Valarie and none of them would argue with their mother. 'When?' he said simply, looking directly at Valarie.

Your dad said you could finish up the term. It's only a week. Then you have to go home. 'Look, I really am sorry.' She started to walk to the door and he followed, knowing that was her polite cue for him to go. When they got to the front door, it had been left open. 'In the day she's fine,' Valarie explained. It's just at night she wakes up and she's terrified.'

JJ gave her arm a squeeze as he walked out.

I DON'T BLOODY BELIEVE IT,' Xavier shouted furiously. Alexia sniffed back her tears and squashed in between him and JJ in his two-seater car. JJ guessed getting pulled over by the police was the least of their worries now. 'Just when we got everything going our way. Bloody typical!' Xavier spat.

'You can't blame her,' JJ said wearily, looking blankly out of the passenger window.

'Stupid Latitia. Why doesn't she bloody get over herself?' Xavier said.

'Look, she saw me, OK!' JJ shouted, his last nerve finally

breaking. 'She saw my true form and couldn't handle it. I couldn't deal with it and I messed with her mind. That's why the Murr had to come in. To sort it all out. I ruined it, OK. Not her.' The anger in his voice trailed off to exhaustion by the end of his sentence and he put his head in his hands. He felt Alexia's hand touch the back of his neck. 'I'll ring Father, OK. I'll sort this out for you both.'

When he let his hands fall and finally looked up in misery, Xavier looked at him strangely, then out of the front screen. 'No, leave this one to me. I'll talk to him.'

JJ was just too exhausted to argue. Alexia already had her phone to her ear. 'Pick me up from the wharf, now,' she said, rudely.

They pulled into the tarmacked area in front of their building and all piled out of the car, but instead of coming up, Alexia just strode away. 'Where are you going?' Xavier called.

She whirled around furiously.

JJ paused on the steps.

'I'm warning you both now. I'm not going anywhere. You ruin everything.' Then she stomped off.

XAVIER THREW his car keys down on the kitchen side. JJ flopped face down onto the sofa as if he'd been shot. Xavier tapped his phone to speak to his father, the king, already scripting out the message he would leave when he inevitably wouldn't pick up.

However he threw him when he answered.

Hello, Son, the familiar lilt of his father immediately said. *I take it Valarie spoke to you?*

'After everything, I can't believe you're pulling us out,' Xavier spat, barely able to speak, he was so angry.

JJ rolled over and leaned up on an elbow to listen in.

'We did everything you said.'

But Valarie, she's a good friend. She's worried sick and it's our fault.

'No, your fault, Dad. Your fault! I'm not taking this and neither is JJ or Alexia. I demand you pull Valarie in. Pull all of them in. Make them understand. You owe us that much.'

JJ sat up, alert, at that.

That's not fair on them, Xavier. What about Latitia?

'Deprogram her if you must, or reveal it all to her, properly. I don't care, just do something. Anything, so we can stay.'

There was silence on the line for a beat and JJ got up and walked over. Xavier looked him in the eye the whole way. He wouldn't be moved on this. He was in the right and he was prepared to fight him. Surprisingly, he just leaned in to listen to his phone. 'I'm with Paige, JJ is with Latitia,' he shrugged. 'I'm not sure what Alexia is, but we've all come too far to let it all go.' Xavier flicked a last look at JJ and delivered his final stroke. 'JJ won't admit it, but he more than likes her. He's changed. We've all changed. Dad? Say something.'

CHAPTER 39

JJ stared at his brother, not believing what he was hearing. How dare he say those things and make those decisions for him. And yet, as he looked at him like he wanted to kill him, what he'd said sunk in. It was true, all of it. He did feel for Latitia. For the first real time in his whole miserable life, he felt properly for another person.

There was something different about her. He'd known it from the moment he met her. It was the reason he'd needed her to see the real him in the first place.

Xavier put the phone to his shoulder. 'Dad said, what do you want to do?' His eyebrows were up while he waited, but there was no pleading in them. He was hard and implacable, like it made no difference to him either way. They would fight over this. 'Think, JJ. Don't be obstinate; it affects us all.'

He could be right, with all of it. Resignation began a slow journey through his body until it seeped into every cell. Maybe he shouldn't fight it. Perhaps he couldn't if he tried.

'You don't have to bind her to you.'

JJ was already thinking that was easier said than done. They'd been moments away from it just the other day.

'If we want to stay, then we have to do something drastic. You have to be brave.'

And there it was. Xavier calling him out on what was stopping him. Fear.

JJ swallowed and balled his fists. Xavier stiffened in readiness. But instead, JJ closed his eyes and said, 'OK.'

'What?' Xavier said in shock. His face brightened and he bounded around saying. 'OK, OK, Dad. He said OK.' He was ecstatic.

JJ watched him, smiling wanly. It was hard to get excited about something that would probably signal the end of his relationship. He watched Xavier's excited nods of agreement and then him clicking off his phone. He put the phone down on the side and pulled JJ into a tight hug, smacking his back loudly.

'What did he say?' JJ said, through the loud thuds.

Xavier put him away from him and, holding the tops of his arms, gave him a gentle shake. 'Don't worry, it's all good.' He went to the fridge, pulled out two beers and opened them.

JJ took the one offered. 'Come on, Xav,' he said, taking a huge swig.

'We're going home for Christmas and Paige, her family and all the Johnsons, are coming with us.'

JJ's heart was beating hard. 'To Soho,' he clarified. It was out of the question to take them all to their castle in Ireland. It would be too much and just blow their minds.

Xavier grinned and shook his head. 'To Filfla!' he said, not able to keep the delight out of his voice.

JJ just stared at his brother and waited for the gotcha. Instead, Xavier just nodded and grinned.

JJ put his head in his hands. He was taking the girl he liked, who was already terrified of the real him, to the centre of the Atlantean world. And her whole family was coming with them. 'Oh my god,' JJ whispered. 'They'll have to deprogram them all.'

EPILOGUE

'Do you really think it's a good idea bringing all those humans here?' Jay asked, shaking his head.

'I could have made sure they had a great weekend at the Bluebell. We could have laid on the charm and they would have all gone home happy.'

Dante swirled the amber liquid and ice around in his cut-crystal glass. Then he looked out of the vast panoramic window to the sea. Human problems seemed so far away when he retreated to his beloved Filfla; spectacular island home and centre of everything Atlantean. He felt very weary and sad about it all.

'What is it?' Jay prompted.

Dante looked back at his oldest and dearest friend. They'd battled and fought their whole lives and still loved each other deeply, but they'd always been on the same side. Their children weren't so lucky; they were the product of prophecy.

'You're thinking of the whole Darkly Begotten thing,' Jay said, now mirroring his sadness.

Dante nodded and watched a shoal of fish swim to the

window and dart away. 'It's started, Jay … I thought … I hoped they'd be much older.' He looked over at Jay and he was thoughtfully absorbing what he'd said. Jay was nothing if not pragmatic.

'And you think bringing them here will help you keep some kind of control.'

Dante let out a sigh and bobbed his head slightly again. It wouldn't be that easy. 'Xavier and Paige are almost there already, you can feel it. So are JJ and the Johnson girl, once she accepts what he is … and Alexia—' He didn't even bother finish that one. The mystery Demidov was a whole other problem entirely. One that he'd have to give his whole attention to. For the time being, he'd concentrate on their two sons.

'It's unlikely they'll end up with these girls for life. They're so young,' Jay said. 'I'm not sure we should be encouraging a bonding that could take away their choice. That's all,' Jay said, shaking his head and draining his glass.

All Dante could do was nod his head in agreement. He wasn't wrong. 'Ah, but we weren't much older when you think about it and their mother was eighteen. Once the hormones kick in—'

Jay nodded reflectively.

'No, we have to take the bull by the horns on this one, Jay. We'll lay it on the line to the families and make them an offer they can't refuse.'

'And what if they do … refuse, I mean,' Jay said, getting up to top up both their glasses.

'We'll soon over run the school and have a strong foothold on the ground in London. They won't have anywhere to go.'

'Our boys might have something to say about that,' Jay said, smiling and saluting him with his glass.

'Neither one is king yet,' Dante said, tipping his glass back at Jay and throwing the contents down his throat. 'And while I have breath in me bones, I'll keep it.'

Jay laughed, just like when they'd plotted as kids. He was in no hurry for the boys to grow up, any more than Dante was.

Dante grinned and Jay narrowed his eyes suspiciously, knowing full well he was up to something. Then he leaned forward conspiratorially. 'Didn't you wonder how every-thing went through so quickly with the school?'

Jay frowned, intrigued.

'I made all the necessary applications two years ago … Then when Dr Henry said the boys had approached him, I was so surprised and impressed, we decided to let them run with it.'

Jay chuckled; he should have known that Dante would have always been way ahead of this. 'And what about the Murr drugs, the social media app? … will you let that continue?'

Dante shook his head and smiled as if they'd genuinely got one past him on that one. 'I have to admit, the toe rags surprised me there, but no harm done. As soon as the request went in for the shipment to Murrtaine someone notified me. Same with the lawyers and the hackers. I've decided to let them run with it and see where it takes them. Watching closely, of course,' he said, tipping his glass at Jay.

Jay had to hand it to him; as usual, he'd thought several moves ahead of them all.

'Nah, bother, Jay. While they're here, getting smitten with their girlfriends and trying to win over their families, every-thing will move into place. By the time they all go back for the new term, we'll really own the school. They just won't know it yet.'

CONTACT T

To receive your two, 21st Century Sirens Novellas, and be the first to know anything relating to T's books, leave your details here: https://mailchi.mp/d18c89c14f50/tstedmannovellas
And please don't forget to leave a review wherever you bought your book, I really appreciate the feedback.
Much love
T
www.tstedman.com
Facebook
Twitter

ALSO BY T STEDMAN

Night Shades Novels (YA)

The Blackwood Curse

21st Century Sirens Series (Adult)

Soul Breather

Blood Sister

Shield Maiden

Tiger Lily

Night Goddess

Darkly Begotten

The Dark Valentines (Adult)

The Watchers

Diablo

The Novellas

Protector

Lost Moon

Non-Fiction

My Migraine Story